NOT THAT KIND
OF EVER AFTER

NOT THAT
⚘ KIND OF ⚘
EVER AFTER

Luci Adams

ST. MARTIN'S
GRIFFIN
NEW YORK

First published in the United States by St. Martin's Griffin, an imprint of St. Martin's Publishing Group

NOT THAT KIND OF EVER AFTER. Copyright © 2023 by Luci Adams. All rights reserved. Printed in the United States of America. For information, address St. Martin's Publishing Group, 120 Broadway, New York, NY 10271.

www.stmartins.com

Designed by Jen Edwards

Library of Congress Cataloging-in-Publication Data

Names: Adams, Luci, author.
Title: Not that kind of ever after / Luci Adams.
Description: First U.S. edition. | New York : St. Martin's Griffin, 2023. |
   "Originally published in United Kingdom by Little, Brown Book Group."
Identifiers: LCCN 2022034036 | ISBN 9781250842206 (trade paperback) |
   ISBN 9781250842213 (ebook)
Subjects: LCGFT: Romance fiction. | Humorous fiction. | Novels.
Classification: LCC PR6101.D3633 N68 2023 | DDC 823/.92—dc23/
   eng/20220719
LC record available at https://lccn.loc.gov/2022034036

Our books may be purchased in bulk for promotional, educational, or business use. Please contact your local bookseller or the Macmillan Corporate and Premium Sales Department at 1-800-221-7945, extension 5442, or by email at MacmillanSpecialMarkets@macmillan.com.

Originally published in the United Kingdom by Little, Brown Book Group

First U.S. Edition: 2023

10 9 8 7 6 5 4 3 2 1

To Riley's fairy godmothers.
And you too, Mum. Obviously.

PART 1

1

It came, unlike me, while I was riding backward cowgirl on what must have been the hairiest man in London.

I'm going to be honest with you, it wasn't my finest hour. I'm not talking about my performance, of course—on that front I'd rate myself a solid 6.5, maybe even 7 out of 10, and I promise you I don't say that lightly. I was giving it all the cries and whimpers of your more talented roster of YouPorn actresses, but being totally sincere, my heart wasn't in it.

But oh, how I wanted it to be.

The date hadn't been great. We'd met through Mirror Mirror, the latest in the long line of dating apps that have haunted my home screen, and from what I could see on my phone, he was . . . well, he was male, single, and conveniently located in London so he ticked the right boxes.

Name: Charles Wolf

That should have been my first telltale sign. The Charles bit, I mean—not the Wolf, although to that point his surname was a bit unfortunate given his disproportionate body to body-hair ratio.

But Charles: not Charlie, or Chip, not even Chaz, but Charles. Like the prince of Wales or the floppy-eared dog. I wondered maybe if it was just the formality of writing down his name—I'm still the full "Isabelle" on all my work emails despite just being Bella—but as he joined me in the cute little pub that I'd suggested, he went straight in with a cheeky banker side kiss and a five-drinks-down-already slur of:

"Belle? Charles. Charmed."

So it was Charles. Just Charles.

Still, it wasn't his choice to be called Charles. His parents named him, the nice vicar christened him, he was the victim here and if none of his primary schoolteachers had given the whole "nickname thing" a go then who was I to blame him for it?

Name: Charles Wolf

Occupation: Assistant Manager, GRM Investments

Again, I told myself. Not his fault.

Not all those who work for investment banks are dickheads, there's just a disproportionate number of dickheads who work for investment banks. Finding the pure gems from inside the sea of rhinestones is, speaking from personal experience, a rummage in the dark that inevitably ends with me crying my eyes out to *Pretty Woman* and thinking that my life would be easier if I was a beautiful West Coast prostitute.

He was probably just great at math or economics at school and teachers guided him to portfolio management the same way that mine guided me toward creative writing. That's a bit of a lie—my teachers guided me to average grades all around but I guided myself to creative writing, and my parents invariably accepted my life choices despite my obvious mediocrity.

But, I reminded myself, someone's name and job title doesn't necessarily define them. I mean, they literally define them, sure, but I know firsthand that I'm far greater than: Isabelle Marble, receptionist at Porter Books Publishing Ltd.

I'm Bella Marble: writer and creator; lover of dogs and fantastic karaoke singer to aughts' classics; four-time winner of Porter Books's annual "most courteous telephone manner" award (an achievement that is still very much on my LinkedIn profile despite the fact that the last time I won was over four years ago now); drinker of wine, pale ales and, if I'm in need of a pick-me-up, strawberry-infused-gin and tonics; a walking advertisement for H&M clothing; queen of animal-based documentary recommendations and owner of more books than the rest of London combined. Ginger, like all Marbles, freckles like the stars, and body type "petite," meaning at one point the rest of the world grew taller and I somehow didn't. I can juggle (ish), cartwheel (kind of), and have a strange love of constructing IKEA furniture.

And I'm a true, hopeless, despairing romantic. Above all things, above my wish to be a writer, above my dream to hug David Attenborough one day, above anything and everything, I want love.

I want what all those Disney princesses had before the producers and writers got better and found independent non-male-oriented story lines. I want a good old-fashioned man to sweep me off my feet and make me feel like royalty, but I'm living in the twenty-first century so I also want a man who treats me with respect and admires my strength and talents for what I'm worth while he rides me off into the sunset and maybe, just maybe, I will find that in:

Name: Charles Wolf

Occupation: Assistant Manager, GRM Investments

Height: 6'3"

Age: 33

🌿 2 🌿

The pub hidden on a tiny side street just north of Chinatown is an old favorite of mine. In the heart of Soho it's easy and convenient for most of London, but it has a beautiful home-away-from-home vibe that's not associated with central London at all. It's straight out of an old English fable: all dark woods, mahoganies, and the strong smell of varnish coupled with an enthusiastically early Christmas tree. It feels like a bit of countryside in the wrong postcode. I love it.

I try to leave it to my dates to pick the place. I think it tells me a lot about them depending on the kind of place they pick but the usual "where should we go" conversation with Charles didn't quite go the way I'd hoped.

Bella Marble
Where do you fancy going? ☺

Charles Wolf
What's near your place?

Bella Marble
I'm sure there's a place that's good for both of us!
Soho maybe?

Charles Wolf
I don't know Soho

Bella Marble
Where do you work then?

Bella Marble

I'm happy traveling to you if you know somewhere
nice?

Charles Wolf

Running late. Be there in 10 x

Bella Marble

Be where?

Charles Wolf

Wrong chat

Another sign maybe that it wasn't going to be the happily-ever-after I'd hoped for, but it wasn't like he was the only guy I was chatting with either. Well, he was, but it wasn't like I wasn't open to chatting with multiple other men. I just happened to not be, right at that moment in time.

When I didn't hear from him I thought about calling the whole thing off, but then it occurred to me: I had the power. I'm a strong female, raised in a house led by a strong female, living with other strong females and watching strong females on television more often than I'd care to admit. Plus, I hadn't had anyone even accept a date with me in months. So I took the lead.

Bella Marble

Free Friday?

Bella Marble

There's a cute pub on the edge of Chinatown?

Bella Marble

Maybe like 7:30?

Bella Marble

I think it might already sell mulled cider

Bella Marble

If you're into that, it also sells beer

Bella Marble

Or wine if that's what you drink

Bella Marble

It's like a normal pub, it sells all drinks, just to be clear

It's not like a specific cider place or anything is what
I'm saying
Bella Marble
I just called them up to check and they won't be
selling mulled cider
Bella Marble
So like, let me know if you fancied it. No problems if
not, obviously
Bella Marble
We could also meet later if you had other plans

I waited five hours after sending that last one and regretted everything. The stupid app interface doesn't let you delete messages or I would have instantly. I was about thirty minutes away from deleting my entire profile, but, like a true prince galloping over the horizon, he texted back.

Charles Wolf
Sounds good to me. Let's say 11

3

Eleven p.m. was a rogue time for a first date, but given how much effort it had been to secure the rendezvous I didn't want to take my chances asking to move it only to find myself alone on a Friday night. Luckily for me, 11 p.m. is basically the new 7 p.m. in Soho . . . at least that's what I told myself as I reapplied my makeup five hours early and tried to coerce a few of the commissioner's assistants to have after-work drinks with me so I wasn't just hanging around. By the time I polished off a shared bottle and finally wandered down Marylebone Road toward the twinkling lights of Piccadilly, swerving around annoying tourist and Instagrammer alike, it was already 10:30 p.m.

Still, I was early and arriving early on a date is never ideal. I thought about circling Leicester Square but given that I'd opted for heeled boots my feet hurt too much to walk more than I already had. Plus I went for a "borderline-work-appropriate sexy" look in a sheer white shirt over my black jeans, and given my autumn jacket is basically a moth-eaten relic, it was too cold just to hover outside.

I picked a corner of the nearly empty pub maybe a bit close to the Christmas tree (it's September now; surely it will die before December?) to try to avoid people looking up at me with those "you okay, hon" eyes as I waited completely alone, not "okay, hon." It didn't help that the place was almost empty. The kind of vibe the pub emitted, all homely and warm, isn't the kind of vibe people come to Soho for on a Friday night, unless you're me, of course.

As 11 p.m. came and went the last-call bell rang out. Charles had already sent me a preorder with some flimsy late excuse so it wasn't an immediate problem, only it did remind me that it was probably not the best idea to choose a pub for an 11 p.m. date. Then again when I'd suggested the place I think I'd anticipated a slightly earlier start time. But he did get there eventually, all politeness and apologies and any thought I had for calling it a night early was quickly switched out for the happy butterflies of budding romance.

"So tell me a bit about yourself."

"Ever seen that Leonardo film?" His accent was cool public school drool, which wasn't entirely unexpected. His stiff white shirt was unbuttoned at his collar and a plethora of thick brown hair was protruding out of his chest like a fur blanket. In fact it was quite easy to follow the zigzag of hair from his chest, right up around the sides of his ears, right around his untamed beard, and finishing with a thick patch of brown sprouts twisting around in no order whatsoever on the top of his strangely square head. I was trying not to stare directly at it, keeping my eyes fixated on his.

"Da Vinci?"

"No, the actor."

"DiCaprio?"

"The film with the fit one from the superhero movies? The blonde?"

I'm sure this game of Articulate! would have immediately put off some women but what some might have seen as off-putting, I saw as a challenge. Movie trivia was my specialized subject. I was in the game.

"Margot Robbie? You're talking about Leonardo DiCaprio and Margot Robbie?"

"Yeah—them."

"*Once Upon a Time in Hollywood?*"

"Na, the one where you see her pussy."

I tried not to wince at the word. Call me slightly prudish but I'm not big on vagina-based terminology. Not on a first date. Not really in general. But the game was on, my cold expensive cider was before me, and the night was young (ish. It was already 11:30 p.m.).

"Oh! *The Wolf of Wall Street*! The Scorsese movie."

"Who?"

"The director—it doesn't matter. What about it?"

"Yeah, well, it's a bit like that."

"What is?"

"My life."

"Oh," I said, all smiles because if this was the one—if this was my Prince Charming—then I wanted him to get lost in my bright blue eyes and not see the confusion and early onset regret that was currently in them. I wanted this night to be perfect, one we could tell to our future generations. The "how we met" we'd tell to our mini ginger mes and hopefully-less-hairy hims. Our little Wolfy children.

"Oh—that's actually quite funny, isn't it," I realized. "*Wolf of Wall Street*, you're Charlie Wolf. Kind of fitting."

"Charles Wolf."

Not his fault.

"Charles. Sorry."

"Yeah, maybe," he concluded, swinging back the £9 craft beer that he'd preordered.

"My, what big gulps you take!" I said, watching the whole thing disappear down him. He wiped the foam from his mouth like a true gentleman. Sort of.

"You a natural redhead?" he asked finally after a slightly awkward silence.

Asking questions—well, that's a good sign. It shows he's interested at least. It might not be the most original of inquiries, but it's something at least.

"I am indeed," I answered, twiddling one of my locks around my index finger.

"You're pretty," he said, and immediately my cheeks exploded a dusty pink. It was the first compliment I'd had from a guy in like . . . months. Maybe even a year. I couldn't stop my heart from fluttering away.

It's not that I think I'm bad looking at all—I don't. I know I look pretty good when I make an effort, only given every girl out there makes an effort these days and most boys don't naturally think "short with freckles" is their "type," I don't think that many people actually notice.

"For a ginger," he added, but I ignored that bit for obvious reasons.

Suddenly I didn't care that he wasn't a natural beauty. Suddenly I didn't care that I could weave his eyebrow hair into a French plait. I was just a girl, sitting in front of a boy, listening to him call her pretty and loving it.

"Thanks," I said, threading a loose strand back off my face and looking down coyly. "You know I—"

"Shall we go back to mine?" he interrupted. I mean, I wasn't going to say anything too breakthrough anyway so like, whatever.

I looked down at my very full pint of cider.

"Maybe another one?" I asked, my voice sounding light and uncaring like I'd seen work in a hundred rom-coms before.

"The bar's shut."

"Somewhere else?"

"My place is like a thirty-minute Uber. We can split it. It won't be more than twenty pounds or something."

This might be the father of my children, I thought. The charm's a little less than I'd hoped, but perhaps he was just shy. Many men are just shy.

Besides, he'd just told me I was pretty. I couldn't keep running from men at the first sign of trouble. Who on earth would there still be if I turned down every man who thought dick first? So I took a gamble.

"Yeah, sure," I said, trying to sound all female empowerment like it was all my idea. Because it was: it was my choice to meet him. It was my choice of venue. I was the one who bought the drinks and now I was the one saying yes.

I was winning at being a modern-day woman. Ish.

Except a £36 cab ride and two hours later I was bouncing on top of him like a jumping jack, screaming his name and trying desperately not to imagine the man beneath me was the aging prince of England.

Not the fairy-tale opening perhaps, but some things, like a good brew of tea, take time.

All was not lost. Yet.

4

Backward cowgirl is great for nosy people like me. While I was up there, dropping it to the beat of "Staying Alive" as per my usual fake-it-till-you-make-it technique and moaning at regular intervals, I managed to sneak a pretty expansive look around his room. He lived in a flat share in Camberwell, a three-bedroom new build with a one-size-fits-all kitchen and generic furniture he clearly didn't put time into buying. His walls had no artwork, his room had no photos—he was by all accounts a psychopath. He did have one shelf, which was lined with all manner of products that I spent the odd bounce trying to make out the brands of. At least looking up at that was time not spent looking down at his catastrophically hairy legs. At one point I considered how satisfying it would be to pour thick golden hot wax all down them and with one rip to pull out fistfuls of thick curls.

But even as I thought it I felt bad.

It wasn't his fault he was hairy.

It wasn't his fault that he'd never been with anyone who'd suggested a little more self-grooming.

This was a man clearly in need of someone to guide him and there I was, ready and open to be the girl who would change his life for the better after we got the awkward first sex out of the way.

Except as a by-product of the hair he must be impervious to the climate because even exerting myself as I was, I was still fucking freezing in his room. I tried once or twice to grab the cover that he was lying on, but his grunts of protest stopped me before I got too far. I tried to change position, thinking the closer I was to him the warmer it would be. Perhaps it would even feel like a nice winter coat in missionary. But trying to turn myself around up there wasn't going down too well either.

My eyes kept going around the room until, just on the floor in front of the full-length freestanding mirror, I saw what looked like a hoodie. The longer I bounced, the longer I looked, the more I was sure.

I thought about asking, but he seemed otherwise engaged so, as casually as I could I dipped down and forward, causing only the slightest bit of discomfort to myself and an awkward grunt from my bedfellow. I scooped the hoodie up in my arms and threw it over me in a move so smooth even I was impressed by my skills. I turned briefly to look back, to see if there was any protest, but his eyes were still firmly shut so I continued as I was, bouncing away.

The hoodie was soft against my skin. He hadn't bothered to take off my bra, but the rest of my torso was having a great time as the felt tickled against it. It was a couple sizes too big for me and bright red, the kind of boldness I wouldn't expect from a man like Charles Wolf, but I guess there was still much we needed to learn about each other.

And there would be time for that. We'd have plenty of time.

Accidentally I caught sight of us in his large mirror. Me, enveloped in a vibrant red hoodie, straddling a man who was 85 percent hair, 100 percent wolf. It looked bizarre. It looked a little tragic. It looked like . . .

A thought came to mind. A thought so small, so outrageous, that I almost wrote it off completely but the longer I stared the longer I realized that—

"Don't move!" Charles instructed.

I could hear the telltale moan of a man just about to—

And there it was. The finished product, all wrapped up in Durex's finest and the thought, like the hopes of my own climax for the night, floated far, far away.

✿ 5 ✿

I climbed off, and as daintily as I could I lay beside him, wrapping my arms around his large hairy stomach and looking up at him like he was my whole world. Because maybe, just maybe, he would be.

Pillow talk is always the best way to get to know someone anyway, I always think. At a bar you're guarded, in a restaurant you're on show, but naked, in bed, post-coitus there is nothing to hide. You're at your most vulnerable, your most humble, your most intimate.

I waited to see whether he might say something first. I even looked up at him sweetly, batting my eyelashes, but a wash of painfully stale beer and what must have been a lunch of Mexican food departed his mouth and filled up my nostrils so I turned my head back down to avoid direct contact.

He shuffled a little and I realized that shyness that I'd spotted in him earlier was coming back. Perhaps my performance was better than I'd thought. Perhaps he was too intimidated to speak up and ask me all the questions he'd wanted to in the bar.

So I spoke first.

"That was amazing," I said. Because that's what you're supposed to say and I was sure with a little ego boost he'd try harder to take me on the orgasm high with him next time around.

"Yeah," he said, a little more unbothered in tone than I was hoping for if I'm being honest, but at least he replied. The door was open now for the most stimulating conversation, the awkward laughs and the humble beginnings of a whirlwind romance.

"So I—"

"I have an early start tomorrow," he said quickly.

Was he kidding? I know what that phrase meant as much as the next girl, but him? Mr. I-have-more-hair-on-my-big-toe-than-most-humans-have-on-their-heads? Mr. I-put-in-zero-effort-and-expect-you-to-satisfy-me? Mr. Big Bad Wolf?

This was my toad that would turn into a prince. This was my diamond in the rough. This was the start to my own happily-ever-after and here he was, fake yawning beside me as if it was the first time a man had ever been that inventive and clever.

"Maybe it's best that—"

"I got it," I said, furious.

I jumped out of bed faster than he'd ever be able to move. I had aerodynamics on my side from Venus-shaved legs while he'd always have the weight of a hairdresser's daily clippings holding him down.

My jeans were on before he'd even turned his head, the rest of my clothes thrown into my bag in anger. I'd sort it out later. I'd sort my whole life out later. I'd sort out my bad life choices and my clean knickers when I got home; for now I just needed to get out of his psychopathically personality-lacking room.

As I began storming out and back through the hallway I heard him shout my name after me.

Unsure, I stopped in my tracks, waiting. He met me at the door, his immense shape—still unashamedly naked—towering over me. He leaned in and, for some reason assuming he was going for a kiss, I shut my eyes instinctively.

"I think you're wearing my hoodie?" he asked.

Fuck him.

Wrapping the hoodie tighter around me I pulled open the door so violently it stubbed his hairy foot. As he cried out in pain, his head twisted back like he was howling to the great full moon.

I didn't look back. Dressed in my brand-new red hoodie, I skipped away and into the night.

6

As soon as I was sure he wasn't following me I did a stock check. My handbag is unfortunately as bottomless as Mary Poppins's magic suitcase, only instead of a handy hat rack and a variety of undoubtedly useful household items like hers contains, mine's filled with miscellaneous crap that no one needs ever. Empty crisp packets I keep forgetting to take out, old lipsticks and mascaras that have probably dried up by now, pens without caps, caps without pens, and gum that's probably wildly past its use-by date. My hand riffles through it all until I find what I'm looking for. I brought out my battered iPhone, breathing a sigh of relief that I didn't leave it behind in Charles's flat.

I clicked on Uber first. It was 4 a.m. on a Saturday morning. Surcharge: 1.6 percent.

I swore, grinding my teeth together in the cold as I checked out my bank account. Buying two drinks and adding that not-actually-shared taxi to the Wolf's house (a taxi! Who gets a taxi from Soho home?) leaves me with a grand total of £19.30 to last me the rest of the month. I check the date: Saturday, September 26. Could be worse, but when I'm cold and want my bed and my fabricated lottery winnings still haven't magically appeared in my bank account, I'm not thinking practically about my limitations. I'm just furious that my magic handbag doesn't contain a fully chauffeured Ferrari and/or Pegasus.

I let out a little scream large enough to wake the cat sitting beside me on a low-lying wall, but not quite enough to scare it. It raised its eyebrow to me, smiling through its adorably cynical face and judging me for my terrible life decisions.

"Don't judge me," I told it. "He might have been the one. Underneath all the . . . the hair. He might have been the one if we'd had time to get to know each other. So screw you."

I was annoyed, wondering how much bad karma you can get if you push a cat off a wall. I'm more of a dog person myself. But stomping my feet and beating myself up weren't getting me any closer to a warm bed, and despite September often bringing a late heat wave with it, given it was near the end of the month it was so cold outside my eyelashes had frozen.

So I sighed.

"Which way should I go?" I asked it eventually.

But it didn't say anything. Obviously. Because it's a cat.

So I consulted the guru of Citymapper instead and went on my way.

7

Two bus rides (one in the exact wrong direction for over thirty minutes before I even realized) later brings us right back now to the present, standing on the steps of my own Balham palace.

A three-story Victorian building split into two flats, the bottom that houses what my mother once described as the "world's most try-hard fraternity" after she spent the night in our kitchen listening to the sound of their evening activities from the floorboards below. There's no noise now, mind, for even those retaining university stamina long past uni still have to go to bed eventually. I walk past their door and up the browning lime-green carpeted staircase to the first floor. The stale mildew smell of the shared space greets me like potpourri, no longer affecting me as it once did years ago but instead bringing a smile to my face. What once repelled me daily has now become the comforting aroma of home.

As I turn the key to my own flat at the top of the landing I can already hear movement. I check my watch: 5:55 a.m.

Should I be worried?

As I open the door the perky face of Annie Palmer gallops toward me, all high ponytail and leggings with a sports bag hitched over one shoulder.

"Good date?" she asks as she passes by, catching the still open front door behind me.

"Nope."

"Shame. See you later."

Just like that she's flying away out into the wide world and beyond.

"Annie?" I call after her quietly, rechecking my watch.

"Yes?"

She turns around and her ponytail flies around with her, almost hitting her back in the face. She's unbearably beautiful, flawless smooth skin straight out of a Maybelline ad except her naturally thick, long lashes need no volume-enhancing mascara to glow. At least she's the kind of person who knows it. There's no false modesty when it comes to Annie Palmer.

"It's a Saturday. Doesn't your body need . . . I don't know . . . sleep?" I ask, exhausted just looking at her. "Sleep is so good."

"Can't. I have spin with the girls," she says merrily, ignoring my look of horror as she closes the front door behind her and disappears away down the stairs and beyond. I stare at the door with an open mouth in tiredness and confusion as I hear her taking the steps two at a time.

Annie's such a freak. Who enjoys any form of fitness class? Who enjoys being publicly humiliated by angry *Baywatch* wannabes and dripping with sweat before they've even had their first flat white of the day? I mean, probably those who have better luck with men than I do, but still. I've done the math: in terms of effort/reward it's just not worth it. I much prefer my own method of sitting back, sipping my skinny latte, and waiting for my fairy godmother to magically appear and deliver me my own, ready-to-go Prince Charming.

When I turn back into the apartment I come face-to-face with a man so beautiful my eyes burn. He stands there as if he belongs there, naked save for a pair of what must be nude-colored underwear that I try not to look at directly. I blink, hard.

Holy shit.

Fairy godmother?

8

And then I remember that if fairy godmothers do exist, they'd probably have a bit more class than just running a naked man delivery
service.

"Bathroom?" he asks. He has a Spanish accent and it gets me hot
and bothered in a way that Charles Wolf never did. His muscles are
sharply defined, his briefs tighter than they probably should have
been. I both must not objectify this man and can't stop thinking
about my tongue running down his perfectly man-scaped snail trail.
He's practically hairless—a far cry from my earlier catastrophe.

I point gormlessly to the door next to the kitchen, unable to
muster words, and the Spanish man follows my wordless instruc-
tions. As the bathroom door shuts behind him I reach immediately
for my phone.

I find Annie's number and text so quickly my thumb hurts.

26 Sep 05:58-Me
I think you left someone behind!?

Annie Flatmate-26 Sep 05:59
Mine left last night. Guess again

Not hers?

The flush sounds and the door reopens. The beautiful man re-
emerges and looks at me again, a little confused. He blinks into the
dim light of the entrance hall and I suddenly realize I haven't moved
an inch since he went in there.

Oh God. I'm being weird and creepy.

The beautiful man shrugs and walks to the only other bedroom on this floor of the house.

"Simon?" I whisper under my breath proudly. "Go you!"

For as long as I've lived with him he's only had one adult sleepover and it was with his terrible cheating ex who he couldn't seem to rid himself of. This was a vast improvement on that scumbag.

Except as the corridor goes quiet again, memories of my own less successful night come back and I realize I'm standing here, all alone again in a house of people much luckier than I am.

I wander up one more set of stairs and instead of turning immediately right to my bedroom, I pause. I look at the door at the end of the hallway. I begrudgingly turn to my right and look at my own lonely, depressing door and I make a decision.

As I push open the door at the end of the lime-green hall (the landlord has a theme—it's a bad one) the creak of aging wood echoes around me. The shaft of light from the hall behind casts itself on the two sleeping figures like a painting. Ellie's lying still, facing up daintily like a true princess under her fluffy duck-egg-blue duvet while Mark is curled around her, his hand gently resting on her stomach for comfort.

She looks worried as she sleeps, but then again she always looks worried. She's a worrier.

I watch them for a little, wondering if I should just turn back, when from out of the darkness I hear my favorite voice in the whole world speak out.

"Bells?"

Ellie's looking at me, her eyes still half-shut. She moves Mark's hand off her carefully as she shuffles them both back to one side of the bed. She turns down the bedding on her other side and, stirring enough to understand what's happening, Mark grumbles something under his breath that I choose not to listen to or acknowledge because I don't need more negativity in my life. Closing the door behind me I take the invitation gladly and jump straight into the bed beside her.

I didn't realize how cold I was until the softness of her winter-weight duvet is over me and her arms are keeping me safe and warm.

"Not the one then?" she whispers sleepily, falling back into a peaceful sleep.

"You're my one," I reply, cuddling into the warmth of my best friend in the whole wide world.

9

I wake up to the glorious smell of PG Tips.

"Wakey wakey, Sleeping Beauty," Ellie says, precariously balancing two mugs of milk-no-sugar as she climbs back into the bed beside me. I can feel the grazing warmth of the sunbeams filtering in through the open curtains as I keep my eyes pressed shut, the sound of two china cups clinking above me bringing a smile to my face.

"Ta-muchly," I reply happily, scooching myself up.

I let my hands reach out for the awaiting cuppa with my eyes still closed and let the steam from the brew unseal my eyelids enough to look around in the harsh light of day.

It's a tragic sight. Beyond my cup of tea lies only a shell of what was once the best room in the whole of Flat B, 13 Elmfield Road.

"No, no, no," I grumble like a spoiled child as I look at the brown cardboard boxes piled up around the floor. I almost spill precious nutrients from my tea as I shake my head furiously.

"If I don't do it now I'll have a proper panic tomorrow morning," Ellie replies, surveying her land sadly. Her wardrobe is already open, clothes piled in some order around it like a shrine to what once was. Her shelves are still filled with trinkets and thingamabobs picked up over the eight years we've lived here together, but there are already key pieces missing—Greg, her polar bear toy, has given up his throne at the top of her bookshelf in swap for a duffel bag; most of her photo frames have been removed, presumably into the bottom of some box already half-packed; the fairy lights that went up one Christmas five or so years ago and never came back down have finally disappeared. If I didn't know better I would have thought there had been a robbery. I wish there had been.

On the other side of the room Mark's boxes already look closed and taped, ready for shipment. I bet he can't wait to get out, the little troll.

"Where is Mark?"

"He's gone to pick up the keys from the real estate agent."

"Already? I thought you said Sunday!"

"Sunday's tomorrow."

"Exactly! Sunday's *tomorrow*."

"Don't worry—we'll still stay here tonight after the dinner. It's going to take us all weekend to move everything over and we have to hand the keys back in at one."

Partly due to my sleep deprivation, partly due to my terrible night, partly due to the unbelievably comforting smell of tea floating up my nostrils but mostly due to my breaking heart, I can feel the tears well up in full force.

"No—none of that now," she tries, but it's already too late. Floodgates are open. Waterworks are inevitable. Her usually worried face turns even more worried.

"Can't you just live here for one more year? What's one more year going to do in the scheme of things?"

"Not this again."

"You'll miss us! The two of you don't know how to live without us. What if you move in together and find that you don't have anything else in common? What if you're bored and lonely and you miss us too much?"

I can't stop the tears from falling now. Black mascara clumps from makeup I'd forgotten to wipe off last night begin spoiling my perfectly lovely cup of tea.

"Then I'll come over and stay."

"What if you break up?"

"We won't break up."

"But what if you do?"

"I thought I was the worrier? Not you!" She's right. I hate when she's right. "Then I'll come and stay forever. Happy? Now tell me about this big bad wolf before my tea gets cold."

❧ 10 ❧

I'd like to say that I'm a good listener, but I've nothing on Ellie. It's one of her most fantastic qualities, but to date I haven't seen a quality in her that wasn't fabulous. She was born to be a psychotherapist, I swear, only she was a woman of far too many talents and she ended up in medical research instead. Every time I ask about her job I get lost, so I've stopped asking, but she's a genius whether I can articulate it or not.

Her listening superpower is probably helped a little by the fact that her mother was my primary schoolteacher. As I outline my series of unfortunate errors from the night before I feel like I'm six years old again sitting cross-legged on the floor of Ms. Mathews's classroom and crying because Tom Anderson scribbled on my pencil case. There's a strange comforting feeling that wells over me as her sympathetic and somehow still not condescending eyes blink back at my increasingly outrageous monologue.

"Well, put him in the bin and move on. Plenty of others out there."

"Are there?" I moan. Even I regret the whine in my voice but I can't help it. It's the younger, less-lavender-smelling Ms. Mathews before me and instinctively I'm acting like a toddler. "Because the way I see it I'm running out of options."

"Oh come on. The perfect guy is just around the corner."

"I don't even know what the perfect man is anymore. Ten years ago I knew. I knew exactly what I was looking for then; someone who loved dogs, wanted kids, and looked like Ryan Reynolds. Now? Now I'll take just about anyone who'll have me."

"Now that's just not true." Ellie's laugh is annoyingly infectious.

"It is! I'm telling you! I've had a decade's worth of rejection at this point and I've seriously reached a stage where I'm looking at a man across the table who has more hair on his face than face on his face and thanking my lucky stars that he said yes to meeting me in the first place. And still, somehow feeling like shit when the smelly hairy man doesn't want a second date with me."

"You wouldn't want a second date with him anyway."

"I want my happy ending, Ellie. I want a big white wedding with a handsome man who will sweep me off my feet." I take a side-glance at her quickly, before changing my tone. "I know, I know. You don't have to tell me."

"Tell you what?" she says, sounding genuinely confused.

"I know you think that weddings are pointless and expensive and that you don't understand why I'd ever want to bother with one."

She raises an eyebrow.

"When have I ever said that to you in your whole life?" she says.

To be fair, she's never actually said it out loud, but I know she thinks it. About weddings generally that is, not specifically about mine. As if to finish my thought she shakes her head at me: "Just because *I* don't want a big dress and a cute church doesn't mean I don't understand why you do. I'll always want for you whatever makes you happy," she says, which is the most Ellie thing I've ever heard. She's literally part angel.

"I know," I say, smiling, "and I know I don't need a man to make me happy but I still *want* one. It's just, apparently, none of them *want* me!"

"There will be one. One who doesn't treat you like crap and kick you out on the street at four a.m."

"They're the only kind that meet me in the first place these days!"

"That's crap. There are still good ones out there. You just have to kiss a few frogs first."

"I've already kissed all the frogs."

"All of them?"

"All London-based frogs, yes."

"What about that new app you downloaded? The mirror one?"

"It's . . . it's like fine. But the problem with London dating apps is that it's all the same people. A new one comes out and we all think it's great, only then everyone migrates over and you find yourself talking to the same men who've rejected you on four other platforms before."

"Right. This pity party needs to end," Ellie says, finishing off the last of her tea decisively. I love it when Ellie gets all action-star Barbie on me. Her usual worried expression is pulled into something much more fierce and fiery. "You deserve someone who treats you with respect, and given that there are nearly nine million people in London I would say it's almost entirely impossible that you've personally kissed all the single men out there. You need patience."

"What I need is you in boy form," I say, trying not to cry all over again.

"Marty?" she jokes.

My face naturally turns to her shelf where her family photo still sits proudly. Trust Ellie to leave that till the end to pack. It's probably going to be the first thing she unpacks too on the other side. Not that I want to think about that now.

Her mum, Niamh, is in the center, being squeezed on either side by both of her children: Ellie on one side and Marty, her elder brother by about sixteen minutes and forty-five seconds, on the other. They're both around sixteen in the photo and I should know; I'm pretty sure I'm the one who took it given the background is my parents' garden.

"Ew," I reply, turning away from Marty's mop of brown curls. "Let me rephrase, what I need is you in Ryan Reynolds's body."

"Technology's getting better every day. In a few years' time that might even be possible, my friend."

Keeping my teacup finely balanced I launch into a hug that I don't want to end. She's been my other half for so long I don't know how to function without her.

She's always been beside me, through grade school, through high school—I mean, despite never wanting to act the part of the bride, she's been my maid of honor all 392 times I held wedding receptions in my parents' sitting room. She was there every single time that my imaginary groom and I cut the cake and when my love and I would ride off into the sunset she was there too, either as the chorus of angelic voices guiding us or—on more than one occasion—as the horse we sat on.

Her hair smells like my Aussie shampoo and certainly not like her own Boots brand but I don't even care enough to mention it right now. Today is not the day. She strokes my tangled mane from out of my face and smiles down at me and I just know things will be alright.

"Now, young lady," she says. Honestly, it's like Ms. Mathews all over again. "I need to pack and you need to write."

"Write! I can't write like this!"

"You promised me that you'd write every day for at least two hours and given I know you've missed the last two weeks, you have a lot of making up to do."

"But I'm hungover!"

"That's not an excuse."

"But I'm sad." I pull my very best Muppet face but she only laughs at my misery.

"Let that inspire you then."

"Urgh!"

I swirl the dregs of my tea and I look at her, wondering how long I can make this last.

"You can always help me pack if you'd prefer?" Ellie replies knowingly. I look at the bags around her. I might like constructing furniture but I hate dismantling things, and packing up eight years of our friendship into cardboard boxes feels as comforting as magpies pecking out my organs.

"Fine. I'm going," I say begrudgingly, pulling myself up and tip-toeing around the destruction of years of flatmate-ship around me.

"Dinner's at eight," she reminds me as I go, "you're on dessert."

I kick one of Mark's boxes aside as I reach closer to the door and that makes me feel a bit better somehow.

"Oi!"

Shit, she caught me. I turn at the door, feigning my best innocent "what me" face that she's not even looking at.

"Yeah?" I say sweetly.

"You keeping that hoodie then?" she asks.

Oh good.

I pull the red hood right over my head and zip the whole thing right up. I smile as I do it, finally taking back control.

"Absolutely," I reply.

11

When I open the door to my cold, crappy room I walk straight over to my writing desk.

I can see that my bed's not made. This comes as no real surprise as I'm the only one who would make it and I clearly didn't. There are a silly amount of empty glasses on every surface and the floor is a bit of a death trap with more discarded clothes and sharp heels jutting out at odd angles than actual floor to walk on. I swear I tidy it all the time, but it takes me about ten hours to clean it and ten seconds to mess it up again so I never know why I bother. I ignore it for now, turning back to the desk before me.

It was a gift from my parents from years ago, back when I first told them I wanted to be a writer. I was like fourteen at the time, and still vaguely hanging on to the idea that the Easter Bunny was somehow real, so I don't know why they took me seriously. But they did. They listened to me, they heard me, and they got me a writing desk because "the first tool a writer needs is a good place to write."

It just proves how supportive they've always been. It's amazing, it is, and I know that, but it's also a bit annoying in the least annoying way possible. I only mean you hear of all these amazing writers who faced conflict all their lives when I've not had one argument with them about my career at all.

I mean, when I got incredibly average grades, were they disappointed in me? No. They told me to find something I believed in and trust my gut. When I come home without a man at my side do they comment? Tell me that I've failed them? Tell me all about how much they want grandchildren and blame me for my failures to ensnare a permanent semen injector into my life? No. They tell me that there is strength in my independence and salute me for not settling.

God, they're great. I wonder for a second if I should text them, just because really, but quickly decide against it. I'll text them later, because Ellie is right: I did say in January of this year that I'd write for two hours a day every day, and given it's September, I think I'm about eight and a half months behind on that target.

My laptop, freezing cold from neglect, sits waiting for me. I open the lid, type my password in, and open up Word.

I look at the blank canvas that is my screen.

I love writing, I do, only what I'm doing now isn't writing, it's thinking about what to write, and that completely sucks.

Once I have a spark of an idea it becomes the most important thing to me. When I'm in the heart of the drama, twisting the plot around like a candy floss stick, gathering depth and flavor, I'm never happier in the whole world, and yet right now, I'm at a complete and utter loss on what to actually write about.

According to Ellie, I needed "more of a routine."

"It's how I completed my PhD," she said, which inspired me greatly because if she can write eighty thousand words on *Epidemiology and Outcomes of Psoriatic Arthritis* without losing faith, I didn't see any reason I couldn't write the next *Bridget Jones*.

She said writer's block was just a mentality to overcome and that I needed writing to not just be spur of the moment but something I did daily, like yoga. Not that I do yoga daily. Or at all, actually. But I get the point so I promised her.

Fucking inspiration. Where is it? What is it? How do I get it and why, when I've had so many ideas through the years, have all of them disappeared into the void as I stare blankly upon my clean white Word document before me? I have a whole world to explore, whole new characters to conceive and shape, and a whole new plot to delve into. Right now however, it looks very much like a blinking cursor.

In search of a spark I look up to the picture of my parents, propped up against a book spine on the corner of the desk.

I don't know which one I'm more like. They're both as ginger as me, which amuses people no end when we're all together. My old teachers used to call us the "Weasleys," which my mum never really understood because she wasn't a big fan of *Harry Potter*. She never really bought into the whole thing, which makes sense once you know she's a Slytherin through and through. My dad's more of a Hufflepuff, which I think should make me a Slyther-puff hybrid, and maybe I am, but it's very mood dependent for me.

Maybe I should write about them?

I look at my screen once again, my fingers poised over the keyboard.

One Lemon Cake for a Lifetime of Happiness

I write.

I sit back, trying to work out what angle I should take. It doesn't need all too much dramatizing, to be fair—it's already something of a romantic fairy tale even without embellishment.

My parents met at school—at school! It's unheard of that those who met at twelve years old can still be as happy and as perfect as they are but it's true. By sixteen they were childhood sweethearts, bonding over chemistry lessons and English essays until, one perfect Christmas in their early twenties, my mum gathered all of their friends and family together, baked my father's favorite lemon cake (that's important—it's the detail that's never missed in any retelling for it is, to date, the only food item my mother has ever made that didn't burn or give someone food poisoning), and dropped down on one knee.

"One lemon cake for a lifetime of happiness," that's what they say. It's the most romantic thing I can think of and that's been the romantic story I've had to compete with all my life.

All through secondary I was just waiting to have an epic encounter in the library that would change my life forever. Turns out I only kissed one boy in my school years—at Sarah Evans's thirteenth birthday party—and his gluten intolerance and (quite soon after) coming out meant that both the lemon cake and the wedding proposal was off the table for us.

So school came and went. University passed me by. A boyfriend or two lingered in my early London life but faded into insubstantial nothingness quite quickly until we reach now, a time where the whole of England's capital seems coupled up with me as the third wheel to all its (according to Ellie) nine million strong population.

Actually thinking about it, I'm not in the mood to write out any love story, let alone theirs. Not while my own is so terrible.

I quickly hit Ctrl+A and delete it.

Not a romance then. Okay, that's fine. So what else should I write then . . . what else . . .

☙ 12 ❧

After a while, staring at the blank screen just burns my eyeballs so instead I take out my phone and do the usual rounds. Martha and her big-nosed wife are on holiday in Dubai. When is she not on holiday? I see a post from Rachel about a new promotion at the job she can't stop posting about—Jesus, it's so unprofessional to use Instagram for job updates. Does she not have a life? Or LinkedIn? A few annoying baby pictures from Rich and Lucy, a depressingly lovely countryside scene from Ricky, and front-row seats to see some indie star I'm not cool enough to recognize for "I-chose-law-and-now-I'm-a-millionaire" Freddie and his current highly successful businesswoman girlfriend. On Stories I see a few meals prepared by some fitness blogger I started following at New Year's and who never really inspired me more than just made me hungry. Ronnie's had a night in last night. Cara had a night out. I scroll through them all thoughtlessly, sipping my tea slowly until a dog video makes me laugh enough to watch it again. I check the user—Marty Mathews.

Of course it's Marty.

I flip onto messages.

26 Sep 10:17-Me
You coming tonight?

I wait a few minutes. I check the time. It's still early. There's no way he's awake unless he's on call.

I scroll back onto Instagram but get bored pretty quickly and search my apps for some inspiration instead. My finger knows what I'm doing before my brain kicks in and I watch on, helpless to stop it as Mirror Mirror loads up its home screen with a mystical puff of smoke.

For what it's worth, I like what they're trying to do more than the usual generic dating sites.

Because the fairest of them should be the right one too, say the words in a fairy-tale font across the screen.

Okay, so their marketing copy is a bit crap, borderline racist when taken out of the folklore context, and completely female skewing. It's a complete wonder that anyone would sign up to something this juvenile sounding, let alone any decent London male. I reckon they're relying on gals like me, brought up on a healthy diet of Disney, and if an app can get enough girls to sign up the guys do follow eventually, I guess. Still, the tagline is way too cringe. I could do better, but that's because I'm a writer. If I was in charge of their motto it would be something like:

"The best of them all should . . ."

No, it's already crap.

"Blowing out the smog of . . ."

Probably best to avoid blow imagery for a dating site.

"Because . . ."

Well, I don't actually work at Mirror Mirror so I don't need to come up with a tagline, but if I did and I was going to it would be better than theirs.

My profile picture pops up to greet me. It's a little glass slipper, a cheap imitation of the Disney version, probably because of copyright issues.

Everyone's profile picture begins like that—an anonymous fairy-tale character or item and their name. That's all you see for a while actually. It supposedly matches you using some black box algorithm based on a set of questions you signed up with, but I think we all know that's code for "complete randomizer." It pairs you up with three at a time and the more you chat, the more you see of the other's profile. For every message you write them a little more of your actual profile picture gets uncovered until, about a hundred or so texts in, you can pretty much see their whole face.

I like that. You put more time into getting to know someone. People can't make quick-fire decisions—unless you're Charles Wolf, that is. He seemed pretty unfazed that we hadn't chatted long enough to even see an outline of a profile picture.

Maybe if I'd seen his hairy, hairy face before we'd met I might have canceled on him instead.

Who am I kidding? I wouldn't have dared.

Charles Wolf must have already deleted me, for where his Gaston look-alike picture used to be a new match has already been added. I try not to feel the "ouch" in my stomach as I click on this new profile instead.

The picture is a bit bizarre. Most of the guys pick the dragons or the princes—a few of the more comedy-oriented ones pick the fish or lobsters—but this one is a little old goblin. I try to work out who it is but I don't really recognize it from anywhere.

Name: Mystery Man

I raise an eyebrow, then realize that there is no one to witness my raised eyebrow so I quickly drop it back to its usual position.

Mystery Man. That's all I'm getting?

I need a few more texts to even unveil his occupation. Is it even worth it for this? An old goblin profile picture and a name of "Mystery Man."

Oh, why not.

I begin typing.

Bella Marble

Well aren't you mysterious

I pride myself on never opening with the usual noncommittal "hey" as I never really know where you go from there.

Mystery Man
Life's too short to be boring

An immediate reply. Keen. Maybe he was even just about to text me first?

Bella Marble

You going to tell me your real name mystery man?

I cringe at my own words. I hate that I can't delete things once I send them. It's like watching a replay of a car crash in real time.

Mystery Man

That would be too easy

Bella Marble

I bet it's something boring like Paul or Mark

I smile at my own internal joke. Mark, boring. Well, that would be flattering to him.

Mystery Man

I'll tell you what, if you guess it I'll take you on the best date you've ever been on

A game? That's upped the stakes a little bit. Usually I'm lucky to get a "hey" back. At least this is something, albeit just a little creepy.

Bella Marble

What kind of date are we talking here?

Bella Marble

I need to know it's worth the effort

Mystery Man

You a Party Girl? Or like a bit of Culture?

Bella Marble

Culture

Bella Marble

Every time

I sit back and I smile. He doesn't immediately text back and my smile slightly fades. Oh dear, have I blown it already? How?

Was it a trick question?

Oh, I made myself sound so uncool, didn't I? Who picks culture? Seriously.

Mystery Man

After-hours tour of the History Museum. Drinks and Dinosaurs. The winning combo

I'm not being funny but that actually sounds amazing. I'm a big nerd at heart and I love museums. When I first moved to London I remember thinking I'd probably go all the time, but life happens and that somehow didn't.

> **Bella Marble**
> How many guesses do I get?

Mystery Man
As many as you want

I check his profile to see how much more has been revealed based on our little chat already.

Name: Mystery Man
Occupation: Entrepreneur
Height: It doesn't matter
Age: Is just a number

Well, that's not helpful.

> **Bella Marble**
> George?.

Mystery Man
Nope

> **Bella Marble**
> Michael?

Mystery Man
Guess again

> **Bella Marble**
> Nigel?

Mystery Man
I'm not an 80-year-old man

> **Bella Marble**
> I thought you said age is just a number?

My phone vibrates and it shocks me, pulling me out of my Mirror Mirror tangent. It's a text, Marty. So he is awake.

> **26 Sep 10:17-Me**
> You coming tonight?

Marty-26 Sep 10:36
Jack's birthday. I'm out

26 Sep 10:36-Me
But it's Ellie's last night!

Marty-26 Sep 10:36
Is she dying?

26 Sep 10:37-Me
If she was would you come out tonight?

Marty-26 Sep 10:37
No. Still Jack's birthday

26 Sep 10:38-Me
You're a terrible brother

Marty-26 Sep 10:38
If she dies I inherit more. Win-win

Marty's usually a frequent flyer around 13 Elmfield Road. Despite being twins, their differences are pretty substantial. Ellie's a home-bird, Marty likes to stay out. Ellie's a monogamist, Marty sticks to a daily one-in, one-out policy. Ellie worries, Marty doesn't care. Ellie is lovely, Marty's a self-proclaimed arsehole.

In reality they're not as different as they like to think. Family always comes first with that clan, at least that's been the case ever since their idiotic father left them to pursue his dreams of living like an eighteen-year-old, ignoring his paternal duties, and backpacking the world with literal eighteen-year-old girls at his side. I'd say that's why the rest of the family is so close, but those three were always a unit even before Stuart Mathews's twatty adventure began.

26 Sep 10:38-Me
Whatever. I'm on pudding duty
You'll miss out on my beautiful homemade pie

Marty-26 Sep 10:38
Like fuck are you cooking a pie

It's a good point. What am I going to do?

26 Sep 10:38-Me
Fine. You'll miss out on my beautiful store-bought ice
cream

That reminds me. I quickly flick my texts over to Annie.

26 Sep 10:38-Me
Hey, can you pick up some ice cream on your way home from the gym? x

Annie Flatmate-26 Sep 10:38
Won't be back till 5 x

26 Sep 10:38-Me
That's fine. Can you pick it up anyway? x

Annie Flatmate-26 Sep 10:38
Yeah sure x

I turn it back to Marty.

Marty-26 Sep 10:38
You can buy me ice cream whenever

Marty-26 Sep 10:38
Jack only turns 30 once

26 Sep 10:39-Me
Can't believe you're picking Jack over Ellie

26 Sep 10:39-Me
What does Jack have that Ellie doesn't?

Marty-26 Sep 10:39
Fit friends ☺

Marty-26 Sep 10:39
If you're out later drop me a line. We're heading to Brixton x

26 Sep 10:39-Me
Whatever loser x

I switch off texts and look at my cup of tea. There's still a small amount lingering in the bottom of the mug. I swirl it around, biding my time.

I look up to my laptop screen. It's gone into sleep mode. I flicker on the trackpad and watch the blank Word document light back up, mocking me in its starkness. I still have one sip left, I reason, clicking on Mirror Mirror one more time.

I switch to Mystery Man.

Bella Marble
Marty?

It's not actually Marty. Marty's not clever enough for this kind of stunt. I've seen some of the texts he sends girls and they aren't this thought out. Normally it's just:

What do you do?

I'm a vet.

Okay, I'm coming over now.

Still, Marty's another boy's name—albeit a bit of a stupid one.

Mystery Man

Keep going

Bella Marble

This is going to be a very long game

Mystery Man

The best things in life are worth waiting for

I switch off Mirror Mirror, drain the last of my tea, and sit up straight, bringing my laptop just a little closer.

Maybe you're right, Mystery Man. Or maybe you're a strange creep whom I should stay well clear of.

Either way, now I should definitely start actually writing something.

Except, here's the age-old problem: what on earth should I write?

13

I wake up and I'm a bit confused.

I'm not confused that I fell asleep. I sort of saw that as inevitable as soon as I lay my head down on the pillow but I'm confused that it's so dark outside. I check my watch: 7 p.m.

It's 7 p.m.? How on earth is it 7 p.m.? I'm also confused that my room's not that tidy. I spent over an hour trying to sift through the piles of mess once I decided that I'd work better knowing all my chores were completed, but it looks like it barely made a dent in the chaos. The nap was a by-product of the exertion given to the cleaning, but the reward seems pretty disproportionate to the success of the task.

I check my phone again to be sure, also a little disappointed that I've been napping for the last eight hours and in that time I received absolutely no notifications. Not even from my mum.

By the time I have a shower and get myself into clean clothes, carefully draping the red hoodie over my closet door, I can already hear the rumble of voices stirring in the kitchen.

Annie's big on presentation. She only got back at 5 p.m. and yet she's dressed to the nines in a beautifully fitted cream playsuit and the kitchen somehow looks like a dining room fit for kings. Candles are lit, the smell of warm homemade food is bubbling away on the hobs, and someone's got a playlist on the go of aughts tracks that hits the right spot.

"Waaay!" I cry out, swinging my hips like a Hula-Hoop as the words tumble out my mouth as naturally as Milkybar Buttons usually roll into it: *"I got a feeling. That tonight's gonna be a good night. That tonight's gonna be a good night. That tonight's gonna be a good, good night."*

"Let the party begin!" Simon laughs from the kitchen table.

"Oi, oi!"

As I turn around Simon's already cracking open a bottle of wine and I'm quick to get my favorite mug ready for it. His blond hair is still windswept from his day's strenuous activities but his small circular eyes hidden under dramatically large lenses still look just as doe-like and innocent as they always do. His usual jumper and jean "straight-out-of-a-preppy-handbook" look has been exchanged for an equally smart shirt-and-chino combo for the occasion, putting my little black dress (six years old and it definitely shows) to shame.

"Sim-oné, my love. How was the gig?" I ask him coyly.

"Better than expected."

"I'd say. You slept with the most beautiful man in the world last night." I lean in, ready for the gossip.

"I'll take it," a beautiful Spanish accent replies. There in the doorway is the intoxicatingly handsome and now fully clothed man from the night before. In the fresh light of (midevening) day he's all dark tan and beach hair like a new and improved James Dean. His tight leather trousers outline clearly to everyone what I saw last night and I try my hardest to stop my eyes from glancing directly down at his crotch. He holds out his hand with the confidence of a TV hero and as I take it I feel my knees weaken.

"Diego," he says. Honestly, I didn't think I had a thing for a Spanish accent but Diego makes it sound like butter melting off his tongue. I want to lap it up like a kitten.

"And did you also like the band, Diego?" I ask, hoping I sound cool and calm but knowing I sound like an annoyingly excitable squirrel.

"He *is* the band," Simon says proudly, smiling up at Diego with knowing eyes.

Oh, of course he is. Of course this beautiful Spanish man is a rock star by trade. Look at his hair for Christ's sake, it looks like threads of pure silk. He's wearing a jock's sweatshirt with an AllSaints logo that probably cost more than my entire wardrobe is worth. One whole year of nothing and Simon finally struck gold.

"How did the writing go?" asks Ellie, wandering in from behind them. Her long blond hair is puffed up, probably as a by-product of the fabulous volume-enhancing powers of my Aussie shampoo she nicked. I still don't say anything. Neither do I say anything about the green-and-blue floral dress she's wearing that definitely lived in my wardrobe for the last few years that she must have helped herself to—although that's more because I can't remember if I stole it from her to begin with.

"It's getting there," I reply quickly. "Ellie, have you met Diego? Diego's in a band."

"Diego *is* the band," Simon corrects.

"Diego's been helping me carry boxes all afternoon," Ellie tells me. She turns to Diego and, actually looking totally fine with being in his hypnotic presence, squeezes his arm like an old friend. "Thanks again. Having the extra pair of hands around was a godsend!"

"Why didn't you ask me?" I ask, mildly annoyed that I wasn't the first choice.

"I didn't want to disturb your writing!" Ellie replies, looking worried at the whole idea of it.

My writing. Of which I have nothing to actually show.

I swallow, nodding acceptance of this very considerate excuse and swiftly trying to get off the subject.

"It smells delish, Annie!" I say, swigging a large swish of Merlot. "What's for dinner?"

"It's my favorite!" Ellie replies, looking down at the dish.

"You have lots of favorites. Which is this one? Specifically."

"It's a lamb, squash, and apricot tagine," she replies excitedly. It does sound delightful.

The others start a whole new conversation on the joys of Moroccan cuisine but within seconds I stop concentrating. I'm distracted by Diego's hand running through Simon's hair. It's almost 8 p.m. the day after they hooked up and Diego is still in the flat.

More than that, he is already meeting Simon's friends. He'd spent the day helping Ellie move.

Simon didn't kick this man out at 4 a.m. Simon didn't arrive late and stay for just one drink (probably, his timekeeping is usually impeccable). Simon didn't do any of the things Charles Wolf did to me, because Diego is beautiful (which is probably irrelevant but very true) and Simon isn't a giant arse.

This is what I'm after. This here, before me, is exactly what I've been looking for. And maybe, just maybe, seeing Simon get so lucky after all this time means that Ellie's actually right: that there is someone out there for me too. Someone who'll stroke through my ginger nest unprompted at a dinner party, if only I can be patient enough to wait for them. Easier said than done; I'm not a very patient person.

"Bella?"

I turn. My daydream has been caught out and Annie's large chestnut eyes are staring at me.

"Sorry, yes?"

"I said I got that ice cream you asked for," Annie repeats, turning back to her pot to stir the large tagine. "Was vanilla alright?"

"Perfect."

"What's for dessert then?" Simon asks.

I look around for backup. Given what Annie's just said it's a bit of a daft question. But it's a question that, confusingly, everyone seems to be looking at me for an answer for.

"Ice cream," I reply.

"With what though?" Annie asks. I pause again.

Oh God. It just occurs to me: Annie's pulled out all the stops, Simon's wine looks at least two payment categories above Sainsbury's basics, and I've just got . . .

"More . . . ice cream?" I say, my cheeks plumping up all red.

"Wait—just ice cream?" Simon joins in.

"Not *just* ice cream. *Ice cream*," I try, but even I feel my argument failing.

"Just vanilla ice cream?" Annie asks again.

"That's not fair, the vanilla bit was your choice."

"I thought it would be a condiment!"

"Since when is ice cream a condiment? Marmalade is a condiment."

"Marmalade isn't a condiment."

"Oh Jesus Christ, Bella! You had one thing!"

"I brought cake!" says the chirpy voice of Mark wandering in through the door.

The whole room turns around to look at him like he is their savior. If it was anyone else, literally anyone else, I'd be so happy right now. I can already feel the heat of my cheeks cooling at the idea that someone else brought an ice cream alternative—only it's Mark. So I'm not.

It's like the minute he entered the whole room cooled for me. He is a literal fun sponge, soaking in the atmosphere and sucking out all the joy I have.

He's a big guy, Mark, so it's hard to miss him and yet he owns a face so forgettable I constantly struggle to recall it. I look at it now, eyeing up the enemy, and my usual confusion at why Ellie is still with him returns all over again.

His nose is rounded at the edges to match the roundness of his silly little face, which is not terrible looking per se, only Ellie's cheekbones are Oscar worthy and completely out of his league. His complexion's "fine," I guess, with wide eyes colored in a deep gray to match his boring soul. He almost always looks untidy and unkempt, which is bizarre because even without makeup Ellie is superstar tidy. She's my height and slim; this man is a human bear. She's an 8.9. He's a 5.7 at best.

Okay, maybe that's a little bit of an exaggeration. It's not like Ellie's perfect or anything. I know she looks worried more often than not, which crinkles her forehead in an almost permanent way. Her little twitchy nose is a bit on the small side and her ears a little on the large. Her blond hair is a bit flat and lifeless unless it pops with my shampoo (I won't go on about it) but like, still. He's so completely beige. Why on earth is she with him? *Why is she moving in with him?*

"Brilliant, Mark!" say multiple voices around the room.

"Sorry, Bella, I know you were on pudding but I passed by a cake on my way and I thought this was a celebration, after all. I couldn't resist."

I roll my eyes. Typical. Here he is, swanning in, taking over my place and doing everything to outshine me. He didn't buy super-fancy wine to outdo Simon's contribution to the party. He didn't make an alternative main course to compete with Annie. Of course he brought a spare pudding. Of course he assumed I'd fail. I mean, I did, in this particular instance, but I still bite my lip in annoyance so hard it almost bleeds.

If only I'd made a homemade summer fruits crumble, that would have shown him.

But I didn't.

I've never been so disappointed in my own preplanning and basic culinary skills.

14

To be fair, I've forgotten all about it within an hour or two. Mostly because I can handle my wine, but what I can't handle is Simon's wine. He's one of those "top up your glass while you're not looking" kind of guys and given that Diego and him want to head out to a bar later they've been gunning it all through our melon and Parma ham starter course.

All I can say is that I didn't pick the playlist, so it's not my fault when Steps's timeless classic "Tragedy" hits Annie's Bose speakers that I accidentally remember all the moves and have to demonstrate them.

"ELLIE! ELLIE YOU GOTTA JOIN ME!" I scream, because it's important to scream these things sometimes and she used to look just like H when we were little with her little blond curtains so really this is her tune.

"Bella." She's killing herself laughing. "Oh God, I don't know if I remember . . ."

"YOU DO! YOU DO! *TRAGEDY!*" We put our flat palms to our ears in uniform fashion. "COME ON!"

I'm way too drunk right now to remember the words, but when has a little lyric confusion ever got in the way of singing? The less you know, the more conviction you need to have. That's all. So with that in mind, I pump up my vocal volume and power through:

"Bunna bump bump baa, bunna bump bump baa . . ."

"TRAGEDY!"

"YES, SIMON!" Simon's right up beside me, hands on ears rather than over them but we'll forgive that. He's usually a bit timid for these kinds of displays but he's clearly a bit pissed too by the glassiness of his eyes. Hurray for tasty wine, that's all I can say.

"When something something, na na naa!" I sing on, wondering if Simon might correct me with the words. He doesn't. Oh well.

Bold move, I suddenly realize, given he has a new beau watching us. I feel a bit bad for a minute as this is clearly super uncool and Diego's a literal rock star, but just as guilt begins to build Diego hops right up with hips that move like Elvis and although he clearly doesn't know what he's doing we've all drunk enough for him to copy the very gawky arm movements that the two of us are doing.

Yes, Diego! It is *that* kind of night.

Ellie used to be the first one up but clearly this is not Mark's cup of tea (what is?) so she's being all shy. Annie's warming the tagine for the second course but even she's bopping as she stirs to fresh beats of the nineties cover.

"Come on, Els!" I bait through the second verse, shimmying her way. She can't resist a shimmy surely. No one can resist a shimmy. Except she's somehow resisting a shimmy.

We're reaching the last chorus; Annie's turned from the tagine especially for the finale beside Simon on our kitchen-cum-size-restricted-dance-floor. Our time is running out and Ellie's still sitting.

Come on, Ellie! You can do it! I think to myself desperately. I don't even know why this matters to me, maybe it's the wine, but weirdly it does.

Just when I think all hope might be lost I hear from out of the (metaphorical) darkness:

"TRAGEDY!" And she's up! Pitch perfect! There's my girl!

And there it is, the dance routine of many a town hall birthday party coming back to us like no time has passed at all. Ellie and Simon to one side of me, Diego and Annie on the other, perhaps the least likely pop band you could possibly imagine but we hit perfect unison as our hands fly to our ears, left up, right up, restart. Shimmy left, shimmy right. Stop right now, shake out the shoulder. Beat after glorious beat. Gesture after synchronized gesture. We're on fire. We're on top of the world.

My God, I love my friends.

My God, I'll miss this.

"TRAGEDY!" all of us cry as the song comes to its perfect conclusion.

All of us except Mark, that is. He's pretending he doesn't know the dance. Even Diego's worked out the dance moves and five minutes ago he thought steps were just the thing you walked up.

"Do you remember the music video for this?" Simon asks, catching his breath.

"What is it?" Sexy Diego asks, falling back into his chair. Sexy *and* up for a laugh? Who is this man? Simon, you champion.

"Who's ready for the main course?" Mark asks in a totally normal tone like nothing just happened, bringing our joy to a startling end.

Seriously Mark, why the long face?

Live a little.

15

As the meal finally ends, Mark stands up and taps against his glass (an actual wineglass like a grown-up, that is—not my fun-filled wine mug. What a happiness vampire).

Because I am drunk—*because I am drunk*—I stand up too.

This is not Mark's night. I know that he lived here too, and I get that, but this is Ellie's night. This is mine and Ellie's night. If there is someone who is going to make a speech about an end of an era, it's me.

"Thanks, Mark," I say with a wink like we'd planned it. Gracefully he sits back down, indicating that he is more than happy for me to speak first. What a prick.

"Ellie, you're my best friend," I say, holding up my mug. I look at all the faces around me. They are finding me mildly hilarious but that's probably just because I'm a good public speaker.

"I love you," I say, and I mean it. I look at her, tapping my fifth or sixth mug of wine against the right side of my chest before quickly remembering and moving it to my left side instead by my heart. Only a minor hiccup. I bet no one noticed.

At this point I realize all the words have already been said. There is nothing else I can say that could sum up eight happy years of living together and twenty-nine years of perfect friendship.

The Spice Girls are playing in the background and it occurs to me that it couldn't be more fitting. Growing up I always wanted to be Baby, of course, because she was the one everyone wanted to be, but Ellie was blond and I was quite clearly the only Ginger in our whole class. I spent years watching from the sidelines as Ellie mimed along to my favorite lines and wore little pink dresses that I always wanted to wear. Then, one day when I was particularly sad about the whole thing, she asked me what was wrong and I told her. After that, she never even let me be Ginger again, adamant that she didn't want to be Baby anyway. There she was, forever more putting on a wig and donning a Union Jack outfit all because she knew it would make me happy, and being the greatest Ginger in the whole wide world. It's the kind of girl she is: putting her friends first, always. Putting me first, always.

"What I want . . ." I begin, the memories of our God-awful childhood dance routines in my mind, *is to go back to that time and start all over again.*

No, says my sobriety, don't say that.

"What I want . . ." *is for Mark to go and for you to stay with me.*

No, come on, Bella. Hold your shit together.

"What I want . . . What I really, really want is a zigga zig ahh," I conclude finally, finishing it off with an unintentional hiccup. Holy shit, they are lyrical geniuses. Thank you, Scary Spice, I couldn't have said it better myself.

"That is all," I conclude, wondering only faintly how long my heartfelt speech must have taken.

"Love you, Bells!" Ellie whispers under her breath to me as the song fades to the next.

"Beautiful, Bella," Mark says, standing up.

No one gave him the memo. We weren't doing speeches. I did mine, because she's my best friend, but that was the only one allowed. Still, Mark begins speaking without anyone asking for it. I reach for another top up as S Club 7's "Reach for the Stars" starts blasting. At least I don't have to listen to him speak then. The early 2000s were a fabulous era for pop. What a tune.

"I just wanted to say a huge thank-you to everyone for accepting me into your family here at Elmfield Road. I've lived in a fair amount of flat shares in my time in London and not once have any of them felt like a home before this one. Diego, I can't thank you enough for your help today. Annie, I don't know what we'll do without your cooking. Simon, well, I'll see you anyway next week for the squash league, and Bella—thanks for always being there for my Ellie."

His Ellie? Presumptuous tit.

"Ellie, this is a real end to an era for you and I know this is a sad moment, but this is also a new door to the next chapter of our lives and I couldn't be more excited to be a part of this with you."

I look over at Annie and sneakily look like I'm vomiting at the table. Annie doesn't laugh with me like I think she should. She shakes her head and turns back to the speaker.

"Now I know this is a bit of a transition period in our lives, but I think, if we're going to take a step out to this new era, why not take a whole damn leap."

He looks around the table and I smile back at him like I'm listening properly but the song's way too catchy for that and right now, I can only focus on one thing at a time. I've got priorities. I wonder if anyone else is as bored as I am.

"Ellie, do you remember Kate and Millie's birthday thing?"

Jesus Christ, he's taking over the whole night.

"Yes," Ellie says nervously. Probably because she's embarrassed he's talking for so long. I know I am for her already. I'm impatient at the best of times, but drunk me hits a whole new level.

"We got on the subject of wedding proposals at the table and you told this story about Bella's parents."

My parents? Why is he involving my parents in this?

"You said that you'd never heard anything so romantic. That it wasn't a big deal, it wasn't on top of the Eiffel Tower or at a fancy restaurant. It wasn't this big song or dance and it wasn't out in the open. It was at home, surrounded by people they loved. You said that her mum cooked up their favorite meal—"

Wrong. Mum can't cook. Dad did.

"—played her favorite music—"

Wrong again. My mum can't stand ABBA, but she played it anyway because it's always been my dad's guilty pleasure.

"—and just as the lemon cake was served her dad brought out the ring and surprised everyone there."

Jesus, Mark, misogynistic much? My *mum* proposed to my *dad*, not the other way around. Key element missed. He's still somehow talking.

"You said that if you ever got proposed to then that's exactly what you'd like. One lemon cake for a lifetime of marriage, surrounded by family on the most perfect evening."

That's not even the phrase. It's: one lemon cake for a *lifetime of happiness*. He can't even get the fucking line right.

But wait—oh God. What is he doing? I suddenly realize the aughts music is still playing. That was always Ellie's decade of choice. I should know. I've been dancing around kitchens with her to early 2000s songs since the early 2000s.

"Well, here we are. I asked Annie to cook your favorite meal, I've been playing your favorite music, and we're surrounded by people we love. The only thing missing is the lemon cake."

He moves over briefly back to the counter and brings over the large white pastry box he'd brought in earlier. He opens it, letting the cardboard fall naturally to reveal a heart-shaped lemon cake, with tiny swirls of lemon zest sprinkling the top and filling the room with intoxicating citrus like a newly opened car freshener.

Sitting in the middle of this stupid cake, in a square neatly sliced out and nestled in the sponge like sitting on its own throne, is a small black velvet box.

Oh shit. No. This isn't happening.

Ellie is crying but he still keeps going, reaching in to the heart of the cake and delicately removing the small box from its cake-based throne.

Put it back, Mark. Put it back now before this gets out of hand.

"I have loved you ever since that first day I met you. I have loved you every day more and more."

Oh my God, this is real. This is actually happening before my eyes. This is a train derailing, a soufflé popping, an egg cracking. She doesn't want the big white wedding. She doesn't want it at all, and if he knew her like I know her, he'd know that. I want more than anything for the sight before me to stop.

"You are the love of my life."

No, Mark, stop it. Stop it right now.

"You are my best friend in the whole world."

No—she's *my* best friend. We're the best friends here.

"Ellie," he says. Oh God no. Please no. But it's already too late. It's happening. It's really, really happening. "Ellie, will you marry me?"

PART 2

1

"To Ellie!" Simon and Diego sing out together. My glass is out close enough for them to clink it with minimal effort on my behalf.

I didn't mean to go out, but this is where the night has taken me so this is where I am, following the newest couple in the household to some bar hidden within Brixton Market where Diego apparently "knows people." Of course he does. As he walked into this crowded bar he seemed to know just about everyone and he's resting his arm constantly on Simon's knee as if parading him around to old friends. He's a complete sweetheart, a real catch, and one night in they're acting like they're on their honeymoon. Why couldn't Ellie find someone like that? Why can't I?

After the tears and the cheers and the hugs all around in the kitchen, Ellie and Mark had retired up to their room. Mark had even dared to turn on the still smiling but clearly being totally fucking serious tone of voice when he suggested that "maybe tonight it might be best if I didn't come join them in bed." Annie too had turned in for the night. She had Pilates in the morning and when she said morning, she meant it.

Only Diego and Simon were left to play with, and given my options I decided that following their guided path out was the best one for me.

"But why?" I say sulkily. "Why should we cheers the fact that she's been coerced into wearing a chain around her finger?"

"Oh come on, she's hardly been coerced," Simon says dismissively.

"But she has! She never wanted to get married—ever! And yet here comes Mark, embarrassing her in front of all her friends and forcing her into a marriage she *doesn't even want*."

"He hasn't forced her into anything."

"Why wouldn't she want it?" asks Diego.

"Daddy issues," Simon replies quickly.

"Men-are-arsehole issues more like," I mumble.

"Well, maybe she's changed her mind?" Diego says unhelpfully.

"Of course she's changed her mind," Simon confirms. "Now come on, Bells. You're her best friend. You should be happy for her!"

"I am! I am!" I say sulkily. "But . . . but he's just so . . . so Mark. Why couldn't she have found someone worthy of her?"

"He seems nice to me," Diego tries.

"Oh tonight he was fine but . . . God, Ellie's like a superstar and he's . . . he's just so normal."

"Maybe normal is what she wants."

"But she deserves so much better!"

"That's not fair," chips in Simon. "That boy treats her like a princess."

"She *is* a princess."

"And she's found someone who treats her like one. Do you know how rare that is?"

"I know. I know."

I slowly swig my strawberry-infused-gin and tonic that Diego didn't even have to pay for. He winked at the bartender and hey, the drink magically appeared.

"You'll find someone who treats you like a princess too," Simon says sweetly.

"I'm not a princess."

"Oh yes you are."

"Honestly, I'm not. I've read all those fairy tales and I've not once exhibited signs of princess-hood. I want to be Cinderella but I'm more like . . . I don't know. The ugly stepsister, I guess."

"You know, it's so funny you talk about fairy stories," Diego pipes up. "When I saw you walk through the door this morning with your handbag on one arm and that bright red hoodie, I thought you were just like . . . oh, what's her name, *Caperucita Roja*."

"Who?"

"Little Red Riding Hood!" Simon translates. Wait—Simon speaks Spanish?

"Ha!" I laugh. "Well, the man I was with was very wolflike. I mean, his name was literally Charles Wolf."

"Charles?" Simon replies incredulously.

"I know. Don't start." I laugh back in response. Trust Simon to be on my wavelength with that.

"Well, maybe that's it!" Diego claims. "Maybe you're just in the wrong fairy tale!"

"Oh yes, maybe that's why men don't want to date me long-term. Because I'm in the *wrong story*. That's where I've been going wrong," I say sarcastically.

"From what I remember, 'Little Red Riding Hood' doesn't end too happily ever after," Simon muses beside me, sipping on his own luminous cocktail. "Maybe Diego's onto something. Maybe you're just in the wrong story."

This conversation is echoing back in my mind. Partly because I'm drunk, of course—I think one and a half bottles of wine followed by two strong gin and tonics is enough to send anyone into the fuzzy wonder kingdom on the edge of sobriety—but mostly because it's strangely a thought I've had myself, not all that long ago.

As I was bouncing up and down on the ridged figure of Charles Wolf last night, wrapped in his red hoodie, I caught sight of myself in the mirror and thought to myself how similar to the story it was.

Ish. I mean. In the story of "Little Red Riding Hood" she doesn't end up performing bestiality and I'm pretty sure there's a grandmother involved somewhere. But still.

If it was true, if what Diego is saying is real in any way, then how do I get myself out of these other fairy tales and back in the right one?

Somewhere between brain cells a genius thought bubbles inside me. "Does anyone have a pen?" I ask excitedly.

Diego shrugs. Simon does the decent thing of checking himself before shaking his head.

"Anyone?" I ask the crowd around me. It's a busy bar but the majority of them are crowded around us, probably because of Diego. He is very beautiful. I'm not sure if I've mentioned that yet. "Anyone have a pen?"

My crowdsourcing invariably pays off as a Sharpie arrives into the fruitful home of my palm. Why on earth anyone brought a Sharpie with them on a night out is beyond me, but I'm not complaining.

I take off one of my heels—a bright red platform that I'd thrown on in the hope that if I wore killer shoes the man of my dreams would finally come out of hiding and ask me to have his babies. On the very bottom of the heel I use the pen to scribble my name and number and I hand it over to Diego. The pen I launch back into the crowd, but if it reaches its original owner it would be something of a miracle.

"Go put this in the middle of the bar somewhere," I instruct. "Maybe in the middle of the dance floor."

"Why?"

"If I'm in the wrong fairy tale then I'm turning it to the right one. I don't want to be the ugly stepsister and I don't want to be Little Red Riding Hood. I want to be Cinder-fucking-ella and to do that, I need to rewrite my story. So here is my glass slipper; the time is almost midnight. With any luck my own Prince Charming will find it and bring it straight back to me, or at the very least call."

"Yas Queen!" says a total stranger to my right, and I feel completely and utterly empowered until I realize they weren't actually talking to or about me at all. Still, I take it.

When Diego returns shoeless I feel like the world is at my one-shoed feet.

"I feel like this could be the start of some epic romance." Simon claps. "How perfectly exciting!"

❦ 2 ❦

When Diego and Simon left they offered to take me with them, but I wasn't done with the night so I stayed on. I was, at their time of swift departure, barefoot, twirling away in the center of the dance floor, and fucking winning at life.

Four gins had reminded me that anything was possible in my life. Drink #5 reminded me that confidence was the key to success. Drink #6, arguably unnecessary, took me past all feeling in my naked feet.

Almost two hours later, here I still am, as Robyn would put it, "Dancing on My Own" under the beautiful twinkly lights of the picture-perfect setting for the meet-cute between me and my one true love. When I first came to the checkerboard floor I saw my missing slipper sitting on a low step heading toward the upstairs bathrooms, but I resisted the urge to go back and collect it. The night was young and filled with such exciting possibilities. Every smile that came my way might well have been him. Every graze of my arm as I spun in happy circles could be the first touch of many. I tried to stop myself from glancing back at it every few minutes and to be fair, there was a period of four or five banging tunes where I completely forgot about it until suddenly, with unbelievable excitement, I realized I could see it no longer.

Now, with the alcohol starting to wear off, I realize how much my feet hurt from being regularly crushed by others and twirling solo so I eventually peel myself away from the strobe lighting and slide into the nearest booth available, placing my one red heel before me on the table, and wondering which of the handsome men remaining on the dance floor will come to my rescue.

I just can't wait to see who it is.

✤ 3 ✤

God, this booth has good lighting. Two minutes in my own company and I'm already on my phone, positioning my solo heel centrally on the table with the dance floor as the backdrop for the perfect Instagram shot. I hover for a while post-filter, wondering what quick witty caption I should accompany it with, except apparently my writer's block seems to extend to basic Insta-copy too. Well, that sucks.

I don't want to waste the shot though so I scroll through my phone instead, about to send it to Simon when I see Marty's last text.

> Marty-26 Sep 10:39
> If you're out later drop me a line. We're heading to
> Brixton x

> 26 Sep 10:39-Me
> Whatever loser x

Even better. I send the picture his way.

> 27 Sep 02:28-Me
> I'm in Brixton!

> 27 Sep 02:28-Me
> Where you at?

I switch over to Ellie while I wait, about to send it to her too when my phone vibrates and my heart leaps. Prince Charming? My heart falls. Marty Mathews. Still, it's something.

Marty-27 Sep 02:31
Back home. Got lucky
Marty-27 Sep 02:31
Whose shoe?

27 Sep 02:31-Me
Ahhh, sucky
27 Sep 02:31-Me
And mineeeee

I send him a picture of my bare feet as proof.
Marty-27 Sep 02:32
Put it back on you idiot
Marty-27 Sep 02:32
You can't walk around Brixton with no shoes

27 Sep 02:32-Me
Thank you Captain Obvious
27 Sep 02:33-Me
Can't yet
27 Sep 02:33-Me
I have to wait until the other one comes back
Marty-27 Sep 02:33
You've lost a shoe?

27 Sep 02:34-Me
I'm Cinderella!

Marty-27 Sep 02:34
Are you telling me you've lost a shoe?

27 Sep 02:34-Me
CINENDERELLA
27 Sep 02:34-Me
*Cinderella
Marty-27 Sep 02:35
Where's your other shoe Bells?

27 Sep 02:35-Me
It's somewhere
27 Sep 02:36-Me
My prince will come

Marty-27 Sep 02:36
You might be waiting a long fucking time for that to happen

Rude.

Marty-27 Sep 02:38
Who you with?

27 Sep 02:38-Me
All the people

Marty-27 Sep 02:38
You're barefoot and you're not with anyone in Brixton?

27 Sep 02:38-Me
. . .

27 Sep 02:38-Me
. . .

27 Sep 02:38-Me
I'm Cinderella . . .

Marty-27 Sep 02:38
God you're a liability

Marty-27 Sep 02:38
Text me your location

Marty-27 Sep 02:38
And for fuck's sake don't walk anywhere until I get there. I don't want you stepping in glass

𝕾 4 𝕾

"Let me guess, Charming took one look at you and ghosted?" Marty laughs as he slides up beside me in the booth. I didn't even see him come into the bar, but that's not too surprising given he interrupted a rather beautiful and vivid daydream I was having about being smothered in a bath of Maccy's chicken nuggets.

He slides a pint glass to me with such force that some of the liquid pours on the table. I reach to save my shoe instinctively before I realize it's only water.

I do my best to hide how happy I am to see him because he doesn't need that kind of ego boost, but in reality I sobered up at least three songs ago and until the fast-food vision took over me I was beginning to feel a bit lonely.

"He still might come," I reply pointedly, replacing the shoe in the center of the table between us carefully.

"Well, I'll tell you what, I'll just sit here until he does, eh?"

He sits back, flicking his Clark Kent bangs out of his eyes as he surveys the scene with a giant smile across his stupid dimpled cheeks. God, he looks so smug right now. He's already got that look in his eye that tells me he won't let me forget this.

His plaid shirt is almost entirely undone, I see, revealing a ludicrously tight white T-shirt beneath that's impressing absolutely no one. Honestly, he used to be such a skinny little thing as a kid, all baggy hoodies and oversized vests, and when he started to fill out he decided—incorrectly I might add—that the whole world needed to see his fitness progress. His hair was probably gelled back when he went out but already the curls have broken free of their confinement in a bad bedhead he's not even slightly conscious of. As relaxed as anything, he lets the music soak into his skin, one bicep curling around almost half the booth as with the other he brings his IPA to his lips. Wait, what?

"Did you seriously just get me water when you got yourself a beer?" I ask.

"I did," he says proudly. "And drink up. I need assurances you're not going to vom in the Uber."

"Are you kidding me?"

"I've got a 4.9 star rating right now and like fuck will you ruin that with . . . whatever this is." He uses his free hand like a wand, pointing it in my general direction, trying to hold back a smirk. Lovely. Just lovely. He's seriously the worst fairy godmother ever.

Still, at least he appeared.

I turn away from him as I sip my water. Actually, it's not bad. Exactly what I needed really. I didn't realize how thirsty I was until it touched my lips but I could literally down a whole fountain right now.

I try not to betray my gratitude with my face; I don't want Marty to think he actually did good.

Most people think Marty's an arsehole, and they're not wrong, but he's always been nice to me.

No honestly—since we were kids he's always been a bit of a tit. He was forever being suspended from school for skipping class or talking back to teachers. There was this period of time after their dad left them that teachers turned a blind eye, but even I remember the English class where he told Mr. Knot that he was a "gluttonous fuckface," and that was years after his dad's shitty departure. They would have kicked him out, only much to their annoyance he was top of the class in most subjects and those he wasn't, Ellie was and she was a golden girl. If their mum pulled them both out of school, as she so often threatened to do, the school's grade average would have fallen by quite some margin. Given Marty was never physically harmful to anyone, he did daily detentions and went on "early study leave" instead.

His "being an arsehole" continued into his personal life too, of course. There was that one time where he missed his "girlfriend's" graduation because he was too busy sleeping with her best friend (I think to this day he still claims "they" didn't put a label on it, although *she* clearly did). He ghosts girls daily and fake numbers others—in fact his sister is pretty much the only girl in the world he has any respect for, and given I'm practically family he just about extends it to me on most days.

"So what is this anyway?" Marty asks, his eyes already scanning the dance floor for any girls he might be able to leave his number with probably. He's so predictable like that. Every outing is a brand-new opportunity for him. "Did the other heel break or something?" He pushes the shoe between us over onto its side with the lightest touch of his pinkie. "They look pretty cheap to me."

"Oi!" I say, leaning forward and flicking him in the abs. There's no doubt in my mind that that hurt my fingers more than it dented his chest. "They were twenty-two pounds I'll have you know. *And* they were on sale. From like thirty pounds or something."

He puts his hands up defensively.

"My sincerest apologies," he replies sarcastically. "For that price they must be made of solid silver."

"No, they didn't break," I reply. His smile's a little infectious, but I can already feel my cheeks flushing pink because I've just realized I have to justify all this somehow and now I'm a little more sober, I'm not sure it's all that justifiable. I mean, Simon and Diego seemed super on board with this whole plan at the time, but something tells me Marty might have a slightly different opinion.

Oh God. Sobering up sucks sometimes. What have I done?

"So what? Someone stole it from your foot? Who steals a shoe?"

Should I lie and just say yes? It's vaguely plausible, I guess. Except it's Marty. I can't lie to him. I never lie to him.

"Promise me you won't laugh?" I ask.

"I don't make promises I can't keep."

"Then promise me you won't judge?"

"I'm already judging." He looks me up and down with an expectant Cheshire cat look about him that makes me cringe so hard already. Regret washes over me thick and fast as Marty runs a hand through his messy dark locks. "I knew this would be worth getting out of bed for."

I take another sip of water to give me courage before I embark on the tragic story that is my last forty-eight hours. I leave out no detail, not for Marty, and maybe he's not the best person to confide in when I need sympathy, but as it turns out, the more he's laughing at me, the more I'm laughing at myself. Within seconds my sad sorry tale of the big bad wolf becomes a piece of pure comedy gold and my attempt to lure myself a Prince Charming tonight might well have been a movie starring Rebel Wilson.

Weirdly, this is just what I needed.

Marty literally snorts the last of his pint, spraying my shoe with a thin layer of Punk IPA as the lights around us go up. Looks like the place is finally closing just as my story meets me in real time.

"Stay here, tit," Marty instructs, standing up and leaving me. He's gone five minutes before he comes back into my line of sight, wandering over the now empty dance floor. I wonder for a second if he's just forgotten where he left me until, soon after, he appears back by my side, tapping away at his phone.

"Well, Cinders, looks like midnight's been and gone already and your shoe's officially nowhere to be found. Bar's not had anything handed in and it's not anywhere I can find."

"Maybe Prince Charming found it after all?" I say hopefully.

"Yeah, or someone's thrown it in the tip already. Either way, it's time to head home." He shows me on his screen that an Uber's two minutes away.

I look at my lonely, slightly wet, and now pretty sticky shoe, then look at the floor. I can already see wet patches everywhere. I look at my poor bare feet and regret sinks in hard.

"I can't believe I lost my shoe in the middle of Brixton," I say finally.

"*I* can't believe you lost your shoe in the middle of Brixton," he agrees, "which is more surprising because my bar for you is already super low."

"Uncalled for," I mutter, standing up on the seat to get a better line of vision for my path ahead. The lights are almost blinding, but at least I can get a clearer view of all the obstacles on the floor. Marty waits, impatiently.

"You want to carry me?" I ask.

"Nope," he replies.

Could have seen that coming.

"You're an idiot, you know that?"

"I'm a romantic," I insist.

"In my opinion, they're the same damn thing."

Suddenly, and without warning, I'm thrown upside down as Marty launches his shoulder into my waist and I curl over it in a fireman's lift that almost knocks the wind out of me.

"What the fuck, Marty?" I cry, shuffling my hands to make sure my skirt hasn't risen up and my bum's not being shown to the world. Really I'm just laughing all over again. Maybe he's a better fairy godmother than I gave him credit for.

"Come on, princess," Marty replies as he bounds ungracefully with me to the exit, "your carriage awaits."

5

The plan was to drop me off first, but the second we hit the first set of lights the part of the story I purposefully missed out in my recounting to Marty—Ellie's engagement—springs back to my mind. All I can hear is Mark's snide little comment about leaving them to it for the night, and instantly I don't want to go home. Marty doesn't care. His place used to be home to all the best house parties when we all first moved here so I've spent many a night kipping on his sofa instead of making it back to my own bed. A quick little word with the driver and we're turning away from Balham completely, heading instead for the small café in Clapham Junction that Marty lives above.

We lower our voices as we ascend his staircase into the kitchen-cum–living room. He apparently lives here with a flatmate called Ollie, but having spent many a night here over the course of the last eight years I have still yet to meet this alleged second tenant, so I can only assume at this point that he is either a vampire and/or imaginary.

If you didn't know Marty (and his unproven flatmate) lived here, you would have assumed that the flat had been decorated by a middle-aged woman from the fifties, but despite the playboy persona most people associate him with, Marty's always liked things looking "quaint" ever since I've known him. He's slow and calculated. He likes dim lighting and delights in purchasing table covers.

He has about a hundred china animals that sit in random parts of the room and stare at you as you're watching TV, judging you for forgetting to use one of his favorite wooden hedgehog coasters. He has a pretty extensive collection of books too, mostly nonfiction unlike mine, but all of them alphabetized and categorized in one of the five bookcases situated in the living room. I think he thinks it makes him look intellectual. I think it makes him look like a try hard, except to be fair, he does read an awful lot and it hasn't failed yet to impress the dates he brings back. To top it all off, it still smells like blown-out candles and potpourri.

While I was in the bathroom, removing my makeup with the help of some face wipes found on Marty's "one-night stand care package" shelf, Marty made up a bed for me on the cute little sofa. When I come out to join him he already has two cups of tea ready for a last pre-sleep chat.

That's the thing about their family: very tea oriented. Nothing can't be fixed with a good cup of tea, it's a principle all Mathewses live by and Marty's no exception. He's got me some jogging bottoms and a large hoodie to sleep in for the night and he's considerate enough to have a glass of water and some aspirin already lined up for my inevitable morning hangover. Always a caregiver, Marty. An arsehole, but a caring arsehole.

"I take it you heard Ellie's news . . ." I say as I curl up under the blankets, pulling on the hoodie.

"Family FaceTime," he replies. "My mum cried her eyes out."

"I don't blame her. I'd cry my eyes out if my kid was marrying *Mark*."

He laughs, handing over my mug. The glorious smell of Yorkshire Gold warms the back of my throat. Boy's got taste.

"Hey now, he's not so bad."

"He's so boring."

"She's boring. They suit each other."

"She's brilliant." I kick him with my cold, frostbitten foot and somehow he magically doesn't spill a single drop of his tea. He just laughs, leaning back on the sofa so we're top to toe.

"Is this jealousy I see before me?"

"No."

"Really?"

"How can I be jealous of Ellie for having a Mark? He's so forgettable I genuinely find it difficult to remember what he looks like."

"Okay then."

"Jealous? Of what? He has the personality of a freshwater clam and he's forever wearing jeans that don't even fit him properly."

"Got it."

"Jealous? How can I be . . . oh fuck I am. Of course I am. I really, really am."

"Tell me why," he says, his voice soft and low, his face finally free of its earlier judgment.

"Because! Because she's going to get married. She's going to go live in the countryside and have kids and a dog while I'm going to be getting rejections from ugly wolf men forever."

"Chiswick is hardly countryside."

"She didn't even want to get married!"

"So, she changed her mind. People change."

"I don't! Apparently."

"Of course you do."

"I do?"

"You're more whiny and ridiculous every time I see you." His voice is still so sympathetic that I don't even take it as an insult, just a mood booster, and it sort of works.

I kick him again in his shoulder lightly and he doesn't flinch much. He probably didn't even feel it. He's built like a bodybuilder these days, which I don't think suits him half as much as his emo teenage phase.

He looks a bit like Ellie, but doesn't share any of her same features. While she has a little nose and large curious eyes, Marty's nose is sharp and his eyes are always half-closed like he's trying to seduce the whole world. While Ellie inherited her mum's strong cheeks, Marty's always had a chiseled jawline instead that for years aged him up awkwardly. It probably came from his dad's side, but I can't say

I remember much about what he looked like and I haven't seen a photo of him for years so it's hard to say for sure.

"I'm so done with London dating," I conclude solemnly. "I am. I want out. I have about as much chance finding love in this city as I have for"—I look around for inspiration. It doesn't take long—"as I have for meeting this 'flatmate' of yours, Marty."

I even do the air quotes for extra emphasis.

"That's not fair. Ollie works weird hours."

"So you say."

"You know what your problem is with men?" he says, like he's an expert. Ordinarily I would have already fobbed him off but given the tragedy that was my life I was willing to take the bait.

"Go on."

"You're not having enough fun," he concludes. "If you stopped looking for this imaginary Prince Charming you keep going on about and started trying to find someone you actually wanted to spend the night with you'd have much better luck."

"Is that what you do?"

"Nightly. It works. I'm having a great time."

I sigh, like a proper hefty sigh. I love a good sigh. I so didn't want him to be right because he's a complete moron but right now, wrapped in his blankets, about to sleep in a flat whose one-night stands bring up the national average by some margin, maybe he wasn't completely wrong. I'd forgotten the last time I just had fun.

"How is the writing going?" he asks.

Sidestep, but maybe he'd sensed he'd gone too far. It was probably my sigh. It was a really good sigh.

"It's . . . stagnated a little. Inspiration is hard to find when you're feeling sorry for yourself."

"Fair," he says, finishing his brew and removing my feet from on top of him so he can stand. "You'll find it soon enough."

"I'm sorry I stopped you from getting lucky tonight," I say finally, relaxing back, ready to sleep.

"You didn't. She's still in my room."

I sit bolt upright, shocked. I look at his door for confirmation. The door doesn't say anything, clearly. It's a door.

"You've been sitting here talking to me all this time—you literally joined me for a drink at the club—when you had some girl in your room?"

He smiles cheekily, winking my way. He removes the mugs from the sofa and leaves them behind me on the kitchen sink. He doesn't even seem like he's in a rush to get back to her. I'm outraged on her behalf, this unknown stranger. What an arse he is.

"You know," he says slowly, elongating his journey back, "maybe you should write about your night with that wolf man. Like a twisted modern fairy tale. It's a funny story. Pretty tragic."

I laugh sleepily.

"I'm glad you think my life is tragic."

"Your life is tragic. Anyway, sleep well, Bells." I lean back down and get ready to sleep but given the eyes of a hundred weird ornaments raining down on me, I don't think I'll be able to get any shut-eye before sobriety reminds me they're not real. "I'll try not to be too loud," he says, finally switching off the lights.

Then he disappears into his room and if the china animal–based judgment wasn't enough to keep me up, the outrageously loud sighs and moans of a woman who I assume must be faking it, certainly is.

✤ 6 ✤

As I wake the next morning (okay, fine, afternoon, whatever, I'm tired) I find a note from Marty telling me he's gone out already and to lock up and put the keys in the mailbox on my way out. It's only a forty-five-minute walk or so, so I keep the hoodie I slept in and steal a pair of trainers near the door that weirdly fit me to make my merry way home.

It's cold out, but otherwise a really lovely day. The trees in Wandsworth Common have turned all shades of amber and orange with piles of leaves gathered below, ready for dogs to jump through. The sun shines as I walk at irregular intervals through the light cloud cover, which is just about as good as it gets this season.

Look at me, embracing the weather. It can only mean one thing: I'm actually in a good mood. Talking it all out has done me wonders. In fact, the closer I get to home, the more I feel a new sense of freedom come over me that today will be a better day.

My phone buzzes as I reach my side of Elmfield Road.

Mystery Man

Any more guesses or have you given up already?

Bella Marble

You going to give me a clue?

Bella Marble

Mathew? Luke? John?

Bella Marble

Is it biblical?

Biblical? Did I seriously ask that? Well, that was presumptuous and weird. It doesn't even sound like me. Urgh, I so wish I could delete it already.

But there it is, Marty's annoying weasel voice in my head telling me to have more fun. Maybe this is what it takes to have more fun. To care less.

So, trying desperately not to care, I google "most popular boys' names," copy the entire list, and paste it.

Bella Marble

Muhammad

Noah

George

Oliver

Charlie

Harry

Leo

Arthur

Jack

Freddie

Jaxon

Ethan

Jacob

Theo

Oscar

Alfie

Archie

Joshua

Thomas

Mystery Man

I like the name Noah

Bella Marble

Is it yours?

Mystery Man

Nope. You'll get there. Keep going

I turn to his profile picture. He can probably see mine already with how many names I've guessed but his is still fogged out, that weird creepy old goblin the only picture I have for him. I've never talked with anyone on this thing long enough to actually see their whole face—only fragments of it. I pocket my phone while I search for my keys.

I jog up the stairs—actually jog—and by the time I open the door I can hear voices coming out of the kitchen.

"Hellooooo!" I say, fresh-faced and full of energy as I bound in.

"Oh, hi," says a short, sharp man's voice I don't recognize. I blink, a bit confused. The man is unpacking a box of cutlery into our communal drawer. He's average height and pretty stoic looking, with a thick head of overly styled blond hair. He looks a bit like a *Die Hard* villain.

At the table sits a woman I don't recognize either. She smiles, nice and relaxed, her pigtails twirling around her fingers.

"You must be Belle," she says, a slight flair of a German accent. "I am Gertie and this is Hans."

"Hello, Gertie; hello, Hans," I reply. They know my name. Strangers are sitting in my kitchen and they know my name. This is strange.

"Are you friends with Annie?" I try.

"Yes, we've met Annie," Hans declares.

"And Simon," Gertie adds.

I wasn't aware that Annie and Simon had that many mutual friends. Especially ones comfortable enough to be putting their cutlery into my drawers.

"Are they around?"

"Annie's doing the yoga and Simon is in bed with . . . what was the beautiful man's name, Gertie?"

"Diggo," Gertie replied.

"Diego," I correct. "The beautiful man is Diego."

So not friends with Diego then.

Then it hits me.

I knew it was a couple moving into Ellie's room, but I didn't know how quickly. These aren't friends of anyone visiting; *these are my new flatmates.*

If the new flatmates have already arrived then—

Without even saying anything else I run out of the kitchen and toward the second set of stairs, taking them two at a time. I run to the end of the corridor and throw open the door to Ellie's room— only it's not Ellie's room. Not anymore.

It's stark and empty, with boxes that probably belong to Hans and Gertie piled up into the corners. The bedding has already been changed. No longer are they duck-egg blue but instead some sort of hypnotic lotus design in strange browns and greens. A hypnotic painting in deep red hangs over the bed for decoration where a framed picture of three ducks once stood proudly.

Eight years of perfection, now a new slate to be made by a couple I'd just made a pretty terrible first impression on.

I walk back to my room and lie down on my bed, but I have a strange mix of energy that I don't know how to place. I pace around, picking up things that don't need to be picked up and putting them back down accordingly. I walk over to the window and look down and out to the road outside that is free from cars. It's 2 p.m. on a Sunday. No one goes anywhere at 2 p.m. on a Sunday.

Except Ellie, I guess.

I need more of a distraction. I need something to take my mind off things.

Before I even know what I am doing I charge over to my laptop and throw open the screen.

Word greets me like an old friend, the cursor blinking away, ready for my active mind. Writing has always been a great distraction before, I just need to dive right in and forget everything else. Inspiration. Where are you, inspiration? Where are you when I—

It hits me quickly. With a surge of excitement and Marty's words ringing, I place my hands over the keyboard.

My Night with the Big Bad Wolf

My fingers type like fire. There's a smile on my face and a glint in my eye that hasn't been there in years as I unleash all my pent-up frustration on my little qwerty keyboard. Fuck you, wolf man, take that! Screw you, terrible dating history. Goodbye, sadness over my fallen flatmate; hello, empowered writer.

With every typed character I'm one step closer to not giving a shit. With every symbol I realize how brief sadness can be. With every hit of that space bar I'm back to feeling more myself than ever.

I'm back in my happy place.

I'm back in my happy place.

I'm back.

28 Sep 10:01-Me
Want dinner sometime this week?
28 Sep 10:01-Me
Just you and me?

The Elsa to my Anna-28 Sep 10:03
Can we try next week sometime?
The Elsa to my Anna-28 Sep 10:03
It's just been a bit busy over here!

I groan. This is how it begins. First Ellie moves out, then she's suddenly unavailable for dinners. She was always available for dinners before.

I want to tell her how fucking brilliant I felt yesterday, how cathartic it was to have my writing mojo back all over again.

Except she's too busy now, apparently.

Get over it, Bella. Moving in takes time. Once she's fully settled she'll be able to meet again like nothing has changed.

Stupid sensible reasoning. You'd better be right.

28 Sep 10:04-Me
Yeah sounds good
28 Sep 10:06-Me
How's the new place?

The Elsa to my Anna-28 Sep 10:06
Cold!

The Elsa to my Anna-28 Sep 10:06
We can't work out how the radiators work yet
The Elsa to my Anna-28 Sep 10:06
And our internet keeps going down on us
The Elsa to my Anna-28 Sep 10:06
It's been a bit of an adjustment

28 Sep 10:08-Me
Do you still have data?

The Elsa to my Anna-28 Sep 10:08
Not enough
The Elsa to my Anna-28 Sep 10:09
Mark's phone has a data plan thing so we can at
least stream movies

28 Sep 10:10-Me
Oh thank God. A life without Netflix is not a life worth
living

"Bella, can you answer that please?"

Maggie pops her head out of the office especially to tell me that, the little narc. Her curly hair bounces like springs as she talks and her glasses fall down her nose an inch.

That's mean. She's alright. Pretty nice actually, but she's new, which means she doesn't know my ways yet.

If I let it ring six or seven times it makes us look far busier than we are. Busy means important. Important means successful.

The longer you make someone wait on the phone at a publishing house, the more successful that publishing house looks. I'm doing them a favor.

To be fair, it's probably been ringing for a good five minutes so far. I was just being distracted by my phone and couldn't be bothered to pick it up. I wonder if Maggie hadn't come out whether I might have missed it altogether. I smile at her in a just about acceptable passive-aggressive way before picking it up.

"Porter Books, how can I help you?"

It's the receptionist. They have a guest downstairs waiting for a Mr. Shipman, but as I point out to the nice young lady on the phone, we don't have a Mr. Shipman within our staff. Thank you and try again.

We share the same building as four tech start-ups and a couple of recruitment companies, so about 50 percent of the time when I pick up to reception it's actually just been misdirected. I hang up and smile at Maggie with a slightly I-told-you-so: "Wrong number."

I didn't used to be like this. Not when I joined.

I remember falling in love the first time I walked through the door. The walls have book posters from decades ago and photographs of book events hosted by some of the most amazing modern authors of the day—the kind I one day hoped to be right in the middle of. Walls are filled with books calling to me to read them—and I can. Whenever I'd like. I'm actively encouraged to read at my desk, which is exactly why I couldn't wait to join the company eight years ago.

I was excellent at my job for the first four years at least. I wouldn't ordinarily make a statement like that, only I was the consistent winner of Porter Books's "most courteous phone manner" and people often told me that my tea runs were always their favorite, as I brought back a little biscuit with every order. I was the first person in every morning and I oftentimes waited until the last person left the building before I dared take my own leave. I was fresh faced, well dressed, polite to everyone, and very ready to please.

Except life happens and four extra years of answering phones later my enthusiasm has curbed slightly. More times than not Instagram is more appealing than the newest bestseller and I grew tired very quickly of watching authors much younger than myself enter the building and leave with a five-figure publishing deal.

Instead of filling me with inspiration to write, it's shoveled down my dreams. Still, the benefits are good, my salary's better than minimum wage, and every so often I get to eat the leftover croissants from a breakfast meeting, so it's not all bad.

"Has Henry Pill arrived yet?" asks Cathy, popping into the corridor. She's the assistant to a few of the execs and incidentally one of my favorite colleagues. Not that it matters of course, but she's also so beautiful she makes eyes burn. Literally. Like, there was this intern once who got conjunctivitis and had to leave after half a day and I'm about 92 percent sure it's because they were staring at Cathy too hard. Many a male author and a few female ones too have asked for her number but as far as I'm aware she's never shown that much interest. She likes wearing pantsuits, almost constantly has a pair of AirPods in her ears so you never know whether she's actually listening to you, and her raven-black hair is the envy of the office. At least I envy it, and I'm basically everyone who matters in the office.

I look around the empty reception area.

"Yes. He's sitting behind the plant," I reply.

Cathy half smiles—it's the best you can expect from her really. She never looks all that happy but I love that about her. She sits down beside me.

"He was supposed to be here at ten. He's late. These new kids—no respect. You'd never catch one of the old-schools being late."

"Is he a translator?"

"An author."

"Oh."

I should probably know that. Any author who walks through the door I'm "encouraged" to have already read a segment of their work. It's part of the deal here. They like to appear as if everyone in the company is a fan. If Henry's book was sent to me I must have missed it, maybe. Or, more probably, I saw it and decided to play Toon Blast on my phone instead.

Just as Cathy hovers the phone rings. I don't wait to pick up this time.

"I have a Mr. Pill downstairs for you?"

"Yes, send him right up," I reply to the nice lady.

Cathy sits down on the swivel chair beside me. She has to greet him anyway so there's no point in going back to her desk.

"So what does he write?" I ask, googling it quickly. Cathy knows I don't read the books and she's not the kind to judge. That's a lie.

She judges everything. But it's because she judges everything that I don't sweat the small stuff with her.

"It's sort of a sex-ography. He meets all these girls online and writes about how crap it is after. Sort of a 'how not to date' guide."

"How not to date him?"

"Worse. He dates women he thinks look tragic then writes about how terrible they were."

"That's horrible. Who even wants to read that?"

"Everyone apparently. I think people like to believe that no matter how bad they are at dates, that there are worse girls out there. It gives them hope. Plus he's pretty funny."

He's apparently twenty-two, according to the wonders of the web. That's depressing for so many reasons. No picture, mind, but I guess if girls knew what he looked like they probably wouldn't agree to dates.

"Is he big?"

"He is on B-Reader."

"What's B-Reader?"

"What's B-Reader?" Cathy replies a little confused. "You work in publishing!"

"I work on phones," I reply, my hand flexing out over my reception desk for show.

"It's this online thing. You publish one chapter at a time and a bunch of beta readers get to leave comments and give feedback."

"Why would they do that?"

"People love to give opinions. And no one has time for a whole novel these days."

I nod, googling it. It's modern life's answer for everything.

"And how did he get famous on this?"

"People liked his work. It's basically like any social media platform: the more likes you get, the more comments, the more popular it becomes, and the more it's read. We're always checking it for the newest writers. I think the scout team will hire someone specific for the job eventually because they've already made a few TV shows off the back of stuff found there. It's a good launchpad."

Just as she finishes her sentence the lift in the corridor opens to reveal a thin, gangly Harry Styles tribute act. He's all limbs, but even from far away he has an arrogance crossed with some kind of stoner chic. He has black hair that looks like it's never seen a brush of any form, probably aiming for a bedhead aroma but mainly looking like a sulky stubborn teenager who never grew up. He struts down the corridor like it's his own personal catwalk, with his clothes looking half picked out by a controlling mother and half like he's worn it for months.

"We're giving this boy a deal worth nearly six figures."

"That's almost one figure for every year he's been on the planet," I whisper back.

"Yeah well. That's how the world works now—Henry!" she calls, walking up to him and greeting him with a firm handshake. I can see his jaw drop. I bet he's never seen someone look both so intimidating and so unbearably sexy at the same time. Good old Cathy. "How lovely to meet you finally. We were just talking about your latest chapters. Why don't you come through now . . ."

He doesn't even look my way. He's a "too good for the receptionist" kind of guy, I get it, but that's alright. I can't wait to see them go, because I've just worked out exactly how I'm going to waste the rest of my day away.

⚜ 8 ⚜

I wait for them to disappear completely before I turn back to my computer. She's opened up a door that I can't close so I turn straight onto B-Reader.com. Signing up only takes a few seconds, choosing the rather unoriginal handle of @B.Enchanted and giving my life rights away as usual by accepting all cookies so the weird data scientists behind the scenes know exactly what I'm up to at all times.

It's bigger than I thought. Almost a million uploads every day, it boasts. The home screen pans through success stories and movie trailers inspired by the works found in the database's archives and a "today's most read," "all-time favorites," "discover new," and "for you" tab all skim through some choices to get me started.

"For you" is a bit presumptuous given I only just signed up, so I click on "today's most read." There's safety in numbers.

Henry Pill is right up there already, coming in at number 14 for the UK.

The Best of the Worst by Henry Pill

Urgh, what a freak. It's a "best of" apparently, which I'm surprised he can even get away with, but it looks like he's got seven full books on the site already. This one's five chapters in by the time I get to it. I can also see some of the comments below.

LOL. She deserved it for wearing that thong!

Ohmygod the dog bit! Still crying!

New chapter out! Is it bad to pull a sicky at work
for it?

Weirdos. Who does this? Who actually comments on new
writing?

I click on to the chapters to start reading. They're pretty crude.
It gets hot and heavy pretty quickly, which, when I remember the
author, makes me feel pretty sick if I'm honest.

She looked to be the runt of the litter, as desperate
for my approval as a balding man is for miracle-grow
cream.

What a prick. These poor women. I click off it and on to someone else's.

Just like that I've fallen down the rabbit hole. Three hours later
and this is the fastest day of work I've ever sat through. I didn't even
notice when Henry Pill left the building. I barely blinked when the
other scheduled guests arrived. I was way too captivated.

It took me forty-five minutes before I read one I liked enough
to comment on and once that started I felt like I should comment
on them all. It was amazing—for every one I read that was actually
pretty funny I read about ten that were so bad I was wheezing at
my desk in tears.

Maggie even came out of her office once or twice, to check I
wasn't somehow dying.

I liked the comments too. I sometimes spent far longer looking
through the comments than I did the chapter itself. I liked the ones
that I agreed with; I wrote back to the ones that I didn't. I loved it. I
was part of something. I was in a new collective. My own personal
not-life-threatening cult.

After reading what I can only consider to be the works of a computer algorithm fired up on a healthy cocaine diet, I turn to the next in line. No comments yet—posted a week ago.

Probably shit then. I love the shit ones.

I start to read it.

My life started the day Kurt Molbury died.

Not the worst first line I've read. Far better than the one I read earlier of: "I loved Katie until the great cow massacre." Yeah—that one went exactly where you'd imagine. Imagery of cow guts spraying into the outer solar system mixed with a pretty crappy love story about two unassuming farmers. I admired the ambition at least.

So this one wasn't so bad. I check the clock—I still have plenty of time to waste before the day's conclusion.

So I begin.

9

And it's beautiful.

It's written like a poem or spoken word, following the life of a young woman so lost she starts to take an active interest in a complete stranger who died the day she was born. The two lives weave like a glorious cross-stitch and before I know it I'm crying.

As I reach the last line I immediately click on the second chapter but it isn't there. Nothing is there. They must have only just uploaded the one, so instead I go back to the start and read it all over again.

Henrietta Lovelace.

I follow her immediately and, before I know what I'm doing, I've read it again for a third time.

I start to write a comment and stop myself. There's nothing I can say to do it justice. How on earth has this got no followers?

Without missing a beat I send it on to Cathy with a little note: "This is so beautiful my heart hurts. Give her a book deal. The world needs to read this."

"I'll take a look," comes the reply, "although we probably can't do much with it until she's grown out her fanbase."

Her fanbase?

Henry Pill gets a six-figure book deal for his drivel and this starlet, this delicate piece of fiction gets only a "maybe if she does the legwork"?

Man, I hate the world sometimes.

I write her a comment: "One of the best things I've ever read. Can't wait for the next chapter."

Eventually I peel my eyes away, moving on to the next one, which pales in comparison, when a notification springs up. It's her—it's Henrietta. I switch back instantly to see.

> @Henrietta.Lovelace
> I can't tell you how much this means to me. I thought about giving up on this, I didn't think anyone was interested in reading my work, but knowing someone's out there is enough for me to persevere. So thank you, stranger.

I'm practically crying all over again when I read it.

I've made a difference. Here is a writer, a wonderful, talented writer, who just needs a confidence boost and here I am, pushing her along.

It feels like an honor.

For about half an hour I can't do anything else. It makes me smile. It makes me feel so good about myself, knowing that great art will be continued because of one comment I made on some bizarre little website. God—if I heard something like that said about my own writing I'm sure that I would have completed one of my many works-in-progress.

Which gets me thinking.

I've written something. Just yesterday.

It isn't long enough to be a book or a novella or anything. It isn't rounded enough to be a short story. It doesn't really fit any of the right sizes for anything, other than perhaps a chapter . . .

No, I can't. I've seen some of those comments on the crappier ones. I've written a few of them myself. I don't want to put my work out there like that only to have it ripped apart by vultures. But then again, what else am I going to do with it?

Maybe getting feedback this early, maybe getting some guidance from complete strangers, maybe that's how I get the motivation I need to keep going. It isn't like any of the comments I've written were mean, just deeply constructive. Maybe that's what I need—a thicker skin and some good old-fashioned cruel-to-be-kind feedback.

Or maybe, more accurately, what I need is another me. The kind of me who replied to Henrietta.

I happen to have the pages in my Dropbox anyway so I can access them pretty quickly on the reception computer.

I reread them at my desk, checking through for the obvious spelling or grammar mistakes, but even satisfied with that, my finger still hovers over the upload button for far longer than I care to say. Pressing it feels like pressing a button to my soul. Maybe it isn't ready yet for the world. I hadn't written it for such a forum; maybe it isn't at the right stage for it yet.

But maybe it is.

Oh what the hell. It's not like I'm doing anything else with it.

With one click of a button my first chapter is unleashed on the world.

❧ 10 ❧

I can't look at my screen any longer. I need the algorithms to work their magic. I can't just stare at it in real time now that the deed is done, so I go and make myself a good cup of tea.

I look at my phone to see if I have any immediate notifications. I don't. Obviously. The chapter was nearly two thousand words and it's only been live for two minutes. They would have had to average over sixteen words a second, and if they read that fast they might have missed the bit about his crack's impossibly high thread count (okay, so I'd embellished just a little).

No notifications. I need to stop looking at it before my brain explodes, so I do the works: trawling social media, flicking through my past messages. Finally I click on Mirror Mirror.

I haven't been matched with anyone new but my old matches have pretty dried-up conversations.

I turn to my mystery man:

Bella Marble
Alexander
Anthony
Andrew
Aaron
Asher
Austin
Adam

Axel
Abel
Alan
Abraham
Antonio
Amir
August
Andres
Adriel
Archer
Arthur
Anderson
Ace
Arlo
Armani
Atticus
Allen
Abram
Atlas
Adonis
Armando

Mystery Man
Oh hello, you
Mystery Man
I was about to text you actually
Mystery Man
I was thinking about you earlier

Bella Marble
Thinking about me?

Mystery Man
Stuck in a long boring meeting and thinking about
how good our date will be

Bella Marble
Did I get your name right then?

Mystery Man
I assume you googled "boys names"

Bella Marble
No

Bella Marble
I googled "boys names beginning with A"

Mystery Man
It's a good technique

Bella Marble
Did it work?

Mystery Man
It might do, but you've got a while to go

Bella Marble
This date better be worth it

Mystery Man
Believe me. It'll blow your mind

"Bella, can you get that?"

Maggie pops her head back around all over again. I shoot her daggers, of course. I don't tell her how to do her job, she shouldn't tell me how to do mine.

In fairness though, this time around, I hadn't even heard it ring.

11

I can smell a faint whiff of weed from the other end of my street. As I reach the door the smell grows stronger.

It's weird—the fraternity crew on the bottom floor are athletes. Alcohol, bring it on, but I don't think I've ever seen a green side to those "lads" before. At least not like this.

As the door opens, the smell completely drowns out the lingering damp smell I'm so used to in the hallway. That's a bit much, isn't it? I don't want to be a complete party pooper but someone should probably say something.

> **28 Sep 18:14-Me**
> Either of you in?

I text the house group. Annie's response comes within seconds. Man—even her thumbs are fitter than I am.

> **Annie Flatmate-28 Sep 18:14**
> Boxercize

Fuck her and her ridiculous sports schedule.

That's mean.

She likes sports. I don't know how, but she does. Still, I wish I liked sports. It's a much better hobby than my own personal favorite pastime of eating carbs and crying to Attenborough documentaries.

> **Sexy Simon-28 Sep 18:16**
> At Diego's!!!

Oh my word, it is getting serious.

Three nights in a row. Both houses visited. Friends met.

He's having a better relationship in seventy-two hours than I've had in twenty-odd years.

Simon sends a picture of what must be the most ridiculous flat I've ever seen. It's all London skyline and river views with a minimalist twist that Marie Kondo would be so proud of. Why on earth Diego chose to stay in a hole like our cheap flat share for two nights is beyond me.

It means, however, that I'm on my own.

Instead of walking up the stairs, I turn and face the door to the bottom flat.

I take one deep breath, intoxicating my lungs with third-party grass, before getting the confidence I need to knock.

The movement inside is slow in response but I can hear the garble of what sounds like a hundred voices echoing around me. No wonder they've chosen to go herbal. They're having a party.

12

The door opens and the self-appointed ringleader of the merry troop, Dom, appears.

His lumberjack beard has grown. Last time I saw him he was dabbling at best but it looks like in the interim he's gone full-blown hipster and it sort of suits him. He's even wearing a short-sleeved shirt. A short-sleeved shirt I tell you! In almost but not quite winter! What a fool.

"Bella!" he cries. He's pissed. There's nothing funnier than a slurring lumberjack. "Guys, guys—it's Bella!"

"Bella!"

"The Bells! The Bells!"

All manner of nicknames start to be fired my way. Their place stinks, but not of weed. It looks more like a dive than my room, although to be fair to them the increase in mess is probably proportional to the increase in bodies. There are six of them altogether in front of me, three of whom live here and three who pretend not to live here and pay rent elsewhere and yet somehow are always here anyway. The noise isn't quite proportional to the noise level I'd heard but—ah, yes. There's a game on.

I look inside at all their glorious faces and my "I'm going to be a grown-up and have a serious face" dissolves instantly. They're a funny old bunch.

They met at university—some amateur rugby thing if my memory serves me, and they look exactly as you'd imagine. They all have the same frame—all broad shoulders and thick tree-trunk legs—but they've all styled it out pretty differently at least so you can just about tell them apart.

Behind Dom, chilling on the sofa and stuffing their faces with stuffed crust, are Dave, Dean, and Donald—no, I'm not kidding. Dave is the only one not to throw some sort of comment my way but that's pretty normal. I don't think I've heard him speak once since I've known them all and I'm a delight. Dean's got a cold by the looks of things; his nose is as red as the Peroni that he's pouring in his mouth but it's not stopping him from being in the heart of the action. I don't think I've ever seen Donald without a smile across his delightfully adorable face.

Sam looks like he's about a bite away from sleeping, draped over the beanbag—and yes I said beanbag. These are nineties babies who never grew up. It wouldn't surprise me if they own a blow-up armchair among their other blow-up items I'm sure they also own. He still manages a "Bella-ma-nella" before shutting his eyes all over again.

Stu is the only sensible one. He is also the only one with a plate for his pizza and a glass for his beer rather than the rounds of bottles by everyone else's feet. He's got his headphones on, working away while the others are all watching some large sports event on the big screen they share. He nods my way but turns his eyes back to his laptop pretty quickly.

The room's dark, and not just because of the lack of light at this time of night in the autumn months. The walls are painted gray, the sofas are all black, and the table's a rich brown. It's their own personal bat cave.

"How can we help my dearest Bellatrix," Dom says. "You want pizza?"

Trick question. I always want pizza. But I am a strong, confident woman who came here to tell them to take their dirty little habits out of the house.

"Ah man—that shit is strong!"

Keno's at the door behind me, another almost permanent visitor—or tenant I guess, who actually knows? He must have just wandered down from the stairs as there's no way he followed me through the front door. He's got his eyes half-shut and he looks like he's power napping standing up. Jesus, that would be a fantastic superpower.

"Yeah, I was just—" Then I stop, looking back up the stairs. "Did you just come from my flat?" I ask.

"Our own real-life Sherlock over here," he says, rubbing my head affectionately as he walks past me. He's the leanest of the group and he's still at least two of me wide so "walking past me" actually involves waiting for me to move and shuffling around.

"But no one's in?"

"The new German lot are."

Hans and Gertie. Of course. Totally forgot about them.

"They nice?" asks Dom, mostly to Keno, which I'm glad of, given I've barely met them.

"They're generous," Keno replies, smiling. He's riding a magical unicorn by the looks of it, high as a Mary Poppins kite.

"Wait—is that smell of weed coming from my place?" I ask, sounding more like my mother than I'd care to admit.

"It's good stuff, man," Keno replies, missing the chair he was aiming for and landing on the floor. The various voices pipe up around me in "Waaaay!" and "Oi oi" in response. Dom wanders over once he's stopped laughing to help the thick fella back to his wobbly sea legs.

"Alright, Dopey, grab some pizza before you hurt yourself," Dom says, pushing him toward the sofa. Keno doesn't need telling twice and I watch him sway toward the food like a zombie finding brains. "So Bella, to what do we owe the pleasure?" Dom tries again.

"Just . . ." I look around them. Gone are the days when I used to do this: hang out with my flatmates as a regular occurrence. This used to be me. This used to have been both of us—Ellie and me.

In fact, it was always Ellie and me and whoever it was who

took the other two rooms. Over the eight years we'd had several winning combos, but Marta and George were swapped for Ronald and Minty when Marta found a boyfriend and George wanted his own bachelor pad. Ronald was switched for Katie when he moved in with his boyfriend and Minty eventually turned to Simon, which was a huge improvement in conversation, fun, and above all, cleanliness. Katie left after a little spat with Simon over dishes, which made the kitchen feel like no-man's-land for a while, and in came Annie to make up the perfect dream team.

We used to always have movie nights on Mondays. We always used to do two-for-Tuesdays at Domino's—even Annie. But then life happened and schedules filled and now it's a Monday and I have two stoners living with me who I don't know and the people I do are having fun without me.

Holy shit, I'm suddenly feeling sorry for myself.

"Nah, I was just saying hi," I say eventually. "Have a good night, guys!" I call out to the room around me but Dom wanders out to stop me.

"Hey hey, it's been ages! You never hang out with us anymore."

"Well, that should change."

"Sure you don't want to come in?" he asks, but I'm already mentally preparing myself for the pity party I'm overdue.

"No—I have leftover curry from last week. Need to eat it before it gets bad."

"Fair enough," says Dom. He turns to the room. "Saturday then? We're all heading out. It's Dave's last night in London."

"Last night?"

"He's got himself a big-boy job out in Australia for the next year, don't you, Dave?"

Dave looks a bit embarrassed by the whole thing and shrugs.

"Yeah, maybe," I say.

"Well, I hope so," Dom replies. He turns to the crowd behind him. Someone's thrown pizza to someone else and it's missed. I can see molten cheese now dripping off a nearby pillow. "Say goodbye, guys."

"Bye, Bells!"

"Bon voyage!"

Come the usual echoes as I trudge back up to the lofty heights of my own self-pity.

❧ 13 ❧

I try to be cool. I do. But there's no cool way of telling someone to waft their baccy into the cool September night and not to hot-box our flat.

I awkwardly knock on their door, the last room on the upstairs corridor, which has a trail of breadcrumbs leading toward it in the form of a pungent odor. Oh how I wish Annie was around. She's usually a no-bullshit kind of girl. I once saw her crush a spider that was freaking the shit out of Simon and me with her pinkie finger. It was so badass I thought someone should make a Netflix show about the incident.

But Annie isn't here. It's just me. And technically I'm in the right as this is a nonsmoking flat.

But I'm still feeling mega awkward as I knock.

"Enter!" calls out Gertie.

So I do.

Jesus motherfuckingchrist. They have turned Ellie's room—they have turned Ellie's sweetheart wonderland—into a sex den. The walls are filled with erotica, the colors are no longer sweet duck eggs and pale pastels but deep reds. I'm pretty sure the contraption in the corner is a sex swing but I don't want to look like I'm staring at it.

"Bella! Won't you come join us?" Hans asks.

He's properly naked. Like completely fucking naked, except he's lying down in a slightly "paint me like one of your French girls" way that actually makes it look less weird and more beautifully artistic. Gertie's got clothes on, just about. She's wrapped in a flowing dress that's more or less see-through at the bits that shouldn't be see-through and bizarrely opaque everywhere else.

Oh please Lord, give me strength.

"I'm . . . actually alright, thank you, Hans. But that's a lovely offer," I add, because I'm trying to act cool. I'm not, I'm tense as shit, but I can't sound that way. I have to sound and act like this is a totally normal thing to walk in on and then when I leave I can call Ellie and she will cringe with me.

"We have plenty to go around," Gertie adds, holding out a doobie.

Just for a second I'm suddenly a little tempted. It's not like I'm doing anything else, I feel awkward enough to need a stress reliever and I haven't smoked weed since my uni days. But I also don't want to be a strange part of their foreplay. I wonder if they were this exposed while Keno was up here.

I have to be strong. I have to do the right thing. But the air—oh man, it's so thick I can feel it on my skin. Here goes.

Just stay cool, I tell myself.

"Erm . . . it's like . . . totally cool or whatever that you're smoking or whatever but do you mind like erm . . . like maybe doing the smoking bit outside? Only, it's pretty strong and like . . . asthma exists—not mine, I'm like totally fine with it but like—Simon has an asthma . . . well, just has asthma really and like it's cool and stuff but if you could possibly take it outside that would be like . . . cool."

"Of course, how rude." Hans says, genuinely affected by my words. There's somehow not an ounce of offense or sarcasm in his voice and—I mean, I just heard my own words back at me and even I would be sarcastic to that. Both of them look genuinely apologetic.

"Consider it done, little petal," Gertie says, and despite it being an ever so slightly condescending thing to say I take it as the nicest thing anyone has ever said to me. At that moment I do feel like a "little petal."

I mean, I'm standing in a small room filled with secondhand smoke, so maybe that has just a little something to do with it.

"Cool, like . . . I totally appreciate it," I say, trying not to count how many times I've just said the word "cool."

At least the deed is done.

As I walk out a sad realization takes over me; it's a Monday. There's no one in. All I'm going to do is reheat days' old curry, watch a David Attenborough documentary, and contemplate things like when I stopped being the "fun one" everyone wanted to hang out with and began being the fun police.

So I quickly turn back around and reach out for Gertie's extended hand. I take a long, hard toke and I feel the wonderful rush of tobacco tickling my throat. Keno is right, it is the strongest I've ever had for sure. Gertie seems genuinely amused by this turn of events and Hans rolls over to reach for his drink on the side table, revealing a bottom as perfectly stoic as his face.

Even I know this is weird now.

Returning to my high horse, I thank them both and shuffle out of the room, wanting simultaneously to die inside and to eat everything in Annie's cupboards.

❧ 14 ❧

I dared not look at my phone until 11 p.m. Partly because that's how long it took me to finish surveying the death-defying animals of the Sahara Desert with my good friend Attenborough as my guide, but also because I was weirdly nervous and the weed didn't help.

I can't help but feel super nervous at the thought of strangers reading my work.

Ellie has read some of my writing before. When I first decided that writing was my passion she used to read everything and tell me exactly how she felt about it, which was always incredibly positive because Ellie is completely and utterly incapable of being anything but supportive. I think Marty might have read a poem or two by proxy of it being on Ellie's desk when they both still lived at home—but he just shrugged so he doesn't count. I guess my parents have read a few things I've sent them, and my English teachers too back when I was younger but other than that, no one ever reads anything.

I know. It's dumb. I'm a writer—I should be sending my writing to everyone and forcing them to read it, but when I start thinking about who to send something to, I start panicking that maybe it's not good enough or maybe they'll be too harsh and critical and maybe I can't handle that and suddenly I break.

So I don't look at my phone. I need time to process what I've done: putting something I've worked on out there into the universe. I need time to prepare myself for the comments.

When the final closing scenes of the baby cub taking its first adorable little steps turns to darkness and the credits roll, I pick up my phone and turn it off silent. I'm ready.

I have a few texts to begin with. The parentals have popped out of the woodwork:

Mummy Marble-28 Sep 20:35
Free for dinner Friday?

28 Sep 23:15-Me
Are you cooking?

Mummy Marble-28 Sep 23:15
No

Father Marble-28 Sep 23:15
I am

28 Sep 23:16-Me
Then yes. Sounds delightful

They're only in St. Albans. It's a twenty-minute train from Kings Cross and given I work on the edge of Baker Street it's not all that complicated to make it up to them.

Marty-28 Sep 21:55
There's a new Attenborough on BBC iPlayer

Marty-28 Sep 21:55
It's brutal

28 Sep 23:17-Me
Just finished it

28 Sep 23:17-Me
Fucking antelopes

28 Sep 23:17-Me
They're such shits

Marty-28 Sep 23:18
For not wanting to be torn apart?

28 Sep 23:18-Me
They're totally pointless and cheetah cubs are adorable

28 Sep 23:18-Me
They should sacrifice themselves
28 Sep 23:18-Me
Poor little Simba

Marty-28 Sep 23:19
Feeling broody are we?

Whatever.

I switch over. My finger hovers over the B-Reader app but—no.
I can't, not yet. I'm feeling a bit paranoid, but to be fair that might
just be the weed. I head to Mirror Mirror.

Two of my previous conversations must have deleted me, for
two new ones have appeared. I have a "hey" from one of them
already. Urgh, so boring. I'm not in the mood to even reply "hey"
back to them.

I click on my old friend.

Bella Marble
Does it begin with a B?

Mystery Man
It does not

Bella Marble
A C?

Mystery Man
Not close

Bella Marble
First half of the alphabet?

Mystery Man
You're getting warmer Miss Marble

I smile at that. There's something weirdly sexy about a last name
in a text. It's like *Fifty Shades* meets *Pride and Prejudice*. Plus I sound
like that lovely old woman detective and that's pretty ace too.

It's time.

I've waited long enough.

I click on B-Reader and wait for it to load.

The app's got a nicer interface than the website. It's far less clut-
tered, one picture at a time scrolling around at the top. I look at

the bottom, waiting for the little red number sign to appear in the corner to tell me how many notifications that I have. I almost can't breathe I'm so nervous.

It takes a while to load apparently. I push my thumb down on the screen so the whole page reloads but still no little red number appears. Maybe that feature's broken in the app.

I press on the "writers" tab anyway, going through to the portal. Yep—there it is. There is my chapter 1: all the relevant ticks are in place; it's fully uploaded; I've agreed to the terms and conditions; I've named it properly and added the right genre. Weird.

I click on the page and the stats come up.

No views? Is it being serious?

I reload the page again but still nothing. No likes, no comments, no views at all. It's been out for half a day. Not a single view in half a day? Where are all the B-Readers? What better things have they got in their lives that makes my chapter have zero views?!

I throw my phone down beside me, then realize how pointless and childish that is and pick it back up again. I read through the FAQs, searching for a reason for this catastrophe.

"New writers—be patient! We have hundreds of new writing samples going up every second. It takes some time for people to see it properly. It won't be long until the views come in so don't be put off by a slow start."

Well fuck them.

I go through all the settings, trying to see if there's something I missed somehow. Under "consents" there's a little checkbox stating that my handle can be made public—that's already checked so that shouldn't be an option.

There's one unticked under the "media" headline that asks permissions for third-party consents to use my handle. I tick that too. Anything to get my name out there. Anything to help people read it!

Then, having exhausted my options, I turn off my light in a strop. Then I switch it back on again to find my phone charger and plug it in, then turn it off again. My mind is still buzzing though.

All I can think about is how much I want to just pull my writing from the site completely. Maybe I should.

No, that's not what I want to do at all. What I actually want to do is wander over to the next room, tuck myself up next to Ellie, and have her tell me that it's all going to be alright and that I just need to be more patient. That's all. What I want is for her duck-egg pillows and her soothing affirmations to help send me to sleep.

But I can't do that. Because she's not there anymore.

So I pick up my phone one more time and I turn to my messages.

28 Sep 23:39-Me

I miss you xxx

There's no other way I can put into words how it feels to be deprived of the other half of my soul.

I do.

I miss her.

So much.

My phone buzzes almost instantly. Like she was waiting for me. Like she knew I needed her.

The Elsa to my Anna-28 Sep 23:50

xoxo

That's all I needed. With that, I can drift off into a calm, peaceful sleep and see what excitement tomorrow will bring.

❧ 15 ❧

Except Tuesday came and went with still no reads on B-Reader. In the words of the band FUR, who I just googled to make this exact point: "Where Did All the People Go?" Work drags and, in the absence of anything new being uploaded onto Netflix in the last twenty-four hours, I spend my night rewatching the same Attenborough documentary again.

29 Sep 22:28-Me
Ok. I feel a bit bad about the whole antelope thing

29 Sep 22:28-Me
They're quite cute too

Marty-29 Sep 23:29
I once gutted an antelope. Part of anatomy

29 Sep 22:28-Me
That's disgusting

Marty-29 Sep 23:30
That's life

I switch to the better sibling.

29 Sep 23:39-Me
Which is better, an antelope or a cheetah?

The Elsa to my Anna-29 Sep 23:50
You are xxx

Wednesday has a very similar quality. I stop checking B-Reader every half hour and start only opening it on the hour mark, which still doesn't help my anxiety as it still doesn't say I have any views. It's a flawed system.

"Patience," I hear in Ellie's soothing voice in my head. "Have patience, Bella."

So I do. I drink copious amounts of tea, read plenty of others' work on the site, and do what I can to forget about it.

Weirdly, it pays off, for on Thursday I have my first spark of hope.

A little red dot with a number has appeared beside the app logo on my home screen. It's half past four and I break my usual "on the hour every hour" rule to check it immediately.

1

That's what the little red dot says: *1*

The knots in my stomach start to grow. The phone rings and, distracted, it isn't until I hear the shuffle of Maggie already en route to me to tell me to pick it up that I do, letting up some nervous new work experience to one of the editorial teams.

But 1.

I hold my breath as the app loads and, with a beating heart, I click on my notifications page.

1 reader has viewed your chapter 1 — "My Night with the Big Bad Wolf."

There it is: proof. Someone has actually clicked on it and read it. I scroll down to the likes and the comments.

Nothing.

Well what does that mean?

Does it mean they like it? Or they don't like it?

I think maybe it might give you the notification as soon as someone clicks on the little "read me" page so I wait for twenty minutes, staring at the screen, wondering when they might comment. But they don't.

I can't tell whether that's better or worse. Did they hate it so much that they didn't feel the need to say anything? Or did they think it was so funny and heartwarming that . . . no, not worth thinking about. Nothing just means nothing.

I need to stop getting worked up about this.

One view is still one view. My work is being seen, by someone who isn't related to me, teaching me, or a Mathews. That is a victory in itself. So I close down the app and, feeling like I am being a real grown-up, pretend to work really hard for about twenty minutes.

❧ 16 ❧

Simon's back for the night, thank God, so I have company as I eat my Nando's takeout dinner. That's right: PERi-PERi chicken, grilled to perfection and covered in a mango and lime sauce that I would quite literally smother myself in if given the chance.

Diego's taking him to France for the weekend. (A weekend trip! A weekend trip, a week after they've met? It's so romantic I feel I should be submitting it to the Hallmark Channel for their next big film.) Diego's got a gig there so it's not a big deal—at least that's what Simon says incredibly unconvincingly.

I finally get to tell someone about the sex den upstairs. It might not be as cute as an epic romantic weekend away but it's still a story that needs telling and it's quite a weight off, I can tell you. I keep my voice low because I'm pretty sure they're upstairs, but Simon's laughter practically shakes the whole flat. He'd make a crap spy.

Mysterious noises have been floating to my room every night since but I haven't seen either of them emerge. The smell of weed hasn't completely disappeared from the house but if they are still smoking inside, it's at least far enough out the window for us not to get a direct hit.

With all the niceties out of the way I get on to what I really want to talk to him about—what I want to talk with anyone about—my one whole reader on B-Reader. I click on my profile to show him when my eyes dazzle over.

There's a new notification. No, not just one . . .

5 readers have viewed your chapter 1 — "My Night with the Big Bad Wolf."

That's a 500 percent increase on my previous tally! Ah!

2 readers have liked your chapter 1 — "My Night with the Big Bad Wolf."

Oh holy hell—Likes! I'm getting Likes! People actually like it! I'm trying to hold my shit together as I read the last one.

1 viewer has commented on your chapter 1 — "My Night with the Big Bad Wolf."

My stomach drops instantly. A comment? An actual comment? I click on it nervously. Are they going to tell me that my main character isn't likable enough? I tried to gloss her over a little with some charm, but given that she's me I found it pretty difficult. Maybe they're worried that it sounds a bit man-hating? Maybe I should have reminded the audience that not all men are terrible, just this one wolflike fool.

Oh God, I'm so nervous I almost can't read it but I can and I do:

@sirreadalot
LOL

There we are: my first comment. "LOL."

Three letters. Three symbolized words. That's what I get, LOL. I'm saying it like it's a bad thing. It's not. It's good. I'm so happy I can feel fireworks exploding behind my eyeballs.

"That's annoying," says Simon, because he doesn't understand.

LOL means laughing out loud. Laughing out loud means I'm funny. I'm funny? Who knew! I'm officially a funny writer. I'm apparently a good writer! I'm a *writer* for fuck's sake. I'm absolutely buzzing.

Our conversation moves on but my mind lingers. I kind of want to write back to @sirreadalot to thank him for the time taken to write a comment, my first comment, just like Henrietta Lovelace did to me.

I actually click on Henrietta's profile while Simon starts talking about the view from Diego's living room. Ah, the luxury of even *having* a living room seems beyond me. Four bedrooms, one bathroom, and one kitchen are all our flat has to offer. I think Simon's bedroom might have been a living room at one point as it's much bigger than all the other rooms, but the landlord obviously didn't feel shared common space was necessary for a flat share.

Looks like Henrietta hasn't had any new chapters just yet but I can see that her following has already begun to grow. My one read has been joined by forty others and six others have joined my first comment. Simon's still talking so I can't read them properly, but scanning my eyes down I see the word "love" in nearly every one. I know I can't exactly take credit but I have a weird sense of pride thinking I'd discovered her first.

I make a mental note to read the other comments later as Simon and I begin to talk about some wild night he had on Monday. (Who even goes out on a Monday?)

"Oh my God, one of them is emerging!" Simon whispers. Suddenly a creak echoes from upstairs. Some light footsteps come tapping across the corridor. "Do you think it's Hans?"

"I hope he's got clothes on this time!"

"I can't believe you saw his Willy Wonka."

"I can't believe you just called it a Willy Wonka."

"Shut up, they're coming."

Not a second too late the footsteps arrive at the kitchen door and there, standing in the doorframe, is neither Hans nor Gertie. Instead, it is a girl in her midtwenties. She is in the middle of pulling up a bra strap as she walks into the kitchen. Her hair is disheveled like she's just backward combed the lot of it. She looks a little red and flustered.

"Your bathroom?" she asks. It's a very normal question as nearly everyone asks it—the bathroom's at a weird angle so the door looks more like the entrance to a broom cupboard—but she is so soft-spoken that neither Simon nor I are able to even hear her the first time around.

I recover from the sight slightly quicker, pointing to the bathroom door and waiting for the click of the latch before even daring to look Simon's way.

"Wait—are they having a threesome?" Simon whispers. "Are they actually having a threesome?"

"We don't know if it's a threesome. We don't know how many more people they have up there!"

The two of us stay silent as the soft-spoken woman flushes and, from the open door of the kitchen, we can watch as she scuttles back up the stairs. Simon and I filter into the hallway as she goes, staring at their door from below like it's calling to us. We stay silent, listening in for extra voices but we hear none. Unable to control our laughter we head back into the kitchen and close the door.

"That room has seen more in the last week than its entire lifetime, I reckon."

"Oh fuck—do you think when they asked me if I wanted to join them they meant . . . in bed?"

"You think?"

"I don't know. They seem pretty out there! I mean, who brings a sex swing into a flat share?"

"You're sure it's a sex swing?"

"Who brings a normal swing into a flat share?"

"Talking of sex swings, did Prince Charming ever get in touch?"

"Who?"

"The shoe in the bar? Your red heel with your digits?"

"How is that related to sex swings?"

"How isn't it?"

I wipe the tears of laughter from my eyes and finish off the last of the Nando's chips. There are no chips better in the whole world than Nando's chips. I soak up all the salt with the broken potato and have no regrets that I've just wasted £10.75 on mango and lime chicken.

"No, no luck. No shoe. Turns out I'm not Cinderella after all."

"No," Simon replies with wide, sad eyes. "Maybe not, but we'll find you your fairy-tale ending. Somehow."

"You know, I think we will," I say happily, because I am happy. I have two whole likes on my writing. Things are beginning to change for me. Things are looking up.

"Now Diego's given me his Disney+ password. Want to grab some ice cream and watch *Moana*?"

"Erm. Yes. Yes, I would, Simon."

An almost perfect evening after an almost perfect day, missing only one key ingredient.

As I lie in bed that night I think about texting Ellie but stop. I don't want to be needy, and she hasn't texted me first yet for a while. I can just see Mark's face sitting beside her, judging me more with every text I send. So I don't. I leave it. Instead, I flick back to B-Reader and head straight back to my notifications.

> @sirreadalot
> LOL

I read. I read it again.

> @sirreadalot
> LOL

"Thank you, Sir Read-a-lot," I think as my dreams finally take over.

I can't help but think this is the start of something epic.

17

Fridays at work always feel a bit easier when I have something to look forward to at the end of it, and going down to my parents' is always a delight.

When work finishes for the day I wrap up extra warm (the temperatures dropped again so goodbye autumn jacket, hello winter coat) and hop on the Met line from Baker Street up to Kings Cross. Before I know it the trusty (albeit eye-wateringly expensive) Thameslink carries me swiftly back to my childhood.

I wander through the little old town of St. Albans with its cobblestones and its magnificent abbey and I'm right back into ye olde land of yore. This is where I grew up thinking fairies hid behind every corner. Behind the Georgian houses and the wood-beamed cottages of Fishpool Street lived all wonder of witches and goblins and wizards, brewing up in their cauldrons that they hid from mere mortals like me, the only proof a thick puff of smoke up their little chimneys. My mother and father had very active imaginations, and I took in every drop of it, knowing that one day I would sit in the highest tower, waiting for my own Prince Charming to rescue me from my evil stepmother. Except I'd never have an evil stepmother, because my parents were perfect together.

I used to think everyone had what I had. I didn't understand why Timothy only had one parent dropping him off and a different parent picking him up on alternate days. I couldn't believe that Zoe had two homes on either end of the same long street. I can remember trying to comfort Ellie by telling her that her dad was probably just on a business trip like my mum sometimes went on because it never occurred to me that he might not come back.

I took for granted how perfect it was to have two loving parents in one home. They didn't argue either. My mum is quite a calm, relaxed woman and lets my dad do most of the worrying for the two of them, which suits him fine. My mother burns food; my father rescues it from destruction. My father plows through the finances with a toothcomb and my mother pays the check. My parents are two halves of a whole. They are each other's better side and their worse. They are the one and only reason I've always stayed true, knowing that my one true love is out there somewhere, even if he's not Charles Wolf or Mystery Man or whoever it is that comes next.

Which is why I am so shocked, so heartbroken, so completely sidetracked when my mother—very casually over my dad's potpie might I add—tells me what she does.

❧ 18 ❧

"A DIVORCE?" I scream.

When I say scream, I really do mean it. It's so shocking to me that my emotions are already taking over me. I'm shaking, my eyes watering.

"Well, a separation at first of course but yes, we'll sort out the paperwork eventually." My mum sounds so easy and free. She sounds like she's asking for the saltshaker.

My dad is looking up at me. His face is twisted into the same knots as my stomach is. He's not a fan of confrontation, that's always been my mother's forte, and although he's nodding in agreement he clearly isn't comfortable with my immediate reaction here.

"I . . . I don't . . . but you are meant for each other. You're a happily-ever-after."

"We were a happily-ever-after. For years and years we were, but sometimes things change, darling," my dad tries. He has a softer touch to my mother.

"Nothing changes!" I reply uselessly.

"Some things change. Days change. Seasons change."

"That's not helpful, Mum."

"Well, it's true."

"What your mother's trying to say is that we've changed. Over the years. But what hasn't changed—and this is important—what hasn't changed is that we still love you very much."

"Really? Or might that change too, Mum?" I spit.

"Okay, fine. I can be the bad guy," says my mum, throwing her hands up in the air, very calmly really given my extreme level of wrath.

"No, that's not fair, Lexie, don't take the blame for this," my dad coughs up. My God, he's too nice. He's too wonderful. Why doesn't my mum see that in him anymore? What's happened since the last time I visited? "Look, we still love each other very much. But sometimes it's what happens when you live with someone for so long. We've been friends now for years. Best friends. And in being best friends we've sort of lost that . . . that spark that . . ."

"But love like yours doesn't die!"

"It isn't dead, it's different," says my mother. I don't believe her. She's even leaning back in her chair like it doesn't matter. I've read at least four *BuzzFeed* articles on what body language means and this one is not fitting to this outrageous scenario that I've found myself in.

"Is it someone else?" I ask. "Is that it? Has one of you cheated?"

"Neither of us have cheated."

"Mum, have you cheated?"

She puts her hands in the air, like she's actually finding this whole thread funny somehow. It's not funny.

"I'm back to the bad guy," she cries, looking at my dad for support.

"Your mother has not cheated," my father pipes up. "Neither of us has cheated. This is not something we chose to do lightly but this is a mutual decision that's been discussed for some time now."

"But . . . but you said finding each other was the best thing that ever happened to you."

"It was." Thank God, maybe she does care that my whole world is spinning.

"Past tense?" I cry, physically cry. Wet tears soak up my pie's remaining crumbly pastry base.

"It is," my dad says, smiling up at his soon-to-be ex-wife. "Because both of us found a friend for life that day, and because of it you were brought into the world. That is the best thing to ever happen to either of us."

"But what about your happily-ever-after?" I ask.

"We've already had it," my mother says, finally leaning forward, "and now it's time to move on."

❧ 19 ❧

What does a perfectly normal twenty-nine-year-old do when she finds out her parents are getting a divorce? I'll tell you.

I pushed the rest of my potpie halfway across the table, spilling my large glass of apple juice—yes apple juice—and stormed up to my bedroom like a spoiled teenager.

To be fair, my bedroom hasn't changed since my teenage years at all, so it was at least fitting. It's still mostly purple and pink with a large painting of a castle across the whole of the back wall. Cartoon animals fly overhead and a fluffy white circular carpet is on the floor. Books from all the years are filling the shelves and piled up on the floor, from *The Very Hungry Caterpillar* to Tolstoy novels I read way too young to even understand them. Posters from all the aughts bands I fawned over are still overcrowding my writing desk in the corner and glow-in-the-dark stars are stuck on the ceiling, although these days the glow feels weak and half-hearted.

I look up at them now, crying my eyes out and lying back on my purple single bed that I somehow never grew too big for.

I know, I know. It's a bit of an exaggeration. But I just didn't see it coming.

2 Oct 19:30-Me
I don't know why I'm handling this so badly
2 Oct 19:30-Me
I moved out almost 11 years ago

2 Oct 19:30-Me

Why do I care whether they are together or not?

2 Oct 19:31-Me

I don't know why I can't stop crying

I wipe the tears off my phone screen but even as I do that new tears land, taking their place.

The Elsa to my Anna-2 Oct 19:31

Because it's your mum and your dad

The Elsa to my Anna-2 Oct 19:31

Of course you're upset

2 Oct 19:31-Me

I literally can't stop crying!

The Elsa to my Anna-2 Oct 19:32

Come for a sleepover and a movie night

The Elsa to my Anna-2 Oct 19:32

We'll watch a rom com and eat ice cream

The Elsa to my Anna-2 Oct 19:32

It's the best cure. I promise

2 Oct 19:33-Me

What?

Watch happy couples get together while my whole
family is breaking apart? No thanks

The Elsa to my Anna-2 Oct 19:33

Then a horror movie

The Elsa to my Anna-2 Oct 19:33

The Shining?

The Elsa to my Anna-2 Oct 19:33

I hear that's got a really healthy relationship in it that
we can learn from

I laugh out loud, imagining her beside me. She spent half her life sleeping top to toe with me on this bed. Even remembering that, knowing it won't happen again, makes me sadder. Life just keeps spinning. I don't know how to stop it.

2 Oct 19:34-Me

Will Mark be home?

The Elsa to my Anna-2 Oct 19:35
He won't bother us

I just can't do it. I want to be around Ellie more than anything, but right now I don't even want to look at Mark's stupid annoying face. He's part of the problem. Without him, Ellie would already be home, waiting for me to return. She'd probably have already begun baking some kind of "feel better cake" all Mary Berry style. But instead she's playing Happy Families with Mark, while my own happy family is breaking apart.

2 Oct 19:36-Me
No, it's alright
2 Oct 19:36-Me
Probably best for me to get this out of my system
alone
2 Oct 19:36-Me
I'm a grown-up
2 Oct 19:36-Me
Apparently

The Elsa to my Anna-2 Oct 19:38
Offer's open. Anytime x

✥ 20 ✥

At one point I hear a knock on the door and, a little begrudgingly, I invite my mother in. She sits at the end of my bed, nursing a cup of chamomile for me that I reject. Even in my upset form I'm clever enough to remember that it should be builder's tea or nothing.

"Are you going to tell me it was all a big mistake?" I ask, barely able to look at her. She smiles.

"There are no mistakes, only learnings."

"You've read that somewhere."

"I've lived it."

Oh, if only I could have my mum's outlook on life. She annoyingly looks like my older, more mature doppelgänger, but her attitude is more like my alter ego. I've never met anyone who is as relaxed as her about just about everything. Honestly, if you told her the whole world would explode in ten minutes she'd still walk at a snail's pace and smile.

I also can't fault her timing, of course. Ten minutes earlier and I was gearing up to scream at her all over again, but now that the reality has set in I'm somehow feeling a lot calmer. Devastated, yes, but at least ready to hear what she has to say.

"I'm sorry about downstairs," I say finally.

"I'm sorry it's not what you want to hear."

"I'm just . . ." I say, hanging my head low. "It's just one thing after another at the moment. Everything seems to be unraveling all at the same time and this . . . this was the one thing I thought I could rely on."

"I know. I get it."

"This is all I've ever known."

"It's all we've ever known too." She strokes back my hair and I let her, but I pull a face anyway.

"Then why?" I ask despairingly.

"Because it's time to move on."

I groan wildly like one of those cheetahs in the Sahara.

"Why is it that everyone's moving on except me at the moment?" I cry like a strange banshee to my window, unable to even look at my mother right now because even I understand how immature I sound. I just can't help it.

She waits for my huffing to subside a little before she speaks again.

"Go on then. Tell me what's going on, love."

I stare at her blankly.

"You and dad are getting a divorce?" I reply. "Were you not part of the conversation downstairs?"

"Conversation? Is that was it was? Sounded more like a tantrum to me."

"Oi!" I say, wrapping my pillow around me for comfort. "You're the one asking the dumb question."

"Well, obviously I know about your father and me. I was asking what else seems to be 'unraveling'?"

She has this weird super talent of actually listening to all the shit I spout. Even I forgot I said that already.

"It's like . . . not even a little bit important right now."

"Is it not?"

"It's stupid."

"I'm sure it's not."

"I don't want to talk about it."

"Don't you?"

"Not with you. Not now."

"Really?"

I hate it when she does this because ever since I was little I've never been able to resist. I start to protest some more but then I hear my voice weakening and I know I'll break eventually. What's the point in stalling?

"I just had this vision for where I wanted my life to be and this . . . this isn't it. Not with work. Not with . . . with love . . . I guess, and now this? The other bits, I mean, whatever, but I thought our family, I thought this was something I didn't even have to worry about."

She nods rhythmically and I find my whole temper subsiding.

"No one ever leads the life they expect to."

"Maybe not," I say, hugging the cushion in tighter to my chest, "but . . . I don't know. This isn't even close."

"Well, what is it you're missing?"

"I'm not *missing* . . . well, maybe I'm . . ."

Why are words so hard to get out sometimes? How do you put it into words when all the foundations you've built through the years suddenly crack beneath your feet?

"I know this sounds stupid, but it just feels like everything I believed in was a lie."

I don't mean to necessarily, but as my eyes glaze over once again I find myself turning to the painting on my wall. I follow each turret of the castle up the same way I used to look at it on nights I couldn't sleep. I'm like so old for it and yet I never once wanted it gone. Not even during my awkward mopey teenage years. My mum follows my gaze and hums thoughtfully.

"If you and Dad can't make it, what chance is there for anyone else?"

My mum smiles as she thinks, not a happy smile necessarily, but the kind of reassuring smile that I didn't know I needed to see.

"We made a real good go of it, you know. We had a real romance. We had a perfect life, we made a perfect daughter, and now both of us are ready to find that all again."

I start crying at her words and she moves in closer so I can hug her. I don't even know if I want to hug her—she's the one I'm mad at—but even when you're angry with your mum you want your mum to be the one to make it better, always.

"People don't just need to have one fairy tale in their lifetime. If the books have told us anything it's that there are plenty of Prince Charmings in plenty of stories. There's no quota for how many stories you get to be a part of in life. Your dad is still the greatest man I'll ever know but our fairy tale came to a close a few years ago now, and it's time we both found ourselves a new one. We're too old to waste time, and too young to not have fun."

"I'm going to miss it," I whimper. "This family, this setup. I'm going to miss it."

"I will too sometimes, I'm sure," she says, cooling me down. The smell of chamomile is actually exactly what I need. As I pull away from her I find the mug has already been transferred from her hand to mine and I can start to feel the hot warming liquid soothing my sadness.

So much change in such a small amount of time. My brain can't handle it.

"You know Ellie's engaged?" I say. I try to sound non-fussed but my voice acts on its own volition. I sound like a sulky teen all over again.

Fuck it, I'm in my childhood bed. My mum's next to me. I'm allowed to act five years old.

"We do. Niamh called us. We sent her an engagement letter already. If she asks, you signed it too."

"To Ms. Mathews?"

"No, to Ellie."

"I didn't know people sent engagement letters."

"Only to people who are engaged," my mother says, giggling to herself. "I can't tell you how strange it is that your friends are getting married. That girl once weed on my best sofa because you'd made her laugh too much after school and now she's getting ready to walk down the aisle. Times are changing, aren't they?"

I nod. The chamomile's already gone. Turns out my mum does

know me after all because it was delicious and I kind of want another cup.

"I don't like how fast it's all going," I say stubbornly. "I want everything to stop. The whole world's moving one way and I feel like I'm pushing against it the other."

My mum stands up, stretching out in some bizarre yoga pose like preparing for the world all over again.

"Then keep fighting, darling. I raised a strong, healthy woman. Now is not the time to conform to banality, now is the time for you to get yourself out there and have fun."

Weirdly, it's Marty's words that echo in my head.

If you started trying to find someone you actually wanted to spend the night with you'd have much better luck.

Is my mum seriously dishing out the same advice as that absolute moron?

"I expect you to be able to handle anything life throws at you, and anything you can't handle you throw straight at me. I'll pick up the slack."

Oh my God, I love her.

She smiles, clapping her hands together like that was the scene-change cue.

"Now your father is anxious and has made your favorite pudding, so shall we go and eat it together now? Or do you want to strop some more?"

❧ 21 ❧

Marty-3 Oct 09:16
Come by the vet's on your way home

3 Oct 09:17-Me
Why?

Marty-3 Oct 09:17
BubbaWubba's been asking for you

It came with a picture like all great texts do. A picture speaks a thousand words and my God, this one spoke novels. It is my favorite being in the whole wide world—a small pug with the beadiest eyes you've ever seen. He's the most helpless-looking creature in the entire universe, and his face is calling out my name for help. He belongs to a mean old lady so Marty always keeps him for a few more hours than he needs so I can give him all the cuddles he lacks at home.

That's a lie. He probably gets lots of cuddles at home. The old lady is mean to humans but my God she loves that dog.

3 Oct 09:17-Me
Me? Specifically?

Marty-3 Oct 09:18
By name
Marty-3 Oct 09:18
Bring chocolate

3 Oct 09:18-Me

Isn't that poisonous to dogs?

Marty-3 Oct 09:19

Bring it anyway

3 Oct 09:19-Me

PMSing are you?

The practice is more crowded on a Saturday. Most people wait until the weekend to work out whether it's worth bringing in their little critters so it's always bustling on the weekends. There are all kinds of small creatures on laps and large dogs plodding along in small confined circles. The posters on the walls show pictures of elephants and llamas but I can't believe anyone has ever tried to bring one of them into the practice. It's on the edge of Battersea. It's hardly in the wild.

I don't understand how some people don't like animals. It confuses the hell out of me how someone can see the fluffy bunny and think that's a terrifying beast. I just see a giant marshmallow in need of a hug. Marty has done an awful lot of terrible things, but becoming a vet was not one of them. It's the forgiving factor in his otherwise pointless life.

The second I walk in, Naomi at the front desk waves me over. I think she knows if she leaves me in the waiting room too long I'll end up snuggling on the floor with a sick bloodhound like last time, so she's swift in getting me out back to the staff room. It's not much. The back wall is a line of cages meant for those whose stay is a little longer than the rest, with an old sofa not far away for anyone on call to get a bit of shut-eye if they have to stay the night. There's a poor excuse of a kitchen at the back with just about enough to make a tea but don't be fooled—the biscuits on the shelf are actually dog biscuits, not just small regular human biscuits. I learned that the hard way.

BubbaWubba's in one of the cages at the back. There are several adorable dogs there, but BubbaWubba's in prime position as I wander over. I swear he knows me, for the second I come close he rolls over ready for a belly rub. The little tart.

I reach over to undo the cage door.

"I don't think you want to do that," says a voice behind me.

It always makes me laugh when I see Marty in scrubs. It's like seeing a small child play dress-up. He's twenty-nine, he's been a vet for years now, but he's still just the annoying little shit who used to do no work and still get much better grades than me. Now it's so unreal. He's in charge of saving lives. Actually saving real living, breathing creatures. Like, how?

"And why not? I thought you said he's been asking for me?"

"He's also been pissing on just about anything and anyone." He comes up to the bars just as BubbaWubba squats and a little line of bright yellow urine slides out from under him. "Liver infection."

"Oh my God, it's actually serious this time?"

"He'll be fine. In a bit."

"You on a break?"

"I have five minutes. You timed it well."

He sits back on the small sofa and in a world-weary way rubs his head.

"Not feeling good?" I ask. I turn back to BubbaWubba. He's too cute not to look at even if he is a weeing machine.

"Just tired." He wipes his face and shakes it off. "Had a girl over last night who kept me up until five this morning."

"Oh, poor you," I say sarcastically. I pull out the Milkybar Buttons from my bag. "This for you then?"

"No—I'm watching my weight."

"Oh," I turn to little BubbaWubba. "Is it actually for the dog?"

"Nah—the chocolate's for you."

"For me?" I say, completely unable to hide my shock.

"Yeah, sounds like you've just been served a shit show. Needed to make sure someone's looking after you."

"Sorry, what?" I'm blinking hard here, so completely confused.

"I heard about your parents."

"Ellie told you?"

That's unlike Ellie.

"No, my mum called this morning. Your parents dropped her a text last night. I figured you wouldn't be in a good state."

He is right, of course. I'd spent a bit more of last night crying. I cried a bit during pudding, and then a bit more when we had coffees after the meal. I'd actually ended up staying over in my old room because I couldn't bear the thought of crying on public transport, but that made me cry more because my mum slept in the spare room and I found it so weird I couldn't help but wail a bit. Plus I tear-stained my jumper and spilled ice cream all over my jeans so I wasn't in a fit state for human eyes. I woke up a new person though. More grown-up. More accepting. I stole some of my mum's jeans (she's as small as I am) and a jumper that matched identically to the one I was wearing (her taste in clothes is disturbingly similar to mine). I may have still been hurting, but at least as I jumped back on the train I was dealing with my hurt in a very respectable and adult manner.

Right now, however, I'm still a bit shocked.

"Sorry—you got me to get chocolates for myself?"

"Yep."

"You got me to specifically buy *myself* chocolate to make *myself* feel better?"

"And you got yourself your own favorite so that's worked out nicely."

I stand there for a second, looking at the sharing bag in my hand like a foreign object. Finally, looking at him with my specialized fire eyes, I chuck the whole bag at his face. He gallops over the sofa for cover.

"You shit!"

"You love chocolate!" he protests.

"I don't love buying *myself* pity chocolates!" I throw all the pillows his way as he still cowers low behind the sofa and watch him wince. Poor little BubbaWubba starts barking, starting off a little wave of barks from behind various cages behind me, all annoyed they can't join in the fun.

"Well, I didn't have time to get them for you so I thought this was the next best thing!"

"You arsehole!" I'm already laughing though, falling back on the sofa right next to where my chocolates landed. I'm embarrassingly out of breath. I didn't even exert myself that much. Begrudgingly I pick them up and tear them open.

"You want one?" I say, stuffing myself with the first handful. He puts his hand up in surrender as he straightens his hair back into place and flumps on the sofa next to me.

"Nah, moment on the lips."

"Fuck you," I say, grabbing an even larger mouthful and stuffing it in my own mouth.

Annoyingly this is actually quite a nice gesture. I do really like Milkybar Buttons. Obviously. Because I'm human.

"I have to go back to work."

"Why'd you ask me here then?" I ask, my breath pretty much back now.

"Just wanted to make sure you were alright." He turns to me, in one of his very rare earnest moments. "Are you? Alright?"

I nod slowly then turn to look at him. It's weird. I see so much of Ellie in him and immediately it burns into my soul. What's the point in putting on a brave face to him? I shake my head.

"No. Not at all really."

He nods, giving my arm an affectionate stroke.

"Go figure," he says, and I can hear his tone has shifted. It's warm, honest, and open. This isn't the usual laugh-it-off Marty I know, but someone else entirely. Someone who actually cares, and isn't afraid to act like it.

I think he's going to hug me and for just a second I realize that I don't think he's ever hugged me in my whole life. That would be completely weird. But it's alright, he doesn't. Instead he jumps up to his feet and wanders back over to the cages. He looks down the line to a golden retriever puppy looking particularly pathetic near the end and unlocks his cage, picking him out and carrying him over. He hands him over like a little Simba.

"What are you doing?"

"This is Jasper. He's cute and, more importantly, toilet trained."

I take Jasper and immediately the little thing licks my face. I'm in love.

"Stay for as long as you want. Put him back when you're done. I'd stay but I have a cocker spaniel with a sore throat who needs me."

"You're giving me a puppy to play with?"

"I'm giving you an emotional-support animal."

"This is the best thing anyone could ever have done."

"I know. I'm amazing. Get over it."

He ruffles my hair as he wanders away from me, picking up a spoon on his way out near the kitchen area to make sure his own hair is back on point.

"You know what you need to do?"

"Steal this dog? Hide from the Bubster?"

"Go out tonight," he replies.

Okay. Totally not where I saw that going.

"You offering?"

"No—I've got a date, but it's not good for you to be moping around all evening. It's Saturday night. You need to dance it out."

"I need to do more than dance it out."

"Yeah you do." He's smiling like he's my own more promiscuous fairy godmother. I know what he means of course. His mind has been on the same one track since his late teens. Usually I'd throw something at him all over again and tell him I want more than just meaningless sex.

But weirdly, just tonight, maybe I don't. Maybe I just need to release some tension. Maybe I need to stop worrying so much and have more fun. It's what my mum told me too—although to be fair she probably wasn't promoting one-night stands.

I sit back and close my eyes as little Jasper's plodding his adorable little paws all over my shoulders. Man, this dog is so perfect.

"You got plans tonight?" Marty asks.

"You know," I say, my mind bringing back the week's events, "I think I do."

Jasper gives a pitiful little howl and I feel like everything's right in the world.

"Good. Tell me how it goes tomorrow. Steal the dog and I swear to God you'll never see BubbaWubba again. Mostly because they'll revoke my license."

Satisfied, he gives me a last wink and wanders back out into the thick of it.

It's not long before Jasper's lapping up the tears down my face and I don't even care. They're not even tears of sadness, just the leftover tears I still need to expel from my system. I've got a puppy, I've got chocolate. I know, just know, I'm going to be fine.

And what's more, tonight, I'm going to get some.

❧ 22 ❧

A few hours later I'm downstairs in the bottom flat of Elmfield Road, surrounded by seven rugby lads and celebrating Dave's last night in London.

I had an interesting start to the night, I'll give you that. I drop Dom a text telling him I'm coming and as a response I get a:

Dom Downstairs Hipster-3 Oct 11:18
BELLAAAAAAAAAA
Dom Downstairs Hipster-3 Oct 11:18
HELL YES!
Dom Downstairs Hipster-3 Oct 11:18
Wear white

I think it's weird that there's a dress code, but not weird enough to comment, so it's a "wear white" night. That's like, normal. Not necessarily a problem. Ellie I know has this amazing white jumpsuit, which I've always wanted to wear anyway so as soon as I'm home I decide to go straight to her room to—

I stop at the kitchen because I get a rather visual reminder of my own stupidity. Annie's in there stirring a vegan curry that smells incredible and behind her, taking up the entire kitchen table might I add, are two very high Germans with more flour on their faces than has made it into the cookie dough they're molding. Both of them are giggling away and Annie, not fond of the greenery let's just say, is grinding her teeth and saying nothing.

So it hits me all over again—*Ellie doesn't live with me anymore*.
God, I'm not used to this setup.

Gertie and Hans have a cookie sheet in front of them waiting, I'd
imagine, for the raw cookie dough to take its rightful place but from
the looks of things, no cookie dough has yet made it onto the baking tray. Instead, it gets rolled up into a little ball, and in a weirdly
sexual way, gets fed into the other's mouth. I watch them for a while
doing this strange rolling, feeding dance and it's wonderfully hyp-
notizing. They're clothed this time, mostly, but Gertie's leg is almost
completely exposed in her maxi dress and every time she opens her
mouth she leans back like she's mid-orgasm and her bare leg shakes.
It's completely weird. How does someone make force-feeding raw
cookie dough erotic? I don't know. But maybe it's just them. Maybe
they make everything erotic.

Annie could not look more uncomfortable if she tried.

"Urgh," I say accidentally. The two Germans pause in their mating
ritual and look up at me, confused. "No, not you!" I say quickly, "I
just . . . don't own anything white." They continue to look confused.
I'm not that surprised. "As you were," I add.

They are pretty compliant, laughing away as they go back to
failing to cook their cookie dough.

"Anything white?" asks Annie.

"Yeah, I'm heading out with the guys downstairs," I say. "Wanna
come?"

"I'm going to stay over at Rachel's tonight," she says, turning to
the German pair and shooting them daggers. Oh dear. Looks like
Annie's not a huge fan of our new neighbors then.

"You sure? Rachel can join too."

"No, she's on a cleanse."

"Of course she is."

"Wanna come to Rachel's instead?" she asks.

Rachel's one of Annie's more common booty calls so no, I don't
particularly want to join that any more than I want to stay in and
hang out with the sensual cookie dough pair. Plus, tonight is not

a Netflix and chill. Tonight is not a bath and iPlayer. Tonight, my friends, in the words of Pharrell, I'm going to get lucky.

"Nope," I conclude, adding proudly, "tonight, I'm planning on having wild sex with a stranger."

"That's unlike you."

"It is."

"Are you alright?"

"Everyone keeps telling me to have more fun, so that's what I'm going to do. Have more fun."

"Are you sure that's how you have more fun?"

"I'm positive."

"Good for you," Annie says, mildly amused.

The Germans behind me move on top of each other, the cookie dough somehow cascading down Gertie's body and Annie's eyes widen like bugs. She turns to me, clearly desperate to fling her curry sauce right over the pair of them, but restraining herself she says, "I have something white you can borrow."

🌿 23 🌿

So here I am, wearing the skimpiest, tightest, most revealing little white number I've ever set eyes on. Annie is the fittest woman I know and all of her outfits aim to show that off.

I knock, happy that I've complied with the dress code until the door opens and I realize that "wearing white" isn't the dress code at all.

Being blue is the dress code. Very blue. The bluest.

They are covered in paint, head to foot, and wearing what I can only describe as white loincloths and strange garden gnome hats to complete the number. Dave's sitting at the table, getting the finishing touches of bright blue paint shoveled onto his face by a very happy and very blue Donald. While the others are all on Guinness it looks like Dean's on DayQuil as—even blue—his nose looks to be bright red. Why on earth he's decided to go out I have no idea, but I can only imagine the others wouldn't accept "actual sickness" for a good excuse not to party. Sam and Keno are both relaxing on the sofa, both of them as high as the two I left upstairs just a minute ago. Stu is the final addition to the tableau. He's blue, but even blue he looks completely unimpressed. This was clearly not his idea, this was clearly not what he voted for, but there he is, a little grumpy blue Smurf in a sea of blue Smurfs. He's actually the funniest of the lot of them and even though I'm shocked, just looking at his serious blue face makes my cheeks crack up into a wide smile.

"SMURFETTE!" Dom yells as he opens the door. He's even dyed his whole beard white for the occasion, a beautiful Papa Smurf if ever I saw it. He goes to grab me and I wince, but his paint has dried so nothing more than a blue smudge lands on my palm. "Time to blue up!"

"No no no no no!!!" I cry.

"Come on! We're Smurfs!"

"Why?"

"It's a throwback to our rugby initiation way back when," someone shouts from across the room, as if that makes sense somehow.

"We need to Smurf you up too!" Dom adds.

"I can't be a Smurf!"

"You can, Bella!"

"You have to!"

The voices all chime up around the room.

"BLUE! BLUE! BLUE," the chants continue. Donald, smiling away as always, starts to move toward me with the face paint. I start to panic.

"NO NO NO!" I scream, pushing Dom away from me and standing, the chair behind me flying backward. "I CAN'T BE BLUE!"

The faces that are now all staring back at me look stunned. My words run away from me before I can even help myself. "Look, I've just had a really bad week. I got kicked out of a wolf's house at four a.m. and I lost my shoe and Prince Charming never found me and my best friend's getting married to an ogre and my flatmate's sleeping with the most beautiful man I've ever seen and my parents are getting a divorce and the Germans upstairs have a sex swing and I don't own a dog and I keep getting told by everyone that I should stop trying to take everything so seriously and I should start just having fun, which I think means I need to have sex with a beautiful stranger tonight and I think that might make me happy and somehow I don't think being covered in blue is going to help my chances!"

I take a large breath of air, my lungs having completely emptied.

I look around the room. All fourteen big, blue-rimmed eyes are blinking at me. Oh God. What did I do? What did I say?

I wonder how I'm going to break the silence. Suddenly, out of the painful quiet one voice cuts through.

"WAAAAAAAYYYYYYY!!!" Donald cries and suddenly, like a well-trained orchestra taking their cue, the others all join in.

"Bella on the prowl!" Dom calls out to the group.

They're all catcalling and cheering me on and suddenly I turn from an absolute weirdo to a superstar. I look down, my cheeks turning as red as my hair, completely embarrassed but the cheers of my name keep echoing around me.

"I'm really sorry I shouted," I murmur.

"No no no, my friend. The apologies are all mine! There shall be no blue for you tonight!" Dom cries, signaling over to Donald.

Donald throws down the rest of the blue paint and exchanges it for his own Guinness, holding it up to the light happily.

"So, plan tonight, boys," Dom begins, rallying around his bizarre congregation of avatars, "first things first, we're going to help Dave lose his virginity. Then second, and most importantly of all, we're going to find our Bellatrix a knight in shining armor!"

Everyone, even those draped over the sofa half-comatose, cheers and laughs. Someone hands me a Guinness to catch up with the others and I do, ready for my night to begin.

From beside me, in the smallest voice I've ever heard, I hear a bashful voice speak up: "I'm not a virgin . . ." Dave says timidly. He's so quiet I reckon I'm the only one to hear him and, if I'm being honest, I'm astounded. Not because he's not a virgin, but because that might just be the first time I've ever heard him say anything in his life. By the time my Guinness is through, the troop of merry men are all on their feet, ready.

Seven Smurfs, little old me, and a collection of pubs filled with eligible bachelors and endless possibilities.

Bring it on.

24

Oh God I'm drunk.

There's no way I was ever going to keep up with the drinking speed of seven rugby lads but my God, I'm giving it a good go. The other perfect thing, of course, is that I haven't paid for a single drink all night. Payday has come and gone, my bank account is as healthy as it has ever been, and here I am being looked after by seven slurring Smurfs around me.

They treat me like royalty. There is never a minute I don't have someone beside me, checking up on me and making sure my drink is topped up, and I realize that in their homely arms I am as safe as I could ever have been. I am having the time of my life, hopping from bar to bar, becoming increasingly less embarrassed to be seen with the full Blue Man Group and increasingly more up for continuing our adventure at the next bar.

The only bad thing about being surrounded by seven blue bouncers, as it turns out, is that it's not the biggest turn-on for the men. I'd be near the bar, chatting with a guy who'd then see one of the Smurfs hand over a drink to me, and suddenly my chances were gone. They'd look at the size of them, look at the color of them, and quickly make their excuses. Without meaning to, I have gone out with seven fully grown face-painted cock-blockers.

Not that it matters. I'm still having a brilliant night.

Somewhere past the stroke of midnight I find myself waiting

in the queue for the ladies' room and before I know it I'm taking a selfie.

> 4 Oct 01:09-Me
> See?????
> 4 Oct 01:09-Me
> I'm ouit!!

Marty-4 Oct 01:09
I'm like a proud parent

> 4 Oct 01:10-Me
> Wigh SMurfs?

Marty-4 Oct 01:11
Don't know what autocorrect's fucked up there

> 4 Oct 01:11-Me
> NOO Actual SMURFSSS

Marty-4 Oct 01:11
Alright Gargamel

I laugh, checking how long I still have to wait. Three more girls ahead of me, so out comes Mirror Mirror.

Oh shit, I'd almost forgotten about Mystery Man. I wonder if he's lost interest. Only one way to find out.

> Bella Marble
> Jon? Pal? George? Ringoo?

Mystery Man
You've already guessed George

> Bella Marble
> I feel lucky toniht. I'm going to ges it

Mystery Man
I can't wait to see what names you have in store for me

> Bella Marble
> What is yor name?

Mystery Man
You can't get me that easily

I'm starting to get really bored. This game was fun when it began but it's starting to feel like a lot of effort for very little payoff. I'm about to go off completely when I see he's doubled up. He's sent another one. I read it, although my eyes are a little blurry.

Mystery Man

Having a good night, Cinderella?

Cinderella?

I know it sounds stupid. I know it does, especially because the cartoon profile picture I picked for myself is a glass slipper and everything. But it feels like . . . I don't know . . . a sign. I feel a power, a strange surge of power. I can do this. I can get his name.

Except then I get a text message and it distracts me.

I turn to my phone, wondering whether—just maybe—someone might have found my shoe. Whether someone might have found my number. Whether it might literally be Prince Charming.

The way my night's going I think it might just happen.

Urgh. No, it's not Prince Charming. It's just Marty. Twit.

Marty-4 Oct 01:17

Text me when you're home safe later please

He's worse than my dad.

Anyway. The night is still young, ish, and a stall just became free so it's not too long before I'm washing my hands and I'm back out into the night.

❧ 25 ❧

The party disbands not long after. It turns out when you're blue, you are quick to get recognized and very quick to get yourself kicked out of the bar. Given that I still loved the whole not paying for anything, I went when they all did and found myself lying on their sofa with a sleeping Sam, a very merry Donald, and an ever quiet (soon to be in Australia) Dave.

Dom got lucky; something about the white beard really appealed to a girl named Karen, who seemed nice enough in the taxi back. They retired early into one of the three bedrooms.

Poor Dean had been coughing and sneezing all night until all the blue around his nose and mouth had completely come off by their own merit. As soon as the front door opened he headed straight for the bed he should have been in all night. Stu made himself a hot water bottle, which I found rather adorable but didn't comment because he still looked a bit angry for some reason and it would have been way too scary to ask. Keno went upstairs to see if Gertie and Hans were about, leaving the three of us finishing the leftover pre-drinks around the sofa.

After an hour or so setting the world to rights, Donald gives a lion's yawn and stretching out, he stands.

"Alrighty, my friends, it's time I make waves."

"Where you going?"

He turns on a *Terminator* voice as he finally reaches the door.

"I'll be back," he says to the room, then bursts into a peal of laughter. Slamming his hand on the door a few times to calm himself down, he wanders out.

I turn to look at Sam, snoring away on the sofa.

"Is he always that tired?" I ask.

"Yeah, I guess," Dave replies.

Dave—actually Dave! Quiet Dave.

Except of course he's the only one to reply. He's the only one left. I look around the room, wondering if it should be time I disappear back upstairs too, but I'm too tipsy and lazy to stand. I sit for a while, letting the calmness of an evening's end wash over me.

"Big day for you tomorrow, eh?" I say.

I turn to look at Dave to see if I've made him uncomfortable, speaking directly to him, but he doesn't seem to mind.

"Yeah, well . . ."

"What made you want to move, if you don't mind me asking?"

Dave looks around at the empty bottles and table still covered in blue face paint. He turns to the kitchen where there's at least a week's worth of dirty dishes piled up. He looks over at Sam, snoring away. I wonder if he'll ever answer me.

"I just . . ." he says quietly. "Life's just a bit . . . the same here."

"Isn't same good?"

"Same's good," he agrees, nodding politely. "I just . . . I think I could be happier than good."

"And you think you'll be happier in Australia?"

I'm sort of not expecting an answer. It's funny, but given how loud this living room is every time I visit, it seems weirdly haunting to be here when it's still, and of all those left, Dave is the one I've never found conversation with. So I don't expect him to start now.

Except, almost as if to defy me, he does.

"I think as long as I'm here I'll stick to the same patterns, and I don't think that's good for me right now," he replies. His voice is so soft-spoken it completely doesn't match his rather burly exterior. I mean, the man's all muscle but speaks like he has none at all. It's adorable really. A little soul in a big body. "I know it's a bit stupid.

I mean, I love this place. I love these guys. But as long as I'm here I'm not . . ."

"Not what?"

"Not growing up." He looks at me like he's said something wrong already and honestly, I don't know him enough to make my own comment. "I've been with these guys for years now and I love them, I do. But this isn't going to stay this way forever and . . . I'm . . . I'm not the kind of guy who does well alone. So instead of waiting for them to all peel off like they probably will one day, why don't I do it on my own terms, you know?"

He shakes his head, looking down at the floor like it's stupid.

I'm a bit too drunk to react, but sober enough to hear him loud and clear. I nod, sipping the dregs of the Heineken in my hand. I'm not sure I want this kind of conversation right now. So I change it.

"So which of you guys actually lives here then?"

Dave smiles, probably as glad as I am that I haven't lingered. He gives Sam a quick glance to check he's still sleeping.

"Dom, Stu, and me, at least until tomorrow," Dave replies. "Sam's moving in after that."

"So Dean's in your room then? That's nice of you—giving up your room for him. He looked like death all night."

"Yeah . . . although," Dave looks awkwardly at the three adjoining doors to the flat, "technically Dean's in Stu's room. Stu's in mine."

"Why is Stu in your room?"

"Dean was in his?"

"But why does that mean Stu takes yours?"

"Just Stu really. It's alright. He cares about that kind of thing more than me. I don't mind the beanbag."

Oh my God. He's not just quiet. Dave is *nice*.

That's his thing, he's just a nice guy. He's the good one in a house of men who most of the time probably put themselves first. He shrugs, all bashful and sweet and my heart just explodes for him. No wonder he's getting out. I've known these guys for three years and I've just assumed Dave was boring, but he's not at all. He's just the one real introvert in a pack of loudmouthed lads.

I turn to my phone. It's getting late. It's probably time I go but even looking at the home screen triggers a memory. I quickly flip to my messages.

Marty-4 Oct 01:09
Text me when you're home safe later please

4 Oct 03:02-Me
Home

4 Oct 03:02-Me
Stop panicking

4 Oct 03:03-Me
No really, call off the search

4 Oct 03:03-Me
But seriously. I'm back

I smile at my own joke, it's not even a good one, and Dave catches me. He smiles too.

"Guy you're seeing?"

"Ew no. Just a friend."

"Just a friend?"

"Not even that. My friend's brother."

Dave laughs a little under his breath, nodding.

"I'm being serious," I say.

"I know," Dave says unconvincingly.

"No—I am. Like he was on a date and everything."

"Okay!"

"No—you're laughing—what is it?" I'm laughing too. I push him and he sways to his side but in reality there is nothing I could have done that caused any form of physical motion in him. The man's a tank and I'm a toy lawnmower at best.

"Well, it's just that's how all rom-coms start, isn't it?" he says, giggling. "The 'he's just a friend' and then . . . I don't know." He's smiling sweetly and I can't even be angry with him, but to be fair to him he hasn't met Marty. If he'd met Marty he'd know.

"He's the one who told me I should get with someone tonight, aaaccctuallllly." I overpronounce it to be clear and Dave calms down.

"Oh yeah. Sorry we never found you a Prince Charming."

"I'm sorry we never found someone so you could lose your virginity."

"I'm not a virgin," he says defensively.

"Well, I'm not looking for Prince Charming," I reply, "so looks like we're both wrong."

"You're not?" He seems pretty confused.

"That's the whole point. I've spent far too long looking for Prince Charming and getting nowhere."

He laughs sweetly.

"Then what are you looking for?"

"I don't know. The Mad Hatter?"

We're both laughing. I turn to face him and watch as his blue face creases up. The face paint flecks off by his laugh lines.

I think I quite like Dave actually.

"What about a Smurf?" he says as we're both chuckling away.

I mean, he's joking. He is joking. He's joking.

Is he joking?

My own laughter stops just before his and—I mean, I don't know how I rearranged myself, but I'm somehow looking him right in the eye.

"I don't think that's one of the fairy tales."

"I thought you don't want fairy tales?"

He's still joking. Except, he's sort of looking at me. I don't know how—I really don't, but my face is quite close to his now. I can feel his breath against my lips but he's still joking. The room's dark. It's late—or rather it's so late it's early. He's still . . .

"Fuck the fairy tal—"

I don't even make it to the end of my sentence. I don't know if it's his head that moves in to kiss me or mine that bends up to his but suddenly his lips are over mine and I can feel his soft touch as he gently strokes at the back of my neck and—holy shit, for such a big guy his lips are soft and—

We both hear a snore. It breaks us apart. I turn. Sam's just behind us, still sleeping away. I turn back to Dave a little shocked. I can't believe I just kissed Dave. I can't believe I've just kissed "quiet" Dave. More importantly, I can't believe Dave's such a good kisser.

"I think . . . I think that—" I begin to say but Dave nods in understanding already.

"It's alright. I don't mind, you can go, I won't take offense. I mean . . ." He shrugs bashfully, and it makes my whole heart warm for him. "I mean, I'm heading to Australia tomorrow."

I look at him, I look at Sam, I look back at him.

"I was going to say I think we should move to the bathroom maybe?" I say.

For such a big guy, my, did he move fast.

❧ 26 ❧

Two incredible hours, three mind-blowing orgasms, and an accidental self-inflicted shin bruise later and the bathroom looks like a unicorn murder scene. You can see our trail of passion marked out in awkward blue smears and smudges across all the white porcelain because—and I probably could have worked it out—sweat and other bodily fluids mixed with body paint means what begins as wild sex with a Smurf turns into a cuddle with a patchy human in a newly redecorated bathroom. The loo seat is covered; the sink's only a partial, which is impressive enough given the angle I was at during that segment of the night; the edge of the bath—well, by the time we reached that rather interesting position most of the blue had rubbed off on the floor, which resembled something closer to an ice rink than anything else.

My white dress, or more accurately Annie's white dress, lost its purity quite quickly into our little efforts, with a comically large blue handprint upon my left buttock that I don't particularly want to justify. I'd care, really I would, only that's the first actual climax a man's given me in, what, five years? Nice guy that he is, he seemed to care a whole lot about pleasing me before pleasing himself, which was beautifully refreshing. It didn't take him long to give me the same effect as my little pink rabbit charges in me three times a week, only with twice the enjoyment and a whole lotta mass to cling to after.

He's a big guy. I like that about him. The walls are just as stained as the rest of the room from where he held me up with my legs wrapped around him, like in those rom-coms with the actresses who are all as light as a peanut.

We land in the bath, or rather, I land on him while he lands in the bath with the shower still on around 4 a.m. like exhausted colorful water aliens.

A shared shower later he's kissing me goodbye and my night with the Blue Man Group is over. He's sweet enough to ask for my number and I'm smart enough not to bother giving it, but thank him anyway for the gesture. It was a one-night gig and we both know it, but he's good enough not to make me feel cheap and I like that.

As I'm wandering back up the stairs, leaving him to clean up the mess we made, I start to realize that after all the shit I've been through, this was exactly what I needed. Maybe, just maybe, Marty was right after all. Maybe this is exactly what I need more of.

No more heartache and lost hopes. No more wild-goose chases and tears to *The Great British Bake Off*. I don't need Prince Charming at all.

Call off the search. Switch off the desperation.

I just need a few more Smurfs and I reckon I'll be dandy.

✌ 27 ✌

I shove Annie's dress quickly into the wash in the hope that it may yet survive the attack.

Like she cares, though. I've lived with her for three years and not once in that time have I ever seen her wear the same outfit twice. Maybe I've done her a favor. Maybe dyeing it will give it a new lease on life in her eyes or maybe, more probably, she'll get a bit huffy and puffy and move on pretty quick.

I crawl into bed but I'm not tired at all. I've never felt so alive. I'm buzzing in my own happiness. I've never had a one-night stand before, or more accurately I have, but the whole one-night-stand bit has never been on my terms. It's empowering. No wonder Annie basks in this feeling. No wonder Marty never wants this to end. How stupid I've been, missing out on this exceptionally wonderful portion of life that has been available to me for years.

I wonder what to do next. Sleeping's not an option, I've already had a shower, and I'm not particularly hungry. I head to my phone for inspiration.

Suddenly I don't care that Martha's still on holiday. Now when I see baby pictures from Portia and Nelly it doesn't make me feel lonely or depressed, it makes me feel sad for them that they can no longer enjoy what I'm enjoying. When was the last time they were spread-eagled over shampoos or clutched over cisterns? When was the last time they vibrated away to three perfectly natural, wonderful, bright blue orgasms?

To be fair that might be what they call Saturday night, but I don't care. There they are with babies and here I am with my baby-making machine. One didn't have to sink for the other to thrive.

I go back on the home screen, wondering what will enthrall me next when I see it. A little ! icon next to the B-Reader app.

How long has that been there for? What with the whole divorce sidestep I hadn't even thought twice about it but now it's staring right at me.

Maybe it's another comment! I think happily. Maybe @sirreadalot has decided to share it with a friend and maybe they've written a comment too.

Oh God, please don't let it be bad. I almost don't touch it in fear—I've just had a wonderful night, I don't want anything to spoil it now. But even as I think it I know I can't wait. I've seen the "!" now. It's time to rip off the Band-Aid like a big girl.

It takes a while for it to load, and then a while again to turn to my writing profile. Each turn of the little wheel on the screen spins my nerves into knots. And to think, I had just loosened up. Now I'm tense all over again.

Thirty-two notifications.

What?

I think I've misread it. Maybe two notifications and my eyes are too drunk to focus? Maybe at a push just the three. I check it again. Nope. It's definitely thirty-two.

Twenty-nine likes, three comments.

My mouth is open but I close it quickly.

Twenty-nine likes? Twenty-nine people like it? Twenty-nine strangers have read "My Night with the Big Bad Wolf" and decided to hover their little mice over the little thumbs-up and decided it was worth the pressure on their index finger to click it??

I cry a bit. Obviously. I'm a crier, still a tiny bit drunk, and this is a perfect crying opportunity. Twenty-nine people like it!

I click open the comments and read them, lapping up the words.

> @hpfangirl
> Sounds like an arsehole. Bring on chapter 2.

"He was an arsehole!" I say out loud in the darkness. Bring on chapter 2? They want more?! Hpfangirl wants another chapter?

Next comment:

> @BeenThereRedit
> Bit crude.

Okay. Not so good. That put me back in my box a little but not enough to forget that twenty-nine people liked it. Twenty-nine! I turn to the last one.

> @mayfleur
> Reckon it's going to go through the same fairy
> tale or mix them up a bit? Loved part 1!

SHE LOVED IT.

Oh my God my heart can't contain itself. First "LOL" and now this?

She's even asking a question. A question! She's interested enough to take an active interest in the book!

The book—the whole book. I hadn't even written the thing as a chapter. That's just the only thing the site would let me upload. She brings up a good question—I don't even know where I go from here. It's not like it's going to be an epic romance between myself and Wolf boy. I doubt I'll ever see him again in my life and even in the fictional world I don't want to picture his hairy feet ever again.

But @mayfleur brings up a good point. Maybe it's not the story of "Little Red Riding Hood" at all . . .

Inspiration sparks in my mind. I'm laughing before I've even reached my laptop screen and as it fires up I know exactly what my chapter 2 will contain.

There it is, the black cursor blinking away, except now it's not looking down at me. Now it's fired up, charged, and ready for my overactive imagination to set it on fire.

Snow White and the Seven Smurfs

I write, although soon after that, the whole chapter basically just writes itself.

❧ 28 ❧

While I sleep the rest of my Sunday away my "likership" grows from twenty-nine to thirty-four. That's a 17 percent increase in just a couple of hours. It made me so happy I almost cried. That's a massive lie, of course I cried. I've never liked math before but when I hear a stat like that being thrown around, suddenly numbers become my friends and boy, do I need some more friends.

The house is still empty, or rather it's still full of two sexually active Germans, but Annie hasn't come back from Rachel's and Simon's still in Paris, probably. Despite me having a wild encounter last night, I have no one to immediately share it with.

So, like all good lonely women in their mid-to-late twenties, I take out my phone.

4 Oct 16:02-Me

Can I come by?

I read through our previous texts and quickly see my mistake. No free dinners until next week. Damn. I miss seeing Ellie's little button nose daily.

4 Oct 16:02-Me

Oh no—sorry. Forgot you were busy

4 Oct 16:02-Me

Let me know what dates work for you next week then!

The Elsa to my Anna-4 Oct 16:06
Of course you can come by but I'm not sure you want
to

4 Oct 16:07-Me
Why wouldn't I want to?

The Elsa to my Anna-4 Oct 16:08
Mark's in

The Elsa to my Anna-4 Oct 16:08
His colleague is over for dinner

I pause.

Not because Mark's in. Of course Mark's in. It's a Sunday. No one does anything on a Sunday other than stay at home. But it actually makes me sad that she's written that in the first place. I know she knows I don't like him, but it's always been so unspoken. Now, seeing it like that in black-and-white, it makes me feel like a proper dick.

4 Oct 16:10-Me
As long as you still don't mind me joining?

The Elsa to my Anna-4 Oct 16:11
Of course not! That would be amazing!

The Elsa to my Anna-4 Oct 16:11
I find Phillip a little boring if I'm honest so thank God!

The Elsa to my Anna-4 Oct 16:11
Ah! I'm making a roast

The Elsa to my Anna-4 Oct 16:11
Do you want a roast?

4 Oct 16:12-Me
Is that a trick question?

The Elsa to my Anna-4 Oct 16:12
Pork alright?

4 Oct 16:12-Me
Why are you even asking?

The Elsa to my Anna-4 Oct 16:13
I don't know

The Elsa to my Anna-4 Oct 16:13

Annie might have convinced you to go vegan or
something

4 Oct 16:13-Me

I haven't changed that much since you last saw me

Oh, but I have, I think to myself. It's strange. I don't want to get ahead of myself but I was never the type to purposefully have one-night stands before. I mean, I've had my fair share of first dates that went well enough for me to stay over, but apparently didn't go well enough for them to ask for date #2. But to go looking specifically for a "no strings attached" hookup? That's a completely different ball game. I was never the type to publish my own work before either—albeit just the one chapter, but still. Maybe Ellie's right to suspect.

The Elsa to my Anna-4 Oct 16:13

See you at 6?

4 Oct 16:14-Me

I'll be the one huffing and puffing to blow your house
down

I practically skip to hers, or rather I skip to the tube and wait for an hour and a half for a slow Sunday service on the District line. I realize quickly that I should have worn a jumper and not just a black tank top under my coat as the tube is outdoors before we reach Turnham Green and each time those tube doors automatically slide apart I'm shivering. Train at its destination, I open Google Maps on the last leg of my journey and still somehow get lost in the side streets until here I am, standing outside their little Chiswick flat.

I don't know what I imagined. I remember seeing the flat in pictures, of course, but given that I scowled at the screen every time it was shown to me, I didn't get a particularly clear view. Now, standing outside and looking in, my first impression is just a little disappointing.

I sort of imagined her to be upgrading. I was half imagining the swishiest of flats, a doorman like in those New York apartment buildings and a full concierge service behind a beautiful marble lobby. Except, of course, it's just another Victorian house. I know she's paying far more for this and yet it's similar, albeit smaller, to the one we shared for eight years together in Balham.

Still, when her little rabbit face appears I'm all "doesn't this look nice," and "what a lovely street," because that's what supportive friends who aren't harboring bitter resentment toward ogre-like boyfriends say.

To be fair, as I walk up the stairs inside and through her new front door, it all begins to make more sense, because the flat itself is the most grown-up thing I've ever seen. Plants, living plants, not like the dead one that rotted on the edge of our kitchen windowsill for two years, are scattered everywhere. The furniture looks like a compromise between comfortable and stylish and not built for tenant living like ours at home are. There is a rug that has actually been hoovered on the floor and coasters on the table, ready. Their kitchen has its own little room that has an actual spice rack, and yes, all the spice bottles are full and ready for cooking. They have matching bowls and a sharp knives set and a stack of quilts next to the television ready in case they get a bit chilly while they're watching TV. I bet they even fold it up again before they go to bed and everything.

Mark's at the table, midconversation with someone who looks equally as forgettable, and I greet them both with a perfect Stepford wife smile like I'm the perfect guest, because this is clearly a home for adults, and I am determined to act like one.

❧ 29 ❧

"We have to write down all the good fairy tales immediately!" Ellie cries, jumping to her feet.

I've just shown her my B-Reader account and she is somehow even more excited than I am about the whole thing. I wasn't allowed to talk about it before the meal because for whatever reason, Mark wanted the conversation to be about him and work only, except performance marketing is really boring and as if to prove the point his work colleague might be the only man in the world I found more instantly uninteresting than Mark himself. They were talking about how "hilarious" the effective CPI prices were at the moment, which is probably the least hilarious thing I've ever listened to.

The second that Phillip (that was his name, Phillip, a suitably middle-of-the-road-would-get-on-with-your-parents-but-probably-will-talk-to-you-about-lichen-preservation name) went to the bathroom after dinner, I couldn't stop the word vomit from spewing into Ellie's ears. Mark had made it pretty clear that the conversation should probably end the second Phillip returned but now, almost ten minutes later, he awkwardly still hadn't emerged from the bathroom (we all knew and said nothing), giving us enough time to delve deeper.

Ellie goes straight for a notebook and pen rather than anything electronic. Proper old-school. I love her more than anything in this moment.

"Right, so you've ticked off 'Little Red Riding Hood' and 'Snow White,'" Ellie says, writing them down and marking them off. If I was by myself I'm sure that's as far as I'd have gotten, but here she was, ready. "'The Little Mermaid'?"

"I have the hair color for it . . ." I say, thoughtfully twisting my strawberry-blond locks. Ellie writes in big cursive handwriting, so unlike the scrawl I always see on her work folders. She's taking her time for me. I love it. "But what would I do for that one? Splash around for a while in the leisure center and hope some lifeguard spots me?"

"You could go down the singing route? You do love karaoke?"

"I'd have to stop speaking though to make it authentic and I'm a big chatterbox. I don't think I'd last. Maybe we should . . ."

"Shall I put a question mark on that one?"

She read my mind. Of course she did.

"Yeah, TBC on Ariel. What are the others?"

"'The Three Little Pigs'?"

"Oh, I think I've already had my fair share of wolves, and I'm not that desperate to launch myself into a foursome just for the sake of my writing . . ."

"That's a good point. I'll just cross off the little pigs."

"'Sleeping Beauty'?"

"That story reads more like a sexual assault than a romance."

"You're right, I don't think I want that at all."

"'Shrek'?"

"That's a great one! And pretty easy I'm guessing—I could probably find a big Scottish guy somewhere. Actually, there's a guy at work who is from Glasgow originally. I bet he has a few friends. I've never slept with a Scot before."

"You know you don't need to now?" Mark chimes up.

Both of us stop. I think we'd both vaguely forgotten he was there.

"Sorry?" I ask.

"Well, it's just . . . it's a story, isn't it?" Mark asks. "You don't actually have to sleep around for this. You could always just use your imagination. Like most writers."

I try to keep the smile on my face but watching him, leaning back in his chair like a fat king at the end of a banquet, makes me want to stick my tongue out and blow a raspberry or something equally immature. I hold back, because—I remind myself—I'm channeling adulthood.

I turn to Ellie, ignoring him.

"Any others?"

"What about 'Beauty and the Beast'?" Ellie asks. "Your name suits that one!"

"'Imprisoned Woman Falls in Love with Wolf Man part two?"

"What is it with fairy tales and hairy scary men enticing beautiful women?"

"Age-old misogyny?"

"Maybe a few need updating."

"It's not the worst. I do like books, but again—I don't think anyone I meet is going to beat Charles Wolf in terms of hair content and I sort of think if I can't do it properly there's no point in doing it at all."

"I'm confused," Mark says, which annoys me, because he's not actually a part of the conversation at all so he doesn't need to be confused about anything. "You're seriously saying you're going to sleep your way through these stories?"

"No," I say. "I specifically said I wasn't going to sleep through 'Beauty and the Beast,' which is why that one can be crossed off the list." I nod to Ellie, who puts a big line through her own handwriting.

"Okay, fine, not that one. But are you telling us you're planning on having these ridiculous one-night stands or just writing about them?"

"I think 'ridiculous' is a bit harsh."

"So you are?"

"I don't see why not."

"It's just a story, Mark," Ellie adds, trying to keep the situation from escalating. "She wants to write it."

"Write it? Or live it?" Mark clarifies. "Because you're making out right now like this is nonfiction."

"It is nonfiction!" I say.

"So you are planning on sleeping with them all?"

"Well, yes. Obviously."

"Wait—you are?" It was Ellie this time. Ellie.

What was going on here?

"Yes, I was. That's what I've just been telling you," I say, only to her. I thought she was on my level.

"You can't just sleep with random men for the sake of writing this B-book or whatever it is." Mark's laughing from the corner and it's infuriating me.

"It's an *actual* book. And why the hell not?"

"Bella," Ellie says, she's smiling sweetly at me. She clearly isn't a fan of Mark's comment but she's not putting him back in his place either, which actually hurts. She looks worried again, but that's normal. She's a worrier. "Bella, you're not actually going to sleep your way through the fairy tales?"

"Why not? I've already slept through two of them."

"But you hated your date with the wolf man, remember? You don't want more of that, surely," Ellie says nervously.

"Well . . . okay . . . no, but they don't all have to be like that one. Dave was amazing."

"Dave?" Ellie asks.

I realize I didn't actually fill her in on the night out, just the writing of it. Maybe that's why she doesn't get it.

"Yeah, downstairs Dave."

"Quiet Dave?"

"Exactly! Quiet Dave! He was the Smurf!"

"So that actually happened?" Ellie looks completely surprised.

"Just because you had one good one-night stand doesn't mean you can just plan for more. It doesn't work like that," Mark joins in again. Seriously, who is asking him?

"Men plan for one-night stands all the time," I snap back.

"But you're not a man," Mark points out. Oh my dear God, my anger is bubbling.

"What, so a man is allowed to sleep around but when a woman fancies sex without consequences, it's suddenly taboo?"

"He's not commenting on the sexism of it," Ellie insists. "It's just . . . it's not very *you*, is it?"

"What do you mean it's not very me?"

"Well, you've never really wanted a one-night stand before."

"Maybe I do now!"

"What, we've been gone a week and suddenly you're a whole new person?" asks Mark.

"Well, maybe I am!"

"Come off it—"

"You guys have moved on in life. Why can't I too?"

"Moving on? You think whoring yourself out is 'moving on'?" Mark laughs.

"*Whoring* out?!" I can feel my cheeks redden, filling with blood that's causing my temple to throb. Ellie says nothing. Absolutely nothing. "I'm not *whoring* myself. I'm *having fun*. Something you probably don't know much about!"

Ellie starts speaking before the end of my sentence so I think she's missed my last comment but Mark certainly hasn't. I can see him biting back words, his eyes bulging. He's like a wind-up jack-in-the-box, about to explode.

"Bella, come on now, let's not argue," says Ellie, trying to act the mediator as always. "It's just for as long as I've known you, you've always wanted the fairy-tale big white wedding ending. I'm just . . . surprised that you've given up on that. That's all."

"I haven't given up."

"Well, you're not going to find a Prince Charming by sleeping your way through all the other characters," Mark says, the judgment distilled in his voice.

"What he's trying to say," Ellie adds quickly, "is that this feels like a step away from what you actually want."

"That's not what he's trying to say at all," I tell her.

Mark puts his hands out to silence us, and that move alone makes me want to throw my room-temperature fizzy water all over him. I restrain myself.

"This is classic self-destruction going on here," he begins to mansplain.

"I don't think I would call having multiple orgasms 'self-destructive,' Mark."

"Look," he says, "I know what with your parents that—"

"My parents? Are you seriously bringing my parents into this?"

"When my parents got divorced . . ." begins Mark but that's really just too much for me.

"My parents are nothing like yours, Mark, don't compare them!" There's a pause after that. There's an awkward flush from just behind me. Looks like Phillip's done with the bathroom after all.

"Look, I didn't mean—"

"I don't care what you meant, Mark. What the hell are you doing talking about my parents?" I turn to Ellie, betrayed that he even knows. I told her, not him, and yet she's just gone ahead and told him anyway. Beyond that she hasn't even stepped in already to put him back in his place. I feel angry and petty and horrible, which I didn't think I'd ever feel in a house belonging to Ellie Mathews. I don't understand how things got to this point but I'm on fire now. I can't stop. I'm biting my lip so hard I'm pretty sure it's bleeding.

"I was just saying, when mine—"

Oh, he's actually continuing. So I do too, stopping him instantly.

"Unlike your parents, mine actually give a shit about each other. One didn't cheat on the other with a bartender half their age."

Mark turns to Ellie quickly, whose cheeks have exploded with color.

"You know?"

"Of course I know! You're not the only person that Ellie confides in, you know! I'm her best friend here, and you might blame your own boring shitty life on the fact that your mum chose to live a little, but me, finally choosing to have more fun in my life, taking back some of the control I've been missing, this has nothing to do with deep-set mummy issues like you seem to have." I regret it instantly. Even as the words tumble from my mouth I'm about to apologize for them, but before I do Mark cuts right in.

"Look, if you want to ruin your life because you can't handle a bit of change around you that's fine, but don't drag me down with you."

"I'm not dragging you down, I'm defending myself. Don't you dare say shit about my parents."

"I was just going to say," he says through grinding teeth like it pains him to do so, "I know what you're going—"

"YOU KNOW NOTHING. You know nothing about me!" I shout. I can hear my words echoing back at me. I think I'm crying but I'm not entirely sure.

He looks like he's about to stop then but, like a steamroller down a hill, he's begun now. He can't stop himself. "You think I don't know you? Of course I know you! I know every single time you've had your heart broken, which seems to be just about every week by the way. I know every single time you're feeling lonely and lost and sorry for yourself. I know every single thought and every single feeling you have, not because Ellie tells me, but because you tell Ellie in *my bed,* while I'm lying there, the third wheel in my own relationship, trying to actually sleep in my own bedroom. Believe it or not, I know you better than I ever wanted to, which is why I know this is going to end in a disaster. This is going to end up with you hurt and crying and Ellie canceling on me *yet again* to spend the night with you because heaven forbid you find any other friends to confide in. So please, hate me for trying to jump in and do the right thing before this whole thing gets out of hand. I should have said nothing. I should just let you get on with it. Go on then. Get all the STIs you want. Be my guest."

"Mark!" Ellie cries. She shoots him daggers but it's already too late.

I stand up before I realize I can stand. I'm by the door before my legs have even felt it. I've got my scarf around my neck before I remember I don't own a scarf—it must be Ellie's, but she says nothing as I fling my coat on over it and do up the zipper.

"No, please stay!" Ellie whispers. "Let's sort this out!"

Mark has stayed in the other room, probably fuming like I am. Phillip's stayed in the bathroom, probably aware of the commotion and staying out of range. I think of his little awkward face lingering inside and twiddling his thumbs. Probably also on the hunt for some air freshener.

Ellie's looking up at me with her big eyes.

"How do we sort this out, Els?" I whisper. "You heard what he said."

"If you just apologize, then—"

"Me apologize? He's the one that should apologize!"

"You both said some things, things you both didn't mean . . ." she adds, trying to justify it. "If you just apologize first I'm sure he'll come back around."

It feels like a bullet, straight to the heart. I try so hard to keep my voice even.

"Why should I go first?"

"Because . . . just . . . you shouldn't have said that about his parents!" she said. "He just acted out, that's all."

She sounds reasonable in tone but the words that are coming out of her mouth floor me.

"Ellie, you're *my* friend. Why can't you be my friend?"

"I am your friend," she whispers. "But he's my fiancé and you just said things to him I can't defend."

I can't say how much that hurts.

I feel a physical burn cascade down every artery and up every vein. I feel like my whole soul is punching the inside of my stomach. I feel my eyes sting with tears.

She would always come first in my life. She always had and as far as I know she always would. But just like that, I was playing second fiddle to that male Maleficent who hadn't even left his chair.

I leave before I say anything I'd regret for the rest of my life and practically sprint down her stairs, ignoring her pleas from above me. I hardly hear them. I can hear nothing but white noise ringing in my skull. I get a text from her before I even hit the bottom step:

The Elsa to my Anna-4 Oct 21:01

Please, I know things got out of hand but we can fix this

The Elsa to my Anna-4 Oct 21:01

You just hit a nerve and he acted out, that's all

The Elsa to my Anna-4 Oct 21:01

If you just say sorry I know he'll do the same! I know it!

There's a pause, and I think about writing something back but I somehow feel frozen in time. Before I can even articulate a reaction another text pings. Maybe she's just read back her own words and regrets it?

The Elsa to my Anna-4 Oct 21:08

I get that you might need some time. Just please, please call as soon as you're ready to talk

The Elsa to my Anna-4 Oct 21:08

I'll be here whenever you're ready

The Elsa to my Anna-4 Oct 21:08

I love you

The Elsa to my Anna-4 Oct 21:08

xx

Holy shit. Is she serious?

I feel devastated, utterly and completely torn in a way I didn't think I ever could be. She's taken his side. She's actually taken that ogre's side, leaving me alone and helpless on the edge of a deep dark wood in a corner of my mind that I don't know how to escape from.

❧ PART 3 ❧

1

I don't feel anything as I power walk down the street. Nothing at all. Not pain, not sadness. It's so cold outside I don't even feel my face.

But of course I don't feel anything, because it didn't mean anything. Ellie and I used to fight all the time when we were kids. She once cut the hair off my favorite Barbie and in retaliation I soaked her favorite polar bear toy, Greg, in malt vinegar. We screamed at each other for hours that day, and yet still by the end of the night we were having a sleepover to discuss the stages of forgiveness, all twelve of which involved chocolate in some way.

Except this wasn't about Barbies. This wasn't stupid and small. Mark had been more of an arsehole than even I had thought possible and my best friend, my ride or die, had seriously just watched from the sidelines and had done nothing. No, worse than nothing. *She had picked him over me.*

Actually scrap that, I do feel something. As I reach the start of Eastbury Grove I know I feel it for sure. I am fucking furious. Each step I take pounds the cement of the lamplit pavement, firing me up. She talked to him about my parents. He used it against me. He used it to pit Ellie against me. How dare he do that? How dare she enable him to do that? Screw him. Screw both of them for making me feel that way.

She had actually picked him over me.

Yet as I turn on Ashbourne Grove, other parts of the conversation repeat in my mind. Maybe I'm the one who should be embarrassed? I'd said some pretty horrible stuff and really, I should have just waited until Mark was out of the room before I told Ellie about any of it. He always judges me. She never does. I should have known to keep my trap shut. If I'd just waited then none of this would have happened. She would never have chosen Mark over her friend of twenty-eight years.

But she had. She'd picked him over me.

Devonshire Road was long enough for my memories to play back the whole argument from start to finish, and just as the rain starts to drizzle down upon me, I get complete and utter clarity. Never had I ever actually questioned my friendship with Ellie, because she wasn't capable of ever hurting me. At least she hadn't been *before he came along.*

One phrase and one phrase alone circles around my head: fuck Mark.

It even feels good to say. So many consonants matched together in two short, sharp syllables. Fuck him. Fuck you. Fuck Mark.

He doesn't know me, he doesn't know what I'm like, and he definitely doesn't know what makes me happy. How dare he speak to me like that?

Dave made me happy. Dave made me really fucking happy.

@sirreadalot made me happy too. In fact all of my readers and likers do. These complete strangers make me happier than Mark has ever made anyone feel in his whole pointless life.

I need to get this out of my system. I need to leave all of Mark's fuckiness and his negativity behind and I need to find what makes me happy.

In fact, that's exactly what I need.

I need an orgasm and I need a story.

That's exactly what will make me happy.

Just like that my feet change direction, no longer heading toward Turnham Green station but away, left instead, and pounding their way down Chiswick High Road until a sign for a wine bar guides me out of the October rain and into low-lit fruity-smelling warmth.

My hair has flattened slightly under the downpour outside but I don't care. I push the straggly bits off my face as my eyes glance over the middle-class drinkers, all laughing in the haze of jazz music and candlelight. It's busier than I'd have assumed for a Sunday evening but it's clear enough to scan across, searching. It doesn't take long.

Two men sit side by side on the copper-colored barstools, freshly refilled glasses of red before them. They look friendly but not friendly enough to make me think they're on a date. They look like they're talking but not deeply enough to not interrupt them. They're male, which means they're exactly what I'm looking for.

I can't tell you the amount of conviction shooting through me as I walk over.

"Hi," I say, smiling like I know exactly what I'm doing.

The two men look up at me, their eyes blinking in unison.

Then it hits me.

What am I doing?

What the hell am I doing?

But it's too late to jump back onto the diving board. Instead I can only plunge headfirst into whatever unknown will come next.

2

"Hi," replies the man on the left.

He's older than me for sure, with hypnotically large brown eyes that don't seem to blink as they look at me. He's smart, but the kind of smart that doesn't intimidate with his sleeves rolled up and his top button undone to give him some room to breathe. His white shirt still looks crisp, his black shoes, gently resting against the barstool, shined to a military degree. His hair looks both practical and stylish, cut short at the sides but groomed at the top in a way you could just tell he'd perfected over the years.

His companion's, on the other hand, is almost shaved down to a spike, as if time spent doing hair was time wasted. He's my age, maybe even younger, and the dark circles around his eyes are made more prominent by his almost sickly pale complexion. Unlike his friend, his generic blue tie is still noosed around his neck and his sleeves still buttoned down as if he'd forgotten all about them. He too is looking up at me, less of a smile across his face and more of confusion.

I suddenly realize that I don't know what should happen next. I look at the man to my right who turns to the man to his right who looks at me who looks at them both, not sure who should be the next one to speak.

Then I remember: I'd just interrupted their conversation. It was probably on me to justify why, only when faced with two actual human faces my newfound anger-driven confidence melts quite quickly.

"How . . ." Oh God, think, Bella, think. "Is . . . is one of you Mark?"

It's a panic question. It annoys me I've even said his name, but it's the only male name I can think of and I have to say something.

"No," says the younger man. I look a bit worried; I look around the bar, wondering what others would do in this situation but then remembering that they probably wouldn't have put themselves in this situation.

"Oh," I say weakly, blushing. "God, I'm so sorry, I—"

"Who's Mark?" says the man with the wide eyes.

In fact, now I'm looking at them, his eyes are pretty unbeliev-able. It's probably just due to the low-level lighting situation but there's something quite extraordinary in them.

"He's . . . he's an arsehole," I say. I try to sound as confident as I came in as, but I sound weak and pathetic like I usually do.

"Did he stand you up?"

"No . . . I . . . I . . ." I look up at the kind, clean-shaven face and suddenly my brain kicks in. Before I know it I'm nodding, blinking down to him. "Yes. Yes, it looks like he stood me up. Again." Again? Where did that even come from? Wow—that just tumbled out of my mouth, easy as anything.

"Tough break," the young man says, turning to his friend like the conversation is over but his friend is only looking up at me. It's worked. The line was cast and I think . . . I think . . . he might be hooked and ready for reeling.

"How'd you meet?"

"Mirror Mirror," I say quickly.

"So that's why you don't know what he looks like."

"Why'd she not know?" the young one asks.

There we have it. Wide-eyes knows the app, the young one doesn't. This can only mean one thing: Wide-eyes is single. As he explains the concept to his friend I look around the bar, trailing my eyes and giving what I can only imagine is a first-class performance in the dramatic arts. I passed GCSE drama with a B. I know what I'm doing.

"You haven't been talking for long then?" the young one asks.

I have to say, I was thinking so hard about how to look stood up and forlorn that I hadn't been listening to their side chat.

"Sorry?"

"If his picture isn't viewable."

"Oh, we exchanged numbers instead, he said he preferred it to silly apps and . . . he just, seemed so great, you know."

"But this is the second time he's let you down?" Wide-eyes asks.

"Third," I say without a beat. Third? Wow, these lies are dropping out now. "I should have known better."

Wide-eyes turns his whole chair around to face me now. It's a swivel stool so it's not exactly difficult, but the body language is incredible. He's single, pretty good-looking, and he's looking at a damsel in distress right now. Even I see the appeal. The younger one looks a bit annoyed but not enough to say anything.

"Some guys make the rest of us look so bad," Wide-eyes says, and I think—I think—he's being genuine. "I'm Isaac. Lovely to meet you."

Right. I'm in.

But you can't just give your name out to a stranger, right? I don't know anything about this man, there's been no pre-meeting chat, no profile to stalk, nothing. I've literally never met a man this way before so I don't know what the protocol is but giving my own name feels weird given the circumstances.

I panic slightly, in the heat of the moment.

"Ellie," I say quickly, because it just feels natural and it's the only girl's name I can think of that isn't my own.

"Max," says the younger man but neither of us acknowledges it.

"Ellie, why don't you take a seat? Looks like you've had a bad night. Let me get you a drink."

3

They say when you're lying you should stick as close as possible to the truth, so I do. My name's Ellie Mathews. I'm a medical researcher. I got a degree in biology at Nottingham and then went on to do a master's at Kings College and a PhD at UCL. I love all things duck egg, prefer tea to coffee, and no, thirty-eight isn't too old when you look as good as Isaac does.

The longer we talk the easier it becomes. Things that take time at the beginning to set right become easy half an hour and a drink in. The younger man bids us good night at one point, claiming he'd only meant to go for one anyway, and Isaac buys us another round and another because the conversation is still flowing.

He's not a fan of the apps either. Mirror Mirror he tried, but he found it a bit jarring to be drip-fed information on someone and he doesn't have time for that kind of thing—not because he can't be bothered but for a much more noble reason: he's a doctor. He's not really able to put in the hours usually needed to get to know someone properly at the early stages. He doesn't have time for the usual "who texts who first" games, because he doesn't have that much "time" at all. He works strange hours and he loves what he does enough to know that the shift system won't end for him in the imminent future. Long hours put off girls as it's not too convenient and he's too decent to want to date anyone in his own hospital—he's seen that end in disaster for a number of his colleagues already.

He's a two-feet-in kind of guy, which I get completely under his circumstances, and which I realize personally when another drink down he's already resting his hand gently on my knee.

He's nice. Very nice. He actually asks whether the whole knee thing is alright, like a gentleman, and I tell him it is, because he's actually pretty decent and I've understood that he's exactly the kind of guy that Ellie needs. The real Ellie. He's funny, he's clever, he's dedicated to saving human lives, he's kind, and he takes an active interest in what my friend Bella is up to (which I describe in some detail as a side step to when he talks to me more deeply about my PhD thesis). He's a hell of a lot better-looking than Mark, he's funny, and he even knows how to make homemade parathas apparently (not that that's relevant, but it comes up naturally somehow and it's still pretty cool).

I am Ellie Mathews for the night, and I'm picking out for her the man she truly deserves, not the man she's settled for. When the barman calls last orders Isaac turns to me like a true gent.

"I'd say I'm sorry this Mark guy is such an arsehole but, to be honest, it's worked out pretty well for me."

How right you are, Isaac. How little you know why.

"So let me get your number and I promise I'll—"

But throwing all caution to the wind, I lean in and cut him off, my lips on his before his last words can free themselves and he's quick to react.

After a slightly PG-13 first kiss I pull away, still close enough to smell the lingering full-bodied red on his hot breath. He's smiling. It's sweet. I don't want sweet though. I'm Ellie Mathews and I'm sweet enough as I am. I need something more.

"Do you live close?" I ask.

He nods, but he's clearly a bit surprised I asked. He's ironically the kind of guy I'd want to be with. Smart, funny, sweet. Interested. He blinks down to me—he's tall too—six foot one. Did I mention he saves lives for a living?

"You know you don't need to—"

"I want to," I say, kissing him again to prove my point. Oh, he's a good kisser. His hand runs around the back of my neck and I know I'm doing the right thing. This is exactly what I need. This is what will make me happy. I very much want to.

Plus I've been lying to him all night. Pinocchio ain't got nothing on me now. I can practically read my next chapter title forming as he walks me the ten minutes to his own flat above a perfectly nice Waitrose because it's exactly how I feel. I'm a free lady. I haven't got a judgmental Mark doubting everything I do. I am single, and happy, and I'm about to have an anatomy lesson with a very learned teacher.

I've Got No Strings to Hold Me Down

$$\mathscr{L} \quad 4 \quad \mathscr{L}$$

The lights are still dim outside, the sun hardly risen over a miserable October morning when I wake. I look around the room, far more adult than any other bedroom I've ever stayed in. It's all modern art and lampshades. His hangers all facing one way, his clothes color-coded, and his bedsheets are actually ironed and clean. I can see the unwrinkled sharp line for where it was pressed going up the center of the duvet. He lives alone, which is a rare find for those in their twenties, but I guess he had a decade's worth of life experience that justifies the extra expense. His mattress has a topper, which gives for a luxurious night's sleep, and the alarm beside his bed is one of those wake-you-up-gently ones which tweeted out a morning song at 5 a.m. when it went off.

He switched it off quickly as not to disturb, and apart from my dreams vaguely traversing through the Amazon rainforest, I didn't really notice. I only remember now as I stretch out in his king-sized bed, completely alone.

It's only 7 a.m.; I have plenty of time before work still, but my doctor's already gone.

He told me last night that he had an early shift at the hospital and by early, he meant far earlier than I had ever wanted to work in my life. At the time I thought it was a line to get me going, but he seemed genuinely offended when I started putting my clothes back on at 2 a.m., so I took them off again, taking my position for my second orgasm of the night.

He wasn't the best I'd ever had, but he was efficient alright. He was detailed in the strangest way possible, using my body like a thermostat he wasn't used to for an hour or so, but after he'd unlocked orgasm number one, the second he was able to reach in under the magic five-minute mark.

I'd asked him, lying in the darkness, his hand gently stroking back my hair, why on earth he'd gone out the night before an early shift.

"Surely you'll be tired tomorrow?"

"I'm a doctor. I'm always tired," he answered, laughing, kissing my forehead, and holding me close like this wasn't the first time.

Everything about the encounter felt like I'd known him for years, which isn't something I'd had much experience in. Pillow talk with him felt wonderfully natural, not at all the awkward "that was pretty good" kind of banter that most men usually tried. He said he found it hard to sleep on normal nights, his mind always racing through the day. He said with or without me he'd have been up, but I got the feeling he was just saying it to be nice.

He'd had a bad day as it turns out. Three fatalities, which he described as "pretty normal in his unit" but he also mentioned it doesn't get any easier. The man he'd gone for a drink with was a new resident, one he didn't particularly like all that much, but he'd had a worse day and he needed company. Given that he hadn't any other plans, he thought he'd go for one.

"Turns out it was a great idea after all" was the last thing he said, before gently the two of us fell asleep cocooned in each other's arms in the most luxurious sheets I'd certainly ever slept in.

Now, the morning after, I get out of his bed and wander into his living room completely naked, which is a freeing feeling I've never been able to have elsewhere. I've always lived in flat shares where naked days weren't a thing and I've never dated anyone else who didn't have a similar arrangement to my own.

Isaac had left me a note on his kitchen counter.

HELP YOURSELF TO ANYTHING.

THERE'S CEREAL IN THE CUPBOARD, OR BREAD ON THE COUNTER IF YOU FANCY TOAST. IF YOU NEED ANYTHING, CALL—YOU CAN DROP OFF THE KEYS THROUGH THE LETTERBOX IF YOU'RE IN A RUSH OR COME BY THE HOSPITAL IF YOU'RE BRAVE ENOUGH.

HOPE I DIDN'T WAKE YOU. HOPE TO HEAR FROM YOU SOON, ELLIE. XX

That last line made my heart drop a little.

Ellie.

He still thinks I'm Ellie. Of course he does. I never corrected him and now it's too late. Even if I wanted to call him again it would be too strange to acknowledge my weirdness, so this truly was it for us.

To be fair, if I was truly interested I'm sure I'd do it anyway. It's early enough that we could just laugh it off in a few weeks—but despite the night being pretty wonderful, I know deep down he's not the one.

I can't even put my finger on it exactly. Perhaps he's just a little too serious for me. He might be the kind of guy who could cheer me up when I'm sad, but I don't see him as the guy who would make me laugh. I don't know, whatever it is, I know this is the end of our road, however nice our road was.

So goodbye, Isaac: you might not have been the perfect guy for me, but you were an orgasm and story alright, and I needed that.

🌿 5 🌿

I almost can't breathe. I don't know how it happened, I don't know why it happened, but there it is.

1,897 people like chapter 1.

1,678 like chapter 2.

4,890 following me.

378 comments.

I accidentally let three calls go to voice mail in my shock as I absorb the comments one by one. Most of them are one-liners—some are grammar police—but there are a few absolute gems. Five-line paragraphs comparing it to other writers—real writers—ones far more famous than I am. Whole stanzas about clever ways I might be able to pick other stories. So many people tagging others—lots of "@GemmaMannaly, this sounds just like you!" and "OMG @DanMFee, you HAVE to read this."

On Facebook I currently have 972 friends, which I would consider a lot given I only really speak to the same five people. A lot of them are randomers from different stages of my life—some school, some uni, a few encounters along the way and in between—but even if all the randomers in my life corralled together and invited a friend to read this with them, I still wouldn't reach anywhere near the 4,890 people who are following my work.

My first reaction is the same as my first reaction to anything. I get off B-Reader, turn to my messages, and excitedly type in Ellie's name, but then I pause.

Her texts linger on my phone.

> **The Elsa to my Anna-4 Oct 21:08**
> I get that you might need some time. Just please, please call as soon as you're ready to talk
>
> **The Elsa to my Anna-4 Oct 21:08**
> I'll be here whenever you're ready
>
> **The Elsa to my Anna-4 Oct 21:08**
> I love you
>
> **The Elsa to my Anna-4 Oct 21:08**
> xx

No. If I contact her then she'll tell me I need to apologize to her precious little Mark again, and I'm not going to do that. I'm not the one who messed up here. If Mark wants to apologize to me then maybe, just maybe, this whole thing will vaporize, but I can't hear her ask me to say sorry again. I can't hear her choose him over me again.

I put my phone down and I'm shaking, a weird hybrid of excitement and sadness and memories of last night's orgasms. No. I can't text Ellie, especially not about this.

But I have to tell someone, so I turn instead to my last messages to draw inspiration. It comes pretty quickly, of course.

> **5 Oct 11:02-Me**
> So you know you told me to write about that terrible date with the hairy man?
>
> **Marty-5 Oct 11:02**
> Yeah
>
> **5 Oct 11:03-Me**
> Jesus that was a quick reply
>
> **5 Oct 11:03-Me**
> I wasn't expecting a reply that quick
>
> **5 Oct 11:03-Me**
> Do you not have a life?

Marty-5 Oct 11:04
Calm it, Bells. I've got the day off

5 Oct 11:05-Me
Using it wisely?

Marty-5 Oct 11:05
Not right now I'm not

5 Oct 11:05-Me
How so?

Marty-5 Oct 11:05
I'm texting you

5 Oct 11:06-Me
Oh come now

5 Oct 11:06-Me
It's not like you have anything better to do

Marty-5 Oct 11:07
You going to insult me some more or tell me about
your writing?

5 Oct 11:07-Me
Both?

Marty-5 Oct 11:07
You have 5 mins. Then you lose me

5 Oct 11:07-Me
Girl?

Marty-5 Oct 11:07
FIFA

5 Oct 11:08-Me
Ok! Ok!

5 Oct 11:08-Me
Well I did what you said, and I submitted it to this
reader thing and I think I've gone viral

5 Oct 11:08-Me
Actually, what counts as viral?

Marty-5 Oct 11:08
Ebola?

5 Oct 11:08-Me
No come on! I mean it!

Marty-5 Oct 11:08
I don't know. How many reads we talking?

I send him a screenshot with the numbers all circled in case he misses them. Then I underline the numbers again in case he misses the circle. Then I make the screen size bigger in case my circling and underlining means he can't actually read what I'm highlighting. I wait a few minutes, doing that terrible thing where I look back though the texts, and when my eyes return to the screenshot I sent I suddenly notice: the numbers have grown.

1,922 people like chapter 1.

1,679 like chapter 2.

4,961 following me.

382 comments.

Oh my word. I've literally gained seventy-one followers in the space of a few minutes. What's happening in the world?

Marty-5 Oct 11:09
That's it?

"Oi!" I whisper under my breath, because I forget momentarily that I'm alone. Then I remember.

5 Oct 11:09-Me
Oi!

Marty-5 Oct 11:09
No, I mean, that's your writing?

Marty-5 Oct 11:09
This looks awesome

Marty-5 Oct 11:09
What's B-Reader?

Marty-5 Oct 11:09
How do I get it?

Ah, of course. He may be a jackass, but he's a jackass who's always had a vague interest in my writing at least. So I send him the link, smiling ear to ear as I watch a few more followers join my wolf pack.

He must be looking at it for his texts come to a halt. I feel weirdly nervous, watching the clock tick on, waiting.

Marty-5 Oct 11:19

This is amazing

Marty-5 Oct 11:19

Really fucking funny

I suddenly release the breath I hadn't even realized I'd been holding.

5 Oct 11:20-Me

You really think so?

Marty-5 Oct 11:20

It's genius

The smile across my face is suddenly ear to ear.

Marty-5 Oct 11:21

Are both these hookups for real?

5 Oct 11:21-Me

I've lived 'em all

Marty-5 Oct 11:21

I'm not going to lie

Marty-5 Oct 11:21

I'm a bit surprised

Oh, not him too.

I can't have this from both of the Mathews siblings.

Marty-5 Oct 11:22

Not for the writing bit

Marty-5 Oct 11:22

That I always knew was great

Oh, it's happening. It's about to happen. I'm about to have to justify my new exciting life—one he promoted, might I remind him. I chew my lip, ready to fight back.

Marty-5 Oct 11:23

But I'm constantly surprised that anyone ever wants to get with you

Ah. So he's not being judgmental. He's just being an arsehole. I'm not surprised. For as long as I've known him he's always been more comfortable hiding compliments in comedy than just saying something nice to begin with. Ellie always blamed it on school. She said all boys were trained to keep things on the light side. It's why she didn't get offended when at her graduation, he just ruffled her hair and called her a "little swot," instead of just hugging her congratulations like the rest of us.

Maybe she's right, of course, but . . . I don't know. I've always wondered if it ran a little deeper for him. His mum's always laid it thick and fast with affirmations, just like Ellie, but I don't remember his dad ever being all that complimentary about anything.

If that's the only male role model he had to base his own tone on then I'm impressed he's even as supportive as he is to begin with.

At least I know when I read the text that this, from Marty, is something of a standing ovation. I'll take it.

5 Oct 11:23-Me
Thanks ☺

So there it is: my own growing following. So where next then, I ask myself. Where next?

6

Mystery Man
Have I lost you?

                        Bella Marble
                     Oh God! Sorry forgot
                        Bella Marble
                  Have I tried Balthazar?

Mystery Man
I'm glad you're still here

                        Bella Marble
        Glad enough to tell me your name?

Mystery Man
I'm not telling you now

                        Bella Marble
          Why not? What have I done?

I'll tell you what I've done. I've just gone and submitted chapter 3. I'm so nervous that I'm about to lose all my followers that I'm biting my nails and distracting myself with any app that will take me. Plus Mirror Mirror is now as much a source of inspiration as it is a platform to distract myself from it.

Mystery Man
No name would be good enough for this kind of
lead up

Bella Marble

Unless you're someone famous and you've been
trying to conceal it from me all this time

Bella Marble

Are you an actor?

Bella Marble

Oh—are you the sexy one from Poldark?

Mystery Man

Don't pretend you don't know his name

Bella Marble

Poldark?

Mystery Man

Yes, I am Aidan Turner

Mystery Man

I have a hard time finding women despite being
scientifically proven to be one of the most handsome
men in the world

Mystery Man

I just googled that. Is that actually true?

Bella Marble

If you read it online it has to be

I'm actually finding I'm enjoying this. He seems, I don't know. Well, he's replying instantly, he's the one chasing initially, and he's got a little bit of what the boys downstairs would call "banter."

I'm not going to lie, I had sort of written him off. Somewhere between this game taking far too long and my new B-Reader success I'd almost forgotten about him completely. I'm a new woman now (granted, I haven't had enough time to *actually* be a new woman but the intentions are all there).

But hey, if he's going to put all the effort in here I don't mind going along with it.

Bella Marble

Go on. Why can't I know your name?

Mystery Man

Because no name can stand this kind of lead up

Bella Marble

Then why did you begin this game to begin with?

Mystery Man

The truth?

Bella Marble

No. A lie please

Mystery Man

I'm Poldark

Bella Marble

The truth please

Mystery Man

I was on holiday

Bella Marble

. . . Congratulations?

Bella Marble

Wait—really?

Mystery Man

Yep

Bella Marble

That doesn't explain anything

Bella Marble

Other than your potential tan that I would have seen if
you'd added an actual profile picture

The more we spoke the more of his profile picture was revealed,
only once the weird old goblin face disappeared I was left with—
you probably could have guessed it—a second bizarre old goblin
face.

Mystery Man

I needed to buy myself some time while I was away

Mystery Man

But I'm back now

Mystery Man

And I owe you a date

Bella Marble

. . .

Mystery Man
You don't want a date now?

> **Bella Marble**
> That's what the name thing was?
>
> **Bella Marble**
> Buying time?

Mystery Man
Yeah

> **Bella Marble**
> Why did you even bother?
>
> **Bella Marble**
> Why didn't you just wait until you were back from holiday?

Mystery Man
It thought it was fun at first

Mystery Man
Then I saw your picture

Mystery Man
And I knew I wanted to meet you

Mystery Man
So I kept going

I know it's stupid. I know. I'm as much a feminist as the next millennial woman who pretends to be a feminist but isn't, despite wanting to be one. I'm still wired to feel like Christmas came early when a boy thinks I look pretty.

Plus I'm riding a high. My new chapter is out, the likes keep growing, and three times today I've had the commissioning editors at Porter Books tell me I look "work appropriate finally," which I'm choosing to take as a compliment.

My picture from Mirror Mirror is a good one. I take a look at my own profile to double-check. It's me at my twenty-first birthday (okay, whatever, so it's a little bit on the old side). It's cropped, of course. You can't quite see them but I am effectively the icing layer between the Mathews siblings' cake. On my right is Ellie, obviously.

She actually made the cake that's before me, lighting my face in a way that makes it blurry enough for my skin to be flawless. Honestly, all the filters in all the world and I challenge anyone who can find a more flattering lighting situation than good old-fashioned candlelight.

On my left is Marty, who—if I remember correctly—paused his riveting conversation with the girl he was chatting with all night, some old work colleague of mine I think, just to make sure his face made it into the frame.

I'm happy in that picture.

I thought everything would turn out well.

I'd moved to London, achieved some sort of passable degree, and I had the whole world at my feet. I wasn't just hoping to become a writer, I was sure I'd be one. I knew that just a year or two of trying and I'd have my first book published—maybe one or two slightly awkward reviews but otherwise an "indie charmer," growing my following ready for book number two.

And yet here I am, twenty-nine, not quite a writer, not talking to my best friend in the world and locked in a stalemate with her shitty partner, child of divorced-parents-to-be, and feeling all blushed because some stranger I don't know said he liked my profile picture.

Mystery Man
I promise I'm not shallow

Bella Marble
I mean, it's a bit shallow

Mystery Man
A bit maybe

Bella Marble
But at least it's a compliment

Mystery Man
It is

Mystery Man
Did it work?

Mystery Man
Can we meet?

I hate that it's working. I should take the high road. Think of wolf man—he called you pretty and look where that got you! He should want to see me because of my intelligence and good humor. But how could he see that until he's actually met me anyway?

Bella Marble

Yeah go on

7

As I sort out the logistics of time and place, Maggie pops her head out of her office. Her hair's all "Rachel from *Friends*" today, which I assume has something to do with the resurgence of the show on streaming devices. Perhaps the nineties are back in style. I hope they are. Then I can reuse some of my hoarding wardrobe I keep meaning to eBay before I remember how much effort it is to put anything on eBay.

I look down at the phone guiltily but it's actually not ringing. Her presence is therefore confusing; as far as I'm aware I haven't done anything particularly wrong. I look up at her.

"Can I help you with something?" I ask in my most innocent voice.

"Yes—Henrietta is about to turn up any minute now," she says matter-of-factly. I blink at her a few times. She blinks back at me. I hear the clock ticktock in the background.

"Okay," I say, a little confused. "They haven't rung from down-stairs yet."

"Oh—no, I didn't think she was here yet," Maggie confirms.

Wow, this conversation is getting difficult.

"Okay, well, I can come get you when—"

"According to Cathy you're the one who found her."

"Cathy?"

"Yes, Cathy told me you found her and brought her to our attention."

What? That's unlike me. I've been terrible at reading the submissions. I always mean so well but I get distracted so easily and, being honest with myself, I haven't been reading anything at all unless you count—

The phone rings and Maggie nods at it expectantly.

"I have a Miss Lovelace in reception for you?" says the nice man from the desk downstairs.

"Yep, send her straight up," I reply automatically before hanging up.

Wait. Lovelace? Henrietta Lovelace?

The B-Reader I found right at the start of this all.

I look at my computer screen to confirm it before I see Maggie's prim and proper nod in my direction. My heart's jumping a little bit, my ears ringing. I can't believe someone I've found on B-Reader managed to break through the first barrier in this ridiculously tough industry.

Because of me.

Looking at the commissioning calendar now, there she is. I didn't even notice. It proves how often I read the calendars to know who to expect through the door. God, when did I become so bad at my job?

Henrietta Lovelace—General Meeting—Maggie Tomlinson and Robert Musgraves.

"Are you offering her a deal?" I ask excitedly.

Maggie's smiling now, realizing I've only just worked it out but being way too polite to spell it out.

"No, no. She's new and her following's slow, but she shows promise and I like her style. The bit about the boat on the ocean—it was beautifully subtle. We don't find that kind of writing done well very often these days."

"The boat?"

Is this the same one I'd read? I don't remember a boat.

"Yes—chapter . . . I don't know, three perhaps?"

God, I'd been so negligent I hadn't even read past that one chap-

ter that had me absolutely captivated. I was so obsessed with looking at my own followers growing that I hadn't thought to look at
anyone else's work. I hadn't even noticed that her one little chapter
I had read had already tripled somehow.

"Oh yes," I lie quickly, "oh the boat. Yes, totally beautiful."

If Maggie notices the lie she doesn't say anything.

"Well, it's a good spot from you," Maggie continues.

I smile ear to ear before I even realize I'm smiling. I don't even
know why I'm smiling. Usually I don't care at all about the writers
crossing through the office—*but this one was found by me.* I feel a
weird sense of pride taking over, like she's my child on the first day
of school or something.

The lift door opens and a nervous, nerdy woman in her fifties pops out, looking around at the wooden bookcases in absolute
wonder.

She's not how I pictured her. I thought she might be younger
somehow. She was new to writing, which usually meant new to the
world, but of course that's not always the case. Even as I look at her
I realize that it has to be her, all black hair scrunched on her head
and wide cardigan complementing her inch-thick glass lenses. She
was someone who had probably been writing her whole life, but
only now had been noticed.

By me.

My work, my rubbish, weird job, has made a positive difference
to someone's life. It suddenly makes my being here feel validated
somehow.

"Keep up the good work, Bella. You've got a good eye." I turn
to Maggie, who's nodding to me like a schoolteacher, handing me
back an A-graded paper. It's like the world's moving in slow motion.
A compliment? From Maggie?

"See what happens when you're not just looking at your phone
all day?" she adds, just as Henrietta Lovelace pushes open the double
doors from the hallway and into our office.

Henrietta smiles at me like an old friend. I wonder if she's going
to thank me.

What were her words?

"I can't tell you how much this means to me. I thought about giving up on this, I didn't think anyone was interested in reading my work, but knowing someone's out there is enough for me to persevere. So thank you, stranger."

"Hello, dear," she says, her voice about ten years older than she even looks. "I'm here to see Maggie?"

I blink back at her.

She doesn't recognize me. Of course she doesn't. She only knows me as my B-Reader handle, @B.Enchanted. She only knows me as the unknown stranger who liked what she saw.

Henrietta's waiting for me to answer but my thoughts are slow, taking in this bizarre situation. I watch her like some bemused fangirl, unable to greet her properly.

Maggie's lost interest in waiting for me, which I don't blame her for.

"Henrietta, Maggie. So lovely to meet you. Can I take you through here?" Maggie cuts in a fraction of a second before the pause is awkward between all of us and although I'm slightly relieved, I'm still annoyed I didn't get a chance to say anything. I watch them disappear into a side office and close the door. Robert, a small, bubbly-looking man, bounces in after.

It's only once they're all gone that I even realize how passive-aggressive Maggie was to me before she left:

See what happens when you're not just looking at your phone all day?

I'm more than a little annoyed now. I look at the closed office door and my annoyance only grows. I should be in that room. I should be talking to Henrietta about how beautiful her words are. I should be singing her praises and asking her to stay in touch, not Maggie.

Almost in protest, I take out my phone and begin to scroll. Except then I put it down. I turn my head to the closed door of the office they're talking in and I wonder what on earth must be swimming around Henrietta's head. This must be so exciting to her, speaking to two well-known commissioning editors in the complicated publishing world. It proves what getting noticed on a platform like B-Reader can really do for you.

Smiling in the happiness Henrietta must be feeling, I turn back to my computer screen and log into B-Reader. There are four more chapters for me to read. I'm suddenly glad I'm not inside that room; I can't wait to delve in.

8

By the end of the week I have—I mean, even as I think it I'm shaking—over 100,000 views.

100,009 people to be exact.

Over 100,000 people have read some portion of my work and have liked it enough to follow me because of it. I don't even know 100,000 people. I've never been in a room with 100,000 people. I wonder how many people I've even spoken to in my life, including all the waiters and the retail assistants and the cold callers, and even that probably doesn't add up to 100,000 people. That's unbelievable. That's stupid numbers. That's my following.

As I'm walking from Angel station to the pub Mystery Man has offered up I get a text.

Mystery Man
I'm looking forward to this x

Texting in the immediate run up to a date? That's a nice touch. A gentleman's touch. I quickly text back:

Bella Marble
So am I x

And the funny thing is, I actually am. I'd forgotten this feeling. This wonderful, nervous, this-could-this-be-the-one feeling. This guy, well, he's pretty funny, he likes games, he visits museums— okay, maybe that's a bit random, but it's still nice.

If I like him, what do I do with the rest of the book though?

Just . . . what, make it up? No, I can't do that. I'm a writer fully dedicated to my art. What if my 100,000+ followers smell the lie? What if what they need is authenticity or nothing? I've literally just seen what B-Reader can do to a writer's career—surely I can't ignore that?

But if he's great then do I just let this potential husband wander away for the sake of a story?

It's annoyingly Ellie's voice that's in my head. Oh God, Ellie. Even thinking about her makes me sad.

I had thought she would have broken before me. I thought I would have received something—some eventual "I'm sorry about what I said—Mark should be the one to apologize and I'm sorry I made you feel like you weren't as important to me as he is," or a "Mark can be an arsehole, I'm so sorry for his terrible behavior to you." What I really would have loved was a "I've finished with him—no one gets to speak to you like that," but even I know that's never going to happen.

But since the texts that night I've not had one message in all this time. Not one call in nearly a whole week. Not one tagged picture of a puppy on Instagram or a Facebook comment under a video of a baby rolling over. Nothing.

She really is giving me time.

She really does expect me to apologize to that shithead.

No, stop thinking about Ellie right now. Think about Mystery Man.

I enter the bar. I can't help but be a little disappointed by the venue. He promised something different and exciting and unique, and right now he's in the most generic bar imaginable. I double-check the text chain three times over to make sure I've got the right place, but it seems I'm exactly where the little marker is on the map he sent. I look back around me. It's not terrible by any means, just incredibly basic. It's modern and glass-filled, with little lights hanging over the ceiling and booths that are dark enough to hide the nightly alcohol spillages. It has a dance floor with a silver glitter ball hanging over it like just about every dance floor ever, and the walls are so clear of paintings it looks clinical. It's totally "normal," which is unlike the kind of vibe I was getting from Mystery Man. But maybe that's not all that bad. This is a first date, after all; perhaps he doesn't want to go too unique this early.

It's full to the brim though—I don't know how on earth I'm supposed to find this mystery man if he is in here. He would know my face, of course, the app would have shown him that, but I have absolutely nothing to go on.

I feel that familiar kink in my stomach from nerves. I can feel my breath tightening in my chest already. I look around but most people are in groups around me. Finding someone solo in this heap is going to be a little difficult. I can only hope that this mystery man spots me first when—

Oh shit.

There he is.

Of course it is.

9

What were Cathy's words again?

"He dates women he thinks look tragic then writes about how terrible they were."

Oh fuck, what am I in for? For there, in front of me, is Henry Pill of B-Reader infamy.

Before I even have time to think about hiding or ghosting he spots me.

"Bella!" His voice is slow and drawn out, like the stoner kids on U.S. TV shows.

I straighten my face pretty quickly. I don't want it going back to the office that I was rude to our latest signed author. His work is worth more than mine to Porter Books Publishing Ltd. I wonder if it's a fireable offense to date a client. I mean, technically he's the one who approached me here, I didn't know who he was, and it's not like I have any say on his book deal.

"So lovely to meet you at last!"

Meet you? But he's already met me. *At the office.* He literally walked past my desk two weeks ago. No one would be that shitty and not remember something like that. Literally no one is *that* forgettable. Not even Mark.

"I have to say, when I saw your profile picture I thought you were pretty, but seeing you now—wow. You're so much more beautiful than I could ever have imagined."

I keep the smile on my face like my job depends on it, but inside I'm already screaming.

I don't know what's harder to swallow, the fact that I really am that forgettable, or that I'm clearly being prepped to be the next chapter in his shitty little six-figure book.

What a little fuckhead.

10

He's making this awkward already.

I go in for a hug; he heads for a handshake. He overcorrects to a kiss on the cheek and as I pull away, he awkwardly leans in for a second kiss that I miss and then pull back in for a late one, only to find him already sitting back down again. He laughs, like this is the first time this has happened to him. It's not, of course, I know it's not, because I've literally read that he's done this before in one of his other chapters.

If I didn't know though, if I seriously thought this was a mystery date, this is the kind of detail I would have agonized over for the rest of the night. I would have lain in bed alone telling myself how stupid I was to go in for the hug.

What an absolute arsehole making women feel that way.

I wonder if I should go. Maybe I should call him up on it, tell him who I am and wish him luck on his shithead-of-the-year entry. Maybe I should disappear.

But I can't. The situation is way, way too juicy. Here is a man who clearly doesn't know that I know who he is, and who clearly is about to sink our date on purpose in the interest of comedy. I'm fascinated to see how this plays out.

Plus, little does he know I'm almost playing the same game. Mystery man turned misogynistic weirdo gremlin? This sounds like a fairy-tale character alright; I just need to work out which one.

"I'm not what you expected?" he asks.

He's confident alright, and although I hate to admit it, close up he's good-looking in a suave skater boy kind of way. Tall and thin, long arms, and untamed ruffled hair. I try not to look like I like what I'm looking at.

"I didn't know what to expect," I reply daintily, sitting down opposite him. He passes over the second drink before him.

"I got you a vodka Red Bull. Is that alright?"

No. No, it isn't. Of course it isn't. This is a date, not a school-girls' club night. I haven't had a vodka Red Bull since I was about eighteen, but I can already read in his eyes that he's testing me. He's looking between me and a drink he knows is probably incorrect and he's measuring me up, trying to get a reaction.

I read this in one of his chapters too. One girl he took out, he spent the evening getting her increasingly more bizarre drinks and watching, as she was far too polite to correct him. She got trashed of course, because that's what way too many spirit mixers does to a human. He wrote a rather poorly constructed sentence about how her vomit ricocheted off the club's wall like a downpour of sticky rum-filled raindrops.

He's not even being original for me. Fuck him.

"I'm not discovering alcohol for the first time so no," I reply stubbornly. "I'm going to get something drunk by adults."

He's surprised.

To be fair, I'm also surprised. I'm not usually this blunt. I expect him to be offended and to call the whole night off, but his raised eye-brow looks more impressed than anything else. I turn away from him, pulling out my wallet from my handbag and standing all over again.

"Do you want anything while I'm up there? Peach schnapps and lemonade maybe? Glass of milk?"

He's staring at me now and I hold his eye contact daringly.

He's dressed up for the occasion, but I'm not surprised given the amount of money I know he's just had deposited into his bank account. His navy jumper looks old but it's clearly new, probably designer, and baggy and shapeless in that high fashion kind of way.

I worried when I left home that my dark jeans and cream satin cami might have been a bit too underdressed given what I expected from this date. I'd hoped to look "cool and casual," topping it with some heeled black boots, fire-red lipstick to match my curled hair, and smoky eyes. Now it feels like a waste of good makeup.

His eyes search my face and I think he's about to snap.

Except instead of breaking, he starts laughing. It's genuine. You can fake the sound but you can't fake the glossing over of water in your eyes. He's actually finding this hilarious. I continue to stare at him, unamused.

"Just one for me then," I reply finally, about to head off.

"No!" he calls after me. "Please, let me. I'll get something for you."

He stands up, pulling out his own wallet from his back pocket. It's smart and leather, the "Cinderella" ball transformation to the twelve-year-old H&M rags that I'm holding.

"Erm, I'm going to say no to that one."

"I insist!"

"I don't trust you not to return with a mango White Claw."

He's laughing again, the tears in his eyes. I'm honestly not that funny.

"What do you want? White wine?" he asks.

"Camden Pale Ale."

"Ale?"

"Did I stutter?"

He puts his arm on my arm and sits me back down. He's really enjoying this. He's properly laughing, enough to turn a few heads around us.

"I got it. I got it, please."

I think about insisting right back, but then I remember how much money he earns and how much I do.

"Sure, but if you come back with a Malibu and pineapple I promise you'll be wearing it for the rest of your night."

11

"So what do you do, Mystery Man?" I ask, half a pint down. "Other than lure women on dates with you with a blurred-out profile picture."

He laughs at that too. Honestly, I don't know why. I'm not being funny. I'm being deadly serious.

"I'm a vet."

"Bullshit. Try again."

"You don't think I'm a vet?"

"I know you're not a vet."

He pauses, weighing up his options.

"What gave me away?"

"Your hands," I say quickly, because I don't want him to know I know. That begs more questions and I don't want them.

"My hands?"

"They're too soft. You can't do anything physical and have hands that look like that."

Turns out I'm pretty good on my feet like this. It's true too—at least it's true for Marty. He's usually got a fresh scratch or two close to his knuckles from a naughty kitten and if you feel the tips of his thumbs they're all worn down from years of overuse. I assume it's the same for all of them. He's just the only vet I know.

"So are you actually going to tell me? Or are we going to fuck around all night?"

He pulls a face like I've just given him the world's best riddle.

"I'm a writer," he replies back, leaning forward. Positive body language. Opposite from the vibe I'm giving off, I'll tell you that. I bet he's read the book on the "art to seduce the ladies" and has taken it as gospel.

"You are?" I ask, fascinated. At least I look fascinated. I'm more fascinated that he's not outwardly lied to me a second time. From the few chapters that I've actually read of his, I don't think he's admitted this before.

"I am."

"And what kind of writing is it that you do?"

"Personal biography," he says, choosing his words well. So he's going full-on truth for me. Let's see how deep this tunnel goes.

"And what makes you so interesting that people might want to read about you?"

He looks around the bar for inspiration. His little mole face looks down.

"I'm not that interesting," he replies. He's smiling but his eyes look a bit sorrowful, like a lost puppy. For a second, just a second, I think he looks a little embarrassed. This is unlike the Mr. Confidence he began as.

I wait for him to continue but he doesn't.

"Apparently not," I tell him.

He laughs again (no idea why, I'm still not being funny).

"Are you always this blunt?"

And it finally hits me: why he's laughing, that is. This is shock. This is the confused laughter of a man who has clearly never been called out for any of his wrongdoings and here I am, my bullshit radar on high alert and my arsehole tolerance at an all-time low. I'm not being funny, I'm being honest, but this is new for him. He's unsettled, he's out of his comfort zone, so he's laughing.

"No," I reply earnestly, before adding in a perfectly pitched-to-be-patronizing voice, "you're special."

He's playing with his drink now, obviously a bit nervous, which is something I don't suppose he feels all that often. This is clearly not the night he planned for. I love that.

"I don't write about me. I write about . . . it's . . . well, I go on dates and I write about them."

"Like this one?"

"Like this one."

I'm astounded. Has he tried this method before? The ultimate truth tactic?

"And what do you say about these dates?"

And—and I'm genuinely surprised by this—he tells me. He even shows me a little bit of what he's working on. He doesn't do it willingly, mind, but I ask him and eventually—a little sheepishly—he shows me a bit of a chapter. I don't tell him this, of course, but I've read it before. It's one of the nicer ones, one of the ones that shows him in a bit of a better light. Only just.

"Well, aren't you the modern-day Romeo," I say, throwing the phone back across the table. He's biting his lip. "Did you not get enough love as a kid or something?"

"Wow, you are something!" he says, his laughter all but gone now but he still sounds genuinely impressed.

"You are too apparently."

He taps his phone nervously, before slipping it back in his overly priced Levi's.

"You really want to know?"

"I don't like waste and I still have a good five minutes of my drink left. I'd say that's enough time to enlighten me."

He runs his hands to the back of his neck, perhaps a nervous tic. The bar's filling up, ready for a true Saturday night. I can see why he's picked the place now too. If he managed to get a girl drunk enough she'd probably end up making a fool of herself on the mini not-quite-a-dance floor. It's the kind of thing I would have done if I thought it would up my chances. He clears his throat, ready.

"You know, I used to be this shell of a boy when I was a kid. I could barely talk to other people, let alone girls. That's why I took up writing to begin with, I guess."

It's like his whole tone has suddenly changed. The confidence he began with has all but been stripped away from him. Like he's finally being his authentic self, so separate from the Casanova I've read all about. So different from the man I first met as I walked into the bar. He continues, his voice suddenly so raw and unfiltered. I have to say, it certainly makes a nice change.

"When I was like, sixteen, I asked out a girl who was being nice to me. She said yes, and I planned this whole thing with dinner and drinks, which I know is a bit out there because at that age no one expects more than just 'hanging out' somewhere and maybe a sneaky can of Stella. Turns out she didn't even know it was a date. It was awful. She spent the entire time talking to me about another guy in the class who she thought liked her and when I told her I liked her, she laughed it off and . . . God, I mean, at the time I laughed with her but the whole thing made me want to never date again."

"So that's why you hate women?" I ask. "Because one girl when you were sixteen made you feel bad?"

"I don't hate women," he says. He's keeping it light but I can hear the nerve I've touched. This date has taken a turn and both of us know it. I pull a vaguely apologetic face, and he gets ready for his next chapter.

"Anyway, I ended up writing it down but pretending that I was her and she was me. I found this site online for new writers so I put it out there . . . and it got a lot of likes. Like, a lot of likes. So I wrote another. Totally fake, mind, all about this terrible date where everything went wrong—even worse than the last one—and I posted it again and there it was. Validation. So I kept going. Writing more and more and making the dates far more ridiculous and the worse they were the more likes it got and . . . I don't know, it sort of just took off."

"Wait—these are fake?" I ask, surprised, pointing to his phone but accidentally pointing to his crotch. He shuffles around a little uncomfortably as I remove my finger.

"Well, they were. At first. Except, when I was like, twenty, I began to run out of ideas. By then I'd grown up a fair amount and some people were actually interested, so I just sort of, took on the persona I'd invented for myself and began doing the dates for real. Turns out the whole 'fake it till you make it' thing works."

I'm about to say something sarcastic and rude but I stop myself, changing tacks. If he's changed his tone, I should probably change mine too.

"How many dates have you been on?" I ask instead.

"More than I can count."

"Jesus," I say, leaning back on my chair and taking it all in. "So what? You pick people who look tragic and hope for the best?"

"No!"

"No?"

He looks at me, shrugging.

"It doesn't matter who the date is with. It's easy to sabotage a date once you've got a good read of someone. Seeing how they react is the interesting part."

"So you're telling me all this to get a reaction from me? One you can write about?"

"No, I'm telling you all this because you might just be the first woman I've gone on a date with who's actually made me laugh. I'd forgotten that feeling. You've got this whole no-nonsense policy going on that's . . . well, it's refreshing. I'm enjoying this."

He's really fucking serious. I stroke back my hair and lean forward, channeling my best Ruth Wilson (sexiest woman alive— have you seen *Luther*?).

"You want my advice?" I ask.

"Are you going to give it anyway?"

"Stop treating women like shit. We feel shitty enough about ourselves without men treating us that way too."

I finish the dregs of my drink, slam it on the table, and wipe down my mouth in a way that would make my father tut at the table. I put my wallet in my bag and do it up, ready to go.

"Let me get you another one. Still on me—I owe you."

I laugh at him this time.

"One's enough, I think," I tell him.

"Come on, you can't go now. I've only talked about myself! I know nothing about you!"

"You've just summed up most first dates I've had, and the other guys didn't seem to care that much about that," I reply.

God, I'm sharp tonight.

"I haven't even told you my name yet!"

"You don't need to tell me your name."

"You're angry at me?"

"I'm not angry."

"You are—you're angry about my writing. I knew I shouldn't have shown it. Women can be just as bad," he says defensively.

"Oh no," I say, smiling slyly, "they can be much, much worse."

I pick up my coat, pull myself out of the booth, and watch as his disheartened little face turns down to look at his own empty glass. I've never seen such a pretty man look so unhappy.

"Well?" I ask him.

He looks up, confused.

"Well?" he replies. I sling my handbag over my right shoulder and tuck my hands into my pockets with a knowing glint in my eyes.

"Your place or mine?" I ask.

❦ 12 ❦

I sit in front of my laptop, back at my own desk after what was only a mediocre night with a man pretty enough to look at, inside an epic river-facing flat in Pimlico that I will never be able to afford. The place was ridiculous. He lives alone, in a two-bedroom flat that he actually owns, where the most obvious feature is a television as big as a wall with devices and consoles spread out beneath it like a smorgasbord of writing distractions. To be fair—if I ever make it I'm sure I'd do something pretty similar.

For a man who's written a lot about how lucky a woman is to ride his magical penis, he wasn't that great. He was clunky and self-oriented as only those below the age of twenty-five can be—without the excuse of too much alcohol to justify it—and when I stopped making the fake noises that I accidentally began out of habit he started to get increasingly self-conscious.

"Holy shit," he said, leaning back once we were done. "That was amazing."

It wasn't, but it was sweet of him to say anyway. I stood up, picking up my clothes and doing the usual shuffle to avoid too much exposure. His room had down lighting, which was flattering, but it was also bright red like a booth in Amsterdam. It screamed new money and young mind and although I wondered at one point whether it might have been romantic, I couldn't help feeling like it was made to have the opposite effect.

"We don't have to lie to each other, we're not invested," I told him.

"It was!"

"It was . . . pretty good."

"Just good?"

I wondered whether I should bother. Oh, what the hell. What was there to lose? At least the next girl along might thank me.

"That thing you did with your fingers?" I told him. He nodded slyly, already proud of himself for a party trick most men think is their specialty but isn't. I continued, much to his confusion: "Slow that the fuck down next time."

I wondered whether he was going to go all stroppy and offended but instead he actually looked a little thoughtful, nodding to himself.

"Noted," he replied, pulling himself up. I sat on the end of the bed, putting on my socks when suddenly, I felt his lips down my neck, ready for a second shot. I'd already had my fill for the night but it was cute. Ignoring him slightly, I stood up, reaching for my coat.

"You're leaving?"

"Early start."

"You don't have to."

I turned to look at him. He was actually ripped, which was surprising for such a tall, thin man. He must have time in his writing, gaming, dating schedule to work out. Maybe they're the only four things he does with his day, full stop. He looked pretty earnest at least, which I admire in someone who's probably about to write me up in some horrific way to impress his next round of readers.

"It's alright. I know how this goes."

"How what goes?" he asked innocently. I laughed, gathering the last of my things and screwing up my hair on the top of my head as best as I could for the night bus back.

"Get some sleep. You'll need it. I need you on your best form when you're putting this encounter down on paper."

"Don't be so stupid, I won't write about this."

"I know you will. I don't care."

"But I won't!"

"Okay, sure," I replied sarcastically. I really don't care. Mostly because I'm about to do the exact same thing to him.

He stood up quickly, jumping in front of me to block my quick escape.

"You don't have to go."

I kissed him, mostly for politeness, before moving past him and out through the living room with the giant TV. Shame I wouldn't get to watch anything on it—although my eyes might have burned from the intense light emissions and close proximity. I heard his voice following me but he wasn't, so by the time I reached his door I knew that finally our chapter together was at an end.

As I reached back to the safety of my own room an hour or so later, I saw Mirror Mirror had one new notification waiting for me. It was him. Obviously.

Mystery Man
Let me get your number at least

Mystery Man
We can get off this stupid app

Now, back at my desk, I look through the past conversations we've had, boy's name after boy's name, and I know I should just leave it. I know I should walk away. I've had my fun. But I can't help it.

Sitting down at my laptop, ready to indulge my 100,000+ readers with another tragic fairy tale gone wrong, I lean back in my chair.

Bella Marble
I'll tell you what

Bella Marble
Guess

Mystery Man
Guess?

Bella Marble
Yes, guess

Bella Marble

If you get it right I'll give you the night of your life

Mystery Man

Guess 11 random digits?

Mystery Man

That's impossible

Bella Marble

It's unlikely. Not impossible

Bella Marble

In fact, I'll give you a clue

Bella Marble

It begins 07

Mystery Man

That's not a very helpful clue

Bella Marble

Same odds as you gave me I reckon

Mystery Man

You never even guessed my name

Bella Marble

I don't need to guess it

Mystery Man

Oh yeah?

Bella Marble

I already know it

Mystery Man

What is it then?

It's the next chapter name of my book, my friend.

Bella Marble

Rumpelstiltskin

Then, without a second thought, I right swipe across Mystery Man's homepage and off he goes, back into the cloud he came from.

❧ 13 ❧

"Hello?"

"Hi, darling, it's me. It's Dad here."

"I know, Dad. Phones have screens now. I saw your name before I picked up. Believe it or not I actually 'chose' to speak to you."

"Oh, good. Well, we need you to come back. Today if you can. For lunch."

"Is Mum cooking?"

"No, I am."

"Good. Why?"

"Because I don't burn food."

"No, why do you need me to come back?"

"We just need to talk to you."

"Are you and Mum getting back together?" I try hopefully.

There's a pause on the line, the kind of deep long pause that doctors give before they deliver bad news. At least I already know this bad news.

Anyway, it's for that reason that I head to ye olde St. Albans for the afternoon, ready to have my heart broken all over again.

11 Oct 09:09-Me

You're not home are you?

Marty-11 Oct 09:09

I am

11 Oct 09:09-Me

Home home?

Marty-11 Oct 09:09

As opposed to home home home?

11 Oct 09:10-Me

No, freak—St. A?

Marty-11 Oct 09:11

Ah, no. On call

Marty-11 Oct 09:11

Need me to be?

11 Oct 09:12-Me

Need?

11 Oct 09:12-Me

Get over yourself Marty

11 Oct 09:12-Me

No one needs you

Turns out my 'rents have dragged me up here because they need me to clear out my room. Well, isn't that brilliant.

They're putting the house on the market, and my choices were for them to pack my room up and decide what's worth keeping, or for me to do it myself. The real estate agents who came seemed adamant that the place would get lapped up pretty quickly, so they wanted to make sure everything was ready.

As I stand at the edge of the same room that I've lived in nearly all my life, smelling the familiar roasted vegetables cooking in the same pans that I've had for Sundays spanning right back to my infancy, I feel like the world is about to explode.

"Do you need a hand?" my mum asks, leaning her head on the door. I try to ignore the fact that she's wearing an almost identical soft blue jumper-and-jeans combo to me, because I'd like to think my fashion style was born out of my good taste and not just an imitation of my mother. Sadly, given she too has freckles galore and her darker shade of red is only due to hair dye ironing out the whites she pretends not to have, I literally look a little like a younger version of her at the moment.

I shake my head. I think I'm likely to break down at one point, but with my mum there with me, I'll be in floods before I've even reached the first bookcase.

"Call me if you need me."

Away she goes, saying her own silent goodbye to the room that she watched me grow up in and disappearing downstairs.

I know it's stupid. I haven't actually lived in this room since my last summer of university and that was over a decade ago. Not very many people in their late twenties still have rooms at their parents' homes, but if I'm honest, I never thought I'd have to say goodbye to mine. It's a time stamp of my history; it's a reminder of the happiness and love that a family brings; it's my home. Except, in a few months' time, it will be someone else's home.

I sit on the edge of my bed, not even knowing where to start. It's moments like this that I could seriously do with a real fairy godmother. Just someone to appear magically when I feel my most lost and make everything that little bit easier.

"You know, I always found that super creepy growing up, but I think I'm weirdly going to miss that castle."

The breath gets knocked out of me instantly. I look up to my door, completely surprised.

"Marty?"

I didn't even hear anyone rise up the stairs and yet there he is, leaning on my bedroom doorframe with his arms folded before him in his blue checkered shirt. The left side of his lips curls up in acknowledgment as he twists his head to survey the giant fairy-tale scene that backdrops half my wall.

"I thought you said you weren't home this weekend?" I ask, unable to hide the smile on my face. I couldn't be more grateful to have a friend right now. "Aren't you on call?"

"I'm on backup duty," he says, shrugging his shoulders. "I'm only on call if the vet actually on call gets called away. It's pretty rare."

"And you came up to see me?" I say sweetly, batting my eyelids for comic effect. Marty laughs but doesn't take the bait.

"My mum called. I haven't been up here in a while so I thought I'd visit."

"Doesn't she call like, every day?"

It's true. I've never seen someone speak to their mum as much as Marty speaks to Niamh. Marty shrugs his shoulders uncaringly, but I can see his cheeks flush just a little.

"You totally came to see me," I say smugly.

"My mum told me this place was getting sold. I figured you wouldn't be too happy about the whole thing and my mum wanted company. Two birds, one stone," he says, picking himself back up to standing and wandering a little deeper into my room. "How you doing anyway? Must feel strange, packing this all up."

He leafs through a couple of the books on my shelves, picking up the odd one before replacing it all over again. Harry Potter, The Northern Lights trilogy: memories, each and every one of them. My eyes follow his as they glance around.

"I sort of feel a bit numb if I'm honest," I reply, leaning back against the bed frame. "I didn't think I'd ever have to do this."

"Thought you'd live in a princess room forever?" he says, smiling, but his tone's still pretty sympathetic.

"No," I reply quickly, my cheeks glowing red before I remember it's only Marty. "It's not like I even live here anymore. But, I don't know, I thought I'd always have a princess room *available* to me forever anyway."

"Yeah, I get it. It sucks when you don't have control over stuff like this," Marty replies, his voice softer than usual. In a funny way it calms me. Maybe he really is my fairy godfather.

Done with wandering about, he walks back a little closer and with a little twist he flops onto the bed beside me.

"Just think of it like this: maybe a new little boy or girl will move in next and look up at that wall every night, just like you did. Maybe it'll inspire them too."

He's lying flat and I'm still propped up against the headboard, but even from the corner of my eye I can see he looks up at me to see my reaction. My mind is suddenly filled with a vision of some other kid, curled up at night with a little headlight under the covers, looking up to that mural and dreaming about their future.

"I guess I never thought about it like that," I say finally, and a lovely feeling of calm takes over me.

We stare at it for some time in a happy silence.

"Or maybe they'll paint over it," I add quickly.

"Yeah, but that wouldn't be so bad though either. A nice blank canvas for someone to start over," Marty agrees thoughtfully, "plus it's probably better for them in the long run. You know that's a giant cock block, right?" I actually snort at that. I feel the phlegm expel out my nose but there's nothing I can do about it.

"I never thought about it like that either." I laugh. That brings me out of my own head a bit.

"You didn't? Well, what did guys even say when you brought them back?"

"I didn't ever bring men back here."

"What, like ever?" He sounds shocked.

"Nope."

"Not one guy?"

I raise an eyebrow at him, still giggling away.

"I was too busy looking for the one to actually sleep with anyone else. At least when I lived here that was the case."

"Jesus." Marty sighs, wiping a tear from his eye. "You missed out."

"Yeah, well, not all of us can be arseholes like you," I say, channeling my true Hermione Granger know-it-all voice as I chuckle through it. Maybe I'm inspired by my surroundings.

"Like me? What makes you think I'm an arsehole?"

"Oh, you know what I mean," I say quickly.

"No, go on," he insists.

For a second I think I've offended him, but he already looks pretty proud of the insult.

Still, I realize that I might have just been rude. I didn't mean to be rude, not to him—I mean, I call him an arsehole all the time, and it never occurred to me he might actually dislike the term.

As if sensing the mood might change he leans over and starts tickling me, and I scream out laughing as I grab a pillow for defense.

"Go on then!" he says, narrowly avoiding the purple pillowcase I try to throw at him. "Tell me! Why am I an arsehole?"

"I only mean," I say, wriggling free of his grip to cool down a little. I wipe the tears in my eyes as he backs off, letting me catch my breath. "You always have a different girl over every night and don't even think about it."

"Girls who know what the deal is and still want to come back with me. That's not being an arsehole. That's being a hero."

What a smug idiot. I don't worry about offending him now.

"Oh come on," I say, "every girl you sleep with is secretly hoping for more than that."

"No, *you* want more than that when *you* sleep with people. Don't project monogamy on all other women just because you're on the hunt for a husband."

"That's . . ." I stumble over my words. He's smiling up at me like he's already won the argument. My competitive streak takes over. "Okay, well, what about that girl from the other week? The one who you left in your room while you came back out and joined me in Brixton? You literally had a drink with me at the bar *and* made me a tea that night while she was just waiting for you all that time! That was a pretty golden arsehole move there."

He puts his hands behind his head happily, rearranging the pillow to get himself comfortable.

"She wasn't waiting, she was sleeping."

"I heard you have sex that night!"

"She *was* sleeping," he says, his eyes glimmering with pride as he continues: "she just woke up when I came back in the room and wanted another round."

"Ha! Well, you still left her! Ergo: arsehole."

"That's not even slightly what happened."

"Oh yeah?" I prompt.

"Yeah," he replies, mimicking my self-righteous tone.

"Enlighten me then."

"Alright, how about this: I got a text from a *certain idiot* telling me they found themselves alone, on a Saturday night, in the middle of a club in London, surrounded by drunk men probably who I can't vouch for, hammered and for some bizarre reason, with no shoes on."

"I had one shoe!" I try badly. I'm laughing, but I can already feel the heat in my cheeks growing.

"So I told this girl—Gemma was her name—I told her what the situation was and that I needed to make sure you were safe and she agreed with me and *chose* to stay. I didn't ask her to wait, just like I didn't kick her out at three in the morning because *that* would have been the arsehole move. I gave her a choice, and she chose to stay in the nice warm bed she was already in."

Yeah, I mean, put like that . . .

"Fine, I'll give you that one," I say finally, a little embarrassed really. Marty stretches out in victory. "Although you're wrong too," I add weakly.

"Oh yeah?"

"I'm not on the hunt for a husband. Not anymore."

He peeks open his right eye.

"Does this have something to do with this fairy-tale sexcapade you've been on?"

"Sexcapade?! Only you would use that word." That makes me chuckle. "You know, I've had more success and more . . . more fun, I guess, in the last few weeks, than I have in over a decade of trying to find 'the one.' Turns out it's a lot less fun finding the fairy-tale ever after than it is looking for the . . ."

"Actual happy endings?" Marty tries with a half smile. That cracks me up all over again.

"I was going to say 'plot twists.'"

Marty closes his eye again happily.

"Well, good," he says. "It's time you started having a bit more fun in your life." What a funny old fairy godmother he makes. "Besides, you don't have to be an 'arsehole,' as you put it, to enjoy a healthy sex life."

"So you don't," I agree. "Alright, alright, I take it back. You're not an arsehole."

I sigh, my eyes still tracing the outline of the fairy-tale castle I'm about to say goodbye to. Weirdly, a different memory stirs.

"Although," I add, "what about the time you called Mr. Knot a gluttonous fuckface?"

"Ha!" he huffs. "Yeah, go on. I was being a proper arse to him. I don't know, I was just angry the whole time back then. I resented any man Stuart's age. Thought they were all scum."

That surprises me more than it should.

I'm not sure I've ever heard him speak about his dad. Not like that. So casually and calmly. I don't think I've ever even heard him refer to him by his real name before.

I go a bit silent, taking it in.

His dad really messed things up for the two of them, Ellie included. I mean, I've always known it in the back of my head, sure, but I guess knowing something and understanding something are two very different things.

I used to be so confused as to why she was never obsessed about walking down the aisle the way I was. I get it now, I think, or better at least. It must be hard to get excited about a big white wedding if the closest example she has of a grown-up relationship is Stuart up and leaving them all like they meant nothing to him.

I never had that. I had two parents who never made me feel like I wasn't good enough. I had two parents who loved me and loved each other. Who still love each other, I guess. Just in a different way.

No wonder Ellie never dreamed the things I dreamed. No wonder Marty's not big on commitment. One man's selfish decision forever shaping the lives of those he so thoughtlessly left behind.

A little beeping noise breaks through before I have the chance to say anything and Marty quickly reaches for the pager on his waistband.

"Oh shit. Cassie's just been called out on a home visit."

"You're needed back at work?"

"Someone should be in the practice. Just in case. Hey, I came to help and I did basically nothing. How about that?"

"You cheered me up. That's something."

"I'm basically amazing." He laughs, jumping up to his feet, ready to leave.

"Thanks, Marty," I say, genuinely touched that he even bothered to come. Even just having him here made me feel better.

He stops by the door, and I think he's about to make another joke, but instead he just nods.

"Anytime," he replies, "anytime."

14

Twenty minutes later I still haven't moved, and not a single bag has been packed when my phone buzzes. I dig it out from my pocket. For whatever reason I think it must be Ellie.

It just feels right to be Ellie.

The number of times I sat on my white fluffy rug and used all my free minutes to text her pointlessly, knowing that in an hour she'd probably be around anyway for dinner. Texting Ellie and being in this room is as natural to me as swimming and being in the ocean.

Except, right now I feel like I'm drowning.

No new messages. Not from Ellie, not from anyone.

I double-check. That was weird. Maybe I'm having phantom vibrations—so desperate to hear from her that I believe she must have texted.

I look back at the last ones she texted, just as I left hers last week.

The Elsa to my Anna-4 Oct 21:08

I get that you might need some time. Just please, please call as soon as you're ready to talk

The Elsa to my Anna-4 Oct 21:08

I'll be here whenever you're ready

The Elsa to my Anna-4 Oct 21:08

I love you

The Elsa to my Anna-4 Oct 21:08

xx

Something about what Marty said suddenly makes me think leaving it any longer just isn't worth it. My fight's not with Ellie, it's with Mark, and yet for some reason I'm punishing her for it with my silence. I don't want to be that person in her life who just leaves at the first sign of trouble.

So what if Mark and I don't get along? Our friendship shouldn't have to suffer for it. Maybe the vibration was trying to tell me something.

I begin to write a text out:

12 Oct 12:02-Me

I miss you. So much

Except I don't send it. Something stops me. Something physical. My phone vibrates again.

Weird. I close Ellie's messages but no one else has texted. That wasn't phantom. I felt that. My whole hand tingled and—no, just checked, but I'm not having a heart attack or a stroke.

Mirror Mirror has no new notifications, no surprise there. B-Reader doesn't either. I turned off notifications because I became way too nervous to keep checking in. Within forty minutes of "The True Rumpelstiltskin" being uploaded I'd already seen likes from over five thousand people. I quickly flick on it now. Bloody hell, my heart's hammering in my chest. It's had over 55,000 views alone just on that one, latest chapter.

It honestly doesn't feel real. In fact, it feels so unreal that I turn it off.

I'm back to Agatha Christie, twirling my mustache and working out the tale of the phantom vibration. I check all the other apps on my phone and come out empty. I check the vibrate settings—nothing.

Then I realize—it's the button I didn't even bother checking because I literally never check it. I have way too many unread emails to even try to look through them. Given I only really use it for online shopping there's no point in sifting through the rubbish unless I know I'm waiting for an ASOS delivery. I do now anyway, desperate for distraction and—there it is, there's the source of the palm twinge. It's *Time Out*'s marketing email telling me the ten most Instagrammable cafés in northwest London. Brilliant. That was worth the wasted five minutes of looking through my phone.

Although—now I'm on mail, I suddenly notice other emails from earlier this week I never bothered looking at.

One from *B-Reader Customer Relationship* from Friday.

That's interesting.

I click on it, hoping I haven't committed any violations that get me kicked out.

Dear B.Enchanted,

I hope you don't mind us reaching out to you directly.

We at B-Reader have been incredibly impressed with your journey on our site. We wanted to get in touch with you as we have recently been contacted by literary agency Hummingbird in regards to your latest entries. Although we would never send out the email address of any of our users, we often like to let our authors know when those in the publishing world reach out to us. You may well already have a literary agent, and if this is the case please do let us know so we do not contact you further on any matter like this.

If you would like us to pass on your email address to the agent at Hummingbird, or any other contact details, please let us know and we would be happy to put you in touch. If we don't hear from you we will assume you do not want them to contact you.

We look forward to your next chapters and hope you have enjoyed your experience with us.

Best wishes,
Freya Baxter
Author Relationship Manager
B-Reader

Oh my word. Oh my WORD. OH MY—

My heart's skipping. My world's spinning. This is everything I ever dreamed of. I mean, not quite, but this is the first step on a road that I've always dreamed of being on.

I reply back instantly.

Hi Freya,

Your email has made my day.
    Please go ahead and pass on my email address to the agent at Hummingbird. I very much look forward to hearing from them.

Best,
Bella

I sit there, in the middle of my room, staring at my phone like it might instantly vibrate again. I google "Hummingbird." It's small, but I recognize some of the authors from the shelves. We haven't published any of their clients but some of our more established competitors have. I look through all of the agents that are listed, trying to work out which one I think it might be.

I realize after what feels like half an hour that it's a Sunday. The email was sent on Friday. I assume this Freya Baxter probably works normal hours like everyone else in the world, so she's unlikely to be online on a Sunday at lunchtime. I'm so angry with myself for not seeing it earlier.

"How's it going up there?" my mum calls up the stairs. "Lunch is almost ready!"

I turn away from my phone and realize it's been way more than just half an hour. The room has still not been touched. I get to work instantly, no longer the sluggish bunny I was but now an efficient turtle that, slowly but steadily, begins the piles of Must Keep and Must Go.

I should be sadder. I should be more nostalgic. But I can't help but feel that in some way, one part of my life is coming to an end, but maybe, just maybe, the next door has just swung open.

❧ 15 ❧

"Bellabon!"

"Ms. Mathews?"

Standing, holding a nearly empty mug of tea by the kitchen table, is my old primary schoolteacher. She looks so much like Ellie, honestly. They're two peas in a pod, just with different coloring and a slightly different nose. Niamh Mathews has flawless skin. I know that's a weird thing to say but honestly it looks Photoshopped and it has been that way ever since I've known her. She's wearing a knitted cardigan like she always has, and some loose-fitting jeans unlike the black slacks she had to wear as my teacher.

"Why on earth do you still call me that?"

"Old habits? Sorry, Niamh—God! How lovely to see you!"

I give her the hug I've been so desperate to give Ellie. There's that familiar lavender scent filling my nostrils.

I realize I never texted Ellie in the end. I should do that now.

In fact, it's even better now. I can tell her all about how the fairy-tale adventure actually worked out for me after all. I mean, I don't need this to be a "fuck Mark" moment—I wanted to reach out even before I found out—but I'm not going to lie, that would be the cherry on top of an already beautiful cake. I can take the high road now and be all "I miss you. I want to see you. The fairy-tale book is actually a huge success and Mark was wrong—he can apologize whenever—but let's put it all behind us and pick up where we left off."

"I hope my son was actually helping you up there and not just causing mischief." Niamh laughs.

"Oh, Marty just left," I tell her.

"I know. Life of a vet! Always running around last minute."

"Are you staying for lunch?"

"No, no, I just came round for a quick cuppa. Wanted to make sure I caught you too before I left. Now, Marty tells me you're writing again?"

That boy speaks to his mother about just about everything.

"Yeah, I am," I say bashfully. "I've actually just been approached by an agent!"

"An agent? You didn't tell us that, Bells," my father pipes up from behind a steaming tray of vegetables that he's delivering to the table. Thank God he's wearing a gray check shirt or our family would have looked like a matching American Christmas card.

"It only just happened!" I reply, still in the afterglow of the whole event.

"Well! We can't wait to see your name on the shelves! My own student—a published author! What kind of book is it?"

Eeek. This is my old primary schoolteacher we're talking about. She's watched me grow up. It feels . . . no, I can't.

"It's just a story about a girl . . . finding love."

"Oh! A romance! I love a good romance!"

"Which agent?" my dad asks, wonderfully excited.

"What's this about an agent?" my mum adds, wandering into the room.

"Bells has gone and got herself an agent."

"An agent?! God, Bells! Why didn't you tell us?"

"I don't *have* an agent, I've been *approached*. And I only just found out!"

"That's amazing! Which one?"

"That's what I just asked," said my dad, excitedly.

"I'm not sure yet. I'll find out next week sometime. But anyway, it's early days. Yes, I'm writing." I turn to Ms. Mathews, who couldn't look prouder.

"God, seeing you guys all grown-up. It kills me, honestly!"

"I know exactly what you mean, Niamh," my mum sings while passing my dad a dishcloth to protect his hands from the oven.

It's a small gesture, I know, but weirdly as I watch it I feel a smile creep over my face. I mean, I've watched my mum pass my dad dishcloths for twenty-nine years now, so it's a pretty normal sight—but I guess that's exactly the point.

With the Mathews family, I mean, Jesus—they had to readjust to everything overnight. Stuart left without warning and Niamh was suddenly left with no one to pass dishcloths to her. Marty and Ellie had to learn how to be one parent down without any kind of transition period like I've been given.

I'm not saying I'm happy about any of this, I'm not, but put into perspective like that . . . this whole "parent separation" thing . . . it could be much worse.

My mum continues: "We have Marty, a qualified vet. You're about to be a published author. And Ellie of course doing the whole engagement thing in a month!"

"They're already engaged. I should know. I was there," I say, remembering my phone. Ellie! I was going to text Ellie! God, with her mum here I got a bit distracted but the universe is telling me to text her now. I can't ignore the universe.

"Oh, you know what I mean!" my mum replies.

"God, sorry, Niamh, we haven't RSVP'd yet," my dad says, placing the juicy beef roast on the kitchen counter.

"Oh, we have," my mum corrects him.

"Oh, you did it?"

"From both of us this morning."

"Oh, great," my dad replies.

"You need to RSVP?" I ask.

"Well, *you* probably don't, love," says Niamh confusingly "You're a given!"

"What's given?"

"That you'll be there."

"Be where?"

"Their engagement party."

"I still can't believe their dress code. It's the most Ellie-like thing I've ever heard," my mum says.

"Well, it is Halloween."

"I can't even remember what I wanted to be when I was young," my dad muses.

"I can. You wanted to be the Easter Bunny."

"Well, I'm hardly going to dress up like that, am I!"

What the hell is happening here?

"Engagement party?" To say I'm hiding the confusion and horror in my voice would just be an outright lie. "You mean, this Halloween? Three-weeks-away Halloween?"

There's an awkward silence in the kitchen. My parents are looking at each other, which I can see through the mirror hanging up behind the kitchen door. Niamh is nodding, unsure of what's going on. No one looks comfortable.

"But of course you know—I sent the evites out this morning! I would have thought you'd have been at her flat constantly to plan it! You guys always seem incapable of planning anything without each other," Niamh says, before she too realizes what's happened.

My phone's already tight in my palm so I click out of Ellie's last message and I hit the envelope to open my emails once again. I scan through, my eyes barely glancing at the B-Reader note as I filter through autumn sale alerts to find it.

Nothing.

I check my junk mail.

Still nothing.

"I sent it to everyone on Mark's list!"

"Mark made the list?"

"He's the one who sent it to me . . ." Niamh says, panicking herself as she's cross-checking on her phone. "Here it is, see?"

I grab it off her, ignoring how rude it is, and scan through the email address list sent to her from Mark's account.

I'm not there. I check it three times. My mum, yes. My dad, yes. But I'm not there.

I know Mark and I had a fight a week ago. I know we all said things. But my best friend is having an engagement party in twenty days' time and apparently her shithead of a fiancé has decided I no longer qualify as a "good enough friend" to go. Ellie Mathews is having a party, a big life-event party, and I, her best friend since infancy, the other half of her soul, am not even invited.

❧ 16 ❧

Niamh left pretty soon after, claiming it must just be a mistake, but I know Mark better than that. That's not a mistake. Not at all.

In the end, I needed help from both my mum and dad to speed up the packing process given that I did very little pre-lunch, and it was performed in near silence while I seethed in anger.

When I left, potentially waving goodbye to the very last meal all three of us would have under that roof, I hardly even looked back at the bright blue door of the house I grew up in. I was so furious, so ludicrously angry and pained that Mark could do this to me.

I was already on the train when my phone buzzed.

Missed Call: The Elsa to my Anna
2 Missed Calls: The Elsa to my Anna

There it is. Her first contact in seven days. A few hours ago I would have been ecstatic to hear from her, but now I know exactly why she's breaking the silence. Her mum must have told her.

Even if I wasn't hurt, even if I did pick up, the train might go through the tunnel and lose signal and I couldn't have that. I didn't want to make this worse than it already was. I needed time. So the third time Ellie tried calling I hung up. I didn't get another call to follow.

I did everything to distract myself. I went on Mirror Mirror and sent random messages to random matches. I scrolled through Instagram photo after Photoshopped photo of people leading better lives than I have and who, unlike me, probably all got invites to Ellie's engagement party. Eventually even that was making me sad, so I went back on the one app that was filling me with absolute joy: B-Reader.

There was comfort in that. Look at my amazing number of followers. Look how it's grown. Look at all these people who like me and respect me far more than Mark Fuckface Reynolds, who apparently deems his partner's oldest friend as "not worthy" of an evite. Fuck him.

I read through some of the thousands of comments:

>   @CatcherInTheLibrary
>   This is the best idea I've ever read!

>   @BookWormsUnited
>   Come on girl, you can find your Prince
>   Charming! #TeamDreamComeTrue

>   @CallieLDawson
>   Can't wait for more!

Can't wait for more.
Can't wait for more.
As I walk from Elephant & Castle train station to the tube, that's all that's in my mind. I need to keep my followers happy. I need some sort of a win. I need them to stay with me while my other friends, my oldest friends, are being pulled away from me. *Can't wait for more.*

I'll tell you who else can't wait for more. The first time I was sad I found my Smurf. The second I found my doctor. My Henry Pill interlude was empowering as fuck and now, more than ever before, I want to feel empowered. Who is going to shag this anger out of me? Who is going to ride me back to happiness?

Can't wait for more.

As the tube pulls up to Balham, I'm wondering which story I can try next. Which is the next fairy tale I can choose to embark on? I need something big. I need the next one to happen quickly. To happen tonight? Is that even possible?

Can't wait for more.

I walk down Balham High Road and turn off at my connecting road. Come on, I must be able to think of something. It's Sunday and despite my growing libido, I don't fancy going up to a total stranger again like I did Dr. Wide-eyes.

I must be able to find something. Mirror Mirror? There's no way I'll get someone to go out tonight with me on there. There are only three of them and I haven't talked to this batch long enough to even see their occupations.

What else?

Can't wait for more.

Can't wait for more.

As I turn the key to my flat I can hear voices floating up from the kitchen. I realize with a sudden pang that I haven't even seen Simon or Annie for a week. Simon's been at Diego's, Annie—well, God knows. She's been avoiding the Germans, that's all I know.

I stop instantly, my senses returning to me. What was I thinking? I don't need a man.

Maybe all I need is friendship.

I head into the kitchen, ready to pour out my heart and soul to my flatmates when, instead of Simon's adorable little dimples and Annie's strengthened glutes, I'm confronted with a very giggly half-exposed Hans and Gertie.

No comfort there then.

There is flour and icing sugar just about everywhere. Gertie is covered in it—more covered in white powder than she is clothing by the looks of things. Her rather interesting choice of top is more like a scarf than anything else, and precariously wrapped in a loop covering just about one of her nipples. She also has rather elaborate, stringy thong-based "shorts" on to bring together the whole ensemble. Hans is no better—both of his pecs are covered in baking powder and his tighty-whities are tight enough that they might as well not exist.

"Bella!" Hans says, as if this is a normal finding.

Oh God, he's high as a fucking kite. His pupils look like they're about to burst into the whites of his eyes' stratosphere. I turn to Gertie, who is piecing together what looks like a gingerbread monstrosity. If it was meant to be a house, it failed.

For a second I think I might blow. Just for a second I think I might unleash all my anger on them and scream but I don't. It's not their fault. Plus, I know it's weird, but I'm actually finding this whole thing pretty, what's the word . . . funny.

"Hello, Hans. Gertie," I say, looking around at all the mess that Simon would freak out about. My voice is strangely calm. Even I didn't expect that. "Are Annie and Simon around?"

"They're both out," Gertie replies, trying to poorly cement a roof onto one half of the structure. The domino effect of her failure causes a whole different section to slide apart and she laughs hysterically at it. I'm not really sure where to look.

"Annie left an hour ago. Simon's not been back for a while. Would you like some gingerbread house? It's filled with goodness," Hans adds, shaking a large, mostly empty bag in front of me with the remnants of greenery at the bottom.

"Wait—are these space cakes?"

"They're space *houses,*" Gertie corrects me. Her movement accidentally knocks a boob out of place and, without even the slightest bit of embarrassment, she shuffles it slowly back in.

I'm not being weird but their accents while they're high are actually comical. Maybe it's the anger bubbling out of me, but everything before me is somehow completely and utterly hilarious. I still can't believe they're trying to make a gingerbread house while high. I can't believe Hans and Gertie are building a gingerbread house.

Oh holy shit.

I've just found my next chapter.

"Can I . . . join you?" I ask.

Gertie turns to Hans and the two share a knowing glance. Gertie breaks off a piece of gingerbread from her painfully fragile architecture and walks over to me, all nineties erotica. As if I'd asked her explicitly, she places it delicately in my mouth. Fuck me, it's sensual. I've never had a carby treat fed to me in such a wildly erotic way. I'm angry, I'm excited, and I'm about to be very, very high.

I'm counting on that. I need all the green courage I can get.

"The more the merrier," Gertie whispers.

17

I'm still confused, still a little high, and am sore in places I didn't know I could ache from. Gertie and Hans. Jesus Christ. There was one point, somewhere in the middle of it all, where I couldn't work out which bits of my body were my body and which were actually Gertie's. It was strangely nice having her around. She was very—what's the word—supportive. She was there at all the right moments and not there at all the others. I've never gone that far with a girl before, but it felt very, very natural. Everything felt natural. I was more high than I'd ever been before and just about everything was making me giggle so it all felt very "one with nature" no matter which way you look at it.

Hans was a beast. He was moving in a way I didn't think humans could. He twisted and he thrusted like an absolute hero and my body was tingling regardless of whether he was in or out of me. Even high he was a stallion.

The clock strikes 1 p.m. and I realize I've not left my room in over six hours. Not to pee, not to eat, not even to get a little fresh air. I walked straight from their room to mine, and I haven't moved since. I'm wearing my penguin pajamas for comfort and the same blue jumper that went from smelling like my dad's beautiful roast to something a bit less identifiable that's still somehow making me hungry. I wonder if that's a bad thing, but then I remember that I have everything I need right in here. I have a laptop, the internet, and over 100,000 friends who all appreciate me much more than anyone else in the world outside.

"Following the Breadcrumbs" is already one of my highest-rated chapters and it only went online two hours ago, but then again having reread it I'm not surprised. Where I was a little prudish and held back in some of the others with some of the more detailed descriptions, for this little wander down fairy-tale lane I went all in. I must have still been high when I wrote it. Who am I kidding? I was completely high when I wrote it. In fact, at the end of the third paragraph I actually put my head down on the pillow, slept for three hours, woke up just after 4 a.m., and continued to write with the help of just a little more gingerbread house.

Given it's a Monday I rang the office this morning to tell them I was sick. I haven't pulled a sickie in about four years so I reckon I'm overdue one. Plus I had overslept my ten alarms. Plus, if I leave my room, I might bump into the wonder twins and, well, one night was . . . well, it was what it was, but I'm way too English and awkward to confront what happened, so I only have one thing left to do: avoid my flatmates for the rest of my life.

But it was worth it. Totally worth it, because look at those followers grow.

18

I double-checked that my email had been sent to the folks at B-Reader, but all Monday as I twiddled my thumbs and napped to more Attenborough, I kept checking my in-box and nothing.

> **The Elsa to my Anna-12 Oct 14:40**
> Please pick up

> **The Elsa to my Anna-12 Oct 14:40**
> Of course you're invited! My mum wasn't supposed
> to send out those invites!

I tried to ignore it, I did, but after a while I couldn't help myself. I feel anxious and weird, probably a hangover effect from the gingerbread, but still.

> 12 Oct 15:02-Me
> I saw the list Mark sent. I know I wasn't on it

> **The Elsa to my Anna-12 Oct 15:03**
> That's because he thought I was going to invite you
> face-to-face! Which of course I was!

> **The Elsa to my Anna-12 Oct 15:03**
> I was going to call you later. I really, really was

Really? Or is this a bad excuse for his actions?

> **The Elsa to my Anna-12 Oct 15:03**
> You've got to believe me!

> **The Elsa to my Anna-12 Oct 15:03**
> Please pick up

The Elsa to my Anna-12 Oct 15:04
I'd love to talk xxx

How does she still not see him for what he is? How is she jus-
tifying him?

I don't even know how to talk to her after this. Sure, the leftover
weed in my system might be making me just a little more paranoid
than I should be about this, but it's also giving me a fuzzy sort of
clarity: Mark has, officially, ruled me out of their lives. He saw
Ellie and I weren't speaking—all because of an argument I had *with
him*, might I add—and he jumped at the chance to strike me out
completely.

I'm sure she'd love to discuss how Mark, the wonderful faultless
Mark, has decided hanging out with me isn't conducive to a healthy
lifestyle. I'm sure she'd love to hear how when I didn't follow her
wonder boy Mark's great advice and nunify myself, that my life fell
to tragedy.

Except it hasn't, my friend. I'm living life to the fullest. I'm living every day like it's my last. Sort of, at least. I mean, if today was
literally my last day, I've spent 90 percent of it in bed desperate to
pee and seriously considering what vessel I could use as a chamber
pot. Not that this would be the worst last day, but this is the hangover to a better last day, you know?

❧ 19 ❧

After my third nap of the day at precisely 5:56 p.m., I wake up to the best email ever.

Hi Bella,

So lovely to be in touch.

We got your email from one of the members of B-Reader, who mentioned that you knew we'd drop you a line. As you might know already, we've read your chapters and we think there's something really promising here.

Why don't we meet up for a chat? It would be great to see where you think this novel's heading, and any other ideas you've had.

Looking forward to hearing from you.

Best wishes,
Becky Hamill
Hummingbird Literary Agent

I google her immediately. She's a new agent. She was an agent's assistant after leaving Nottingham University with an English degree, and a few years ago made the transition to take on her own clients. She even has an assistant by the looks of things—who she's

CC'd into this email too: ConnerDash@HummingbirdLiterary.com. An agent with their own assistant? I know that's such a small detail but it makes me know she's legit. She's winning at life. She has everything she needs. And she's interested in me.

She looks friendly in her picture. She's wearing a woolen jumper and a long pleated skirt, her dark hair is short and spiky and her face is warm and round. She's also got a dog on her lap, as every literary agent should. One of those lady dogs from *Lady and the Tramp*.

I love her instantly.

I stop myself from replying immediately.

I must not sound too keen.

I must not be too keen.

After an hour I justify that enough time has passed.

Hi Becky,

  Sounds great!

No, too enthusiastic.

Hi Becky,

  That sounds lovely.

No exclamation mark, which is better, but I sound a bit, I don't know, dated.

Hi Becky,

That sounds great.
  Let me know a few dates that work for you and I'll see what I can make work.

Looking forward to meeting you,
Bella

I hover over the send button with a little butterfly telling me to rewrite it again but just when I think I will, I pull myself together. That's everything I need to say. The time has come, so I press down on the button and just like that I can hear the familiar swoop of my email floating out of my screen and into Becky's.

I sit, staring, waiting for my in-box to ping all over again. Nothing. I look away from the screen in case it's my eyes that jinx it. I look back at the screen. Nothing.

I look at the clock.

7:02 p.m.

Ah, yes, that might have something to do with it. I google the business hours of Hummingbird Literary Agency: 6 p.m. close. Damn.

I reread Becky's email again and, with a dramatic flair, I throw myself back on the bed in gleeful happiness. A literary agent, emailing me. And not because they want to check up on the arrival of one of the clients to my place of work—because I could *be* one of their clients.

I could be a writer. An actual, real, writer.

My head swims around with her one little line: *It would be great to see where you think this novel's heading.*

Wait. Where it's heading? She probably wants a chapter-by-chapter summary—a list of all the men in all the fairy tales outlined.

I sit up, just as dramatically and the blood instantly rushes to my head in a wave that sends me back. What next? I don't have anything else planned. I don't have anything in the pipeline.

So where to begin, Becky? Where to begin.

❧ 20 ❧

12 Oct 23:02-Me
You staying with Rachel this week?

12 Oct 23:02-Me
Does she have 10 friends?

Annie Flatmate-13 Oct 05:59
Maya's at the moment

Annie Flatmate-13 Oct 05:59
10 friends?

Annie Flatmate-13 Oct 06:01
How's the house?

Annie Flatmate-13 Oct 06:01
Is our kitchen ruined forever?

13 Oct 09:02-Me
Depends. In some ways it's become more useful

13 Oct 09:02-Me
If you run out of flour I don't think they'll mind you
using some that's stuck to the walls

Annie Flatmate-13 Oct 09:03
I can't deal with that right now

13 Oct 09:03-Me
You going out with the girls at all this week?

Annie Flatmate-13 Oct 09:05
Which girls?

13 Oct 09:06-Me

Any girls. 12 of them total would be ideal

Annie Flatmate-13 Oct 09:06

I don't even know 12 girls

I switch over.

13 Oct 09:06-Me

Do you think 12 Dancing Princesses is too obscure?

Marty-13 Oct 09:06

As what?

13 Oct 09:06-Me

As a fairy tale you tit

Marty-13 Oct 09:06

Never heard of it

13 Oct 09:06-Me

Barbie once did a film of it

Marty-13 Oct 09:06

Yes, and I watched all Barbie movies

Marty-13 Oct 09:06

?!?

Marty-13 Oct 09:06

Know your fucking audience

13 Oct 09:07-Me

Know your fucking fairy tales!

13 Oct 09:07-Me

Google it

Another text rears its ugly head.

The Elsa to my Anna-13 Oct 09:08

I just read your last chapter on B-Reader

The Elsa to my Anna-13 Oct 09:08

I thought it was amazing. Really funny, really warm

The Elsa to my Anna-13 Oct 09:08

No wonder it's so popular

The Elsa to my Anna-13 Oct 09:08

I really am proud of you

The Elsa to my Anna-13 Oct 09:09

Please call me when you have a second x

I don't have the headspace for this right now. Something great's just happened to me, and I don't want to be weighed down by some flimsy excuse she has to cover Mark's back. No, thank you. I switch it back over as Annie's text saves the day.

Annie Flatmate-13 Oct 09:10

Actually, I'll tell you exactly where there are 12 girls

Annie Flatmate-13 Oct 09:10

You free Thursday night?

13 Oct 09:10-Me

If you find me 12 girls in one location, I'll see you there

❧ 21 ❧

Fuck her.

I mean, I actually like her, but of course it was never going to be the night out I was hoping for. It's 7 p.m. on a Wednesday night and Annie's on a detox. I could have guessed it, but I had more faith, and so here I am, standing outside Dancercise with ten other women and one man (close enough) who all look about a quarter of my size.

The instructor comes in, all cheery and hair tie and "this is only going to hurt for a second," and regret sinks in pretty hard.

"And slide to the left!" screams the General, a woman perhaps half my age who apparently has the correct qualifications needed to boss me around and make me want to cry constantly. I hop awkwardly to the right, because I'm slightly uncoordinated and at this point, I'm so delirious I think just doing one action, no matter what action, might be enough to stop her shouting. My eyes are blurry with sweat and tears as I collide with the poor girl on my right. She bounces back quicker than I do.

"And hop to the right!" Screamy McScreamerson screams. I hop-jump in one direction and then spin in another when I see someone else doing it and assume I can too. Turns out I can't. Turns out spinning in a circle is something reserved only for the most dainty of those among us for instead of twirling, I'm galumphing toward a wall. When the darkness, as it inevitably does, comes for me, I accept it with open arms.

✤ 22 ✤

My eyes are blurry, still darkened at the edges, but the face that hovers before me is a beautiful image to behold. Suspended above me, eyebrows curved to concern and smelling far sweeter than his surroundings, is a man touched by the gods themselves. He's all Idris Elba meets Musclemania and I can feel my whole body shake in anticipation.

My eyes peel back into reality. The dreamy white light that surrounds him is just the harsh, luminous glow from the dance studio. I'm exactly where I fell.

For a hot second I'm mortified. Hot because I'm still a sweaty mess, mortified because here is a good-looking man with big brown eyes blinking at me, and I'm still feeling like the whole world is spinning sideways. I can hear how strained my breathing is. How long have I been out?

"Careful now, don't sit up too quick," he tells me in a voice silkier than silk, and I feel myself melt.

Wait—this is it. This is exactly what I was hoping for: my savior come to save me; my knight for the night. My next chapter is already forming.

This beautiful stranger is the same man who was in the room with us twelve dancing princesses. It's the only man I even had a shot at to make this work and even though I've made a total buffoon of myself here he still is, coming to my rescue.

Fucking bull's-eye.

"How are you feeling?"

Oh, this wonderful man cares about my feelings. He cares about me. That bodes well for what's about to happen next.

"My hero," I flirt shamelessly.

"No, just Bill, I'm afraid."

This whole sleeping-through-the-fairy-tales thing is proving itself to be far too easy! I never realized how simple it was finding men to sleep with.

I turn to look behind him. Most of the girls are leaving already; others are putting their shoes on. A few of them even look like they've had time to shower. Annie's missing, but then again she was never one to linger. All the better for this fantasy to play out. This is just perfection—I couldn't have written it better if I tried.

"Hi, Bill," I say, trying to sound all coy and sweet.

"How are you feeling?" he asks again.

"I'd feel better with a drink in my hand."

"You want some water?" he says, turning to reach for his own bottle. What a true gentleman.

"No, no . . . a drink drink."

"Oh," he says, laughing. There's a literal twinkle in his eye. It flashes back at me as he smiles.

"Fancy joining me for one?" I half smile, lifting myself up to his level so we're eye to eye.

"For a drink?"

"For a very strong drink. I could do with the company."

My hand finds its way to his knee. I blink my eyes up at him. This is too easy. Way, way too easy. I'm good at this. He smiles at me, all charming and wonderful. Oh, tonight's going to be fun.

I can see the title already forming:

Twelve Dancing Princesses and He Picks Me

"So? How about it?" I ask.

"No."

Did I mishear him?

"No?"

"No. I can't."

I feel a stone hit right in my gut and it's all I can do not to fall right back down again.

Oh holy shit.

He's rejecting me.

"Y-you can't?" I stutter back like a total idiot. I want the ground to swallow me whole and never spit me back out again.

"Sorry—I just—"

"No, no, it's . . . no, it's cool, I . . . I meant just a . . . it's fine."

"How is she?" says a girl hovering in the background. It's the instructor. Oh God, this is only going to get worse. "How are you, hon?"

"I'm fine, I'm fine."

"No headache at all?"

"No, I'm fine," I swear. She kneels down, her sergeant face now filled with concern. All I want is for her to leave. All I want is for them both to leave.

"You're sure? There's nothing I can get for you?"

I don't know how many more times I have to tell them before they leave but finally they stand up.

"Ready then?" she asks him, her hand on the small of his back.

That's weird. Or is it? I look between them, a little confused before it suddenly hits me—oh shit, Bill is the instructor's boyfriend. I just asked out the instructor's boyfriend.

Well, isn't that just peachy. It makes sense. Beautiful, incredibly fit man, beautiful female dictator; they match up perfectly, I'm sure. There goes my chance for a fairy-tale night to remember. What a waste of physical exercise.

"Coming," he replies, and then turns back to me with his big brown eyes. "You really going to be alright?"

I nod, like a brave little girl at the doctor, and he smiles a tragically good-looking smile back.

"Get home safe," he says sweetly, as he follows the woman who just spent an hour traumatizing me out the door.

He leaves me there, broken and flustered on the floor, wishing I could rewind time. I can see my bright red cheeks glowing out at me from all angles like a neon light in the surrounding mirrors of the dance hall. A full 360 degrees of the ruby-red sweaty disaster that is me. I look like Elmo.

I close my eyes, hoping they never open again. What on earth did I do that for? Why did I set myself up for that? What was I thinking?

I can't tell what's sorer: my thighs or my ego.

23

"It's a whirlwind! Every time I think I can guess what might happen, it's like the whole story twists in another direction! I mean, 'Following the Breadcrumbs'—where did that even come from?!"

After the Dancercise disaster, this meeting has certainly cheered me back up again.

I laugh loudly, throwing my head back and almost spilling my drink.

I love her.

I love her I love her I love her I love her.

She smells like fresh daisies, and although she's my age—maybe even a little younger—she has this worldly wonder about her like she's an expert in everything. I hang on to her every word, sipping the tea she bought me and wondering what I have ever done in life to deserve this £2.30 brew with the amazing Becky Hamill of Hummingbird Literary Agency fame.

She's taller than I imagined and her hair's grown a little longer since the website photo was taken. Her dark bob now sits just above her shoulders like a French princess with her fringe pinned back by a hair clip to signify that she means business.

She's wearing a bright yellow dress, which is daring for mid-October, but despite the sporadic cold showers outside she makes it feel like spring. The place she's taken me is cozy, the kind of place built for writers and pastry lovers alike and now, at 4 p.m. on Friday, it's filled with the incredible Becky Hamill and little old me.

"So, what next?" she asks.

I have never been so prepared for a question in all my life. I outline the next chapter nice and clearly. I'm watching her face more than I'm even hearing my own words.

"We're talking right in the middle of the dance floor, his naked thrusting bottom reflected in all three-hundred-and-sixty-degrees of mirrors."

Okay, fine, so I gave fake me a happy ending. The story wasn't a story otherwise, and I didn't have enough time to even find another man in the meantime to make up for it. I say "time," what I really mean is that that one "no" has knocked my confidence no end, and I couldn't face another rejection before this meeting. I couldn't be in a bad place for it, so I took what I had and I made it a perfect success story. Dancercize meets *Fifty Shades*. Five chapters for five successful one-night stands.

I notice the glint in her eye fade just a little. She looks, what's the word for it, a little . . . disappointed.

"What's . . . you don't like it?"

She can smell a lie. I know she can. Oh God, why did I even try to lie to her? She can see right through me!

"No, no! I do, I'm sure you'll make it brilliant on paper, it's just . . ." She looks hesitant. I lean forward, trying not to react too obviously, but I'm so nervous I'm shaking. "Do you mind?"

Yes, I really mind. I've fucked it. I've lied to her and now I've messed everything up.

"No, no, fire away!"

"Well, it's just, a bit tame compared with the last one, you know? I mean, you've already ramped it up bit by bit already. It almost feels like you need to push the protagonist even further down this road, you know? Really explore just how far she'll go."

Okay, well, not quite what I was expecting. Tame?

Oh God, she's right. It was tame. What I just described to

her was incredibly PG-13 when Smurfing a bathroom and riding two different forms of German-originated thighs has much higher stakes. I'm running out of ideas.

Well, of course it was tame—it didn't actually happen at all. This is what happens when I don't have actual truth to write down. Tame is what happens when I don't have real-life experience to back it up with. My imagination is boring and "tame."

I nod, feeling like I've just ruined everything. This was my one chance for an agent. This was my first little taste of success, and it's fading away into nothingness because I didn't have a wilder night. Because I didn't have an *actual* "night" at all.

Becky checks her watch and makes one of those "where's the time gone" comments that I don't fully listen to because I'm already in a confusion spiral.

"So what next? What's the next stage?" I ask, trying not to sound desperate.

"Well," says Becky sweetly, "as you can imagine the run-up to Christmas is always a little busy over in publishing, but why don't we check in again just after the New Year? We'll keep an eye out for new passages, of course, but if your subscribers keep growing at the same rate I think something really exciting could come of this."

"Of course," I repeat absentmindedly, trying not to hide my disappointment. Whatever words came out her mouth, it wasn't: "Let me represent you." It was more like: "I'm interested, but your ideas aren't good enough to sign you now."

"Well, I have good plans on how I can really push the whole thing further, I can promise you," I say quickly, trying to sound enthusiastic.

"Oh, I very much look forward to that then!" she says, collecting her things and leading me out of the nice café.

"Keep your eyes peeled."

She turns at the door, her yellow dress sashaying behind her as she reaches out a hand and takes mine. She's so professional. I love her. I really, really love her.

As I say my goodbyes and begin to back away, I try not to look as sad as I am. I feel my phone vibrate and I look down to my screen only to see—surprise, surprise, *The Elsa to my Anna* is calling again. I would pick up, I would, only I need to work out exactly what I'm going to say in order for her to realize the truth: that Mark is just not the man she thinks he is. Until I have that, any conversation we have will just make me sadder. I'm already feeling defeated. I can't deal with Ellie right now too.

"Oh, Bella?"

I turn, dropping my phone into the depths of my handbag as soon as I hear Becky's sweet voice.

"You know, you really aren't what I expected," she says, blocking my fast exit.

"Oh no?"

"Not at all really. You are so lovely and warm and happy and your protagonist, well, she's a piece of work, isn't she!" She looks me up and down in a nice, comforting way and I feel instantly so much better. I smile genuinely at her this time as she finishes off her thought. "It's funny what assumptions we make about an author based on their body of work. I love a writer who can put herself in someone else's shoes as competently as you can. It shows real talent, you know?"

Real talent.

That's what she said. That's what I have, only little does she know I only seem to have it when an experience is actually authentic.

And my God, this meeting has made me realize how much I want this. My first real taste of being an actual author. It's a dream come true—or one of them at least. I can't just let this slip through my fingers. I just can't.

So I guess there's only one thing for it: I need to find me some plot twists, ASAP.

❧ PART 4 ❧

1

My adventures are off to a flying start. I've never been so determined for anything, because if I can impress Becky Hamill, my dream career is waiting for me.

Plus, and I know this is petty, but I figured out while watching *Lilo & Stitch* over the weekend (I tried to find a story there for me to copy but failed) that if this works out then I can go shove a big fat I TOLD YOU SO straight into Mark's stupidly forgettable face (perhaps it was the ugly mad scientist monster that brought him to my mind). I can go back to them with my head held high. I can prove he was wrong about everything and Ellie—instead of making excuses for him—will be forced to see what I already see clearly: that he's had it out for me from the start.

He's never liked me, I've always known that, but now Ellie will see that too. No longer will she pick him over me. No longer will she blindly side with him. She'll see my success and be back by my side faster than lightning can strike.

I decide to hang back on the Dancercise princesses, because I want to show Becky I can take notes and I haven't been able to make up a new angle for it. If she needs something truthful, then I'm going to give her something truthful. I'll deliver her and my 332,078 (and growing!) other followers some good old-fashioned X-rated fairy-tale truth on a platter.

And so it is that I find myself hanging out après work on Monday evening outside a bar close to Buckingham Palace. It's arguably the biggest tourist trap in the capital, and I've already found three potential candidates lined up and ready. I sip on a large glass of Merlot and catch eyes with all three: red shirt, white shirt, blue shirt.

Red shirt doesn't keep my eye contact for long. I'll come back to him. White shirt smiles back at me but then a female nearby notices and smacks him one. Not white shirt. Blue shirt seems interested, that could be promising. He's with a large group of other men at what might be a bachelor party, but I hold him for one second—no, red shirt has already left the building. Blue shirt it is.

After fifteen or so minutes of blinking hard and smiling coyly, blue shirt fast approaches. The closer he gets, the more I realize quite how perfect he is. He's bigger than your average human, in nearly all dimensions but less in a rugby boy way and more in a "likes donuts" fashion. I don't blame him. They're delish. He's not terrible looking by any means, but a little out of proportion perhaps. His hair's a bit patchy and as he opens his mouth, I can see there's a tooth missing near the back. I just need one more thing. Just one more.

"Excuuse my Eenglish, but can I buy you a der-rink?"

There it was. That glorious French accent that I was looking for. The game is officially on.

The more we talk, the better I know it's going to be. He used to be a boxer, semi pro, but retired after a knee injury and now coaches for a living. He's visiting for one night and one night only (box absolutely ticked there). He's from—no, I mean it here—the very center of Paris. I can see the name forming in my mind already: "The Ex–Heavyweight Champion of Notre Dame."

Except when he said one night he really meant "one night." His flight is at midnight and given we met at 8 p.m. and he only told me the whole flight situation at 9 p.m., it only left us half an hour or so to find a location and get busy with it. I tell him he can anyway, sounding all sultry and strong, but he just laughs. I am way *way* too English to correct him, so I thank him for my drink and head off to re-plan topsy-turvy from the beginning, avoid the German pair, and have an early night.

I'm trying not to feel like this is a rejection. It was bad timing, that's all. Ignore it. Get over it. Shake it off.

On to the next.

❧ 2 ❦

On Tuesday I check my B-Reader account only to find I have 341,181 followers now.

341,181. I don't even know how to process that number. It makes me so happy, so incredibly proud, so validated.

341,181 people.

Although that's also another 341,181 people waiting for a chapter 6, of course, so I really better get a move on.

I do a quick Google search and inspiration comes almost immediately.

See, I've passed the same busker on three consecutive days on the journey back from work last week, and it looks like he's still there. He's just in the corner of Baker Street station by the Metropolitan line and despite not needing to walk that way, I do. With a collection of yummy mummies watching, he has pied piper vibes here, just a little less creepy and with a guitar. He's not bad either—a little rugged around the edges perhaps, with a shaggy beard and casual hoodie-jeans combo, but he's probably not far from thirty. And he sings like James Bay, which I love—smooth and silky.

I stop by him on the way back from work and I hover in the background. I stay for three songs because any more and I'd feel like a stalker. The first is some upbeat tune that my dad might listen to, not really the perfect vibe. He starts singing something more modern after that—sounds a bit T-Swifty to me but I can't place it. I don't know the tune but I'm nodding my head to the music and he catches my eye by the second chorus. He smiles, all charm as he returns his attention to his guitar. Good—that's a good sign. He thanks a young girl who puts a pound in his guitar case and he catches my eye again. Another smolder—this time I see it clearly. I smile back, this is really going great. The third song is his last for the day and, looking right into my eyes, he tells the small crowd it's a love song.

Yep. I'm in there. I quickly take out a scrap of paper from my bag, only to remember that's not something I just have in my bag. I dig deep in my pockets and find nothing more than gum. A little desperate, I shovel out the gum, ripping the paper around the outside. It's just about big enough for my eleven digits, and I write my number with my emergency black eyeliner. I hold it out, making sure it's just about readable. It's good enough.

As his song comes to a beautiful conclusion and the small crowd comes forward to drop in loose change, I drop in my number.

That's it, that's the deed done. I turn, all coy and sweet, and I begin to stroll away, making sure that my walk is extra sassy, but I hear a voice call out behind me. I turn and—yes, that's right, it's him. Even better. I thought it might have been a setup for another night but if he wants to get started right now I'm very game.

He approaches me quickly, abandoning his case for a minute. He holds my number in the palm of his hand.

"Yes?" I ask, blinking.

"Don't throw litter in my case. I'm working here."

Oh God, is he . . . serious?

"No, it's not litter it's my—"

"I don't mind it when people watch and don't cough up a couple quid at the end, that's life. But don't just toss in rubbish. It's disrespectful."

"No, no, it's—"

"Just take it and find a proper bin, okay?"

I gulp, wordless. He's being completely serious and pretty loud. A few of the parents are nodding to their children, all of them tutting their heads at me. Oh my God, I feel like I'm back in school again. I feel incredibly awkward and I need to go.

"Sorry," I mumble. I turn and I flee, knowing I can never come back.

I spend the rest of my route home wondering why the hell I didn't point out more clearly my number was on it. Maybe then things would be different. Maybe we would have laughed together: he'd have apologized and I'd have been all up in his pied piper right now instead of where I am, sitting on a crowded tube trying desperately not to catch anyone's eye.

But I didn't. I didn't say anything, because apparently I was channeling my dad's hatred for confrontation and I froze. So I'll never know what could have happened there.

Confidence—that's what I need more of, and that's just a mindset. I can do that. I can definitely do that.

My determination comes back to me instantly, ready to fire me up again.

As a side note, I also need to find a new route into work now.

3

I wake up on Wednesday feeling so much stronger already. I shrug off any bad energy I'm holding on to and I'm ready for whatever adventure this new day brings.

It's perfect timing, of course, as on a lunchtime walk I pass by an indie clothing store that has a frog logo on half their clothing. That's close enough for some kind of story, I reckon. Maybe I can do the whole "kiss a frog" thing after all.

Just as I pass through the door I feel my phone buzz with a call. Thinking it might be Becky Hamill I rush to it quickly, but no: *The Elsa to my Anna.*

I bite my lip, wondering if I should pick up anyway. I literally haven't spoken to her in so long I can barely remember what her voice sounds like. And I know her, she's a worrier and this is exactly the kind of thing she'll be fretting over.

But in some ways, I want her to fret over it. I want her to know what Mark's doing, ruling me out of her life like this. What it might be like if he got his own way. Maybe then she'd realize how toxic he really is.

Mind, maybe I should tell her that's what I'm doing, just so she knows, you know?

I look up, torn, when that frog logo catches my eye again.

No, I can't pick up now. I need to catch me a frog, so I can prove to her just how right I am and just how wrong Mark is. I can call her after that.

With a power akin to a superhero's I walk over to the cashier's desk and I ask out the only guy working there. His name is Carl and he too wears a polo neck with a little frog on it.

"No, thanks," he says quickly.

He doesn't have a girlfriend or anything. He just doesn't want to. Oh God.

As I leave the shop I know I can't call Ellie yet. I just need one win first, then I will.

Sure, that stung a little, but I can't let it pull me down. I'm a strong, confident woman and the next chapter's out there somewhere waiting for me, I just need to find it first.

4

Right. It's time I changed this all around. It's time that I turn these no's into yes, yes, yes. No more feeling sorry for myself and no more bruised ego. Come on, woman, I tell myself. Let's live the fairy tale.

On Thursday I head to the hairdresser's and spend £95 on extensions. I've never had hair as long as this. I always cut it when it becomes even slightly annoying to maintain, and as it trails right down to my bottom, I can tell already that this will be a nightmare. But it's alright—it's expensive, yes, but if it makes its way into the book it may be paid back to me as an expense or—at the very least—tax-deductible. I keep the receipt just in case.

I walk straight out, salon ready, long hair flowing, and head directly to the Shard, the tallest building in the city, with its open view of London. It's a tower if ever I saw one, and about as close to Rapunzel's as I'm going to get. Now I just need to find myself a prince.

The bar on the thirty-third floor is full, which is good. Full means more chances, and I need as many chances as I can get by the way things are going. I order an extortionately priced drink and sit on a barstool that becomes available. I look around, trying to catch someone's eye and playing with my long, long hair, trying desperately not to reach into my pocket and just start playing with my phone like I normally do when I'm alone. The view is actually annoyingly far away and I don't want to give up my barstool, so gazing out dreamily into the London vista isn't really an option. Needless to say, my phone ban doesn't last long. Within twenty minutes I'm on my phone, no eye contact returned, and after two solo drinks and no more action than a glance from a creepy man in a polo neck I decide it's not happening.

I throw out the receipt for the hair extensions in a bin outside. Well, that's £95 for nothing.

5

It's the weekend and I've had too many rejections to even count them. I never knew I could feel so shitty about myself. I never needed a man to validate me, but I've somehow found myself asking men to validate me, and coming out wanting.

Home alone, I open up a bottle to celebrate my failure and misery and, with no one to share it or (more accurately) judge me, it goes pretty quickly. I open another because it's there and (as before) no one is around to stop me or comment.

I wonder once again about calling Ellie. That stupid engagement party is in a week now and we still haven't talked about it. Maybe I should just forgive her and move on already, maybe that's what will make me feel better about this week, putting this shitty Mark crap behind us.

Except as I take out my phone I feel it immediately slip through my fingers, crash landing on the table below me. Thank God for solid phone cases, I think, cursing my slippery fingers until I remember that slippery fingers are one of the more obvious signs that sobriety has already left me.

No, I can't talk to Ellie. Not while I'm like this. I'll be overly emotional and dramatic and even I don't trust what I'll end up saying.

So instead I text Simon. He's the only one left I might be able to hope for.

25 Oct 17:30-Me
You coming home tonight?

Sexy Simon-25 Oct 18:16
House party

25 Oct 18:16-Me
Can I join you?

Sexy Simon-25 Oct 18:17
It's one of Diego's friends. Not sure it's cool to invite
extra

25 Oct 18:17-Me
I'm not a stranger!
25 Oct 18:18-Me
Oh please can I join?
25 Oct 18:18-Me
Please
25 Oct 18:20-Me
Please
25 Oct 18:25-Me
Please
25 Oct 18:30-Me
Please
25 Oct 18:34-Me
Please

Sexy Simon-25 Oct 18:35
I'll send you my location

✫ 6 ✫

I wake up in my own bed with a sour taste in my mouth. I have literally no idea how I got here. Like none at all. Did I dream the party?

I see a note taped to the back of my door. Oh God, this isn't a good sign. It's Simon's serious handwriting. It's all sharp letters and very clear punctuation. He was angry when he wrote this, I can tell. It's the same handwriting that was so often found on passive-aggressive notes stuck to dirty plates or left spillages during the Simon/Katie house fight before Annie moved in.

Maybe I'm wrong. I'm probably wrong. Please let me be wrong.

JESUS CHRIST, BELLA, WHAT'S WRONG WITH YOU AT THE MOMENT? I'VE NEVER SEEN YOU LIKE THAT BEFORE!

Oh God. I wasn't wrong. He is angry. What did I do? I can't remember . . . it all just feels like a surreal blur. I keep reading.

YOU SMASHED A CHAIR WHILE TRYING TO DEMON-STRATE SOME SORT OF RAPUNZEL THING . . .

Oh God. I did, didn't I? I'd half-forgotten I did that. The bruise on my left bum cheek reminds me of the very real memory and red shame plants itself all over my face.

THEY'RE LETTING YOU OFF FOR THAT ONE, BUT
THEY SAY THEY'RE GOING TO SEND DIEGO THE CLEANING
BILL FOR THE RED WINE STAINS ON THE SOFA.

Oh shit. Yes, I vaguely recall that too. Where did I even get red wine from? I was on white before I left.

YOU JUST STARTED MINESWEEPING EVERYONE'S
DRINKS, SOMETIMES EVEN OUT OF THEIR HANDS . . .

Ah, yes. That's where I got it from.

. . . AND YOU ENDED UP THROWING UP IN NOT ONLY
ONE BUT TWO OF THE BEDROOMS BEFORE I COULD GET
YOU INTO A TAXI HOME.
GET HELP. GET SOMETHING. I JUST CAN'T BE
AROUND YOU LIKE THAT. DIEGO SAYS IT'S FINE, BUT
IT'S NOT. I WAS TRYING TO MAKE A GOOD IMPRESSION
AND YOU'VE BLOWN IT FOR ME.

Guilt peels over me like a slowly sliced apple skin. What did I do? I close my eyes briefly and a wave of nausea runs through me. Quick-fire mental snapshots of the night's events pound my head one by one like a slap in the face.

I open my eyes quickly to get rid of them, no longer sure if the sickness I feel is because of the leftover alcohol or just pure regret. Probably both.

TEXT ME TO LET ME KNOW YOU'RE ALIVE. I DON'T
KNOW IF I'LL TEXT BACK. STAYING WITH DIEGO FOR THE
FORESEEABLE FUTURE.
SIMON.
P.S. WHAT HAPPENED TO OUR KITCHEN WHILE I'VE
BEEN GONE? IT LOOKS LIKE A WINTER WONDERLAND?!
SERIOUSLY?

Technically the kitchen isn't actually me. That's still Hans and Gertie's baking leftovers but that's not even slightly worth correcting right now.

Last night was a complete disaster, right off the Richter scale, to end an already disastrous week. At least my midweek rejections only hurt me. Now I've somehow dragged Simon down with me. Simon. Sweet Simon. Generous, wonderful Simon.

I make a grab for my phone instantly.

> 25 Oct 10:23-Me
> I am SO SORRY
> 25 Oct 10:23-Me
> So completely sorry
> 25 Oct 10:23-Me
> So utterly and horribly sorry
> 25 Oct 10:23-Me
> I don't know why I did that
> 25 Oct 10:23-Me
> I don't know why I've done any of this
> 25 Oct 10:23-Me
> I think I'm just lost and confused and I was acting out and I NEVER wanted to hurt you in all this
> 25 Oct 10:24-Me
> I just didn't
> 25 Oct 10:24-Me
> Let me know how much it all cost—I'll pay it back immediately. I promise
> 25 Oct 10:24-Me
> I'm just so so so sorry xxxxxxx

I stare at my phone and all those little ticks beside my messages double tick within seconds. He's read it then.

I even see the three little dots appear showing me he's texting me back. I feel sick but I stand my ground, bracing myself for impact.

And then those three little dots disappear.

And no text comes through.

That's so much worse than an angry text. I feel the burn through every vein and artery in my body like quick-drying cement.

I think I got it in my head that I was trying for some sort of Goldilocks angle maybe, drinking drinks that don't belong to me, sleeping in their beds . . . but all I've done is just fuck up beyond repair, leaving me with no fairy tale, no happy ending, no dignity, and what's worse, no friends at all.

7

I literally don't know what to do with myself. I try calling Simon at one point, thinking hearing his voice—even if that voice is shouty and furious—might somehow make me feel better. But he doesn't pick up. He's not ready to talk to me.

It's fair enough, of course; I wouldn't be ready to talk to me. Not after what I did. I really fucked it. I really, really fucked it.

I pace around my silent, lonely room with only my thoughts for company and memories replaying in my mind—not just of last night but deeper. Darker.

Snapshots of the whole last week begin hitting me one by one. Every single rejection is played out in slow motion. Every failure is caught from every possible angle. Every friendship I put on the line without so much as a second thought.

What is wrong with me?

It's like I've been possessed recently. Like this folklore book and these unknown strangers who follow me became the only thing that mattered.

That's not right. That's not me.

I've always prided myself that I was a nice person, and yet overnight I've somehow become this selfish prick of a human, not caring who I've taken down in the process. All because of fucking, shitting fairy tales that didn't even come true.

When I think about it, when I properly think about it, there's no excuse for any of my actions since this whole book began: Simon—well, it's pretty obvious where I messed it up there, but it's not just him.

I basically guilted Marty into dropping his own plans and picking me up from the club the night I lost my shoe, and I don't even remember thanking him for it. He paid for the Uber, he let me stay the night, and I just stole his hoodie and a pair of his trainers the next day and left without a word. I didn't even think to say thanks, or return the clothes. I can still see them now, thrown unwashed into the corner of my room.

I fucked things up for Annie too, of course; I ruined her white dress without any form of an apology there. Plus when *I asked* her to take me to a place with twelve women—something she then did—I didn't just leave her unthanked, I bitched about it too. Like she didn't just do exactly what I asked to help me, because she was being a good friend.

And with Ellie.

Oh God, Ellie.

Without this book we'd still be speaking right now. We'd still be sending each other bad memes and TikTok videos. Mark and I wouldn't have exploded at a dinner party (one that I invited *myself to* I might add) and I'd not only be going to her engagement party next weekend, I'd have probably helped plan it with her, with or without Mark's approval.

Mark's a shithead, sure, but he's her shithead. And I didn't have to like him to support her. People hate their friends' partners all the time, that's normal, but you suck it up, you keep your mouth shut, and you stay there for them regardless. You don't scream at them across a small, beautifully decorated table after a delightful homemade pork roast dinner.

Except I got the slightest hint of success and I deemed it more important than the happiness of my own best friend.

I take out my phone, not really sure what to say until I've already hit send.

25 Oct 11:06-Me

> I'm sorry for ignoring your calls
> **25 Oct 11:06-Me**
> I'd give you my list of excuses but none of them
> make any sense, even to me
> **25 Oct 11:06-Me**
> I've just been all over the place at the moment

My phone rings immediately. I stare at her name as it vibrates away in my palm—*The Elsa to my Anna*—and my finger hovers over that accept button. Only I can feel the tears welling up inside me.

I can't actually pick up. I'll break on the phone and that's not fair.

To her, it's not fair.

> **25 Oct 11:08-Me**
> I can't talk right now

I lie.

> **25 Oct 11:08-Me**
> I just wanted to let you know that I hope you have a
> really fun night next weekend
> **25 Oct 11:09-Me**
> I really mean that

Her reply back seems instantaneous.

The Elsa to my Anna-25 Oct 11:10
Please, come to the party
The Elsa to my Anna-25 Oct 11:10
It was all this big misunderstanding, I swear. Of
course I want you there
The Elsa to my Anna-25 Oct 11:10
I can't imagine it without you

For what it's worth I don't think she's lying. I think she does want me there.

But Mark doesn't want me there.

If I go, Mark's sure to bring up something, some comment or . . . I don't know. I can't trust how I'll react, especially after my performance at Simon's party. I can't promise I won't get too drunk from nerves and cause a scene, screaming at him all over again.

So I think about it. For one long second I really, really think about it.

25 Oct 11:12-Me
No, I can't

I text, before quickly adding:

25 Oct 11:12-Me
It's just better for everyone if I don't go
25 Oct 11:12-Me
But that's alright
25 Oct 11:13-Me
It's your night
25 Oct 11:13-Me
We'll celebrate together another time
25 Oct 11:13-Me
And we'll catch up after
25 Oct 11:13-Me
Properly
25 Oct 11:13-Me
I love you xx

I can already see the dots of her replying to me but I quickly mute her WhatsApp and quit the app for safekeeping. She'll fight, because that's who she is, but I need to stay true: this isn't about me, it's about Mark and Ellie, and if Mark doesn't want me there, I shouldn't be there. I can let them have this one night, Bella-drama free. Simple as that.

Plus there's something else I need to do right now.

If this fairy-tale book is what got me into this mess, then it's time I found my way out. And I know exactly what I'm going to do.

8

I could have just left it, of course. It would have been easier to say nothing and let the chapters that exist be it for me without another word on the subject. Perhaps it would have been easier if I just deleted my B-Reader account altogether.

But the longer I sat, the more those memories kept circling and I knew I had to get them out of me.

Plus, all I've done is write about how great I am and how easy it is to sleep around when that's just not true. I've exhausted myself, I've humiliated myself, and I've brought down countless people with me.

I want that shame, I want all of that embarrassment to be out there for all to see. I want all those strangers to judge me, the same way I'm judging myself right now. Added to that I want to tie it all up neatly in a grand finale, a final moral to my story, a real ending.

So I walk over to the writing desk my wonderfully supportive parents gave me and as I so often do sitting at that table, I look up at the picture of them together.

I've been a shit to them too, of course. They're going through something, something huge, something that perhaps they even needed my support with, and instead of listening to them or asking them about how they feel about this life change, I've just acted like a spoiled little child who didn't get their own way.

So I write that.

I write all of it. In one unfiltered stream of consciousness I write about every single one of my failures, removing all of the gloss from my main protagonist and revealing her as the fraud she is. As the selfish prick she's become.

Within a few hours I have it all on paper, every single fuckup ready for the jury to start their judgment. Names are changed, of course, but that's it.

Finally I finish it all off with a chapter title:

Losing My Glass Slipper and Other Tragic Failures of a Modern-Day Princess

That's good. That sums it up alright.

I read through it once, and once only, before finally I hit send on my closing chapter, drawing an end to it all. With a little swoosh, it flies off, into the screens of 410,674 people who I no longer care about.

9

Then I delete the app.

I might want them to know what a terrible person I am, but I don't want to read their comments confirming it. I'm already feeling shitty enough about myself not to need others to make me feel shittier.

That's just the first step, of course. I know now the extent of the pain I've caused, and it's time I started doing something about it.

I head straight to the kitchen. Partly because my room was beginning to feel like a little prison cell, but also because I feel like I need to do something positive and there's something else I can do here, something practical.

I might not be able to apologize to Simon face-to-face yet, but I can make his life easier. He likes a clean kitchen, and at the moment, our kitchen is still a powdered paradise. Looks like Hans and Gertie haven't bothered to clean yet. Nor are they in to ask them to.

It doesn't matter if it wasn't my mess, it's a mess that affects him—that affects Annie too—and although I can't begin to make up for the issues I've caused them both, I can certainly do something about the one right in front of me.

I put on my rubber gloves, I fish out all the available cleaning products from under the sink, and I get to work.

Two hours later and the whole room sparkles. Honestly, I don't think it was even that clean when I moved in to Elmfield Road close to a decade ago. There is no hint of flour, no surface left stained; the floor is so clean I would lick it (except the very strong smell of bleach probably should tell me not to do that).

I step back, admiring my work. Okay. That's a step in the right direction at least. A very small, very insignificant step, but a step nonetheless. And it feels good. It feels great, in fact, to be cleaning up my shit.

Only now I've run out of immediate steps and I can feel the silence of the empty flat fill me up like water into a sinking ship.

I walk back to my room, pacing around it and wondering what else to do. There's so much crap everywhere: piles of books that have fallen over, coats thrown into the corner, clothes littered all over the floor.

Inspiration once again takes over; suddenly I know exactly what to do next.

✣ 10 ✣

I knock on the door so hard my knuckles hurt. It's cold enough for gloves, but despite my handbag having pretty much everything else under the sun in it, warm clothes were apparently not included.

I also didn't phone ahead, which of course I realize now is incredibly rude this day and age. Who does that anymore? Who just turns up uninvited?

There's no answer for some time and it occurs to me that he might not even be in. People often aren't in, not unless you plan ahead.

But before I turn away I start hearing footsteps pounding down the steps.

"Bella?" Marty questions as the door opens. He's wearing some red-checkered pajama bottoms and a plain black hoodie, his hair a complete mess.

"I brought over your hoodie and your trainers. I'm sorry for keeping them so long."

Marty takes the plastic Tesco bag from my outstretched hand, clearly a little confused. He looks into it like it might be some trick, before turning back to me.

"Bella, are you—"

"And thank you," I continue quickly before I forget, "for picking me up that night in the club. You left your warm bed to make sure

I was safe and I didn't thank you then, so I want to thank you now. So thank you."

He blinks a few times, looking back at the Tesco bag like it might hold some of the answers.

"No problem," he says finally, his voice quiet and soft. Well, that's that then. Another step taken. That's good. That is good. Isn't that good? Why do I still feel so shitty?

"Bella, have you been crying?" he asks.

"What?"

"Your eyes. Your makeup's running down."

"Oh God," I say quickly, reaching up to cover myself.

I didn't exactly check myself before I walked out of my flat, but of course I look like death. I haven't groomed myself properly since the mess of last night.

"No, I've . . ." Except, as if by magic, his talking about me crying suddenly reminds my tear ducts that they work. "Yes, I've . . ." Oh God, I've begun to cry.

Hold your shit together, Bella. For fuck's sake.

"Come in," he says, pushing open the door wider. I shake my head, rubbing the tears from my eyes.

"No, no," I say weakly, "you're probably with someone, or doing something . . ."

"Just get inside, you idiot," he says affectionately.

I do what I'm told, of course, sniffing back the tears.

It's like it's all coming back to me in an instant. Someone's being nice to me, and suddenly I remember all the reasons why no one should be nice to me. Because I don't deserve anyone being nice to me. Not right now, for sure.

Marty follows me up the stairs, walking immediately toward the kitchen while I stand a little awkwardly in the center of the room.

The TV's paused on a snapshot of the Antarctic, a blanket thrown roughly over the arm of the sofa where Marty clearly just discarded it. Under the hundred eyes of all the scary little animal ornaments there's leftover pizza on the side table.

I've interrupted a night in.

"I should go," I say quickly, "I didn't mean to . . . I only meant to—"

"The kettle's already boiling, so sit down before you hurt yourself," Marty says, fetching the usual mugs.

I'd argue but I've suddenly realized quite how much I need company right now. Just having a person, any person, is exactly what I need.

Before I know it, I'm sitting with my legs crossed on the edge of the sofa, a hot cuppa in my hand.

"You want to talk about it?" Marty asks, taking his seat.

"No," I reply quickly. Because I don't. I really, really don't. The last thing I need is for someone else to hear me whine about my own problems. Not when I've been so negligent about the problems I've caused others along the way.

Marty nods, looking me up and down like a robot, scanning for signals. Finally he shrugs. He picks up the remote, signaling to the TV.

"You've seen this one yet?"

I look at the screen. I'm behind apparently. The last one I saw was with the cheetahs. I shake my head.

"Good," he says finally, sitting back and throwing the covers over us both.

He hits play.

There is only one thing missing, of course. I've been on sofas watching documentaries with Marty for as long as I can remember, only it's never *just* with him.

God, I want to see Ellie so badly. I want her here, wrapped up beside me and watching these little penguins waddle around with us too.

So much so it hurts.

But she's with Mark. She's with Mark, and right now I need to let her be with Mark. I need to be better at being a supportive friend, even when I don't agree with her life choices. And if I can't be that now, I can at least stay out of their way until I'm ready to try.

I'm doing a good thing. I'm doing the right thing. But still. Ellie.

God I miss her.

As if sensing I'm missing something, Marty pushes the plate of his leftover pizza toward me. I'm actually starving, so I take a piece before my stomach answers for me.

"Thank you," I say, because I've finally remembered how important it is to say that, even when it's the people closest to us doing things they do all the time.

"No problem," he replies, as we sit on opposite ends of the sofa, sipping our tea, eating the pizza, and I try to not think about Ellie at all as David Attenborough's dulcet tones take us both on a journey far, far away.

❧ PART 5 ❧

1

Work's the biggest drag of them all. I can feel the hours draining me dry, every tick of the clock a slam against my already aching skull. Monday sinks to Tuesday. Tuesday lingers back to Wednesday. Wednesday peels around to Thursday until the engagement party looms ahead of me.

I know I've decided not to go and all, and I know deep down that's the right thing to do, only it stings to know I won't be there for Ellie at this point in her life. It physically aches.

Mind, the only silver lining, of course, is that at least I don't have to see Mark. I can't bear to see his smug little face, telling me he was right after all—that this whole fairy-tale thing turned out to be a disaster just as he foretold. Annoyingly I'm thinking about it all so much that I can weirdly see his face everywhere, haunting me like a spirit from the underworld. Where the front covers of a hundred books line the bookshelves and every single cover is just his judgmental face, hovering over me and staring me down. All of the photos of all of the authors on the walls are just Mark, succeeding in life where I'm failing, a painful "I told you so" all over his smug little forgettable bearlike face. The Post-it Notes around me are in Mark's handwriting, the voices on the phone are all Mark, the person getting out of the elevator and walking toward me is Mark.

Oh shit, wait. I rub my eyes.

The person in front of me *is actually Mark*. Like, literally, actually Mark. In the flesh. His annoying beady eyes blink up at me.

"Mark?" I ask, completely and utterly confused. "You're an author?"

"Not that I know of."

"What are you doing here?"

"I need to speak with you."

"How did you even get in?"

"Security isn't exactly tight here. I needed to see you."

"But I'm at work?"

"Yes, that's why I came here."

The phone rings. I look at the phone. I look up at Mark. I look down to the phone.

"Do you think—"

"I need to get this," I say, interrupting him. I pick up using my most professional voice, the kind of voice that got me Porter Books's best phone manner four years in a row (four years ago). "Porter Books, how can I help you?"

It's reception. Obviously.

"I have a Mr. P—"

"Send him up," I say instantly, spotting Cathy approaching. It must be someone for her and I need to get Mark out of here before anyone notices this. I hang up the phone.

"When do you get a break?" asks Mark.

"I don't."

"What, no lunch break? No coffee break?"

"No."

"Are you just saying that because you don't want to speak with me?"

Saved by Cathy. She comes in all sexy and low-cut white dress shirt. Honestly, she was born to be a model. Lord knows why she wanted the publishing life. She could be living it up on some yacht right now.

"Hi, Cathy, I was just telling this . . . delivery man . . . to leave."

"Oh," she replies, unbothered. Mark doesn't move. Neither does he correct me. He just lingers, awkwardly. Cathy shrugs. "Okay. Well, do you know if Henry's arrived yet?"

I turn to Mark, scowling that he didn't get the hint.

"He's just on his way up—Henry?"

"Yes, Henry."

"Henry Pill?"

Cathy looks at me like it's a trick question.

"Yes . . ." she replies slowly.

Oh shit. Henry Pill. I haven't seen him since—I need to get out of here. I need to hide. I need to . . .

"Mark, I have a break right now. Let's go." I sprint out from behind the desk and grab my coat.

"Wait, what?"

"Cathy you're alright to bring in Henry, aren't you? And get one of those interns to cover me for a bit. I need to get a coffee with this . . . delivery man to discuss urgent delivery-based matters."

"Yes?" she says, confused. I'm already out the door. Mark is stumbling slowly after me.

"Mark, come quickly! It's now or never. I mean it!" I sprint double time, my finger slamming hard on the lift button and praying that the lift I'm asking for comes quickly. It does, opening to—thank God—no one. I dive in. This lift faces the other so I stand as close to the wall as possible as I slam my finger down on the ground-floor button. Mark rushes in behind me, finally at my speed.

"Are you alright?"

"I will be!" I say tensely, as the doors finally start shutting. It's literally just in time. I can see the opposite doors open on the other lift and the stupid face of Henry Pill emerges. His eyes are naturally facing forward. I jump behind Mark, who stands pillar rigid as the doors finally close shut. I've never been so thankful for his bearlike physique and my smaller-than-average height, as he covers me completely. I breathe out, one long sigh of relief. Thank God. This is why I need to start reading the bloody schedule.

"You wanna tell me—"

"Nope," I reply quickly.

Mark nods, falling back into a deathly silence as the lift slowly sinks to the bottom floor. Well, at least I managed to escape one shit show. Bring on the one I've fallen right into.

❧ 2 ❧

He puts down the coffee he's just bought me on the table between us, and a fruit juice for him. It's a cappuccino, cinnamon sprinkled on the top, not chocolate. Just as I like it. I didn't even request it. That somehow annoys me more than it should. I sulkily bite my lip.

"Thanks," I utter, because I'm too polite not to. I take a sip. It's delicious. He's picked this artisan coffee place just a little down the street and I've actually always wanted to go but couldn't justify the price of the coffee. It's very Nordic. Clean-cut wood and little stools rather than chairs. Something smooth and calm is playing in the background as he takes a seat before me.

"Look, this isn't a . . ." He looks at me as he swirls the glass his strange green juice is in. "I feel I have to . . ."

Here it is. Here's the "I read your last chapter, I was right, apologize to me and get over yourself" lecture. He looks around the café for inspiration. He's vastly inarticulate at the best of times, although I'd never imagined he'd stall on an opportunity to take me down. Especially one where Ellie isn't even here to check him. This is going to be brutal. "Look," he concludes, "I just wanted to say sorry."

I swallow. I don't know what I was expecting but it probably wasn't that.

"Sorry?"

"Yes. Sorry. I'm sorry for what I said that night. I'm sorry for how I reacted, I'm sorry for the invite mix-up, and I'm sorry it's taken me this damn long to even apologize to you. But I'm sorry. I'm so completely and utterly sorry."

There's a weird pause. I try to look at his face.

"Did Ellie put you up to this?"

"Ellie doesn't know I'm here."

"Oh."

I look around the coffee shop, half expecting to see Ellie's face lingering. I'm not entirely sure I believe him. I take another sip of my delicious Danish coffee. He nods, accepting the silence like he almost deserves it.

"I know I should have come earlier. I know I should have called or texted or . . . something. But I was too selfish and . . . I don't know. I just didn't."

My lips press shut, shocked. That's definitely not where I thought this conversation was going. I wait for him to continue.

"I've known since I first met Ellie how much you mean to her. I've always known you were a large part of her life. Our first date I think she talked more about you and your life than she even did about her own and if I'm honest, how much she cares for people, how much she takes an active interest in their lives—it's one of the reasons I fell in love with her to begin with. But with you it's more than that. She relies on you. You're her rock and I'm . . . well, for a long time I was the person she turned to only when you weren't available. I know that us moving away from you was a big deal, but for me, having Ellie that little bit more to myself, well, I know it's selfish but I loved it. With you just that little bit less available she told me so much more than she'd ever told me before. She confided in me about all the little bits of her day that she usually only saved for you: what she ate for lunch that day, what she was thinking when she was walking back from the station, her reasoning behind picking chicken for dinner over lasagna, the whole works. It meant more to me than I could possibly say and when I found out that you were coming over for dinner that day I got so worried that . . . that it would end and I'd be playing second fiddle all over again so I told Ellie. I told her that I was worried and she told me I had nothing to worry about but I knew she was worrying about it anyway because—"

"She's a worrier," we say in unison. I'm confused why he used that term. That's my term for her, not his, but there we are, saying it together.

"Exactly, she's a worrier. So I was nervous and on edge anyway. I said so much that I didn't mean, words I had no right saying and when you quite rightly fought back to me, Ellie had my words already in her head so she didn't fight me either. As she should have. As you both should have.

"And I should have said sorry immediately. Once I cooled down, I realized what I'd done and I knew I should apologize but . . . with you guys not speaking, suddenly I became the person Ellie would speak to about everything. Well, about you mostly. About how much she missed you. About how much she was worried about you. About how much she wanted to see you again. She was telling me night after night just how sad she was that you weren't by her side and I loved being her 'you' but then it dawned on me that . . . if I were actually 'you,' she wouldn't have any of those problems to begin with. In fact, everything she was telling me, I actually had the power to fix. Except instead of fixing her problems, I was just listening to them and nodding like a complete tit."

He was shaking his head.

"God, when I say it out loud I realize what a total prick I've been." He turns his whole head back up, looking me square in the eyes. "I have been an arsehole of the largest magnitude."

He takes a sip of his juice. I'm not sure if I should speak but he doesn't look done so I leave it a bit longer.

"You know, I was reading your chapters. They're really quite brilliant. I mean that. You've had us laughing and crying and, well, anyway, I was reading these chapters and it got me thinking who I was or who I'd be in the fairy-tale world and . . . and after a while I worked it out. I'm in that one about the long hair."

"You think you're Rapunzel?"

"No, Ellie's Rapunzel. I'm the old hag who wants her all to my-self and keeps her far, far away and . . . I hate myself for it."

He puts a hand to his heart, like it's literally aching.

"I don't want the reason you guys aren't speaking to be because of me, I just don't. Ellie needs you in her life and I've been shutting you out. Please. Please, forgive me but more importantly, whether you can forgive me or not, please come back into Ellie's life. Please come on Saturday."

Wait—did he seriously just *own up* to shutting me out? And apologize for it?

"I never set out to be the villain in this story. I've never loved anyone more than I've loved Ellie. I didn't ever believe I could love as much as I love her. Without her I'm literally nothing." He looks up and coughs as if that accidentally tumbled from his mouth. "That's way too cheesy, I know."

I didn't know Mark was capable of something as nice as that. He's always been way too boring. He smiles a little awkwardly at me.

"I still need to apologize to Ellie. I can only hope she'll not hate me forever for the way I've acted these past few weeks. I can only hope she still wants to marry me."

Oh my God. He's welling up. I don't even know where to look right now.

"This isn't what I meant to say." He wipes away a tear before it has time to land on his reddening cheek. "What I meant to say was I know Ellie needs you there on Saturday. This whole email list thing was a misunderstanding, I swear, see—look at the list yourself." And before I even say anything he tosses over his phone to my side of the table and I look down at the screen he's opened for me. "None of the bridal party are on it. Check it—her cousin Charlotte's not there, or Hannah from her work. My groomsmen aren't there either. They weren't ever on the list. None of you guys were, because we weren't planning on inviting you *by email*. Please, see for yourself!"

I don't think I'd even know his groomsmen's names to check

through, but he's right about Charlotte at least. I slowly push the phone back his way and he pockets it.

"I hadn't even got around to telling my own best man before that list went out, so it's all been a complete disaster. Our internet broke on us again and I worried that I wouldn't actually be able to hit the send button once we'd told our closest friends, so I stupidly sent the mailing list and invites over to Niamh while I was at work. Long story short, our wires got mixed and she went ahead and sent them all out immediately. Not that I'm blaming Niamh, it was clearly my fault, but look—you're her maid of honor, for Christ's sake. She needs you there more than she needs me there, I can tell you."

Maid of honor? I swallow hard but even still my throat feels like sawdust.

"Anyway I didn't mean to . . . ramble . . . I'm just . . . I just wanted to say that I'm sorry about that. And I'm sorry for being an arse back then. And I'm sorry for being an arse now. I'm just, so, completely, sorry."

I stretch out my hands around my mug, trying to take it all in. I'm literally too shocked to even know what my face looks like right now but it can't be that encouraging as Mark swiftly looks down and away.

"I don't want to make you feel uncomfortable. I know you're supposed to be working, I don't want to take up all your time or get you in trouble or anything."

Oh God, I need to say something. He's just done this whole thing and I should say something. I should definitely, definitely say something. Shouldn't I?

Only I'm finding this so hard to process. Never in a thousand years would I have expected this from Mark. I'm in complete shock.

"Look," he says, before I say anything, "I really, really hope you'll be there on Saturday but . . . I understand if you're not. For what it's worth, I've always liked you. A lot. I know I'm not always your favorite person but . . . I'm not so terrible. Not always. Maybe one day you'll like me too."

With that he stands and, with a quick, slightly awkward pat to my shoulder on his way out, he leaves.

"Mark, I'm—" I begin.

But it's too late.

I hear the little woodwind chime of the door tinkle away as it opens and shuts behind him. This place couldn't be more Nordic if it tried.

It isn't long before I collapse into loud, awkward sobs. I'm pretty sure the whole Danish café is looking at me but I don't even care.

That was Mark, the Mark I thought incapable of human decency, doing exactly the right thing: apologizing. Taking ownership of his actions. Trying to set things right.

Can it be? Can it really be, that perhaps he's not such a villain after all?

3

When I make it back to my desk everything feels eerily quiet. I don't notice at first, my head so full of thought, except usually even at reception I can hear some of the commissioners on the phone but right now there's next to nothing.

A little confused, I pop my head into the rooms behind, only to find most of the desks in the open plan part of the office empty. My mind immediately drains of the last hour as a sweep of anxiety pans through me. Oh God, what have I missed?

The few people remaining—mostly assistants—are all anxiously whispering to one another, all of them staring at the largest meeting room on the floor. I follow their gaze through the glass walls and see that all the lead commissioners have gathered inside. It looks serious.

I quickly run back to my desk at reception and check through the diaries but I can't see anything. No email went around, nothing that would ordinarily cause a meeting like this. I know it's not my job to take an interest in things that happen on the "other side" of the office, but curiosity gets the better of me. Plus I'm scared I've missed something and if I have, Maggie will have a go at me later—better to be prepared for that now.

Luckily for me, Cathy's just by the drinks counter, waiting for the coffee machine to whir out another cappuccino that I assume she's about to bring in with her. I rush over to her quickly.

"I was gone like an hour," I whisper. "What on earth happened?"

"Henry Pill happened," Cathy replies, shaking her head. Even at the sound of his name I swallow hard.

Oh God, Henry.

Instantly my mind fills with horror. I can't help but wonder if this is all because of me. Maybe it was a fireable offense to sleep with a client after all? Maybe they found out somehow and are talking about what to do with me?

I try to keep calm, telling myself how stupid that would be. Why would all the commissioners be pulled into one room to talk about how to fire me? That's absurd.

Still, something looks wrong here and I want to know what.

"Go on," I say to Cathy, trying to keep my cool.

Cathy looks at her cappuccino, still thankfully halfway through its cycle.

"He's apparently had a change of heart," she says. "We thought he was coming in to discuss book cover ideas and then he gave a whole speech about how he wants out of the whole deal. He's apparently sick of making girls feel 'demeaned' as part of his day job, saying that his actions could lead others to try similar stunts and ruin vulnerable people's self-esteem. He says he doesn't want to set that precedent. Not anymore. Looks like he's finally grown a conscience."

I feel my stomach drop.

"Did he say why?"

"Well, apparently he had some girl ghost him and he found this trending story on B-Reader that he thought might have been about him. He didn't give us the details, only that he realized how it made people feel to be exposed like that and it made him see the 'error of his ways.'"

Oh shit. Oh shitty, shitty, shit. Henry read my work?

"So he's pulling out of the book deal?" I ask. "Can he even do that?"

"I mean, technically not, he's already signed the contract, but when they brought in Jenks to talk to him about it all she agreed to new terms. We'll publish his next book instead, whatever that is."

Sally Jenks, the CEO of the whole company. She's sitting at the head of the long boardroom table now, I see, nodding away seriously to what one of the commissioners is telling her. I turn away before I accidentally catch eyes with anyone in the room.

Honestly, I think I'm going to pass out.

"Is she pissed?" I whisper, trying to stop my hands from shaking. If they find out that girl is me I'm out of here for sure. Maybe worse.

"Pissed?" Cathy says, shaking her head. "No, she's relieved! Apparently the meeting went really well between them. Once Henry was gone she called all of the commissioners together to tell them what a close call it was. She said that Henry might have been a famous name, but that's no excuse for the company to promote any voices that amplify the mistreatment of women. She said we're better than that, that we got lucky this time but that we need to make sure that an author's popularity isn't affecting our own values in what we publish."

Say what?

"So . . . this girl that ghosted him—that's a good thing?"

"It's good," Cathy replies. Relief floods through me in an instant. "It's probably good for the whole female population, but it's definitely good for us."

I try not to give anything away but I can feel my heart pumping overtime.

"So what is this?" I ask, nodding back to the boardroom.

Cathy picks herself up, clearly reminded she was just on a coffee run.

"Jenks wanted a personal rundown of everything coming up to ensure nothing else being published flagged any potential PR issues. I should probably get back in there." As she starts sashaying back I start to feel weirdly dizzy, not sure how to digest this news. She turns and I try to keep my face expressionless. "Oh, and if you're not doing anything at your desk, do you want to see if you can find that girl's writing on B-Reader? Henry didn't give us any clues to what it might be called or anything but maybe you'll get lucky."

"Why? Is she in trouble?" I ask, unable to hide the adrenaline I'm feeling. "The author, I mean. Is the author in trouble?"

"God no!" Cathy laughs. "I just really want to see Henry Pill getting a taste of his own medicine. I'm sure we all do."

✤ 4 ✤

The meeting lasts for the rest of the day, so there's not much to do in reception. It suits me just fine; it takes about an hour for my adrenaline to subside and after that I just sit there, replaying the day's events in an unending loop.

I go through various stages of feeling terrible, then guilty, then nervous, then proud that Henry Pill changed his mind because of me, and then terrible all over again.

Because he read my work, probably. He read it, and it made him feel like shit. I've made someone feel like shit. And even when I've done it to someone as terrible as Henry Pill, it's still not a nice feeling.

Why did I never think that this fairy-tale sexcapade was a bad idea? That it might hurt someone? Why did no one tell me that it was a mistake?

Well, someone tried to tell me. Mark did. At the start of all of this, he was trying to tell me and I just didn't want to listen.

Oh God, Mark.

As I retouch my makeup in the bathroom a few hours later, Mark's apology lingers in my mind.

Yes, he said bad things that night, yes, they hurt, but instead of holding his ground or stubbornly holding on to resentment like I've been doing all this time, he's taken the upper hand and apologized.

In his own twisted way, all he was trying to do was stop me

from feeling . . . well, like this really. To stop me from having the
regret I'm living through right now. Wrong method, sure, but good
intentions.

Great intentions, actually.

What a good egg.

Why did I never see that before in him?

Why did I never realize that Ellie picked a good man?

Because I never wanted to see it, that's why. Simply put, he
wasn't the perfect guy in my eyes, so I didn't want him to be the
perfect guy in hers.

But she did. And now, against all odds, I understand. So what
if I find his stories painfully dull? Ellie must like them. Somehow.
She must be able to look past the forgettable ogre-like exterior and
see . . . well . . . see her own Prince Charming . . .

God, I feel so stupid.

I've been making so much about myself, when it just isn't.

Now Halloween is looming and their engagement party is coming, and I know for absolutely and completely certain that right
now, this isn't my fairy tale at all. She's the Cinderella here, I'm just
the resentful stepsister who's finally seeing the error of her ways. I
wouldn't miss her ball for the whole world.

5

> 31 Oct 10:36-Me
> You coming tonight?

Marty-31 Oct 10:36
Obviously

> 31 Oct 10:36-Me
> . . .

> 31 Oct 10:36-Me
> What time will you be there?

Marty-31 Oct 10:36
Why?

Marty-31 Oct 10:36
Need a chaperone?

> 31 Oct 10:36-Me
> It's dangerous for a young girl to be traveling alone

Marty-31 Oct 10:36
You're not young

> 31 Oct 10:36-Me
> Fuck you

I don't know why I even bothered texting him. I knew he'd be no help.

Marty-31 Oct 10:38
Text me when you're outside and I'll come meet you x

31 Oct 10:38-Me

Thx x

The pub is in Chiswick, and I love it. Of course this is the kind
of place Ellie would pick for her engagement party. I can't think of
a more Ellie-appropriate place anywhere. It has a fireplace, and the
brick is exposed like something from a Harry Potter novel, ready
to take us to the magical otherworld if we know the right pattern
to tap on the walls.

True to his word, Marty's outside, standing in the freezing cold
waiting for me as my car pulls up. It just comes as another brutal
reminder to me that as a breed, the Mathewses are kind and they're
loyal, and for my own stupidity I've been acting like a spoiled child
and pushing one out of my life.

I'd rectify it tonight.

The Mathews before me is wearing a white boiler suit with
wings, like a badly made angel in a nativity play, and he's wearing
a Bluetooth headpiece in his ear like it's the aughts. Honestly it's
all over the place. I step out, the cloak over my Norwegian bunad
(I had to google that word) keeping me warm, but he bundles me
in through the door so he can breathe freely again without the cold
pinching at his breath.

"Oktoberfest barmaid?" he says. "Sounds about right."

"God you're immature," I say, looking down and checking myself. My ginger hair is in pigtails but it's fighting to get out. I had
to custom-make most of my outfit but the traditional Norwegian
dress I was aiming for, the long black floor-length skirt, the white
shirt with a colorful Nordic pinafore, looks pretty darn authentic
I'd say.

"I'm an Arendelle princess, I'll have you know."

"That's not what you wanted to be when you grew up?"

"It's what I want to be now when I grow up."

"You're ridiculous. Plus you chose the wrong *Frozen* sister. The
other one gets the better songs."

"Whatever, freak. What even are you?" I ask.

He points to the wings like it's obvious.

"A flying sperm?" I try.

"Buzz Lightyear," he corrects, rolling his eyes.

"Like hell did you ever want to be Buzz. All this judgment for me, and you didn't even like *Toy Story*. You found the next-door neighbor kid too scary and wet your pants that one time."

"I was like four when that happened."

"Still happened."

"Well, maybe this is me overcoming my fear."

"You should have been . . . I don't know . . . Doctor Doolittle! You loved that film!"

"No, *you* loved that film. I would just watch it with you."

"Isn't that why you became a vet?"

"I surprisingly didn't base my career choices on some kids' movie."

"Liar."

"I based it on what women most want to hear when you tell them what you do for a living."

It was my turn to roll my eyes as I turned to look at the rest of the room. The thing about old friends is that their engagement parties are so completely filled with people you also know and love. There are people we both went to school with, work friends of hers who became close friends of mine as the years went on. There's her family (which is my family) and my family (which is her family) and although there are those in the crowd who probably belong to Mark, I couldn't feel more at home among these people.

Over by the bar my mum (a fresh-from-the-costume-shop fire-fighter) is in the corner chatting with my dad (he did actually come as the Easter Bunny, bless him) and Niamh (a less embarrassing ballet dancer). I wave over to them and they all wave back over to me, prompting me to join. Not yet though, there's something else I have to do first. My eyes keep scanning around me.

"Your parents are still on such good terms," Marty points out.

"They're still best friends."

"You'd have thought, what with the divorce and all . . ."

"Just because they're getting a divorce doesn't mean they can't still be besties."

Marty laughs.

"That's rare. You're lucky."

My eyes turn back to them now, laughing away together at some joke Niamh has made and I suddenly see it.

Marty's right, of course, it's just taken me a while to get there. I *am* lucky. I'm more than lucky. I was raised in a loving household, by a mum and a dad who still love each other to this day, just in a different new way. One of them didn't have a midlife crisis and disappear like Marty's dad. There was no illicit affair like Mark's. They had an open and honest conversation that led to other open and honest conversations, which led to today, them having a perfectly happy conversation together with my primary teacher, as relaxed as anything. They too, like everyone else in my life, have evolved to the next stage. I smile, watching them as proudly as a parent watching their own children play.

"SmElliee!" Marty calls beside me. I turn, as if in slow motion.

There she is. She's dressed as—oh holy shit.

She's dressed as Elsa. Literally. Her blond hair is braided to one side. Her blue dress is—I mean, wowzibar. She's stunning. She's beautiful. She's my Ellie. She's literally *the Elsa to my Anna*.

"You two are such weirdos. You know *Frozen* came out when we were long into our twenties, right?" Marty chimes in.

"I don't care," we both say in complete and utter unison.

She blinks, staring at me nervously. Marty looks between us.

"I'm going to get us all shots before anyone thinks we planned this and that I'm the singing snowman."

He leaves. We both don't move for some time. It's like there's no one around us. It's like it's just us. She speaks first but I move first, grabbing her hands in my hands.

"Bella, you came!"

"I can't believe I almost missed it."

"I'm so sorry that—"

"I'm the one who should say—"

"I've missed you so—"

"I've missed you more I—"

We both pause. We both swallow. We launch into the world's longest, best, most beautiful hug that the world has ever seen. There she is, a modern-day princess. Here I am, a disastrous mess from the Middle Ages. The Elsa to my Anna, the queen to my princess, the bride to my bridesmaid.

"You have every right to be angry with me," she says. "I should have told him about your parents."

"I'm not angry. He's your fiancé, and I never told you not to tell him. And I know, deep down, he was just trying to protect me too."

It occurs to me in this moment that these last few weeks have been utterly and completely pointless. A waste of time and energy.

I was channeling all my anger at them, when that wasn't what I was really mad at.

I was really just angry that things change.

I was angry that I couldn't stop them.

I was angry for all the wrong reasons.

Even as the hug ends I can't let go of her hands. I feel like all my apologies are being channeled from my palms to hers. I squeeze them tight and she squeezes them right back, not pulling away.

From just behind her I see the smiling figure of Batman. I assume its Mark. It's actually hard to tell because it's one of those proper face masks but I assume no one else would be staring at us the way he is if it isn't Mark. Quickly I see him get pulled away, deep in conversation with a Pikachu and a Power Ranger.

"I'm so happy for you, Ellie," I tell her.

"You mean it?"

"Mark's such a great guy," I say. Because he did a shitty thing, sure, but he owned up to it and apologized. As someone who has accidentally done a lot of very shitty things to people I love recently, I know a little of how difficult it is to take responsibility like he just did. "I really, really mean it."

And I do. I squeeze her hands once again just to prove it.

Knowing that she'll always be there when I need her, knowing that I'll always be there when she needs me, knowing that we'll never be far no matter how far we are, I finally let go.

6

The warming tones of David Attenborough are already on as our soundtrack as we climb onto the sofa. Marty's opened a packet of crisps, ready for us as a polar bear starts ripping open a seal before our very eyes.

As the party wound down, Ellie and Mark disappeared in a Batmobile Uber. I meant to talk to Mark, I did, only it turned out that our paths just never crossed. He was in a room of his friends and I was in a room of mine and despite being in a rather iconic outfit, I barely even saw him through the crowd, let alone got the chance to talk. Marty and I shared a cab in the same direction. Only the drive was long and as sobriety eventually found me, I remembered how little I wanted to be around Hans and Gertie. So, naturally, I'm staying with Marty.

"Didn't want to pull?" I ask.

"Half the people in that room were related to me. What's your excuse?"

I sigh. I'm so good at sighs.

"I'm over sleeping with random men. It's complicated and confusing and rejection hurts like a bitch. Not that you know."

"Are you kidding? I get rejections all the time!"

"Liar," I laugh, "you have a girl every night just about."

"I get rejected every night too. Sometimes multiple times before I find someone."

I look him in the eye and he doesn't blink. I have no idea if that means he's being truthful but . . . well, he certainly looks truthful.

"How do you do it? How do you pick yourself back up again?" I ask. He laughs at that.

"I know it doesn't matter. I don't care about those girls so I don't care that they reject me. When I finally go for it with someone I really like, if I get rejected then, well, that will be a different story completely."

I can see his cheeks start to glow and I think about pointing it out or making fun of it, but I don't. I turn away before he catches me staring.

We slump back into a comfortable silence as the polar bear treads around the screen like a messiah, another poor little seal trapped before it helplessly.

"So you're all made up then?" he asks, throwing himself back to get more comfortable.

"With the bear?"

"With Elmo."

I throw a crisp at him just as the seal is ripped in two. Both of us wince.

"How'd you know we were fighting?"

"Are you kidding? God, I've never had so many texts in my life from her. 'Can you check Bells is okay?' 'Have you heard from Bells at all today?'"

"Your impression of Ellie is horrific."

"She's horrific."

"She's perfect."

I throw another crisp his way. He's quicker this time. His hand comes out and it rebounds back in my face. It's quite an impressive hit. The bear pans away to little bear cubs. From the horror comes beauty. Despite just watching this beast tear up a pair of adorable-looking seals, I'm suddenly completely and utterly in love with it.

"Did she really ask about me?" I ask, trying not to sound like a girl talking about her schoolyard crush.

"She's a worrier," he says, leaning back into his own chair. "She worried. What with your last chapter I'm not surprised."

"You read that?"

"Of course I did. Looks like you've been served another shit show."

"I think I've served myself a shit show."

"Don't blame yourself."

"I do. Utterly and completely. Going out every night, trying to sleep with randomers—it's not me. I've spent the last few weeks trying to prove I'm someone I'm not. I don't want that life. What on earth was I thinking?"

"Well, what do you want?"

Big question. I take a deep breath, not entirely sure I want to even think about it. I still feel like I don't deserve what I actually want. Not after everything I've done. But then I remember it's Marty. If I can't tell Marty, who can I?

"I can't help it. Everyone just feels like they're ticking off their goals around me while I'm stuck in a vacuum. I want my writing dreams to come true and, well, I want what Ellie has. For as long as I've known I've wanted the big white wedding."

"Then do it."

"Easier said than done. I don't have a publishing deal."

"Then self-publish."

"I don't have a husband either."

"You don't need one. Send out fancy invites, throw on a white dress, have an expensive day all about you. That's what I'd say. A man doesn't need to be involved."

"You're the one who told me to sleep around!"

"I certainly did not."

"You did! You said to find a man I want to spend the night with!"

"That's not what I . . . I only meant that you're so focused on the ring at the end that you'd let your standards slip completely just to get one. So you throw yourself a wedding. You celebrate you. That way you can give up on all this fairy-tale wedding malarkey and find yourself a guy you actually want to be with."

I raise an eyebrow at that, unable to hide my smirk.

"Straight from the relationship guru himself."

"I'm not doing so badly."

"Your longest relationship is maybe two hours long."

"Nonsense. We're twenty-five-plus years strong, at least."

"I don't count."

The little cub on the screen fell over and it's so cute, it's Instagram-worthy.

"So that's why you were there for me then? Because Ellie asked you?"

"Nah, I don't listen to my sister if I can help it," he replies. "I have my own reasons."

"Do those reasons involve me being the most beautiful human in the entire world?" I say, batting my eyelids.

I think he's going to laugh but he doesn't. Instead he turns to face me, looking me up and down.

"Sure. Go on then," he says.

That knocks the breath out of me instantly. Did I . . . did I hear him correctly?

"What, no sarcastic comment?"

He shakes his head, turning back to the screen, but I can see his mind's elsewhere.

"Are you sick?"

"No, I'm not sick."

"Are you drunk?"

"I don't watch Attenborough drunk. He deserves better."

"Then why aren't you telling me I look like the guts of that dead seal?" I ask seriously. He reaches for the remote and pauses David completely before he turns to look at me, his cheeky glint slightly subdued. It's probably the lighting. Probably.

"Because you don't look like seal guts," he says, his tone so strangely serious. "You never have. In fact, if you're asking me, I've always thought you're beautiful."

The whole world has paused around us.

He blinks at me, breathing so slowly I can see the rise and fall of his chest. I keep my eyes on him, trying to work out what on earth is going on. What on earth *is* going on in his mind? What is he thinking?

He puts down the crisps, nice and calmly, as cool and calculated as he always is. I can barely move as that same hand winds itself around the back of my head. He looks at me, daring me to stop him, but I can barely believe what he's doing until—oh Jesus Christ.

His lips are so soft they should be in commercials, and so completely unexpected as they wrap around mine like they were meant to. Like they were meant to? Wait, what? What am I saying here? He's kissing me. Marty Mathews is kissing me. We're kissing. We're—

He pulls away, looking me in the eye to try to read my face. I don't suppose there's much there apart from complete confusion.

"What was that?" I whisper.

"Do you want me to stop?"

I look him in the eye. What's happening here? I can't tell what's come over me but here is Marty Mathews and here is me and he's asking me a serious question. An actual question.

I shake my head.

"No, keep going," I say, pulling him in closer by his T-shirt until his lips are back on mine.

Things get heated quickly. Before I know it, he has me lifted around him (my God his arms are strong!) and back to his room where he lays me down, his lips barely leaving mine in all that time.

I don't know how much time passes. I don't know what's happened to Marty for him to become this . . . well just *this*. I don't know what the hell happened to Attenborough or those polar bear cubs in the other room. All I know is that my whole body is tingling and Marty's lips are warm and soft on mine, as my whole body slides farther and farther down the bed.

The sheets smell freshly laundered. All I breathe in is a hypnotic mix of Tide and, well, Marty. Marty's smelled the same since I've known him. Except now it's intoxicating.

"We should stop," he says, pulling away. He doesn't sound convinced.

"We should." I don't either.

"Before this goes any further," he tries, even less certain. "You've sworn off men."

"I have." I trail my last word. "Although . . ."

"Although?"

I take a deep breath in, regaining some of my lost oxygen while my brain ticks away in the background.

"I mean . . . technically I've just sworn off strangers. You're not a stranger."

I look at him. I don't know what comes over me but suddenly I'm back on top of him, my lips heading down his chest and my hands undoing his belt. He stops me. I look up at him, wondering what I might have done, but all I see is that perfect half smile come back again with a fire behind his eyes. It's so fucking sexy right now. He somehow manages to rip off his own belt and slide his hand back and around my Nordic pinafore until suddenly I'm completely topless and tight within his arms. It's like a magic trick I didn't even see coming. He stops, hovering one last second.

"Do you want this?" he asks. "Do you actually want this?"

I look up at him, his face so kind and sweet. The face of Marty Mathews, the boy who lived next door (ish), hovering above me shirtless and so hot I could feel his heart pulsing down on me.

I nod. Holy shit, I want this, and in a move smoother than I've ever witnessed before, he twists me around and, without me even realizing how, dims the lights.

❧ 7 ❧

I've had good first sex before. I know it's not impossible, but with Marty it almost felt inevitable. It wasn't just good. It was like he already knew exactly what would make me cry out, and he hit every single position that would take me there one by one. He was slow and deliberate, like he was in just about everything in life, but in this it acted very much in his favor. He made every single fiber of my body stir and shake. He made parts of me I didn't even know I could feel suddenly erupt.

After an hour of feeling the highest I've ever felt in all my life, we both fall back, but not away from each other as the wave cools down around us.

We're both out of breath.

We're both warm in each other's arms.

With his hands around me one way and mine over his another, we cradle each other softly into a much-needed sleep.

8

The light's peeling through Marty's blinds and it catches my eye, waking me up from my power nap. I'm so unbelievably comfortable. Somewhere between his memory foam mattress and the curve of his arm around the back of my neck, I'm in the most comfortable place I've ever been in my whole life.

I open my eyes and there he is: Marty Mathews. His chest rises and falls in smooth, wavelike motions that almost lullaby my eyes to fall back asleep again. Except a thought keeps me awake, one that hits me hard.

Holy shit. I've just slept with Marty Mathews.

I look up to him and he's stirring. I wonder if I should move, get out of his way and laugh this all off instantly but for whatever reason, I don't. I stay as I am: still somehow topless and curled around him like my own personal pillow.

"Morning, Bells," he whispers, one eye peeling open to look at me.

He's got a funny morning face. He's the kind of person to whom mornings are the enemy and I can see it in him, now. If the light wasn't so strong through the windows he would still be asleep, and we both know it. He rubs his face with his free hand, checking his watch on the bedside table for the time. He groans at whatever answer he faces.

"What's the sound for?"

"I'm on call."

"You have to leave?"

"Not unless they call me," he replies, throwing his watch away. He probably aimed for the side table but missed by a country mile. It makes me laugh, which makes him laugh, which makes his chest pump double time and my head bump up and down, which makes both of us laugh more.

"Does this feel weird to you?" I ask, looking up to him once we both cool down. He strokes back my hair from my face and pulls me in closer.

"It feels normal," he says, kissing my forehead. His hand gently floats down and grazes the curves of my hip and I feel myself melt into his arms.

"But like, is it weird that it's normal?"

He laughs again, his soft hand turning back and ruffling my hair over my face. He stretches up for a second and I think he's trying to pull away. I move slightly sideways on cue, but he pulls me back with a sleepy grin on his face.

"Oi, where do you think you're going?"

"Oh," I answer, curling back into place like I fit there, because, strangely, I do. Everything feels so natural with him. It's natural when he lifts up my chin and kisses me all over again. It's natural when he holds me in his arms. It's all just so, unbelievably, natural.

"But . . . you're Marty," I whisper.

"I'm Buzz Lightyear, my friend."

"I'm serious!"

"You're serious? Well that changes everything."

"I mean it! You're *Ellie's brother*."

"Ouch."

"Ouch?"

"I would like to think we've known each other long enough for me to be more than just 'Ellie's brother.'"

"Well, yes. But you're that too."

"And?"

"And we just had sex."

"We did," he concludes.

He smiles like a conquering hero and I kick him under the covers.

"Well?" I ask.

"Well what?"

"Well, why isn't this weird?"

"Calm down, Bells."

He pulls me into his chest, probably to shut me up more than anything, but it's warm there and he smells like leftover aftershave, which makes me happy.

"Because . . ." he begins. "Because I always thought this would happen eventually."

I feel something bubble deep within me. My cheeks literally glow at that, I can feel their radiation. Trying to get out of my own head, I giggle.

"You think you can sleep with anyone." I kick him again. "God, you're so full of yourself."

"No, I didn't mean . . ." he says. He peels back and looks at me before turning back to look at the ceiling. I turn too, looking at the swirling pattern above us and letting it hypnotize me as Marty speaks. His voice is cool and soft, sweeter than his usual harsh sarcasm. It relaxes me so much I almost fall back to sleep all over again.

"You're not anyone, are you? You've stayed over here a thousand times. That sofa outside is practically your second home. You being here *is* normal."

"But I've never slept in here . . ." I say, looking around the bedroom.

He laughs.

"Consider yourself upgraded."

"I'm being serious! You're my best friend's brother!"

He ruffles my hair affectionately as he stretches out.

"I might just be her brother to you, but you've never been anything but Bells to me." I feel myself literally melt. A sweet wave of pure joy circles through my skin, sending goose bumps right up my spine.

"But why isn't this strange? Why does this just feel right?" I ask the world.

Marty answers for it: "Because some things just *are* right. Right in a way you don't even have to question why. This is clearly one of them."

He smiles, kissing me, his lips soft against mine as he holds me so close I think nothing else matters around us.

ꕥ 9 ꕥ

After a while, Marty gets up to make us both tea like a true hero (and like a true Mathews). Left alone in his room, I find a T-shirt on the floor and throw it over me.

It fits me quite nicely, which I already knew to expect before I'd even done it. I remember I used to always steal his shirts after a sleepover with Ellie. She was always a little skinnier than me and in her tops I always felt lumpy and gross, but in Marty's I was always comfortable.

My phone's on low battery so I find a charger on Marty's side of the bed and plug it in. There's a message from Ellie and my heart flutters in my chest.

It feels so good to be back on speaking terms.

The Elsa to my Anna-01 Nov 10:06
Did you get home safe?

A tricky question. Technically speaking I'm still not home. Best to deflect

01 Nov 10:36-Me
How's the hangover?

The Elsa to my Anna-01 Nov 10:36
Worth it

01 Nov 10:36-Me
Going out raving again tonight??

The Elsa to my Anna-01 Nov 10:36
I would, only I have very important plans I just can't
cancel

01 Nov 10:36-Me
Oh yeah?

The Elsa to my Anna-01 Nov 10:36
Yep. Lord of the Rings marathon

01 Nov 10:37-Me
I see. Yes. Vital that
01 Nov 10:37-Me
Send my love to Gandalf
01 Nov 10:37-Me
And Mark

The Elsa to my Anna-01 Nov 10:37
Will do xxx

I can't help but smile from ear to ear as I flick over to my emails. My heart drops again. Oh God, it's Becky Hamill.

I haven't spoken to her since my last tragic chapter. She's probably telling me I've fucked it. She's probably telling me that I stopped being funny and outrageous and I've turned a corner she can't follow me down. Oh shit. I close one eye as I click on the email, as if that might hide the terror a little longer but then I remember, it's alright. It's alright to have a bit of bad news. I've had a great twenty-four hours. I can handle a bit more rejection now.

Bella!

What an absolute triumph. Have you seen this yet?
It's everything I was hoping for and more. What a twist to your character—making her more and more tragic until she's at breaking point.
I wonder, what's next on her agenda? Will she actually get to meet Prince Charming after all?
I'm very excited to see how this goes!

Best wishes,

Becky Hamill x
Hummingbird Literary Agency

I read it through twice. What the hell? What's happened? What have I done?

There's a link. I look up at the door. I still have time; I can hear Marty pacing around his clean kitchen. I click on the link.

Top 10 B-Readers in the UK Right Now

I scan down the list, a little confused. The top two I recognize, their names were always somewhere on the site when I clicked on the app. The third I think I've maybe seen before but the fourth . . .

No. It can't be?

> @B.Enchanted
> Ever wanted to live the fantasy? This new
> B-Reader is living them all! Enter the world of
> fairy tales in a way you've never read them
> before with this debut author.

It's *BuzzFeed*.

And that's my handle.

My handle is being shared on *BuzzFeed*.

What is going on?

It doesn't go into any details at all, but there it is on the list. Number 4. I literally can't believe it. I scan down the article—there are already hundreds of comments on this article alone with a link straight to my page on B-Reader.

I check it out. I deleted the app so it's not like I've been checking up on it at all.

Oh my.

One million followers. I have one million followers on

B-Reader right now and even as I'm refreshing the page, that number is growing.

My life's about to change. I can feel it. And right on cue, my phone starts to ring.

✤ 10 ✤

Marty comes back, his chest bare to the elements and his hands filled with steaming mugs of joy. He carefully balances them as he shuffles back in beside me.

I barely look at who is calling before pushing it to voice mail and returning to the *BuzzFeed* article.

"Look!" I say, shoving the phone under his nose. He laughs, somehow not spilling the tea he's trying to hand me as we exchange like for like. I watch his eyes as they read the article.

"That's amazing, Bells!"

"That's more than amazing!" I say, accidentally burning my tongue on boiling tea. "The agent loves where I've taken the story. She just sent the nicest email ever! I was so worried she'd hate it. I was so worried I'd blown my chance and—"

My phone blasts out. Another call.

Caller ID unknown, so I flick it straight to voice mail again. It's probably someone trying to get ahold of me "for some accident that I was involved in that wasn't my fault." I take another sip and burn myself accidentally. That's the second time that's happened.

"It probably needs time to cool," Marty says, fitting himself in. "Your name's not on the article. Did you do that on purpose?"

"None of it was on purpose—I didn't even know it existed until just now."

"Did you not give some sort of permission?"

"No," I say warily, "but when I signed up they asked for a bunch of permissions like this. I thought it might up my chances of being read in the first place."

My phone blasts out again. Marty hands the phone back to me.

Who calls these days? I look again. Caller ID still unknown. Wait—could this be Hummingbird Literary Agency maybe? They've tried three times now.

"It might be the agent. Can I?" I ask.

"By my guest," Marty says, reaching out for his phone to pass the time.

I take a deep breath. This could be it, I tell myself. This could be representation or, alternatively, a cold call about my nonexistent car's extended warranty. Only one way to find out.

Nervously, I answer.

❦ 11 ❦

"Hello?"

"Hi, Bella?"

"Yes? Who is this?"

"I don't . . . this is strange but . . . but I just found a shoe with your name and number on it."

I pause.

"Sorry, what?"

"I'm just near this place in Brixton and I found this shoe and it weirdly had your number on it."

I pause again, not quite understanding before—oh my God.

The shoe.

The "Cinderella" shoe.

The shoe I left in the bar all those weeks ago *in Brixton*.

My heart was already fluttering before my phone even rang but right now, I feel I'm soaring over rooftops.

It's worked. It's months after, of course, but I put out a shoe in the world looking for a Prince Charming and, on the very same day that the agent writes to me asking what's next, here is a man calling me about it.

"Sorry—I shouldn't have . . . called like this . . . I know it's weird but like . . . I don't know, this feels a bit . . . like 'Cinderella' or something."

"Cinderella"?

He's . . . what? Speaking my language? Is this a sign?

I can't believe this. An agent likes me, I have a *BuzzFeed* article about me, and here is a man on the other side of the phone returning my red stiletto. The stars have frickin' aligned.

"Hello? Are you there?"

"Yes, yes, I'm here," I answer.

"Did you . . . lose a shoe?"

"Yes actually, yes, I did."

"Oh good, it *is* you." His voice is soft, filled with a beautiful stillness while my mind is exploding with fireworks. Oh my word. This is it—my next chapter—Prince Charming's revolutionary entrance.

"Look, I know this is . . . well, who knows, but I'm just recently single and I sort of believe in fate, so—you don't want to . . . grab a coffee maybe?" he asks.

I remember Becky's email.

Will she actually get to meet Prince Charming after all?

I mean, I thought this book was over. I thought that last chapter was something of a curtain closer, but . . . now I'm wondering if it was just the perfect plot twist to something else completely. Maybe an actual romance of some sort?

I wouldn't have sought this out or anything, but given it's fallen on my lap like this I just have to meet him. I have to meet the man who found my shoe. The stars have aligned, for God's sake. You can't turn your back on the stars.

"Well, I should return this shoe at least?" he says to my silence.

I'm not thinking anymore. All I can think of is Becky's next email to me.

I find words are coming out of my mouth before I can stop them.

"I'm not in Brixton right now but I can be ready in like . . . I don't know, two hours?"

❧ 12 ❧

"So? What did she say?" Marty asks, blowing into his tea.

I'd forgotten where I was for a second. I blink around the room—it's Marty's room. Of course it is, only I'm so excited my brain's not taking anything in. Marty beside me seems very calm right now. I don't know how he can be. I'm bubbling to boiling point.

"Who?"

"That agent?"

"No—it wasn't her—you know that shoe that I dropped in that bar a few weeks back? The one with my number?"

"The night I came and picked you up?"

"Exactly. Well, turns out it's not such a failure after all. That was someone who's just found it. They want to meet."

Marty laughs.

"Someone actually found it?"

"Yeah—he said he saw it in Brixton somewhere. I don't know where."

"He?"

"Yeah—I'll need to ask him where it was. I just assumed it would have ended up in some garbage truck somewhere."

"Why?"

"Because it's been so long since I left it."

"No—why does he want to meet?"

I laugh at him this time. I take a large sip of my tea and my whole tongue scolds me for it. I need to put this cup down before I do myself more damage but for whatever reason, I don't. My mind is way too preoccupied.

"To give me back my shoe."

"Why would he want to do that?"

"Because he still has it. I said I could head over in a couple of hours."

"Well, that's dumb."

Dumb?

I blink a few times, wondering if I've misheard him. I'd assume I had, only his face seems to agree with the sentiment. I feel something pause inside me, like the roller coaster I'm on has come to an abrupt halt mid-ride. I swallow.

"Sorry?"

"If I found a shoe on the streets of Brixton with a number on it, you think I'd go out of my way to return it?"

I blink some more, unable to control my eyelids.

"Well, no, but you're you, aren't you?"

"I'm most people in this situation. You spot a stray shoe on the street, you leave it where it is. You don't pick it up, let alone call the number. Why would someone do that?"

I pause, trying to remember the exact words on the phone call. If he's heard it he'd understand.

"Well, he said he believed in fate and—"

"Fate?"

"Yes, he said that he was recently single and he believes in fate and then he finds this shoe with my number on it and—"

"Sorry," Marty says, shaking his head a little in disbelief. He's smiling but it does feel a little forced. "Are you going on a date with this guy?"

"Just a coffee."

"A coffee date?"

I bring the tea to my lips without thinking, before I pause again. Slowly I put the mug down on the side table. I suddenly hear what he's hearing.

"It's not . . . a 'date' date."

"Jesus Christ, Bells." He puts his tea down and runs his hands through his hair.

"You're making it sound so . . . it's not like that, Marty," I tell him. I feel like he's reading this all wrong—this is Prince Charming we're talking about. The Prince Charming I set up in one chapter returning for another. This is exactly what my book has been leading up to.

"Are you kidding me right now?" he asks. His face is all flushed and his hands ruffle his hair even more out of place.

"Look, I just want to hear his side of the story," I say, trying to sound reasonable. "It's not a big deal."

"It's a pretty big deal, actually. You're still lying in my bed for fuck's sake, and you've just gone and organized a date with another guy!"

He's not listening to me here, and I can see his mind already coming to its own conclusions.

"No, I'm telling you it's not like that!" I say quickly, putting my lava brew back down on the table. "It's not like a *romantic* date. It's not about sex anymore. He's just the perfect next chapter! Marty— this is Prince Charming in real life!"

I smile in a bad attempt to keep the conversation light and happy. He's looking back at me, deadly serious.

"He's Prince Charming?"

"In the book! Exactly!"

"Then who am I?"

"Y-you?" I ask, stuttering a little. "Well, you're not anyone."

"Even fucking better." He goes to get up but I move quickly, trying to root him to the spot as I spin around and grab his arm.

"No, obviously you're not *no one*," I try to correct, "you're just Marty, you know? This isn't exactly a *thing*, is it?"

"This isn't a thing to you?" He looks hurt, betrayed.

"I meant it isn't a *fairy-tale thing*. This isn't *book-worthy*," I say, smiling cheekily in an attempt to change the tone. Hopefully he'll start laughing with me like he usually does and clear this thick smog that's settled between us. Except he doesn't. Not even a little bit.

"This is just getting better and better," he says, lightly tugging his arm away from my grip, head buried deep into his hands.

"'Worthy' isn't the right . . . I didn't mean that either. Marty—I didn't think you'd even want to be part of my book!"

"I don't!" he cries.

"Then this shouldn't upset you!"

I can hear his breaths deepen and slow down, clearly processing. How I wish I could start this all over. He's just got the wrong end of the stick. I sit back a bit, hoping the extra room might give him space, except his processing time is taking way too long for my anxiety levels to cope with. I was on such a high after the call and now I just feel slammed to the ground. As the silence continues I can feel my patience slipping away into something else completely. I'm starting to panic. I can't trust what's about to come out of my mouth. Finally I break.

"Fine!" I say. "Fine—I'll add you to the book! Are you happy now?"

"Am I happy?" He lifts his head up and he's laughing now, but it's not good laughter. It's not good laughter at all. "Believe it or not, not everything here is about your book!"

He turns, looking me square in the eye, and suddenly I wish that he'd put his head back into his palms so I don't have to face those disappointed eyes staring back at me.

Marty breathes deeply, his laughter fading away and his voice calm and collected.

"I feel pretty shitty if I'm being honest here."

"Marty, this isn't about us. This is strictly professional here— you've got to know how much that means to me. This could be my heroine's happily-ever-after," I try.

"You think you're going to get a happily-ever-after with this shoe stranger? Maybe you should stop looking for some magic ending and realize what's actually right here in front of you."

"*You* literally just told me you don't want to be in the book, and now you want to be the fairy-tale ending?" I can hear my voice picking up speed.

"No, that's not what I meant!"

"Then there shouldn't be an issue here!" I can feel my pent-up anxiety pushing me past reason.

"Of course there's an issue! You just slept with me and you've lined up your next date already!"

"It's for a *book,* Marty!"

"This isn't your book right now. It's your life. It's *my* life. And you, being like this, this isn't the Bella I know."

"The Bella *you know*?" I don't know why I'm mad, but I am. I don't know why I'm crying, but I am.

"The Bella I know wouldn't make me feel this . . ."

"This what?" I shout. When did I start shouting?

"This cheap."

There's a stunned silence. My madness drops away and floats into the void.

"I get it. You have an agent interested in you and that's exciting, yes, but it doesn't give you leave to treat me like some one-night stand you've just hooked up with."

My emotions are still bubbling near the surface. Too close to the surface. I have no control anymore.

"But you are!" I cry.

I didn't mean that.

I mean, I didn't not mean that, I have no idea what this is, but I didn't mean it to sound like that. His face has dropped.

Perhaps one of us might have broken the silence eventually, but his pager beeps and he looks over at it, cursing.

He gets out of bed immediately, throwing on clothes.

"Where are you going?" I ask.

"I'm on call."

"Are you actually?"

He looks at me like he can't believe I've even questioned it and he throws over his pager for me to see. I nod, not daring to admit that I have no idea how pagers actually work, and I place it delicately back on the side table.

"I'm so sorry," I begin. "I didn't mean . . ."

"No, it's good. I'm glad I know where I stand."

He's already fully dressed, jeans and a smart gingham shirt, his usual smart-casual. I don't know how that even happened so quickly. I haven't had time to correct myself.

"Marty, please—"

He looks up, his hand running through his hair to whip it back in place.

He looks at me for a long second. I think he might just leave but instead he turns quickly and walks back over to the bed. I see it as if in slow motion.

His steps are fast, methodical, his path clearly set. Before I know it his hands are around the back of my head and he's lifted me up and around into a kiss I never want to end. He knocks the breath right out of me, the softness of his lips melting me into his arms.

He pulls away finally, and I feel my whole head spinning. I almost fall back but he catches me, holding me close, our foreheads almost touching. I've never wanted to be held so much in all my life and even as I feel his warm hands around me, I don't want them to ever let go.

"I get it, this isn't something you expected. Maybe it's not even something you hoped for."

His hands leave me and I feel it pierce into my gut. He turns away, picking up his backpack from the corner of the room, and moves quickly back to the door.

"I didn't expect to be your Prince Charming or whatever, but I also didn't expect to feel like just any other guy with you."

He's not even looking at me. How do I change this around? How do I stop this?

I need to say something. I need to apologize more clearly. I need to say, well, anything, for Christ's sake, but for whatever reason I can't. My lips stutter, my heart hammers—there's nothing coming out.

"Enjoy your date," he says.

And with that he goes, closing the door behind him and leaving me with two cooling cups of tea and a heavy heart.

✌ 13 ✌

It's overcast outside. I tried calling Marty, but as it turns out his phone was right beside me, buzzing away. He forgot it, as he left so quickly.

I wait for an hour, wondering if he might come immediately back, but even I know that's not the case. An emergency vet call-out is expensive if nothing else, and usually takes far more time than a regular appointment. I also don't have time to wait all too much longer. I just told this date that I'd be in Brixton in an hour and—

It's not a date, I tell myself, because Marty's not there to tell him. It's not a real date, it's a professional liaison. That's all. Get over it, Bella, it's time to meet Prince Charming.

I take a shower, stealing his towel (because I've forgotten where (or even if) he has spares), and realize the only clothing I have here is a full-length Norwegian Anna costume. Not ideal for a first date.

It's not a first date. It's just a . . . coffee outing. It's—

I stop my thoughts. Come on, I can make this work for me. I use the little black slip that was under the costume and reach into Marty's cupboards. This boy wears the same things now that he did when he was fourteen. I swear to God, as I'm moving the hangers around I recognize every single shirt he owns. I pick out a few, smelling the usual Marty homey smell of fresh detergent (how the whole family keeps that smell in their clothing I don't know) before I realize smelling his clothes is weird, and I finally win the mix-and-match outfit game with a checkered shirt I've stolen many a time before from him.

It's not exactly a ball gown, but who cares? This isn't exactly a date *date,* it's just a formal meet and greet. It's a shoe return. It's . . . it doesn't matter.

I'm still half expecting Marty to come home. If he did, maybe I'd tell him how little this means to me. Maybe I'd tell him his re-action was out of place. Maybe I'd choose not to go after all—if he had done the same to me, booked some date with someone while I was still naked—God, I don't know how I'd feel. Maybe I should blow this guy off anyway. Maybe I should—

Jesus Christ, Bella, get your shit together. It's not exactly like Marty and I are a thing. It's not exactly like he's ready to propose. We slept together. One time. Friends sleep with each other all the time and it means nothing.

This is my book.

This is important.

If he really cared about me, as a friend, he'd understand that.

Without a second thought I slam Marty's front door behind me and begin my walk to Brixton to meet my own, universe-given, Prince Charming.

14

He's beautiful. He's got a little bit of multiple beautiful people all patched together. He has Zac Efron's eyes and James Franco's lips. He has Penn Badgley's smolder but Chris Pine's smile. His hair's all Kit Harrington meets Henry Cavill and he's built up like a Hemsworth.

He smiles as he meets me and greets me with a kiss on both cheeks like a true gent. He holds the door open for me to enter and he buys me a coffee from a little independent café close to the tube, asking exactly how I'd like it. As I find us a seat I see that he has a nice long chat and a laugh with the barista, which is always a good sign.

"You know," he begins as he hands over my drink, "I don't want to come across too much too early, but I feel a bit like I've struck gold."

Oh my God, I'm blushing. I have a very pale complexion and I can feel the heat of a thousand fires burning at both my freckled cheeks.

"No, really," he says, "when I saw your number on the shoe I thought it could be fun to meet up, but I never in a million years would have guessed you were are beautiful as you are."

He takes a sip of his espresso and instantly I'm thinking George Clooney.

Here is a beautiful man. Here is a completely drop-dead-gorgeous man, who fate has brought me together with in a way that sets my whole head spinning. Here is a perfect rom-com beginning.

But all I can think about, all that I see when I look into his beautiful ocean-blue eyes, is that this man before me, my own modern-day Prince Charming, isn't Marty.

15

By the end of the coffee I'm sure of it.

He's funny, he's sweet, he makes me laugh, and he takes an active interest in my life, but the more he talks and the more I listen, the more "not like Marty" he becomes. He has this sophistication about him that Marty just doesn't have. He uses words like an absolute wordsmith, describing his family and friends in such beautifully vivid detail, while Marty tends to just stick to the facts. He was everything I had been looking for in my life and more, he was a regular Mr. Right, but most importantly of all, he wasn't right for me.

"So where did you find it?"

"Find it?"

"My shoe," I say. "You know, that night I looked everywhere in that bar and I couldn't find it anywhere."

"By some bins," he replies, breaking up my thought.

"By some bins?"

"Yep, sitting beside some bins."

I'm laughing now.

"You pass by a shoe by some bins and you decide to check it out some more?"

"Well, it had a number inside it. That's what caught my eye."

I nod away, laughing as he turns the conversation on, and I try not to think about Marty Mathews.

As we walk out of the coffee shop together he turns to look up at the sky. It's almost, but still not quite, ready to chuck it down.

"What do you say before the heavens rain down upon us to moving this coffee date on to a proper drink? I don't know the area all that well but maybe down here?" he says, pointing down the side street toward Brixton Market.

"I'm . . . I can't," I say finally, Marty's stupid little face the only image in my head. "This was lovely though. Thank you for the coffee."

"No! We can't end it here, not like this. Let me take you out again, some other night. Tomorrow?"

"No, I don't think—"

"The next night? Or later tonight even?"

Bloody hell, cool it, tiger. I stay strong.

"I don't think it's a good idea," I say quickly.

"Ah, but you have to see me again. I didn't bring your shoe with me this time! Let's re-create the Prince Charming moment later this week. I can fit the shoe to your foot, it'll be just like the fairy tale."

That's . . . weird. It's just . . . he's really pushing this whole fairy-tale thing.

"Oh," I say. I realize it didn't even occur to me that he didn't have it on him. I pause, looking around. "You just said you don't know this area well, so do you not live close?"

"I don't," he says coyly, "but I can go back to yours if you want."

Oh Jesus, that wasn't an invitation.

"No, it's just . . . you found the shoe today and now you're saying you don't have it on you."

"I didn't find it today," he says quickly. "I just happened to be in the area today and thought I'd try my luck."

"So you kept it all this time? My number?" God, his smile is charming but a little voice is niggling inside my head. He nods. He has a lovely nod.

But it's not Marty's nod.

Marty's voice, Marty's annoying, smug little voice, is in my head.

"You said 'inside.' You found my number 'inside' my shoe, but I wrote my number on the heel."

"That's what I meant."

"What color was it?"

"What color?"

"Yes, what color was the shoe?"

He's laughing but I'm not anymore, because Marty's voice is ringing loudly in my ear and I realize that so much about this encounter is just not right. A perfect Prince Charming, found in the perfect way, who shares all my same interests just happens to pop up the day after I get highlighted on *BuzzFeed*?

"Black?" this stranger guesses. No. Wrong. It was red. It's all coming together now. Marty's voice is still in my head and he's completely and utterly right. Who finds a shoe and goes out of their way to return it?

Who finds a shoe with a number and chooses to call that number at all?

I look at Prince Charming and it all becomes so clear.

"You know I'm @B.Enchanted, don't you? You've read my chapters."

For one second, just one second, I think he's going to lie. Then he smiles.

"Caught red-handed," he says smugly.

"How did you get my number?"

"A friend of a friend heard you talking about your fairy-tale mission at some house party last weekend. Apparently you were handing out your number to anyone who'd take it."

Oh God, the party Simon took me to. I really was drunk that night. Simon's still not speaking to me.

"So what . . . this was . . . some sort of plot twist?" I ask, looking back at the café.

"No, I'm . . ." He's really smiling, like this is all some game, but I'm furious. "I'm a journalist. Thought it might be fun to see where this fairy tale went."

"Oh my God, oh my God." I hang my head low, feeling my palms ball up into fists. "How could I be so stupid! You were planning on using me to write your own story?"

"Hey, hey now. Look, I didn't mean anything by it!"

"You're an arsehole! How dare you do that to someone?"

"Bit rich coming from you!"

"What's that supposed to mean?"

"Rumpelstiltskin? That Dr. Wide-eyes guy? You're going to tell me you haven't been doing the exact same thing? Using men for your own writing?"

"That's not true, I—"

But then it hits me.

That's exactly what I've been doing.

I've been using men to write my story.

My mind is on fire. Marty was right. Marty was right about everything.

This isn't the Bella I know.

This isn't the Bella I know either. I've turned myself into someone completely unrecognizable. This isn't my story because this *isn't me*.

"This isn't who I am," I whisper to myself. My head's swimming, I'm ignoring the white noise blast given off by Prince Fuckface beside me and suddenly my phone buzzes.

Marty?

I scramble to my phone. What else did he say?

Maybe you should stop looking for some magic ending and realize what's actually right here in front of you.

He's been right there in front of me since I was a kid. He's always been there for me. It's him. It's always been him.

I need to tell him. I need to tell him what a fool I've been. That a man who can see me for who I am is exactly the man I've always wanted to call my own Prince Charming. I can tell him everything.

This is the happy ending to my story. This is the perfect climax—the perfect grand finale. I'm so excited as I look at my phone I literally feel my heart skip.

Except it's not Marty.

Father Marble-01 Nov 15:06

We just had an offer on the house, darling x

Mummy Marble-01 Nov 15:06
The paperwork will take some time to sort through, but we wanted you to know before anything else happened
Father Marble-01 Nov 15:06
Give us a call if you want to chat x
Mummy Marble-01 Nov 15:06
Anytime

I stop for a minute, blinking into the cold reality.

Shit. I wasn't even thinking about that. It comes back to me like a wave: the divorce, selling the house, my whole perfect childhood crumbling away into lies.

It's amazing that your parents still talk.

Marty's voice, there again. I read back through the texts. Both parents together in one group chat. Maybe that is amazing. Maybe that's more than amazing.

You're lucky . . .

I am lucky. I'm very lucky. Because who was there to comfort me when I found out about the divorce in the first place? Who was there to let me play with dogs and give me chocolate (that I bought myself)?

It was Marty.

Marty Mathews.

I don't even bother to say goodbye to the stranger who caffein-ated me. Instead, I turn and I run to my own perfect happily-ever-after.

❧ PART 6 ❧

1

I skip to the end of the road and then, somehow, find myself jogging when I get through the traffic lights. It's not like me to jog. It's not like me to partake in any form of physical exercise at all but especially not the evil "j" word.

Except I am. For Marty Mathews I'm jogging. I start in the direction of his house before my brain kicks in and I turn instead to the station (it's like 5K between Brixton and Marty's, and even fired up I don't think I'd make it without copious breaks and Brunch Bars). I push through the turnstile, jogging on the spot on the platform in frustration while I wait the three and a half minutes for the next train to arrive. Once on, I pace up and down the carriage, as if that might somehow help the train speed up. The double doors finally slide open and out I jog into the crowd at Clapham Junction. Just like that I'm jogging up the staircase and down again to the exit, with only a minor pause as my pass doesn't scan the first time.

On I go, running up St. John's Hill and ignoring the fact that I'm quickly overtaken by a jogger at least twice my own age until I cross the road (looking both ways, obvs), heading straight toward Marty's street. It's seconds later that I'm pounding on the door like a madman.

No one answers but a few people in the street turn to look at me weirdly. I bang again.

"Marty?" I call, as if the banging might not have been enough.

"He's at work."

A woman greets me, standing at Marty's open door in loose-fitting pajamas. She's beautiful, glorious tanned skin and black hair circled on top of her head in a high bun. She's tall in a way that makes my small look completely insubstantial.

"Oh." I stare at her like I might understand. "Who are you?"

It dawns on me that I've seen her face before. From years ago actually, leaving the flat the morning after some large house party. I feel something inside me plummet. Oh shit. Is this . . . is this one of his booty calls?

"Are you serious?" she asks.

"Are you a friend of Marty's?" I ask, not even wanting to know the answer for fear it might cut deep.

"You're literally always sleeping on our sofa when I leave the house. I'm pretty sure you're the reason I need to buy twice as many makeup wipes, and you don't know who I am?"

Her makeup wipes? No, I use Marty's one-night-stand shelf in the—

Oh shit. Actually . . . actually that does make sense. Why would he have ever invested in makeup wipes? It's not a one-night-stand shelf, is it?

My eyes naturally fall down as I'm thinking and I see the train-ers on her feet. They're the same ones I borrowed to walk home on the night I lost my shoe, the ones I returned last week. The shoes that weirdly fit me despite Marty's feet being almost twice my size.

Except it wasn't weird. Because they weren't Marty's shoes at all.

This is the mysterious flatmate?

"Ollie?"

No, it can't be. Ollie's a man. Isn't he? I've always thought he was a man. Except she's looking at me and she's very, very female. Why on earth had I not even considered that his flatmate might have ever been female?

I suddenly start laughing. Loudly.

"You drunk?" Ollie asks.

Fuck I'm bad at first impressions.

But it's funny. It's really, really funny, for all I can remember are my words from all those weeks ago:

I have about as much chance finding love in this city as I have for meeting this "flatmate" of yours, Marty.

"Do you need me to call someone?"

I try to stop laughing. She's still here, staring me down, and for good reason. I'm all over the place right now.

"No—I . . . I need to go," I say, already moving away from her and back toward St. John's Hill. "I need to . . . it's lovely meeting you!"

But she's already shut the door and I'm en route for my own, very real, ever after.

2

I turn back toward the station, and before I even know what I'm doing, I turn my floppy jog into an Olympic medal–worthy sprint just as the first raindrops fall.

It threatened it all day but here it is. The rain begins falling and it looks like it has no intention of stopping. The streets have emptied, because people generally prefer not to be cold and wet if they can help it, so I make good time as I reach the main road and turn to the high street. Under the bridge and on, past the Sainsbury's Local and the takeaways and the various nail parlors, with each step spraying water up my own cold legs.

Just as the vet's comes into sight I can see Marty, locking up shop with an umbrella overhead. My heart pounds against my chest as my feet clobber their way painfully toward him, galloping like a racehorse through the turmoil that is London rain. He has a completely confused look on his face as he turns and finds me sprinting toward him.

"Bella?" I see him say, mouth open in confusion, but it's the only shape he's able to make before I launch off the ground like a lion leaping for its prey. There's mild terror in both of our eyes as I'm hovering in midair, the true leap of faith, which I am completely unable to stop as my limbs fly out toward him. He drops his umbrella, ready for my inevitable descent, and it rolls away.

Except we needn't have worried—I land a little farther away

than I thought, because it turns out judging distance isn't my strongpoint. I take one more pace forward before he even has a chance to speak, and grab Marty's face like my life depends on it. Before I can even catch my breath my lips are on his.

He's slow to react, which I can't blame him for—my jump was pretty fast paced, which is very unlike me—but his hands fit themselves around my back for stability if nothing else.

This is it.

My real-life Prince Charming.

Everything my book has been leading to.

Everything my life has been leading to and it's here, holding me in the rainy streets of London like the perfect happy ending.

🌿 3 🌿

I pull away, looking right up into his big brown eyes, so completely unsure what he must be thinking. The rain is as heavy and as dramatic as any good chick-flick ending—it's the perfect setting to my perfect ending. I smile, looking at his stupid little face, and my heart warms but the nerves are unstoppable. There it was, my grand gesture, and I can only hope and pray that my feelings are reciprocated.

It's funny. In all the movies, music is always playing for this kind of scene. Something big and dramatic like Katy Perry's "Firework" or whatever new song the cool kids are listening to, but in reality there is nothing. No, not nothing. Nothing would be better—very cool and atmospheric, but it's worse than nothing. Our soundtrack as I stare into his unblinking pupils and wait for his verdict on our highly romantic kiss is the sound of my piglike heavy breaths as I'm trying desperately to refill my lungs.

Marty opens his mouth, shaking his head before he closes it again. I need him to speak. I need him to do something. I need something to drown out my heavy breaths before they ruin the moment.

And he does.

Just when I'm beginning to lose hope, he pulls through for me.

A noise burns through the silence, only it's not the heartfelt monologue I was hoping for. It's Marty's unfiltered, uncensored, incredibly stupid laugh. I mean, he's pissing himself. He's shaking so hard he stumbles back a little for balance.

I shake my head in confusion, about to speak my mind except then I catch my reflection in the window of the vet's behind him and I stop myself, realizing how ridiculous this has suddenly become.

I don't look like a delicate flower caught in the eye of the storm at all. I look like a drowned rat. In the movies it's always so romantic in the rain, but here I'm cold and wet. My ginger hair is dyed dark as it clumps on my head, weighed down even heavier with the Rapunzel extensions I chose to keep in, and I can feel dark mascara already running from my eyes. I look almost exactly like the Joker.

Marty's still laughing. Of course he's laughing. That's what he does, laughs at me. That's what he's always done. On every occasion, at every opportunity, he's always laughed at me.

No, not at me. With me. Because now I'm laughing too. I'm laughing because this is all too much and I'm soaking and I look like shit and Marty Mathews is making me laugh by laughing at me.

"Marty, I . . ."

But I can't get the words out. I can't get the words out because I'm cold and shivering and laughing too much to unscramble them. I had a whole speech planned in my head:

Marty, I can't believe it's taken me so long to realize but you're the real Prince Charming I'd always hoped for. You've always been the ending of my fairy tale . . .

It was a whole thing: funny, sweet, dramatic, and romantic, the whole damn package.

Only now, here, right before him, it makes no sense whatsoever. When Cinderella runs into Prince Charming's arms he doesn't *laugh* at her. He doesn't even smile at her. He's incredibly serious and somber as he sings her praises and showers her with compliments. Except I wouldn't want any of that at all—of course I wouldn't. That wouldn't be real. This here, someone laughing in my face about the disaster movie that is my life, is the most real thing there is.

New thoughts come. They expand as I look into Marty's wide, utterly confused eyes that are filling with more liquid laughter tears.

Of course he didn't sling me back and kiss me again. Of course he didn't burst into song or cry about how much this means to him; it's Marty. I know Marty. That's just not the kind of thing he would ever do for anyone, no matter how much he loved them.

"You're not my happily-ever-after."

I don't even know what I'm saying until I'm saying it, but I just about cry out the words through my erratic peals of laughter.

"Okay . . ." he says, and I'm impressed he can even say that. He's laughing at me so hard he looks winded.

And just like that my giggles switch to something else completely. The feeling hits me like a brick wall to the head. I feel exhausted from all of it; from the anger I felt for Mark; from the pain I put myself through by ghosting Ellie; from the disappointment of a thousand rejections; from the pressure of the novel; from my earlier physical exercise; from this silly level of rain around me; and, most of all, from the memory of this morning. Without much warning I stop with the laughing, my tear ducts open like the heavens above me, and suddenly the water streaming down my face is my own production line.

I don't pretty cry either. I can't pretty cry. I can only bawl and that's what I do: cold, wet, and miserable, I throw my head back and widen out my mouth into a weird howl to the not-quite-risen moon.

"Woah, steady on. What's all this?"

"I . . . don't know anymore . . ."

"Okay," Marty says, unsure how to react to this bizarre breakdown before his eyes. He stops laughing pretty quickly. "It's alright, I get it. I don't have to be your happy ending or whatever. You can stop crying about it."

"I'm not crying because of you, God, get over yourself!" I cry, laughing a bit more, which throws him off. It throws me a bit too, to be fair. "No, I meant—I don't want you to be my fairy-tale ending because . . ." For just a second I can see my reflection in his big eyes and I have a moment of pure clarity. This isn't the romantic climax of a movie. This is my real, unfiltered life. "Because I'm not in a fucking fairy tale at all, am I?"

Marty doesn't know what to make of this. I don't either, really. I sort of had a point but my head's a bit confused, and I'm shivering more than I am speaking.

"I'm no Cinderella," I say, defeated. "I'm not even close. I haven't lost everything I own. I don't have to work for shitheads. I don't have shitty evil family members who make me sleep with the pigs."

Marty raises an eyebrow, a cheeky glimmer in his eye.

"Are you seriously crying right now because you're not sleeping with pigs?"

"I'm crying because I know that everything I've messed up in my life is because *I've* messed it up. *Me*. Cinderella, she deserves a fucking prince at the end of her story, but I'm just an idiot. A very cold idiot."

As if on cue, my body shakes involuntarily. Quickly Marty whips off his coat, throwing it around my shoulders and bringing me closer to his chest. God, he feels so warm. I can immediately smell that familiar detergent float up so welcomingly into my nostrils.

"I thought coming here, I thought I was going to tell you that you're everything my book's been leading up to, but you're not."

I can feel his heartbeat against my ear as I'm pressed to his chest and I feel so safe in his arms. But I need to see his face for this, so I pull myself back, just a little.

"But only because you were right. So right: this isn't about the book. Not at all. In fact I told myself I wasn't going to have anything else to do with the book, and yet one little email from that agent and I threw myself blindly back into it, forgetting once again about all those around me."

Marty wipes the tears from my eyes, his face suddenly so soft and calm.

"I promise I won't make that mistake again," I continue. "I treated you like shit this morning after an incredible night last night, and all because I was so caught up in this fairy-tale rubbish that I didn't realize you weren't just any man. You're one of my best friends. I'm sorry. I'm really, really sorry."

He blinks at me, hard.

"It's alright," he says seriously. I wait a second, thinking there might be something else to it, but there isn't. He's genuinely heard me. And he's genuinely accepted my apology.

I feel like a weight has been lifted from my shoulders. I feel so unbearably happy I could cry all over again, but I don't. I've done enough crying.

"Good," I say.

"Great," he replies.

"Do you forgive me?"

"I forgive you."

"Friends?"

"Friends?"

Oh God, was the apology not enough?

As if to prove me wrong he pulls me forward using the lapels of his own coat and spins me around him, holding me effortlessly with his ridiculously toned arms, and as he plants his lips on mine we kiss like there's no tomorrow. We just seem to fit into place, my nose curving so perfectly around his, our eyelashes fluttering as one as his lips warm my whole damn body from the freezing fucking rain.

As the kiss comes to its own beautiful conclusion, leaving a smile across his face, he places me back one foot at a time onto the ground.

I don't think I ever realized how good it could feel to own up to my own wrongdoings. To accept them entirely rather than blaming something else. To ask forgiveness.

A thought triggers in my mind. Suddenly I know exactly what I have to do.

"I have somewhere I need to go," I say dreamily.

"You do?"

Marty looks instantly confused. After what's just happened I don't blame him.

"I do. But I'll . . . I'll call you."

"Call me?"

"I will," I say, smiling in reassurance. "So you can tell me where we're going for our first actual date."

That seems to placate him. He nods, whipping his hair back in place.

"Sounds good to me." Marty smiles, and my word, I want to stay. I want to stay so badly I almost do. But there's one last thing I need to do, something I should have done a long time ago.

I kiss him one last time for good measure and I pass him back his coat.

And just like that, I'm running in the rain all over again, this time toward my good old friend the District line.

4

It isn't until I'm outside of the little townhouse in Chiswick that I even question why I didn't go home and get out of my wet clothes. I had time. I had all the time in the world actually, because it isn't like they're expecting me—I know for a fact they're having a quiet night in and not expecting any guests at all. Maybe they're even having sex.

Ew, gross. I don't want to think of them having sex. In my eyes they never do. It's 8:42. Even if they did have sex sometimes, no one has sex at 8:42 p.m. I take the gamble and knock. A few minutes of wondering whether I'm making a huge mistake, and suddenly the door flies open. There, standing wrapped in a cushy gray dressing gown, is the real hero to this story, only as I've worked out, this isn't really my story at all.

"Mark, I hope you don't mind—"

"Oh my God, Bella, come in, you're soaked through!" Mark cries as he hustles me in quickly. Before we've even reached their actual front door he's stripped himself of his dressing gown (thankfully revealing a boxer/T-shirt combo underneath) and circled it around my shoulders in an effort to warm me up.

"Come on in, I'll get you some of Ellie's clothes to change into."

How perfect this man is. Friendly, kind, respectful. I've just shown up at his door unannounced and he's making me feel like I live here.

"Mark," I say, wrapping the dressing gown tightly around me for emotional support. It's so warm, like someone's just lit a fire around my tummy and I'm loving it. "Mark, I need to tell you something."

"Well, let me get you a jumper first. Ellie's just inside—"

"No, before that. Now." I look at him, scanning his face for something to hate but I find what I've always found, really . . . absolutely nothing.

"Mark, I'm so, so sorry for just about everything I've ever done or said to you. I just can't apologize enough for the way I've treated you over the years. Since the day you walked into my life, you have been nothing but nice to me and I've been nothing but rude to you, and I'm sorry."

His eyebrows are raised in surprise and I think he looks a little bit like a cartoon character but I try not to think of it too clearly. I can't have distractions. I need to get this out and I need to get it out now.

"The truth is, you're perfect for Ellie. I know that. I've known that since the first day I met you, and I think that's why I've been so hard on you. The other guys Ellie's seen over the years, I've always known it wasn't that serious but with you it was different. Different means change. And I don't do well with change."

I close my eyes, trying desperately not to see his face for fear it might stop me or break me down, and I can't cry anymore. I've cried enough over boys, I've certainly cried enough over Mark, and I need to hold it together.

"You scared me, because I knew with you being so perfect for her that she wouldn't need me anymore when I still needed her. But I know now how wrong I was. What I want is for her to be happy. More than anything in the whole world I want her to be happy and you make her happy, so I'm so, so sorry for treating you so badly."

"There's nothing to be sorry for."

"Well, there is. There's a lot to be sorry for. For starters for not giving you guys space. I was in your bed probably more than I was in my own and you guys needed your alone time so I wasn't respecting your boundaries."

I check myself, standing in their corridor on their quiet night in.

"I'm still not respecting your boundaries apparently, but I'm sorry. That will change. I'll . . . I'll call in advance and I'll plan things better and I'll give you the space you guys need, I promise.

"And that night—I'm so sorry for the things I said about your mum—it was stupid. So stupid, I didn't mean it and you were only trying to help—"

"There's blame to share, Bella, I—"

"No. Stop it. You took me to a coffee shop and you bought me a delicious overpriced coffee and apologized, and I just sat there and let you make me feel all high and mighty."

"I overstepped."

"You didn't overstep. You were protecting me. And you were right, it was a mistake. This whole fairy-tale escapade has just been one utter disaster after another. I should have listened to you but I was an idiot and I didn't. So I'm sorry. For all of what I just said and also for making your incredibly warm and lovely dressing gown so completely wet."

There was a pause.

"Are you done?" he asks. His voice is light, soft, even humorous.

In the dim light of the corridor I peel open my eyes to see Mark standing before me, his arms wide, ready for a hug. It's the nicest thing I've ever seen. Finally, perhaps even for the first time since I've met him, we hug out all our problems. He's such a good hugger too. He's a bit bearlike, and his warmth, coupled with the comforting warmth of the dressing gown, honestly makes me forget about my "being soaking" thing. It's delightful.

"Separately," I add, still tight in his arms, "where did you get this dressing gown from? Because I think I need one."

"M&S."

"M&S! I should have known."

"They also do matching slippers."

"Of course they do."

"Now," Mark says, pulling away from me with a smile across his face. He has a nice smile. I don't know why I've never noticed how nice his smile is. Not as nice as Ellie's, mind, but still nice. "Come on in. It looks to me like you could do with a cup of tea."

Oh my word. Tea? He's turning into a Mathews already.

❧ 5 ❧

When I finally enter the flat I can tell Ellie heard every word. Partly because of the smirk on her face that she is so completely incapable of hiding, but the real giveaway is the set of very warm PJs that are waiting for me on the end of the bed.

"I don't need to stay—I was just stopping by," I say weakly, trying to put this whole "boundaries" thing into practice.

"Stay!" cries Ellie. "It's still horrible outside. You might as well wait for this storm to pass."

"Really—I should go."

"I insist," says Mark. "We're about halfway through *Return of the King* so you'll have to catch up quick."

"Extended edition?"

"Obviously," he says as he lingers by the door for one last second.

He goes to make the tea as I change, leaving Ellie and me a few minutes to talk about all the important things we need to discuss in private.

"I think Merry is the most underrated of the hobbits," she says, looking at the paused movie on their screen at the end of their bed. Ellie's tucked in already, looking cozy as anything. "He's clever, he's forward thinking, he's fun. I think I like him best."

"He's the dull one. Pippin has the better lines."

"Pippin's an idiot."

"A very pretty idiot. Who can sing. I certainly would."

"Over Legolas?"

"He's not a hobbit."

"Over Legolas anyway?"

I towel dry my hair with a small towel Ellie throws at me as I deliberate on this very important decision.

"Yeah, go on. Legolas is a bit too good-looking. Aragorn on the other hand . . ."

I check out my hair in the mirror. It's frazzled out in all directions. I doubt I'm any match for Liv Tyler right now but a gal can dream.

"God, there are so many men in this story," Ellie says thoughtfully. "Hey! After your fairy-tale book is over maybe you should try Tolkien characters for the sequel?"

"What, sleep with orcs and old bearded magicians? I think not!" I laugh. "Anyway, I'm done with all that."

"Done with magicians?"

"Done with one-night stands. Done with rejections from men I don't even like and trying to find validation from strangers. From now on I'm back to finding the one."

"The one and done?"

"The one and done."

"Sounds like a good plan," she says, her golden smile warming my heart. "Thank you."

"Thank you?"

"Yes. Thank you." She's not talking about Tolkien anymore. She's looking at me squarely in the eyes and has her mother's face on. She's whispering too, her voice dropping a decibel so it doesn't travel through the closed door. "For saying all that to Mark. It means so much to me."

"It was overdue," I tell her. "I'm so—"

"No. No more. You've done it. You've said it. We move on."

I nod. She nods.

It's done.

"What do you want me to do with my wet clothes?" I ask, my voice returning to a normal tone.

"Isn't that Marty's shirt?"

I look at the soaking-wet shirt I've just peeled off me and try to stay calm so my cheeks don't fire up red.

"Yep."

"Just shove it in the laundry basket. I'll get it back to him eventually."

Good. All clear then. I turn back to the warm clothes laid out for me and I dive right in.

Ellie's PJs are the kind that you imagine grandmas wearing, but to be fair, she has always been a grandma since the day I met her. They're all pinstripe and collar, sagging in places to hide any lumps and bumps that older age might naturally spring on a person. Not that she needs it. She's the most naturally toned person I know for someone who does little to no exercise and still eats burgers most days.

The one I'm wearing is red and blue, not too dissimilar to the ones she's got on in blue and white that are peeking over her duck-egg duvet.

It's just like her old bedroom, just turned around a little bit. The drawers that were always on her left are now on her right, but even the picture frames are in the same order on the top of it; the built-in cupboards take the pressure off her tiny little wardrobe that's fitted nicely into the very corner of the room by the window; even the fairy lights are back up again over the other half of the room. She might have moved multiple tube stops away, but her room hasn't changed even a little bit.

I love that. In such a small amount of time I can look around and see beyond a shadow of a doubt that this is Ellie's room.

She waits for me to hang up the towel over her door before she folds down the duvet to her right.

"So Pippin's your one?" she asks as I bound in beside her.

"You're my one," I reply, snuggling into her. Because she is, and she always will be.

Right on cue, her other "one" pushes open the door holding three cups of tea and balancing a large bowl of freshly popped popcorn close to his chest. It's honestly Michelin award–winning service, this. Like clockwork, Ellie takes the popcorn and a tea and seamlessly passes it over to me before taking her own. As Mark tucks himself into the other side of the bed, I finally realize how magical this moment is.

"Careful, the tea's hot," Ellie tells me.

"I know the tea's hot. You don't need to tell me the tea's hot."

"I just worry that you might burn your tongue."

"You're *worried* about that?"

"It's just the kind of thing you would do!"

"You're such a worrier," Mark and I say in unison. We smile at each other too. Honestly, it's so cheesy that if I wasn't loving every single second of it I'd probably have to vomit a little.

Mark picks up the remote and does a stock check of the situation.

"Ready?" he asks.

"Ready," I reply.

As the sweepingly brilliant soundtrack by Howard Shore begins, I turn my face away from the screen and look at my two bed companions, realizing quite how perfect this moment is. Here I am, tucked in beside my best friend in the whole world and her real-life Prince Charming. If anyone was the mean old troll, it was always me from the beginning, but no more. No longer will I resent Mark for being my best friend's best friend. No longer will I pretend to sleep or yawn at his (probably still slightly boring) stories.

I can't wait for them to get married. I can't wait for them to have kids. I can't wait for them to begin this next chapter together.

"Bella?" Ellie asks just as Aragorn looks forlornly into the distance. I quickly realize that, as ever, we're on the exact same page. She's going to tell me exactly what I've been thinking. She's going to repeat exactly what I've just thought to myself.

Married or not, she'll always be the other half of my soul.

"Yes?" I ask.

"You didn't sleep with my brother, did you?"

Oh.

Shit.

PART 7

1

"Diego! Are you ready for the cue?"

"Ready and waiting, princess!" the sexiest man alive replies, holding his acoustic guitar in one strong hand (as if he could look any sexier). His white shirt follows the curves of his rippling muscles, with smart leather trousers to top off the James Dean glow about him. He's sitting in the shade of a beautiful old oak tree, just at the back of the growing congregation as they slowly wander to their seats.

"Fabulous!" I reply. "Ah! Simon! When did you get here?"

I go over to greet him. My, Simon's upped his style now. His suit might still be tweed, as I'd expect, but it's navy blue and chic as hell. He looks like a Chanel model. He smells like one too.

"You look bellllla!" Simon replies in an Italian accent. I do a swirl in my bridesmaid dress, feeling like the belle of the ball.

"I am," I reply coyly. "The most Bella of them all."

It's floor length and ocean blue, with sparkles swirling in all directions. The lovely hair and makeup lady who arrived in the morning spent about an hour wrestling my hair into one long plait and it's just about holding in place with about a year's supply of hair spray pinning it down.

I haven't seen Simon in a long while. He was the next person I said sorry to, all of what . . . six months ago now. My little stunt over at Diego's friend's house left me feeling so terrible that I even dug deep into my pockets and spent the most I had ever spent on a bottle of wine to send their way to apologize. He couldn't have been nicer about it, but what with him moving straight in with Diego, he suddenly moved sadly out of my life. Mind, the two were made for each other, I'm telling you.

"I hear Annie's moving out now," Simon tells me.

"She is indeed!" I reply. "She's moving into a house with some of her exercise-y friends, I think, somewhere in Angel."

"Crossing the river, how brave!" Simon whispers to me. "Do you know who you're getting in yet in her place?"

"Oh! No, actually—I'm moving too! Just next week."

"How exciting! Who with?"

"Well, no one actually." I shrug my shoulders, taking a big deep breath. "I'm going to try living by myself for a little."

"God, how grown up!"

"I know, right?" I reply. "Time to start moving in the right direction for once rather than trying to pull everyone else back with me."

"Well, you can probably afford it now, eh? What with the promotion and all," Simon says.

"Only just!" I laugh. "My new role doesn't pay that much more!"

"I didn't know you changed jobs. Where did you move to?" Diego asks.

"Well, I haven't exactly 'moved' moved. I'm still at Porter Books but I've changed departments. I'm a scout now—a talent scout."

"That sounds fun," Diego says, smiling.

"It is! And a lot more fulfilling than answering phones, I'll tell you. I didn't realize how much I loved finding new talent until I began, but now I'm so annoyed I didn't work it out years ago. In fact, the first ever writer I found, Henrietta Lovelace is her name, she literally just signed a deal last Thursday for a two-book deal and I'm still reeling."

"But what about *your* book?" Simon asks, "The fairy-tale guide? I thought Ellie told me something about a deal or an agent or . . ."

"Ah," I reply. "Yes, yes, there's that too! I'm just editing it again now, although it's changed a bit since we last spoke. It's less of a guide now and more a . . . I don't even know. A sorry tale of a girl who found herself fed up with London dating."

"And does she find her Prince Charming?" Diego asks coyly. I laugh. We all do.

"You'll have to read it to find out, I guess," I tell them. From the corner of my eye I spot Diego's watch. It looks vintage, which I love, but more importantly, it tells me the time. "Oh crikey! I need to head back upstairs, but let's chat more at the reception."

I give Simon a little wink, which I instantly regret. Who winks these days? Ew. But I turn to Diego anyway, hoping neither of them noticed. "I'll give the signal as I'm walking out. Be ready!"

"I'll be looking out for you, beautiful," Diego says in the sexiest way possible.

I rush back inside through the large double doors, waving hello to the odd guest I pass as I go but I don't stop. There'll be plenty of time later to catch up with old friends, now's the time for action.

It's only when I make it back to the large open double doors of the house that I take a moment to pause, running through the checklist in my mind: music prepped, guests almost seated, groom ready.

Mark's standing at the front, talking to Niamh, who is already crying her happy eyes out. In an act that genuinely warms my heart, I watch as he takes out the small handkerchief in his suit pocket and offers it to her. What a gent.

Just as I'm about to turn away he looks my way and we catch eyes.

He looks, well, good actually. He scrubs up nicely, wearing a smart fitted suit—now one handkerchief down—with his sleeves rolled up from the heat. He smiles as he sees me, so sweetly I feel my own knees melt.

He looks like a real prince; no nerves at all behind those pupils, only pure excitement. I can see it from here. I can feel it too. He smiles at me and I can't help but smile right back at him. He's the perfect man for my best friend and I really, truly couldn't be happier.

There's only one thing left for me to do now: find the bride.

❧ 2 ❧

Ellie Mathews, soon to be Mrs. Ellie Mathews (she's keeping her last name), is the most beautiful bride in all the land. Her hair is loose, but lightly curled at the edges, and her white jeans (yes, jeans) are lined with small flowers that match perfectly with her garden-picked bouquet. With a lace white T-shirt and pristine white trainers to match, she is, by all accounts, the fairest of them all.

I stand behind her, the most proud friend in the whole world, realizing that I literally, properly, couldn't be happier for her. She is a real-life magic princess, and when she opens her mouth to speak I just know that sweet birdsong will come from her lips.

"I'm so nervous I think I'm about to wee myself."

Okay, maybe not birdsong as such.

"You're just nervous."

"I'm being serious!"

"Then I'll find you a cup," I reply, laughing. "You ready?"

She looks again at the mirror; she's shaking a little. She turns to me and smiles nervously.

The moment's broken when a knock echoes against the door.

"Oh God, what's happened?"

"Stop worrying!" I say quickly. "It's probably just the girls coming back. I'll get it."

I walk across the spare bedroom that we've hidden ourselves in while the wedding party arrives out in the garden below. I've never seen a wedding more relaxed in all my life. Ellie never wanted a big white wedding when she was younger, so I wasn't at all surprised when she told me her plans. She wanted something fun over formal, and Mark's dad had a garden big enough for her small congregation of close friends and family so that was that. Balloons and bunting hung between trees, lanterns swinging from low branches. It is the most homely wedding in the whole world, the most Ellie thing I could have ever imagined.

Charlotte, one of Ellie's bridesmaids, had a bit of a spillage disaster with enthusiastic morning mimosas, so she and the other bridesmaid, Hannah, nipped off to the bathroom to wash it out just as I'd arrived.

Fully expecting to see them reappear, I throw open the door.

"About time, you two. I thought—oh!"

I blink twice.

"It's you."

"You sound disappointed," Marty replies.

He's standing there looking like a Ken doll, blue suit matched with a blue bow tie. His hair's slicked back but even with a comb through it still looks a bit ruffled up.

Oh, how things can change in half a year.

"I'm always disappointed to see you."

"Like fuck you are."

Just like that he grabs me and swings me back, my blue gown swirling like a carousel as I fall into his arms. I'm already laughing before his lips touch mine and when he almost drops me he joins in.

"Get off me, you buffoon!" I giggle as he lifts me back to my feet, nibbling at my ear. As far as maid-of-honoring would go, I would say this behavior is certainly unprofessional. I began this morning determined to be the best maiden possible. At least before the champagne toast.

Still, I didn't see him last night as I was in Ellie's bed, so I have missed those arms around me. I give him one last kiss, knowing I'd have time for a lipstick top up before aisle walking.

"How's the ugly duckling?" Marty asks, nodding to the door

behind me. He's got that sparkle in his eye that never seems to fade while I'm around.

"Swanning it like a princess."

"I'll take your word for it." He checks his watch. "You guys are behind."

"Charlotte had a dress malfunction. We'll be down in a sec."

Marty nods. He actually looks nervous, which is not normal for cool, calm Marty Mathews. I see it so rarely in him but there it is. Of course it is, his baby sister (or at least "marginally" younger sister) is getting married and here he is, ready to give her away.

"You're looking sharp," I say, running my hands down the inside of his jacket to try to cool him down. He smiles, not his usual confident smile but something else, something . . . something special. Weird how little I ever saw this side to him before. Amazing how much I love it.

He leans in for one more kiss, our noses lightly bumping as we pull apart. It's not long before we're joined by my fellow bridesmaids as they bundle out of the bathroom together. Charlotte's got a cardigan on over her bridesmaid dress. I'm guessing removing the stain wasn't as successful as they'd hoped then.

Marty shakes off whatever moment he was feeling and smiles bright and bold, his usual cocky self.

"I'll be downstairs," he says, smoothing out his hair, as if that actually did anything.

"Oi!" I scream after him as he begins to wander back down the stairs. "Aren't you going to tell me I'm pretty?"

"Nope," he says, a little too quickly too.

What an absolute arsehole.

"You're beautiful," he adds. Oh, what a little charmer. Boy's got moves. "Now hurry the fuck up, Bells. We're all waiting."

3

"Was that Marty?" Ellie asks as all of her wedding party bursts through the door.

"He's just downstairs now."

"Is everything alright?"

She looks at me all anxious and wide-eyed. I smile her back to calm.

"He's just being his usual prickish self. Nothing to worry about."

"Good."

"I'm so so so so sorry, Ellie!" Charlotte cries.

"I don't mind! I like that cardigan!" Ellie smiles back.

"I can find another dress or . . . I can ask . . ."

"You're good, Charlotte, calm down. She ain't no Bridezilla."

That's the kind of no bullshit policy a maid-of-honor should always distill. Charlotte's giggling. She's a bit drunk because she's only just turned eighteen and hasn't learned how to drink multiple mimosas and stay sober yet. She'll learn. Not that anyone here minds. This is a party after all.

"Do you guys want to head down?" Ellie asks them sweetly.

"Are you ready?" Hannah asks.

"As ready as I'll ever be!"

With one last round of hugs the other two flee first, but we hover for just a second, taking it all in. Ellie checks herself in the mirror one last time, tweaking her T-shirt sleeves pointlessly.

"I haven't seen you like this with anyone before," Ellie says finally, picking up her bouquet. "Is Marty your 'one'?"

I look up at her, all white dungarees and flowers, and I can't help but laugh.

"Today is not even a little bit about me, Ellie. I'm not going to dignify that with an answer."

"Oh come on! I need something to distract me! I'm about to fall flat on my face in front of sixty-five people!"

"I'll catch you!"

"Just tell me! Is he? The one?"

I walk over to her and squeeze her hand one last time as a single (ish) woman.

"How many times do I have to say this? You're my one," I reply.

She throws her arms around me and we hug like there is no tomorrow. As I start welling up I pull away from her. My makeup took way, way too long to fuck it up this early with tears.

"Now come on. Marty's outside ready to walk you up the aisle, Diego's ready with the wedding march, and Mark is ready at the altar . . . garden . . . thing. It's time."

I look at her, the perfect fairy-tale princess and my best friend. This is just as I'd always hoped it would be, me by her side, ready to give her away (metaphorically speaking—Marty's now waiting downstairs to do the actual honors). It's just like we're ten years old again in the living room, our toys the ready audience. Ellie cries one solo tear and I mop it up with a flower petal I rip off my bouquet. No one will notice. Hopefully.

"Nothing's going to change after this," she says quickly. "You know that, right?"

"Oh, it will," I reply as I hear the band start up. I hug her one last time. "But let's give this chapter a grand old finale before the next one begins, eh?"

I extend my arm for her and she takes it, and we walk off hand in hand into the (metaphorical) sunset.

It's our own classy ending to our own classic story.

And I know now, with absolute certainty, that it's better than any fairy tale out there.

ACKNOWLEDGMENTS

Thank you first and foremost to all my family. You are the greatest people on earth and have always been my biggest support, so it's very convenient that you are related to me.

My friends too, the best humans you can find, and all of whom asked me how my book was going even when there was no book. You know who you are, and you believed in me long before I believed in myself, so I can't thank you enough.

Special mentions to my very first readers, Steph and Kirstie, and to Sara, Peter, and Emma too, all of whom have read many samples of my writing over the years and have been far too kind to me about them. Of course thanks go to Rich, for being there always and giving me the confidence to hit send in the first place. Thanks as well to all my London girls: every brunch and gin-filled night out with you gives me a new buzz to keep up writing.

To all my English teachers from primary school through to sixth form, because even though I went on to study math, I spent years falling in love with literature thanks to you.

Everyone needs an agent as brilliant as Watson, Little's Megan Carroll. She championed me, supported me, and helped make my own fairy tale come true.

I don't even know how to thank the wonderful Alexandra Sehulster, Anna Boatman, and Sarah Murphy. You made me better, bolder, and helped me fall more in love with my own characters. I've loved every second of working with you.

To everyone at St. Martin's Griffin, and all those who helped bring this story from my little screen to the shelves. Thank you, thank you, thank you.

And one last thanks to Riley, for choosing to come into my world and change it in all the best ways. May you only read this when you are much, *much* older.

ABOUT THE AUTHOR

Richard Turner

Luci Adams (she/her) started out working on tax returns before moving into copywriting, creating social posts for Apple Music, and assisting with Amazon and BBC productions at Working Title Television. She now works as a senior analyst at *The Guardian* by day and writes uproariously funny and inventive rom-coms by night. *Not That Kind of Ever After* is her debut novel.